FIVE KIDS
AND
ONE GUN

FIVE KIDS
AND
ONE GUN

A GAME TO THE DEATH AND HOCKEY
LIKE YOU HAVE NEVER SEEN BEFORE

BRYAN STEVENSON

authorHOUSE®

AuthorHouse™
1663 Liberty Drive
Bloomington, IN 47403
www.authorhouse.com
Phone: 1-800-839-8640

Published by AuthorHouse   07/17/2012

ISBN: 978-1-4685-8738-8 (sc)
ISBN: 978-1-4685-8737-1 (hc)
ISBN: 978-1-4685-8736-4 (e)

Library of Congress Control Number: 2012907112

CHAPTER 1

Friends to the End

This book is inspired only in part by a true story.

It was the kind of friendship you hoped would last a lifetime. In this case, the lifetime was shorter than the average. As you read on you will catch my drift.

It takes me back to a time back in middle school when my brother and I hung with friends. I guess hoping the friendships would last a lifetime. But no matter how good things are, nothing lasts forever. Like some friendships from the past, whether it be as simple as a group change, or a sudden death. Everything seems to happen for a reason. But as it happened in this instance, until death do us part.

Joe, Paul, Zack, Ted and Ron had been friends since pretty much day one. Day one being the beginning of elementary school. Now it doesn't happen that often, unlike other friends who meet at that age, friendships seem to fade as life changes. Not these boys though, they seemed to stick together until the bitter end, you could say.

Its the graduation from elementary school to middle school where change usually takes place. All your friends seem to disappear. Either they go to different schools, or they just get bored of old friends and meet new friends, leaving the old friends behind. But not in this little group. These five boys seemed to stick together through thick and thin. In fact, as fate would have it, they all ended up in the same school and the same classes.

It was like things didn't seem to change much as far as their friendship went. Other than the new school and new teachers. I mean these boys did everything together. They hit on girls in the hallways together. They hung out at recess, noon hour and even made time to work on projects after school. It really was a unique friendship they shared.

It was on this Friday in particular that these boys had looked forward to most of all. It was the day they figured they would finally reach manhood. No, sorry to burst your bubble, it had nothing to do with sex. But it was the first weekend by themselves, without any parental supervision whatsoever.

They plotted and planned this weekend for what seemed like forever. They even conjured up a letter, supposedly written by the school. It was a permission slip, saying the school was taking them on a weekend camping trip. There was even a twenty dollar fee involved. Pretty sneaky if you ask me.

The bell rang for the last time this week and the boys had it all planned out. They would first meet in their usual spot, the bike rack at the back of the school. Joe was already sitting there waiting for the rest of the boys to show up. He was a little more excited than usual because he had great news.

"So did you get it?" Asked Ron, in anticipation. "Hold on man! We gotta wait for Ted to get here first!" Snapped Joe. "Okay, okay." Pouted Ron. That was about the time Ted wandered his way towards them. "Alright boys, the moment of truth is here and now!" Announced Joe, as he unzipped the zipper of his backpack with an excited look on his face. The boys all gathered around in a little circle and glared inside the backpack. Their eyes lit up like little bright shiny stars.

But that was short lived. Joe wasn't about to get caught with a bottle of booze on school property. So he closed the bag up before peering eyes caught a glimpse. He put the backpack on his shoulders, unlocked his bike, and led the way towards the graveyard. This was the next stop on the list.

There wasn't a lot of chat on the way to the graveyard by the woods. It was more or less a race against the wind. Everyone was too excited and just wanted to get to their destination. But this was just the first stop before they headed out on their way.

As soon as they got to the graveyard, they all literately threw down their bikes and ran to the forest trail, known as the devils path. Everyone had a job to do and a certain amount to gather up for the weekend. This was a place where everything was stored during the course of the week, so as not to arouse any sort of suspicion of what they were really doing.

Joe had the job of lifting a bottle of booze from his dad. This was what he called his fool proof plan. What he did was, he saved an old rye bottle his old man had previously thrown out. Then each day, he would sneak a bit of rye from his dads bottle and fill it up into the bottle he saved. But after his dads second bottle of rye for the week, it got dangerously noticeable, so Joe filled it up with water.

It really wasn't until Thursday night that Joe thought his fool proof plan would work, but he was waiting for it. "Joe, how would you like to pour me a drink son?" Asked his father. "Sure thing dad!" Replied Joe. Then he grabbed a glass from the cupboard, and walked to the basement where his father kept the booze. Joe knew what he had to do, and the watered down rye never even had the chance to reach the glass. His plan was now fool proof and with a loud shattering of glass to the concrete floor, the bottle full of water and rye for coloring had broke.

Joe made his way back upstairs with his head hanging low. "Sorry dad." He said. But his dad never spoke a word. Instead, with a quick firm back hand, he smacked Joe on the side of the head. Then he made his way to the back door and with a slam, he was out and gone. Joe assumed his father was off to the beer store to get another bottle. It was a small sacrifice to make for him and his friends, Joe thought to himself. But it *would* make for a more enjoyable weekend. He never mentioned it to anyone of the other boys, he took this one to his grave more or less.

Paul on the other hand, was the one who got the permission slips together. He also gathered everyone's twenty dollars and arranged for someone to buy them all beer. As well, he swiped some cigars from his old mans desk and bought everyone smokes for the weekend. With the left over money, he bought more food.

Zack had the job of getting whatever tools they needed for the boys project. He gathered up tape measures, hammers, nails, wood and a chainsaw. Anything to do with building, since his father was a carpenter by trade.

Ted had the job of getting food. But not just food, he had to get snacks such as chips, stove top popcorn, candy, that sort of stuff. Of course he had to get steaks, hotdogs and hamburgers as well. Enough meals to last the weekend.

Ron had the job of grabbing a one horse motor with a pulley system. It wasn't as difficult as you would figure though. His dad owned a small engine repair shop and there was always spare parts lying around. Over a period of time, Ron was able to rebuild an old lawnmower engine. It had everything he needed for what he wanted to use it for. He also had to bring along some fishing rods, baseball gloves, matches, paper and his pellet gun.

Your probably wondering how the heck the boys planned on hauling all this stuff around eh? Well first of all, they have to travel from the devils path, three miles down an open road. Then they had to bike down a gravel road for about a half a mile. Near the end of the gravel road, they would make their way through a thicket of forested cottonwood trees. All the while fighting poison ivy and blackberry bushes. But they *did* have the help of Zack's little red wagon.

Ever since the boys all met in grade one, Zack had been toting around his little red wagon. No one made fun of it, at least no one in the group. Besides, it really didn't matter what anyone else thought. The fact was, every time the boys got stuck and didn't have room for whatever, Zack's red wagon was always there. Like today for instance.

Once everyone had established what they brought, and what they needed for the weekend, there was nothing left to do but put on the backpacks and head out. But not before covering up everything on the wagon. What people couldn't see, they wouldn't be able to comment about. That was how the boys looked at it.

It was time to begin the long bike ride to the forest, which had recently been declared the historical cottonwoods. It was a peaceful place that is located on the outskirts of town. The freeway, along with the train tracks, were on one side of the forest. The Fraser river was on the gravel road side, which is the way they came in. No one could hear you scream for miles in the daylight, never mind the pitch black of the night. I guess that is what made the trip so important for the boys. Alone at last, just the five of them, along with the sounds of the forest.

They reached the gravel road within a couple of hours. Just another five or ten minutes left before they make their way through the dense forest. There was not much daylight left at this point. At least, not as much as they would have hoped there to be.

They finally reached the point of their journey, where there was some *actual* work involved. The boys all dismounted from their bikes, and set them on the other side of a fence. This would begin their walk through the forest. But before doing that, they had to cover their tracks. Ted and Zack grabbed fallen tree branches and began sweeping the gravel road to hide the bike tire tracks. Ron, Paul and Joe began handing everything over the fence and down the trail.

Once the gravel road was swept and everything was over the fence, it was time to hide the entrance to the trail. So all five boys sprang into action and put the living tree branches, they had pulled back and tied ever so gently, back in place. Then they spread out dead tree limbs and branches to cover the trail. Shaping the blackberry bushes like they had never been trampled through.

It wasn't long now before the five boys reached the end of the trail. The place they would be spending the remainder of the weekend. Everyone set their bikes aside, and began pulling branches away from the entrance to a big old naturally hollowed out cottonwood tree. When all the debris was cleared, the boys all stood back and looked for a brief moment. The tree was so big you could have parked a small car inside the tree itself, literately. But what a beautiful sight it was.

Inside the tree was about a ten foot drop below ground. But the boys had built a platform for an elevator they had been working on. The motor was the last thing the boys needed to make it work. They already had a cable hooked up. It was just a matter of getting the motor installed.

The boys stood there for a moment, each in their own thoughts of what the elevator was going to be like when it was all done. At least until Paul spoke. "Okay guys, we're burning daylight here! So let's get something done eh? It ain't gonna build itself!" Paul was the bossy one of the group, but it was enough that the rest of the boys seemed to snap into play at those words. He was probably the smartest kid of the five, so everyone listened.

Narrator,

Well I sure hope these kids make out well. I tried to build a tree house for my two children. A little late in life though mind you, but better late then never. At least that's what I thought at the time. I kept going over to the mother of my kids house and continued building it. It was an add on to an existing playground with a slide and swing set. Above it, on a high up branch, I built a floor. Then I added walls, along with a window and a doorway. I spent quite a bit of time building and bringing materials over. When out of the blue I got a heck of a shock. The ex decided she was moving out of town. The landlord tore the tree house down. Lesson learned, never build a tree house for your own kids at a place where your ex is renting. Oh, and by the way, this historical cottonwood forest, *really* does exist on the outskirts of my home town.

Joe took the cover off of the wagon. He asked Zack to give him a hand lifting the motor out, after taking everything else out by himself. Then they placed it in the spot that was built for it, just inside the tree and off to the side.

"So hey boys, when are we gonna bring some girls out here?" Asked Joe, as he took a swig out of the bottle of rye. Paul didn't have to look at Joe to know he was into the booze. "Hey man, we don't have much daylight left. So why don't you put the bottle down and give us a hand, so we can get at least *something* accomplished! Besides, I think it would be better if we all started drinking at the same time, so you don't pass out and miss out on our first night together eh?" Finished Paul, in a sarcastic voice.

Joe muttered to himself, something no one else could understand but himself. Then he began gathering all the tools they usually left behind, so as not to keep dragging them back and forth to town. Paul on the other hand, started barking out orders as usual. "Hey Zack, why don't you fill the chainsaw up with gas. I think it's about time we got some walls up today." Zack wasn't the confrontational type, so he pretty much did what he was told, with no questions asked.

The other boys were the same way, but there was a good reason for that. You see, Paul's story was a little bit different. His home life wasn't exactly the best, and all the other boys knew that. Quite often Paul would show up to school with black eyes and harsh bruises all over his arms and such. Sometimes, he didn't even show up to school for days at a time he looked so bad.

But none of the other boys ever mentioned that to him. It was a very touchy subject, and past experience taught them to hold back their tongues when it came to Paul's home life. They all learned that lesson, after Ron and Paul both showed up to school one day with black eyes. The boys didn't have to ask what happened, they just knew. Ron *did* however tell the other boys what happened, so the subject was best left alone.

That's not to say the teachers never confronted him about it. In fact, they often grilled Paul and his friends about it. But that was a dead end subject and the teachers never got clarity. Paul loved his father very much, and he would have flipped out on the others for saying anything.

His dad was an alcoholic and often beat him up. But its been happening all his life, so he just assumed it was a normal childhood. He tried everything he could to make his father proud of him, because Paul looked up to him. In the end though, no matter how hard he tried, he just knew that was *never* gonna happen.

So for the remainder of the day, construction of the tree house was under way. The boys had built a floor about thirty feet up the tree on a couple of thick branches. The walls were then built on top of the floor. Then they stood them up, nailed them down, and braced them to the tree. They built a window large enough for each of them to be able to view the forest and all of its surroundings.

After the walls were up, the boys took a moment to sit back and enjoy their work. It was a great place to sit back and enjoy nature as well. High up in the tree tops, there were eagles nesting and feeding their young. You could see squirrels gathering food for the winter, and watch the deer frolicking in the forest. Above all, you could hear the sound of the different birds singing. It was the perfect place to get away and just forget about you problems.

It was around six o'clock when they finally finished for the day. The first night without any parental control, and a weekend to remember for a lifetime. But they *were* starting to get pretty hungry. "Okay boys, I don't know about you, but I'm starving! I think we should call it quits for the night!" Spoke out Paul. There was no argument from anyone, except for a race to the ladder leading down.

Ron was the first one down and on the ground scrambling to gather wood for a fire. This kid could eat all day and not gain a pound. So his nickname was Worm. The human tapeworm, but Worm for short. Everyone was down by now, and each played their part in preparing the first meal of the weekend.

Joe crumpled up paper in little balls. Then he placed them on the fire pit along with dried tree branches on top. Zack grabbed a couple of large rocks to rest the metal rack on in order to cook above the coals. Ted pulled out a bag of pretzels to munch on for everyone. He also dug around until he found plates and cutlery. Paul was the cook for the night, so he pulled out five of the juiciest marinated steaks the boys had ever seen.

Ron was still gathering wood in the forest. When he figured he had enough, at least to make dinner, he brought the wood to the campfire. Then he lit the crumpled paper in the fire pit. It wasn't long before the fire was ablaze, so Ron added more wood to keep the fire going strong. But Ron wasn't done yet, he asked Joe to give him a hand to gather enough wood for the night.

Paul stirred the coals around now and placed the rack on the two rocks. The fire got hot enough to throw the steaks on the grill, so that is exactly what Paul did. It didn't take long before the boys could smell the heavenly scent of campfire cooking, and did it ever *look* delicious.

Ron and Joe seemed to be on quite the mission. By the time the steaks were done, they had pretty much gathered enough wood for the entire weekend, never mind the night. It was getting dark by now anyways, and unless you had a flashlight, there was no use continuing the hunt for wood.

Steak and pretzels, what an odd combination. But the boys didn't care, they were hungry. It didn't take them long to devour dinner. Once the steak was gone, the pretzels seemed to fill their appetites. Not one of the boys spoke a word for at least a minute or two. But what the steak wasn't able to fill, the pretzels more than made up for. But after a while the pretzels began to develop an unbelievable thirst for the boys.

Zack was the first to reach for the bottle this time. He took his first healthy swig from the bottle, then quickly passed it on. As soon as the whiskey was down his throat, he made a sour face and ran for the nearest cooler full of beer.

Then he cracked open a beer and started guzzling it like he was dying of thirst. Before he knew it, the other boys were right behind him, grabbing beers and doing the same thing.

After the boys all had a beer in hand, they made their way back to the lawn chairs in front of the fire. Ron added more wood to get the fire roaring, and Paul pulled out five cheese dogs with five long sharpened sticks. "Okay, I went first the last time we were out here, so I think it's time for someone else to go first." Said Paul.

All eyes were fixated on Joe now. He was the best at telling stories. "Oh alright! What do you guys wanna hear? A story? Or Lies?" Asked Joe. It was no competition, Joe could tell a great lie and one hell of a story. "Tell us a story!" Yelled Paul. "Story man!" Screamed Zack. "Yeah, what he said." Answered Ted, in a lazy voice. "Yeah man, give us one of your creepy stories dude! Wooohooo!" Shouted Ron. Yes, you could tell *he* was catching a buzz.

CHAPTER 2

A Story or a Myth

"Deep in these woods . . ." Joe began. "Okay, pass me that bottle! You guys wanna hear a story or what?" This was about the only time Joe became talkative. Another swig from the bottle and a sip of beer later, his story began to unfold.

"The story goes back quite a few years. In these very woods, there was a young boy around eight years old out hunting with his father. They were down to their last crumb of food at home, and this was their only means of survival. With only a few minutes into their hike through the forest, Leroy's dad spots a deer and signals for his son to keep quiet."

"Then he pulled his son aside and whispered quietly into Leroy's ear." "Leroy, we have to be as quiet as mice. This is the prey that will get us through the winter. So follow me and try to keep up. I don't want you getting lost. Do you understand?" "Leroy nodded, and they began to stalk the wild creature."

"At least they started out together. But no matter how hard Leroy tried to keep up with his father, he was just too fast. Before Leroy knew what was going on, his father began to fade in the distance, until he disappeared out of sight. The only thing left to do, was to follow his fathers footprints in the snow."

"A couple of hours had passed by, and there was still no sign of his father. He did however manage to keep following his fathers tracks. But about this time, it was starting to get dark, and Leroy was getting worried. That wasn't the worst part though. The sky was beginning to rumble with thunder, along with wide spread flashes of lightening that started to fill the sky. Just when Leroy thought things couldn't get any worse, it began to rain. Huge raindrops started pelting down upon little Leroy's head."

"Leroy began to panic. So he screamed out for his father, but there was no use. Between the thunderous sounds from the sky, along with the lightening and rain, he would have had a doubtful time hearing the sound of a bear trudging towards him. Never mind hear his father, or his father hearing him for that matter."

"Leroy was scared, now more than ever. He remembered what his father taught him though, if he ever got lost in the woods. Moss *always* grows on the north side of a tree. But it was getting too dark, and fast. So it seemed like everywhere he looked there was moss. But in this case, Leroy was taught by his father *not* to panic."

"The sky was no longer visible either, the trees blocked his view. But there was still enough light to notice a cave like entrance to a hollowed out tree. So he made his way inside as careful as he could, so as not to fall in the deep hole he noticed. Which he almost fell into. As it turned out, it was the exact same tree we picked to build our tree house in." That is where Joe paused his story. He wanted to see what the reaction of his friends would be.

"Your not seriously gonna end the story here are you?" Asked Ron, sounding disappointed. "Pass me a smoke and another swig of that rye, and we'll see where that takes us." Replied Joe, with all the confidence in the world. Zack gave Joe a smoke, Paul passed him the bottle, and everyone scrambled to find him a light. Ted found his lighter first, so he lit the smoke for Joe.

A healthy guzzle from the bottle, a few sips of beer for a chaser, and a few drags from his smoke. Joe took his time as he enjoyed the crackle of the fire and the nightly sounds of the forest. No one spoke a word for a moments time. When Joe was ready, he continued.

"Leroy sat inside the tree as quiet as a mouse. His mind seemed to be racing in a thousand different directions. He was worried about his father. He wondered if the rain would ever stop, and he tried to imagine what life would be like if he knew who his mother really was. Fear was beginning to set in, but wait. What was that? Leroy heard several footsteps outside the hollowed out tree."

"Leroy got up as nervous as could be. He was now standing just outside the entrance, and could just barley see the shadow of a deer." "Dad? Is that you?" "Leroy called out. But there was no answer. The deer obviously got startled, because Leroy could hear it making a run for it. The sound seemed to be getting closer to him and then, a loud gun shot echoed throughout the forest, and the deer dropped to the ground right in front of Leroy." "Dad?" "Said Leroy, barley able to mutter the words. He could see a faint view of his father's shadow on the other side of the fallen deer. Leroy dropped to the ground in the next instance, clutching his chest."

"Leroy? Leroy!" "Yelled Leroy's father, as he rushed to the aid of his son lying on the ground. Leroy could feel the warm fluid filling his cold hands above his chest. The last thing he remembered, was a flash of lightning flaring up the sky, and a sorrow filled look on his fathers face."

"Leroy's father held Leroy in his arms, screaming in anguish, with tears streaming down his face like a raging mountain waterfall. Then he laid Leroy back down upon the ground, and folded his boys arms across his little chest. It was a gruesome sight to see. Leroy's father flicked his lighter to see Leroy's blood soaked clothes. Then he clutched Leroy's lifeless body and cried out." "Leroy! No, not my boy! Leroy!"

"After which, he began shaking his sons body frantically. But Leroy would not move. So he took his jacket off and covered Leroy up in disbelief. He slowly got up and began yelling as loud as he possibly could. But the pain was too much for him."

"He dropped to his knees, rifle in hand, and said a quick prayer aloud. When he was done, Leroy's father took a last look at his surroundings, and one last look at his son. Then without giving it another thought, he cocked that rifle, and pointed the barrel towards his mouth. As the butt end of the rifle lay resting on the ground, he pulled the trigger. He would see no more." Joe paused for a quick moment.

"Wow man! Is that the end?" Asked a curious, yet impatient Ron. "If you were quiet long enough, you will probably find out man! Now, if I may continue? Or is that too much to ask?" "Sorry Joe. Okay, I'll shut my mouth." Replied Ron.

"It wasn't more than a few days later, when a fellow hunter wandered through the forest. He was a good friend of Leroy and his father. He noticed their car parked on the gravel road leading to the river. But the car seemed abandoned, and the windows were broken. So he decided to go look for the two of them."

"The hunter came across the bloodstained grassy area where the rib cage from the deer still lay. But it was stripped clean. The hunter knew this wasn't the act of wildlife. He was a professional hunter and knew the signs all too well. But after searching the area, he could see no trace of footprints or drag marks of any kind."

"They say sometimes late at night, you can hear the crackling of twigs, followed by the sound of a deer collapsing.

If your wandering in the forest at night that is. People even say you can see the shadow of the deer Leroy's father shot. As well as the ghostly figure of its hunter parading around in the night. Those are just rumors of course. But, it *has* been said, that these woods *are* haunted."

A silence brewed among the five boys for a moments time. Then a crackling sound could be heard. It seemed to be coming from the entrance to the tree. "Quiet." Whispered Ted. Everyone turned around at the same time. In fact, Ted, Zack and Joe were getting ready to run. But Paul put a stop to that in an instance, after looking around of course. So he got up and casually walked towards the entrance to the hollow tree.

"Ron you stupid ass! You scared the living crap out of us!" Yelled Paul. Then he walked back to the fire and sat back down on his lawn chair. Ron followed behind him with a huge grin on his face. Not one of the boys talked for a couple of minutes. Instead, their eyes got lost in the light of the fire.

But Ron could hold back no longer, he bust a gut laughing out loud. "Okay boys, who's next?" Ron asked in the middle of laughing. The other boys joined in the laughter as well. It was then that Zack spoke out. "Okay guys, I think it's time I said my peace." "Alright boys, let's give the man the floor!" Blurted out Paul.

"Okay, first of all, if the stories are true? Then these woods really *are* haunted. They say it is the reason they named this the historical cottonwood forest, because of what happened. But I *don't* think the bodies were buried at the edge of the forest like they say. I think they were buried *right* here, where we have our fire pit." Finished Zack.

"I have to agree with Zack. I also think this is where most of the ghostly sightings occurred, if anywhere. Hell this is where it all went down! I mean, haven't you noticed some of the weird things that have been going on here, since we first started building this tree house?" Nobody answered. "Come on! You can't tell me I'm the only one out of all five of us who has had things go missing or misplaced!" Snapped Ron. The boys sort of half shrugged their shoulders.

"I hate to say it man, but he *is* right." Paul began. "A couple of weeks ago, I left my brand new hammer in the spot I usually do. But I searched that spot a hundred times and never found it. That is until today, and I was the first one up the tree. I made sure of that. So I *know* it wasn't any of you guys." Finished Paul.

"Are you sure you never moved it and put it back in the same spot? Only you just can't remember?" Asked Ted. "Okay, then explain why my brand new hammer broke the first time I got to use it, *after* finding it again?" Asked Paul. "Faulty hammer?" Asked Ted sarcastically. "Grab a grip buds. I checked the hammer out thoroughly before I bought it. Besides, I used it the first weekend and there was nothing wrong with it." Finished Paul.

"Okay, since we all seem to be on the same page here, I guess I can add something to this conversation. Now I don't believe in ghosts or anything like that, but, did any of you guys replace *every* nail on the ladder with a screw?" Asked Zack. "What?" Asked Paul, in surprise. "Uh, no!" Snapped Ron. "Not me." Said Ted. "Me neither." Replied Joe. "Well, I guess we seem to have a mystery on our hands then." Said Zack.

"Okay guys, I think we are *all* getting a bit off topic here eh? So why don't we drop all the stories and get on with the night *eh*?" Snapped Paul. The other boys seemed to agree. Just then Zack heard something in the woods. "You guys hear that?" Everyone went silent. Until Joe started to laugh, after noticing the shadow of a rabbit that was cast on the hollow tree, which was reflected from the fire light. Everyone broke out laughing after that one.

But the boys heard many sounds that night, and decided to set up a watch. Even though they didn't want to admit it, the stories seemed to make them really think. In any case, this idea seemed to set the boys minds at ease.

One by one the boys left the campfire and climbed up the ladder to the tree house. The last soul survivor was Paul, but he wasn't alone. He was clutching a pellet gun in one hand, and a drink in the other. The more he drank, the harder he clutched onto the pellet gun.

Ron didn't need to be woken up to know he was next on the list for *his* watch. He was already down, and by accident, he startled Paul. So bad in fact, that Paul literately peed himself. "Hey Paul, I just thought I'd relieve you so you can get some sleep." "Holy crap man! You scared me half to death!" Yelled Paul, still clutching the bottle and the pellet gun.

Ron noticed Paul's wet pants, but he never spoke a word. Instead, he grabbed a hold of the bottle and pellet gun from Paul's hands. Paul was still a little nervous. But he got up, climbed the ladder, and went to bed. After changing quickly of course. This was *never* mentioned to the other boys at all. It was their own little secret, and that is just the way it was.

Ron did alright for the next few hours. He just took sips from the bottle, while he took to target practice, aiming at some empty beer cans he had set up on a nearby log. The time passed rather quickly though. Before he knew it, Joe came down, after waking up with a thirst. He eyed out the bottle right away and decided to take over for Ron. They exchanged good nights, and Joe stayed up until daylight, where Zack would take over.

It was around ten in the morning before the boys woke up. It was time to get ready for the day. Ron was the first one up. The first thing he did, was to start stirring the coals in the fire pit. He was drinking water from a nearby creek like it was going out of style. Anything to quench his thirst, but he wasn't alone. They were all thirsty by this time.

More wood was added to the fire. Once there was nothing left but hot coals, the metal rack was placed on the two rocks. Then a frying pan for the eggs was set on part of the rack. The rest of the rack consisted of hotdogs. The smell of roasted hotdogs and fried eggs seemed to drift into the nostrils of the other boys, before they decided to join the feast. Paul had a bit of a rough night, so he stayed in bed a little longer than the rest of the boys. But it wasn't long before he was down. The smell of food got him up, so he helped prepare breakfast as well.

His morning started off a little different then the rest of the boys though. Instead of lapping up cold water, he walked straight towards the beer cooler, and started the morning off the way he thought it should begin. With the cracking open of a cold beer.

There wasn't a lot of talking this morning. The boys were more hungry then anything. They prepared breakfast, they ate, and they put everything away once they were done. "I got a great idea! Why don't we all go fishing this morning boys?" Exclaimed Ted in excitement. There was no argument there, and so it was settled.

CHAPTER 3

The First Fish

At the drop of a hat, the boys ran to gather up their fishing gear. It didn't take them long before they all met by the fire pit. Then it was time to start out their walk through the woods. "You guys wanna hit the mouth?" Asked Ted. "Sounds good to me." Said Ron. "I'm game!" Said an excited Zack. "Let's go." Said Joe. "I'm in." Paul added, after the last sip of his beer.

They knew the river as well as they did the forest, but there was a little bit of a hike involved. It was a place where two different rivers meet. The mouth was located about a half mile through the forest from where they built their tree house. If you went a certain way though, you had to trudge through a marsh. They learned that the hard way one afternoon.

"Which way do you guys wanna take?" Asked Joe. "Well there is no way I'm getting wet today! So we may as well hit the trail we made." Replied Zack. "I get the rock!" Yelled Paul. "I get the pool!" Yelled Ron. The other boys looked at each other, and what started out as a casual walk through the woods, turned out to be a race for a fishing spot.

By the time the boys reached the place they were going to fish, they were a little tired. So it was more like a walk to the spots they wanted, no longer a run. Paul walked straight for the big rock that stuck out over the riverbank. Ron went to the pool he had picked out. Ted went to another big rock, where you had no choice but to get wet in order to fish off of it.

Once you had established a fishing spot, it was yours for the day. It's the way they always fished. As far as Joe and Zack were concerned, they always fished together. They absolutely could *not* fish without fatties. They usually had a couple already rolled up for *just* such the occasion. So they fished in passing distance of each other. They had a saying when they fished. If you don't catch a fish, at least you'll catch a buzz.

It wasn't more than a couple of minutes after fishing lines hit the water, when those two famous words were shouted out. "Fish on!" Yes, it was Paul with the first fish on for the day, as you may have already guessed. "Well he *should* have the first fish on!" Zack muttered to Joe sarcastically. "After all, he *does* have the best *spot,* as *usual.* Just my luck! Joe, spark that fatty eh!" Finished Zack. Sounding impatient after hearing Paul yell out first.

Paul landed the first keeper of the day. It was a good size pan fry trout. He *did* think of asking Ron to take a picture. But just as he was about to spit out the words, *he* was stopped by those same two words *this* time. "Fish on!" Shouted Ron, with much enthusiasm. He wasn't the only one who had a fish on though. "Fish on!" Yelled Zack. "Fish on!" Yelled out Ted. "Fish . . ." Joe begun, but realized it wasn't a fish he had on. It was some sort of snag. Snapping the line in the end seemed to be his only choice.

Now that everyone but Joe had caught their first fish of the day, he knew what had to be done. So he got out the camera and took pictures. They all shared a little time on the bank together to smoke a fatty or two.

Soon after though, Joe broke out the video camera and took up filming the boys for the day. He figured it would be nice to catch each of the boys in their little moments of glory. He actually got some pretty amazing footage. It was enough for him to think that *maybe,* he would get out of cleaning all the fish. When everyone was done for the day of course.

The boys caught quite a few fish during the course of this day. But they only killed what they were going to eat. The rest of the fish were just for show, so they let them go. Dinner tonight would be fish over an open campfire. Joe *did* get out of cleaning any of the fish though. He was satisfied to be elected to cook however. It sure beat cleaning the fish, *any day.*

The walk back to the tree house seemed a lot longer than the run to the river. But it was an enjoyable walk. They had only fished a couple of hours, but Paul pressed to get back and do some work before nightfall.

Everyone had a job to do when they reached the smoldering fire near the tree house. Their duties just seemed to fall into place. Joe prepared the fish with garlic butter and lemon peppers stuffed with onions. Then he wrapped the fish in tinfoil. Ron ran the cable through the pulley system of the motor. While Ted, Paul and Zack started building a floor on top of the walls to make way for a second floor.

Narrator,

Pretty high tech tree house if you ask me. But if you got the knowledge, why not put your mind to good use? Especially with a working elevator inside a hollowed out tree? You gotta give these boys credit. It is well deserved. Let's see how dinner turns out, and if this elevator is gonna work by the end of the weekend shall we?

Joe gave Ron a hand for a little while, and passed boards up to Paul as well. When he was through with that, he stoked up the fire and set the wrapped fish on the metal rack. By this time, the boys were getting really hungry. So it didn't take long for them to all gather around the fire with plates in hand.

Fish wasn't the only thing on the menu for tonight. Joe spent a few minutes dicing up carrots and potatoes into little cubes. Smothered with butter, onions and seasoning salt wrapped in tinfoil. It was enough to hold back everyone's tongue until every single morsel had been devoured.

For dessert, Zack sparked up a fatty. "Have I got a surprise for you guys!" He said after a he took a puff and passed it on. "Oh yeah? let's hear it buds." Replied Paul. "Okay, you asked for it." Said Zack in anticipation.

CHAPTER 4

The plantation

Zack was the first to break the circle. He began walking to a nearby blackberry bush, about twenty feet from the other side of the hollowed out tree. The other boys followed, still puffing away on the fatty, until Zack made a sudden stop and paused in one spot. "Okay man, what's up?" Asked Paul. "Yeah man, like we have never seen a blackberry bush before. What's your point?" Added Ted sarcastically. "Why don't you guys open your eyes and look a little closer?" Asked Zack.

It wasn't until Zack picked up a small marijuana plant in his hand, and held it up for the other boys to see. "Woo dude. Where did you get these?" Asked Paul, who noticed the rest of the plants right away. "I got them from my dads shop. He won't miss them, he's got thousands. I brought ten for each of us, and I figured we could go plant them tomorrow." Finished Zack.

The other boys could not keep their eyes off the fifty little baby plants hidden in amongst the blackberry bushes. Once the novelty wore off though, one by one they got back to work. Now they *really* had something to look forward to. That soon came to an abrupt end though. Things just didn't seem to be working out as planned, and the boys started getting annoyed quite easily over the littlest things. So Zack made the call.

"Okay guys, this isn't working out. So I say we each take ten plants, and we get out there to plant them before dark." All eyes were on Zack now. But everyone seemed to agree. Tools were dropped and a race for the ladder to get down was on.

Once they were back on the ground, Zack handed out ten plants to each boy, along with some powdered slug bait and a jug of plant food each. Including himself I might add. Once everyone had everything they needed to plant, it was a hunt to find homes for their plants. So they all set out.

It wasn't more then a few hundred feet from camp, where Ron seemed to find a nice sunny spot to plant his first one. So each of the boys decided to plant one a piece as well. They all watched Zack plant his first. After which, they followed him and did exactly what he did. He dug down and set his plant in the dirt, making sure he covered the roots. Then he watered the plant from the jug of food. Last but not least, he sprinkled a ring of the slug bait around the plant.

"A couple of things you might want to know. First of all don't pee near the plants. That will steer the deer away, but it will attract the bear. So stick sharpened sticks around the plant. Deer won't try and eat anything that will poke their eyes. Bear will smell human, and think there is food buried underneath, so they will dig it up. They smell your scent on the roots. But they will just toss the plant and walk away." Added Zack.

While he explained what to do, the other boys planted exactly the way they watched Zack. Once the holes were dug and the marijuana was planted, fed, and slug baited, it was time to move on to find the next spot. Which didn't take too long in finding.

Zack found an absolutely perfect spot to plant. It was in a rather large opening between the forest of trees. Nothing but blackberry bushes. "You don't expect us to plant in the middle of these blackberry bushes do you?" Asked Paul. "You can plant wherever you want. But that is what I am going to do!"

Snapped Zack. Then he ran his fingers in the dirt to show the others how rich the soil was.

"Look, from what I've been told, blackberry bushes are the best place to grow weed. They seem to naturally have everything marijuana needs to grow. There are so many roots that grow in the ground, that it loosens up the dirt, making it a great place for the plant to stretch its legs and grow strong." finished Zack.

That was all that needed to be said. By the time Zack had finished, the other boys were making trails through the blackberry bushes. They made little clearings in the middle of the bushes until every last plant was in the ground.

Each boy marked their own plants in some way or another, so they knew who's plants were who's. But it was beginning to get dark, and not one of the boys thought of bringing a flash light, so they made their way back.

It wasn't as far back to camp as the boys thought. In fact, daylight was still upon them by the time they arrived. But they got a hell of a shock as they neared the fire pit. That's where every boy stopped in their tracks momentarily.

"Hey man! I *knew* there was something going on around here!" Shouted Paul. "Aw man, who ever it was, broke one of the saw horses. Now how the heck am I supposed to cut floor joists?" Exclaimed Ted. Everyone looked at the campsite, and then at each other, shaking their heads.

The campfire was completely out now, and there on the ground, right in front of the boys, was an open bag of chips. "Hey man, who was the dumb ass who left this half eaten chip bag here? Why don't we just mark a trail for them?" Finished a sarcastic Paul. But every one of the boys shook their heads no.

"Okay man, I'm not pissing around here! Obviously someone here ate the chips and broke the saw horses! Because it sure in the hell wasn't me! Which means it has to be one of you guys!" Snapped Paul. "Well don't look at me man! I was the first one to lead the way out to go plant!" Snapped Ron right back.

"Joe and I were right behind him, so you can count all three of us out. If any one of us should be blamed, I'd say it was you two! You were the last ones out and down the trail." Replied Ted, looking right *at* Paul and Zack. "Hey, we may have left late, but we passed all of you on the trail! We have *all* been together ever since!" Snapped Zack.

But this didn't stop Paul from letting his frustrations get the best of him. "Okay this is complete crap! Which one of you idiots brought someone else out here? I mean, who in the hell else would have done this?" Screamed out Paul. "Look man, just because things got a little screwed up around here, it doesn't give you the right to go pointing fingers!" Snapped Ted.

"Hey guys, you really think the stories *are* true? Do you really think the forest is haunted?" Asked an inquiring Ron. "Look man, the stories are just something we made up to help pass the time." Added Paul. "Uh yeah, let's get back to reality a bit here eh?" Said Zack. "No man! You guys got it all wrong! The stories really *are* true!" Snapped Joe. Then he walked away. "Wow, I wonder what got into him?" Sighed Paul. After that little outburst, the subject was dropped. So the boys got the fire going and kept themselves busy until supper.

It was getting dark, and fast. But that didn't stop Ron from finishing up what he started. It was time to see if this elevator was going to work, once and for all. After adding gas to the engine, he put the cap back on the little fuel tank, and called the other boys over. "Okay boys, let's see if this sucker works!" Ron yelled out.

Ron pulled the rip cord a couple of times, and what do you know, the little engine came to life. "Now for the real test boys!" Ron shouted over the noise. Then he stepped on the platform. Next, a remote control unit he designed and installed to a side rail, was ready for the big test. It was time to take the first ride to the top. All Ron had to do now, was press the button. But this was the moment of truth, so he took his time.

"Okay dude, are you gonna try it out or what?" Asked an extremely impatient Paul. With that being said, Ron pressed the button. The boys stood back and cheered Ron on as he slowly started to rise. The elevator was working and Ron couldn't be any more happier. By the time he got the elevator back to the ground, the beers were being handed out and the hamburgers were just being flipped over.

The burgers were starting to smell really good. So Ted slapped some cheese on. Then he handed out a couple of hamburger buns to each of the boys. Beers and burgers were on tonight's menu, and who could argue with that? Zack brought out a bag of chips, and the feast was on. Who could have burgers and beers without chips?

Narrator,

Well it just goes to show, you can do anything that you set your mind to. This is a saying pa used to always say, he still does in fact. "There's no use starting a job if you aren't planning on finishing it. Put your whole heart into it or it's not worth doing at all." Good words to live by. Actually pa is sitting behind me as I write, talking up a storm. Lol. Let's see what these boys are up to for the night shall we?

After dinner, fatties were sparked for dessert, and the night began. "Oh yeah, I forgot, check this out guys!" Zack said out of the blue. Then he pulled out a pistol from his bag. All eyes were on Zack now. He took the safety off, and started shooting at a nearby can that one of the boys threw on the ground, not far from the fire. That got things started. Paul got out the other pellet gun, and they set up cans on a low branch of the closest tree.

Joe pointed a flashlight towards the targets and the cans were knocked off one by one. There was a bottle set up on the branch as well, but no matter how many shots it took, the bottle stayed on the branch. The pellet guns were passed around so everyone got some shots off. But there was one rule, no matter how drunk the boys got, there was no pointing the guns at one another.

This went on for quite a while, at least until they ran out of pellets that is. But that didn't seem to stop them at all. "You sure you don't have any more pellets Zack?" Asked Ted. "I just checked the bag and couldn't find any. Why don't you guys check inside the cans and around the target area?" Suggested Zack. In fact, by the time he *finished* his sentence, the boys were already looking for flashlights and searching for pellets.

To tell you the truth, the boys were surprised at how many pellets they *actually* found inside the cans themselves. But that was it, searching the ground seemed to be a dead end after a while. So, they loaded up the pellet guns and used up the few shots they had left. That didn't last long at all. It was time to find something new to occupy their minds.

It wasn't long before a new party favor was born. The simplicity of tying up a couple of garbage bags together, as well as a knot every foot or so. Then it was hung on a branch of a tree with a bucket of water underneath it. "Okay, check this out boys." Said Ted. Then he took out his lighter, and lit the bottom end of the plastic garbage bags, removing his hand right away so as not to get burned. After which, he stood back to watch.

The boys were a little confused at first. But it didn't take long before all eyes were on the burning plastic. It was like a laser show that seemed to light up the dark forest. From the sounds of the dripping plastic, to the sight of the beautiful colors streaking down and landing inside the bucket of water. It was the strangest sound, but it sure caught every single boys ear, and put a smile on their faces. It didn't last very long though, but it sure looked and sounded cool.

CHAPTER 5

The Diary

It was time to smoke some more electric lettuce, and figure out who was up next for the next story or lie. All hands seemed to point in the direction of Ted. Joe could tell a great story, but when Ted was drinking, he could tell a great story to beat all *hell*. So he took a couple of puffs from the fatty, a big gulp of beer, lit a cigarette, and began. "Okay, you guys are probably getting sick of this story already. But, since you already heard the beginning, then you may as well hear the end." Ted began.

"Now from the story I got, there were no bodies found. The only evidence that was found, were the bones from the deer. The hunter got the police involved after finding no trace of Leroy or his father. The detectives did however find a trace of blood, believed to be that of Leroy's. They also found a single bullet in the place his body once lay. His father shot himself as well, according to police. They found a tiny piece of his ear, but that was it. His body was never found either." Ted paused to take a sip of beer.

"But the story was covered up so as not to spread a widespread panic. Things were a little different back then. It's not like you could hook up to the internet and find out whatever you wanted. They mostly relied on television, radio or the newspaper. These were the only ways to control the public's knowledge."

"So did they ever find the bodies?" Asked Ron. "No they didn't as a matter of fact. The evidence was put away, and the investigation turned it into a cold case. Two coffins were filled with rocks and they were buried right here where we have our campfire tonight. Not at the edge of the woods as people thought. There is one story people seemed to believe though. They say that Leroy and his father come out of hiding from time to time, wandering these woods at night. It is said, that they live underground."

"What? Uh, I think this story is getting a little too out of hand here. I mean, living underground? Give me a break!" Interrupted Paul. "Hey man, do you wanna hear the story or what?" Snapped Ted. "Yeah man, let the guy finish!" Zack spoke out, giving Paul an evil glare, much to the other boys surprise. "Hey man, why don't you two go scrap it out in the woods and let Ted finish the story eh!" Joe yelled out. "Why thank you Joe. Now if I may continue?" Ted waited for a second or two, but not one person said a word, so Ted went on.

Ted took a healthy drag from his cigarette. Then he cleared his throat and continued his version of the story. "One of the investigating officers eventually leaked out parts of the investigation to his son. Which in turn got out to the public." Ted let out one last cough, and the words literately began rolling out of his mouth.

"The bullet they found, was thought to have been pulled out from Leroy's chest. This is how they knew he had been shot. As for his father, a piece of his ear was found. But when he put the gun to his mouth, the power from the gun made his arm flinch to the side, only taking off a part of his ear. That was one more thing they tried to keep from the public, along with the mark on the ground from the butt end of the rifle. They did however find the rib cage left over from the deer. But it was stripped clean and more than likely used for food. There was no evidence to support the fact that another animal did it."

"So where did the bodies go then? Asked Paul, sounding confused. "You know, if you guys would let me finish, without interrupting, you might find out!" Snapped Ted. The crackle of the fire and the sounds of the forest were the only things heard for a minute or two. So Zack lit up another joint, passed it around, and after taking a pull himself, Ted continued.

"The investigation went on for a couple of more weeks. No one was allowed in or around the woods surrounding the historical cottonwoods. They searched every inch of the forest before calling it quits. After the yellow tape was taken down and the investigation was considered closed, one detective decided to take matters into his own hands."

"His name was Santose, and once he knew there was no chance of him being seen going in, he wired himself up and went in the forest alone." "Wired? What do you mean by that?" Asked a curious Paul, getting *right* into the story. "He had an ear piece and a microphone, so he could record every step he made. But he was smart, on the other end of the microphone, was his wife, listening to every word he spoke. Now the only way to do this, is by acting out the characters, so bare with me." Ted took a second to light up yet another smoke before continuing.

"Now as I said before, the officers name is Santose and his wife's name is Nina." "Testing, testing. Can you hear me Nina?" "Loud and clear." "Replied a voice, on the other end of the listening device." "Okay Nina, I want you to record this, and I want you to break to radio silence until I am done." "Replied Santose." "Okay radio silence is now in effect." "Said Nina." "Okay, I have my flashlight out and I am right beside the tree where the blood had been spilled. There is something peculiar about this tree, which I believe will lead to the clues that are needed to close this case. I am going with my gut feeling, and I am walking towards the hollowed out tree."

"For a moments time all Nina could hear were footsteps." "As I near the door like entrance to the tree, I notice some sort of hair sample. I have never seen a hair sample like this before in my life. A key to this case in which detectives *obviously* missed." "Santose pulled the hair particle from the bark surrounding the entrance of the tree, and put it into an evidence bag."

"I am now pointing my flashlight inside the tree. But oddly, there is about a ten foot drop below the surface." "Then Santose screamed suddenly, and there was silence." "Santose? Santose!" "Nina yelled into the microphone. But it was no use, he never answered, and Santose was never heard from again. The end."

"What do you mean the end?" Asked Paul, sounding disturbed. "Yeah man, you can't end the story like that! There has to be more to the story!" Yelled Ron. "Okay, you guys wanna hear more? Then spark up a fatty and pass me a beer!" Ted demanded. So Paul reached in the cooler, grabbed a beer and passed it to Ted. Zack immediately sparked up a fatty. He took a puff, passed it to Ted and the story continued. After *he* took a puff and passed it on of course.

"Okay, scrap everything I said in the last few sentences." Then Ted went back into character, describing what Santose was saying to his wife. "Wait a minute, what's that sound? It seems to be coming from inside the tree. I am pointing my flashlight down the tree hole, and, what's this? Nina, are you getting this?" "Yes Santose, what's happening?" "Asked Nina." "The earth is moving. It looks like, that of a thousand dew worms coming up through the ground. But I don't see any worms! Wait, what the hell?" "Santose lowers his voice to a whisper."

"Santose needed to get a little closer and observe what was going on. But there was no way to get down unless he were to jump. So he attempted to scale his way down with the help of some tree roots. They were sticking out everywhere, and it seemed like the only way he was going to get any answers. Once he reached the bottom, he spoke again."

"The ground seems to be lifting up and, it looks like some sort of door is opening up. But, that's impossible. Nina?" "Yes, I am still here Santose. What do you see?" "Asked a frantic Nina." "It, it looks like some sort of creature! Oh no, no, Nina do *not* come looking for me! Nina!" "Those were the last words he spoke. Nina tried answering back, but there was no reply."

"The young married couple always had a back up plan, if something ever went wrong. This was the time to execute their plan. She knew there was something wrong, so she followed through with everything they had preplanned. Once Nina did everything she had to do, it was time set out and go find her lover." "Aw, how romantic." Sneered Paul. "You wanna hear this or not?" Snarled Ted right back. "Okay okay, sorry man! I'm listening." Cried out Paul.

"The last thing on Nina's list, was to grab a prepacked emergency bag. It had everything she needed in case things went wrong. Still recording, so she could document everything, Nina got into her car and set out for the historical cottonwoods. It took her no time at all to reach her destination. She blew every stop sign and red light on the way there."

"Nina arrived on the dirt road and parked behind Santose's car. She was in such a hurry, she never even turned off the lights. She just grabbed a high powered flashlight and the emergency bag. It was pitch black out, but this wasn't exactly the first time Nina had been out here. The forest was a little scary at first, but she found her way with no problems."

"Immediately upon arrival to the hollowed out tree, Nina raced to the cave like opening, and shone her flashlight down the ten foot drop, just inside the entrance. As Nina stood there gaping down the hole, and without any warning at all, the ground gave way on her. Nina screamed loud as she fell, hitting the bottom with a thump. But the landing was softer then she anticipated. The flashlight was still shining, so Nina made a grab for it and started digging the freshly dug soil frantically with her bare hands."

"Nina dug for what seemed like forever, and it just felt like she wasn't getting anywhere. So she took a quick break, and leaned up against a large tree root. But just as she was going to start up again, the ground began to shake underneath her. Nina noticed the dirt beginning to move around her, so she backed up as far as she could. Then, from out of nowhere, an elevator of some sort started to rise up from the dirt."

"Nina screamed out loud. The next thing she could see, was a bright light, and a door opening up. But that wasn't all, a hairy arm reached out and grabbed a hold of her leg. The next thing Nina knew, she was on top of some strange creatures shoulder. The last thing she remembered, was the door closing and the sound of an elevator going down."

"Two days had passed by now before Nina awoke. But was she ever surprised to see who she woke up to staring her in the face." Ted stops to light a smoke and take a few drags. "Who? You can't stop there man!" Snapped an anxious Paul. "It was Santose!" Ted said quite fast. "Santose? Is that really you?" "Nina asked, quite surprised." "Yes my dear, it really is me." "Whispered Santose softly."

"Oh thank goodness Santose, I had a terrible dream. You were out investigating in the forest, so I rushed out there with the emergency bag, and I fell in this deep hole inside the tree, and the next thing you know, this big hairy creature put me on his shoulder and took me down this elevator underground, and then I woke up to you looking at me. Oh, I'm glad it was only a dream!" "Finished a long winded Nina."

"Uh, dear, there is something I need to tell you." "But just as he said those words, Nina pulled herself up and started hugging Santose. That's when she screamed out in a high pitched voice. Loud enough to break a wine glass. Nina fainted one more time and Santose could not figure out why. That is, until he looked behind him."

"It was Motimer, the same creature who pulled both Santose and Nina through the wooden doorway inside the underground elevator. Santose couldn't blame Nina in the least, for fainting one more time. After all, it isn't every day you see a big hairy creature as huge as Motimer. But as Santose had already spent the last two days with the creature. He learned secrets beyond his own belief and was only interested in learning more."

"It didn't take long before Nina awoke this time. Just in case though, Santose had Motimer wait outside the room, until he told Nina everything." "Where are we Santose, and what have you done with my husband?" "Snapped an enraged, half groggy Nina." "Listen honey, I want you to be calm and let me explain everything to you. We are in some sort of underground city. Now the only one I have met so far is Motimer. Uh, before you say anything." "Santose stopped talking for a second, as he cups the palm of his hand over Nina's mouth."

"Once Santose knew he could say what had to be said, he pulled his hand away. Now this is going to come as quite a shock to you. The reason you fainted, is because the creature who pulled us down here *is real*. But I have spent the last couple of days with him, and he *is* friendly. The main thing though honey, is that we are here together." "Here? Where is here? Can't we just go home? Baby, I just wanna go home!" "Nina cried out."

"There is *one* little problem with that my dear. You see, we are in a magical place called the Packs, and uh, well, we are not allowed to leave. But baby, this a place people only dream of. Now I have *yet* to see the *actual* city, but we have a chance of a lifetime here. I think if we just give this place a chance, we might, actually enjoy it." "Finished Santose."

"I just wanna go home! Can't we just go home?" "Pleaded Nina." "But as Santose was about to speak again, he stopped short to notice Nina faint one more time. So Santose pulled a blanket over Nina, and went back out into the hallway."

"Hey man, before you start again, there's a couple of things that don't make any sense. If nobody is allowed out of this underground city of yours, then how did the story get out? I mean, don't you think we would have noticed some sort of entrance way there by now? It just doesn't make any sense how *you* know all about this story, and we are just hearing about it now." Finished Paul, as sarcastic as he could get.

Narrator,

It was a bit of competition between Joe and Ted for telling the best stories. But there was one key piece of evidence found in the tree house, which Ted kept to himself at this time. It was a diary someone had either forgotten, or just wanted it to be found. But this was something Ted figured he would share with the others after time.

Ted never *did* answer Paul, instead, he reached for the cooler and cracked open another beer. "Do you wanna hear the story or what? Because I know everybody else would *love* to hear the rest of the story." Replied Ted, as calm as he could be. Paul shook his head and shrugged his shoulders, with a grin on his face. But he never said another word, so Ted continued.

"The door opened to the little room where Nina lay. Santose turned around in surprise." "Nina, are you okay?"

"Asked Santose, rushing to Nina's side." "What is going on Santose? I'm confused." "Replied Nina, as she looked out into the dark and dingy hallway." "Look, I'll explain everything to you, but first, I would like to show you something, okay? Then I'll answer all your questions." "Nina nodded her head yes. So Santose led her down the hallway."

"The hallway seemed endless, and Nina was getting anxious about what Santose had to show her. But then Santose spoke." "I can see the entrance just up ahead. Nina my dear, you are about to embark on a sight that will make history!" "Shining his flashlight around what seemed to be some sort of arena, or so Nina thought. Santose stopped dead center in the middle of the rather large room." "Nina, I want you to wait here for just a minute. I'll be right back."

"Santose raced towards a wall, nearest to the entrance of the hallway they had just walked through. He shone his flashlight around, until he found a rope hanging from the ceiling. He gave it a pull, and then rushed back to Nina's side with much excitement." "I don't understand, what's this all about Santose?" "Asked Nina impatiently. But her question was already being answered for her."

"The room starting shaking fiercely and it startled Nina, so she grabbed a hold of her man tightly. Then a monstrous sound, like the rolling of thunder, could be heard coming from the ceiling. Santose watched the look on Nina's face as he smiled. The expression on her face seemed to go from scared, to excited, in a matter of seconds. The ceiling above them seemed to be shifting to one side like a huge door."

"As the ceiling moved to one side, the room began to light up. Nina looked around at her surroundings in fascination, to see it was nothing like she had anticipated. She was standing in the middle of a large room, which seemed to be the beginning of a maze of tunnels. There were tunnels everywhere she looked."

"On the walls, Nina could see hundreds, if not thousands of paintings. They were painted in such an array of colors, that they seemed to light up the entire room themselves. But as she turned her head up towards the ceiling again, Nina's mouth literately dropped. The ceiling was open wide enough for her to notice the most beautiful sight she had ever seen."

"Isn't this amazing Nina? You are *actually* looking up at the bottom of the Fraser river sweetie!" "Nina stood there looking upwards, practically breathe taken." "Oh!" "Screamed Nina, as she noticed a huge sturgeon swim above the glass bottom of the river." "Is that really the bottom of the river? It seems so, unreal!" "Exclaimed Nina, as she gripped a firm hold of Santose's arm." "Yes it is my dear, can you believe what you are seeing here?" "Answered Santose." "The couple stood there motionless, as they watched schools of fish seemingly gliding by, just above the glass bottom. It was truly a miraculous sight."

"You could tell the sun was out and shining, for it lit up the whole room. You could even catch a glimpse down some of the hallways. There were windows and doorways everywhere they looked. But this was just the beginning of the adventures yet to come. Their eyes were directed back to the river above them, and they stood their watching the many species swim by, for what seemed like forever."

CHAPTER 6

The Spell Room

Ted paused the story for a moment. He got up off his chair and started running. "Sorry guys, I gotta pee!" He yelled out. Well that seemed to start a trend, because everyone got off their chairs to take a bathroom break. In good time to I might add. For the sound of thunder could be heard, followed by streaks of lightning that lit up the forest for seconds at a time.

"Okay boys, I think it's high time we took this party up to the tree house." Ted said, as he ran towards the fire pit, grabbing anything in sight that would get wet. Joe and Zack helped gather up what they could, while Paul motioned Ron to give him a hand. "What's up Paul?" Asked Ron. "You gotta give me a hand man, and quick! We have to get a tarp up above the next floor, or we are all sleeping in puddles tonight." Said Paul, as he rushed up the ladder.

Zack filled the little gas tank of a little generator he had taken from his fathers shop. It was collecting dust in a corner anyways, and he didn't think his father would miss it. But this would be a good enough time as any, to see how long it will stay running. After he gets it started of course.

"Hey Paul!" Yelled Zack. "Yeah man!" Paul yelled back. "Throw me down the male end of the cord!" "Okay! Hey Ron, will you please pass Zack the end of that extension cord?" Asked Paul. Ron didn't argue, he just didn't want to get wet. So he passed the male end of the cord down, and tied the other end to a board nailed to an inside wall. Then he finished helping Paul with the tarp.

Zack and Joe rode up the elevator with everything they had picked up, which they didn't want getting wet. Ted waited until they reached the top before turning off the lawnmower engine, so as not to smoke everybody out. Then he climbed the ladder to notice a light on inside, by the time he reached the top.

Sure enough, no sooner did the boys get their last knot tied to the inside bottom of the window sill, the rain came. But they seemed to have everything under control. The floor was literately covered with sleeping bags, so everyone had a spot. A lamp was hanging from a floor joist, in about the center of the tree house, so there was light. To keep warm, the boys had an electric heater they plugged in.

The boys crawled into their sleeping bags and tried to keep warm as best they could. While Paul pulled out another bottle of rye he had stashed. He took a stomach warming sip and passed the bottle around. After which, he passed everyone a beer chaser to wash down the hard alcohol taste.

Then the rain started, it just seemed to be getting worse, and loud. So Zack pulled out an old battery operated radio. Anything to try and drown out the sound of the nasty weather. It worked, but the rain pelting against the tarp *was* pretty noisy. So the boys chatted amongst themselves for a spell.

"Ah, this is the life. Now all we need up here, is some girls." Said Ron. "Yeah, for once in your life Ron, I have to agree with you." Answered Paul. "Yeah man, I say the next time we come out here, we should each bring a girl. I mean, it's not like we don't have plenty of room. Especially since we *are* adding a second floor." Implied Joe.

"Okay, now that we *are* on the subject, who all here has done it?" Paul blurted out. "What? You mean, been with a girl?" Asked Zack. "No man, I mean been with your mom!" Added a sarcastic Paul. "Of course I mean with a girl. Anyone else besides me?" "I have!" Replied Ron sternly. "Yeah, and who would that be?" Asked a curious Zack. "Denise Valemont. My parents went away for the night and I nailed her in the living room." Said Ron in excitement. There was a slight silence.

"Holy crap! What? If my memory serves me right, that was the night *we* were supposed to hook up. At least now I know why I got *ditched*." Said Zack, taking a huge sip from the bottle. "Oh, I'm sorry man. I never knew!" Ron replied, apologetically. "That's okay man. No worries. It just goes to prove, you can't trust *any* girl." Said Zack.

"I nailed that chick Sabrina, two weeks ago in her parents basement." Said Ted, all proud like. "Shut up! I did that girl about the same time!" Yelled Ron. "Yeah, girls *are* a strange breed eh. Hey Ron?" Asked Ted. "Yeah." "How do I taste?" "Ha ha, real funny *Ted*!" Let's just say, the bottle seemed to be disappearing rather quickly after the truth started coming out.

Narrator,

What young man doesn't think about girls? It's in their nature. But as the truth was slowly being revealed, the boys soon lost interest in the subject. It sure would be a nice thought to get some girls up to the tree house though. But hold that thought, let's see if Ted's going to break out and continue his story.

"Okay guys, I think we better change the subject before a fight breaks out. Besides, I wanna hear more of Ted's story." Paul spoke out. "Yeah man, that sounds like a great idea." Added Joe. "Alright guys. You want a story? Then pass me a beer and I'll get started again." Said Ted.

"Nina broke out and grilled Santose in a series of questions. One by one, he answered them as best as he could. In fact, after Santose showed her the glass bottom of the Fraser river, it was time for her to see where they were going to live." "Where are we going now Santose?" "Asked Nina." "There are a couple of people I'd like you to meet." "With that being said, Santose took Nina back down the hallway he seemed to be getting to know so well."

"There was a door not far from the room where Nina had awaken after fainting. This is where Santose stopped and began to knock. Nina was about to say something, when the door opened." "Hello Leroy. This is my wife Nina, the girl I was telling you about." "Said Santose." "Hello Nina. My name is Leroy." "Leroy replied, as he reached out to shake Nina's hand. Nina shook little Leroy's hand with a smile on her face." "So your the boy we have all been looking for?" "Nina asked in surprise. But Leroy did not answer her. Instead, he motioned Santose and Nina to follow him."

"On an armchair in the next room, sat Leroy's father. As soon as he noticed Nina, he got up off his chair in a hurry." "So this is the lovely Nina. Hello. My name is Andy. I'm sure you have already met my son Leroy." "Replied Andy." "Yes I have and, hello to you as well. This sure is a lovely home you have here." "Nina commented." "Why thank you Nina. Come with me and I'll give you a tour." "Said Andy."

"Nina followed Andy throughout the spacious little home. The bedrooms were very nicely decorated and roomy. Leroy had the smallest bedroom, which he didn't mind at all. But when Nina seen the kitchen, she practically fell in love with it. It had everything a kitchen needed, and she loved cooking. It was *just* as big as the bedrooms, if not bigger."

"Once the tour was over, they all gathered in the sitting room to relax." "Leroy and I were just about to prepare something for dinner, and you two are welcome to join us if you would like?" "Suggested Andy." "That would be wonderful, I'm starving. What are you having for dinner?" "Asked Nina." "Well we were thinking of having deer meat, but I am not the greatest cook in the world." "Replied Andy." "Oh, well I can cook just about *anything,* and I would be *more* than happy to cook for everyone." "Exclaimed Nina."

"Can I help you?" "Asked Leroy, sounding excited." "You sure *can!* With your father's permission of course." "Replied Nina." "That is fine with me. It's been a long time since the boy and I had a home cooked meal." "Added Andy, sounding grateful to have a woman around the house." "If you boys are hungry, then I'll get started. Come to the kitchen with me Leroy, and you can show me where everything is." "Said Nina, in a soft spoken voice."

"Leroy followed Nina into the kitchen and they began to get everything in order. Leroy brought out some potatoes from the cupboard, so Nina asked him to peel them. Next, she searched the kitchen and found carrots, onions and some green beans. So she peeled the carrots, chopped them up, and put them in a pot. Nina also clipped the ends of the beans and put them in another pot. After which, she diced up the potatoes and put them in a separate pot, along with chopped onions. Then she added water, along with a little salt to each pot, and prepared the deer meat for the oven."

"The table was then set, while the deer meat was in. Fifteen minutes later, Nina turned on the elements for the potatoes, carrots and beans. While the food was being cooked, Nina decided to join Santose, Leroy and Andy in the sitting room until everything was done."

"Wow, dinner smells really good Nina." "Said Andy." "Yes, my wife is a *very* good cook. Wait until you taste her cooking though. I have been spoiled for many years with her fabulous meals." "Santose complimented." "Why *thank* you *both.* Dinner will be ready in about twenty minutes or so. Leroy was such a *big* help, I couldn't have done it without him." "Nina added. Leroy sat back on the couch with a big smile on his face."

"Leroy was full of questions for Nina, and she answered them to the best of her knowledge. After a while though, she seemed to lose her train of thought, and almost forgot to check on dinner. But the buzzing sound of the timer started going off on the stove, so Nina rushed to the kitchen to serve a most heavenly spread.

Once the water was drained from the pots, Nina placed them on the kitchen table. Then she pulled out the meat from the oven, and called the boys to the table. By the time the deer meat was put on a platter and set on the table, the boys were already at the table digging in."

"Wow, you are an amazing cook my dear. I haven't tasted something so delicious in, well, quite some time. She's a good cook eh Leroy?" "Asked Andy, in between bites." "She *really* is dad." "Answered Leroy." "Nina, you are the best cook, I swear." "Added Santose, as he got up to give her a kiss on the cheek. Nina smiled as everyone seemed to enjoy her first meal prepared in the underground."

"After dinner, Leroy gave Nina a hand with clearing the table and washing dishes. Andy asked Santose to join him in the sitting room for a couple of puffs of tobacco from his corn pipe. So while Leroy and Nina cleaned, Andy and Santose smoked and engaged in an after dinner conversation."

"Nina?" "Yes Leroy." "After we finish the dishes, would you like to take a walk with me and check out the spell room?" "Leroy asked." "What's a spell room?" "Asked Nina." "It is a place I found when I was wandering the different hallways. I guess you could say it's a library. But I never seen a library like this one before! I never *did* view the inside though, I just peered through the window." "Replied Leroy in astonishment."

"Well it sounds pretty exciting, but, I'm afraid your gonna have to ask your dad first." "Replied Nina."

"With that being said, Leroy nodded his head and walked into the sitting room to ask his father." "Dad?" "Yes son. What can I do for you?" "Asked Andy." "I was wondering, could we take a walk to the spell room after Nina and I finish cleaning?" "Asked Leroy." "I think that would be a fine idea son." "Replied Andy." "Oh thank you father!" "Said an excited Leroy, as he gave his father a hug." "If Nina says yes, will you come with us Santose?" "Leroy asked, as he turned his head to look at Santose." "Sounds like a good plan to me!" "Replied Santose."

"Santose answered Leroy without even knowing what the spell room was. But Leroy was already racing back to tell Nina the good news. So Andy told Santose it was a place they never got the chance to explore, but *now* seemed as good a time as any. All he knew, was that Leroy came back one day all excited after noticing a sign saying, spell room. The room seemed to be full of books, from what Leroy explained to Andy. Santose was more than overjoyed to discover more about the underground and its history."

"After the kitchen was clean, Nina and Leroy went to the sitting room and discussed the plan. It wasn't a lengthy discussion though, Santose wanted to get started right away. So the four of them got themselves ready to go. In fact, it didn't take them long at all. Before they knew it, they were out the door and down the hall."

"Along the way, Leroy kept everybody's minds busy as they walked in the direction of the room full of paintings. You could tell he was excited, Leroy explained some of the adventures he had already experienced, in his short visit to the underground. It seemed to pass the time rather quickly as they neared their destination."

"We are here!" "Shouted Leroy in excitement. His voice echoed as they drew closer to the entrance of the large room." "This is the same place where we were *earlier* Santose!" "Nina cried out." "Oh, so you already seen the spell room?" "Asked Leroy, sounding disappointed." "No, we never got that far. I just showed Nina the glass bottom of the river." "Replied Santose." "Yeah, isn't it awesome? I come here quite often to look at the fish. Oh look, there it is!" "Announced Leroy."

"Leroy ran ahead to one of the hallways he knew so well. He just peered through the window until everyone else caught up to him. The door to the spell room was next to the window, and it had an ancient look to it. Like it was built in the eighteenth century. It was a rather large wooden door with a skeleton key hole for a lock. The door handle itself was black, and the door was beautifully hand carved."

"Leroy turned the handle, and the door made an awful loud creaking sound as it opened. Like it hadn't been opened in years, maybe centuries. As they walked inside, it was like that of a haunted house. They had to brush away cobwebs as they entered the spell room. It was nothing like any of the foursome had expected. As far as they could tell, they were the first ones to enter the room in a long time. Everywhere they looked there were layers upon layers of dust. It *was* kind of creepy at first."

"As they walked by shelves full of dusty old books, there, in the middle of the room, was a glass case sitting on top of a very unique hand carved platform. Nina walked right up to the case and immediately, a bright light turned on inside the case. This seemed to attract the others attention as well."

"The glass case was the only place in the whole room, that didn't have the slightest trace of dust on it, or around it. Inside, sat a rather large but beautifully bound black hard covered book. There was an inscription in big letters written in gold, so Nina began to read it out loud." "Ancient spell book of the nineteenth century." "As she continued to read on, underneath, were smaller gold letters." "Dating back to the eighteenth century."

"There's something mighty peculiar about this book. There isn't one speck of dust in this area at all! It's like, like *magic!*" "Exclaimed Leroy. But just as he spoke those words, the glass case began to open. Everyone stood back, glaring at the book case In fascination. Not one person spoke a word for the next minute or so."

"Nina was the first person to make a move towards the book. Once she got close enough, Nina opened the book. On the first page was a list of names and signatures. As she flipped through the pages, she began to read different spells silently to herself. After reading a few spells, Nina noticed that every spell was signed with a signature."

"The others seemed to lose interest in a hurry, so one by one they left to wander through the library. There were books of a vast variety. Books about sorcery, witchcraft as well as wizardry. There were spell books in every section. From spells to cure sickness, to spells that would change your appearance. Spells to make you younger, and spells that would age you. There were how to spells and how not to spells, love spells, reincarnation spells, the list went on."

"Santose and Andy were off in a corner smoking from the corn pipe, when they noticed a book that seemed to catch their eyes. It was a spell in which you could cast upon yourself, and would never have to shave again. Leroy on the other hand, was busy exploring the library by himself. He was admiring a book that made him curious about his mother. That is, until Nina wandered up behind him and startled him."

"What kind of book are *you* reading Leroy?" "Nina asked." "Oh, you scared me." "Said Leroy." "I'm sorry, I didn't mean to sweetie." "Replied Nina, sympathetically." "That's okay. I was just skimming through the pages in this book, and for some reason, I got really curious about my mother." "Said Leroy, with a baffled look on his face." "Aw, may I ask you where your mother is?" "Asked Nina."

"Leroy closed the book he was looking at and put it back on the shelf." "To tell you the truth, I don't really know. I don't think I have ever met her. I did ask dad about her a few times, and all he said was that I would see her soon enough. But I could tell by the expression on his face, that it didn't seem to be the right time to ask him. So I never brought it up again." "Oh that's a sad story Leroy. Well maybe your father will answer you when he feels the time is right." "Nina replied, trying to comfort Leroy."

"Thank you Nina. There are a few things I've been wanting to get off my chest and, well, dad seems to draw a blank when I ask him certain questions. I'm just glad you and Santose are here. Now I have someone to talk things over with." "Leroy said, as he gave Nina a hug, and she almost drew a tear." "You can talk to me about *anything* Leroy, and I'll be happy to answer any of your questions." "Replied Nina." "Thank you. I'm going to hold you to that." "Said Leroy, with a smile on his face."

"At that very moment, Santose and Andy rounded the corner." "You trying to steal my best girl away from me Leroy?" "Santose spoke out in a joking manner." "No, we were just talking." "Replied Leroy, acting a bit shy. Then he wandered off to the next row by himself."

"Andy was quite surprised as he glanced at his watch, to notice the time had gone by rather quickly since they entered the library. So he caught up with everyone else, as they seemed to be once again drawn back to the ancient spell book in the glass case." "You guys wanna get going? It's getting a bit late."

"Announced Andy. At this point, everyone seemed to agree, so they started heading towards the door." "Did you have fun Leroy?" "Asked Andy." "Yes sir, I sure did dad! Do you think we can all come back tomorrow?" "Asked Leroy." "Woo, there young tiger cub. Let's not get too hasty here and intrude too much in this nice couples lives eh?" "Replied Andy."

"Oh no, it's no bother at all Andy. As I already told your son, he can confide in me anytime. He is a fine young man and we would be more than happy to accompany you." "Said Nina." "Well that's very kind of you ma'am. I wanna thank you both for the dinner, and for joining us for the walk." "Replied Andy." "No problem, we really enjoyed it ourselves." "Answered Santose."

"The walk back was peaceful, nobody really said much. Leroy counted over a hundred different doorways down the dark and dingy corridor. Each door leading to one amazing room after another, and every one of them unique in their own way. Although Nina and Santose seemed to lag behind, Leroy and his father payed no never mind. The pair just figured perhaps they needed to be alone."

"Santose noticed something wrong with Nina." "Is there something a matter dear?" "Santose asked." "No, there is nothing wrong with me at all dear, why do you ask?" "Replied Nina." "Well, ever since we left the spell room, I noticed somewhat of a change, and, you seem a little distant. Like your deep in thought." "Replied Santose. But Nina was reluctant to answer Santose at first."

"I don't know, after spending the day with little Leroy, I guess it made me think. I mean, what I'm trying to say is that, well, you always told me that because of your job working as a detective, it gave you second thoughts about having children. Because of the different way you had to see the world. Well

Santose, I think I want to have a kid of our own." "Blurted out Nina. Santose was speechless for a brief moment."

"To tell you the truth Nina, I *did* have a different outlook on life, and about raising a child. But that was when we lived up there." "Santose replied, as he pointed upwards with his index finger." "Except now, we are in a different place altogether. In fact, I think it would be wonderful to have a kid!" "There was a short silence."

"Nina's face instantly lit *right* up as she looked into Santose's eyes." "Good! Then we can start tonight!" "Santose knew *exactly* what that meant. So he stopped to give her a kiss, full on the lips, as he held her soft hands in his. She kissed him back with *much* passion. But when they realized Leroy and his father were no longer in sight, they took each other by the hand and ran to catch up."

"Oh well *you two* seem to have a certain glow about you." "Andy said, as he couldn't help but notice Nina and Santose smiling from ear to ear." "Do *you* wanna tell them or shall I?" "Asked an excited Nina, looking at Santose as she spoke." "Let's say it together." "Exclaimed Santose." "Alright!" "We are going to have a baby!" "Nina and Santose both shouted out together."

"Well that's wonderful news! Do you hear that Leroy? Your going to have a little friend to hang out with soon." "Replied Andy." "Oh well that's great! So if you have a boy, can I help you name him?" "Asked an excited Leroy." "Why *sure* you can Leroy." "Replied Nina." "So do you two know when the due date is?" "Asked a curious Andy." "Well, we sort have *just* decided to have a baby. So we absolutely could *not* wait to run up and tell you the good news!" "Nina answered, sounding as excited as she could be."

"Nina and Santose were arm in arm as they walked behind Andy and Leroy. They were still smiling as they reached the door to their new home. In fact, they could not wait to get inside and head *straight* towards the bedroom. Andy opened the door and they all trailed through the door opening." "Would you two like to join Leroy and I for a tea?" "Asked Andy. But Santose and Nina both faked a yawn." "Uh, I'm *really* tired. What about you Nina?" "Oh, yes, it's been a long day, so we are going to bed." "Replied Nina."

"Oh okay. Well you two have a great sleep then, and we will see you in the morning." "Andy said as he nodded, and gave them a wink of an eye." "Good night." "Said Leroy." "Hey, maybe we can all do some more exploring tomorrow, if you guys are up to it that is?" "We can discuss that in the morning Leroy, but until then, you both have a great night." "Replied Nina." "Good night everyone." "Said Santose, as he grabbed a hold of Nina's hand, motioning her to the bedroom." That was all Ted said for a moments time.

"What are you stopping for *now* Ted?" Snapped Ron. "Yeah man, you were just getting to the steamy part!" Added Joe. "Hey man! Can't a guy get a quick beer break? I mean, it's not like I see any of you guys doing anything besides sitting there. You know, like twisting one up for instance? Hint, hint." With that being said, Ted got up to go for a bathroom break.

So while Ted was gone, Zack pulled out a bag. "Holy crap on a cracker bra, that's *quite* the bag you got there! Where the hell did you get that?" Asked Paul. "I scooped it from my brother man. I caught him in the middle of a cut down, so he offered me this, and a lot more if I kept my mouth shut. It's pure hydroponic hash bud man!" Finished Zack. "That smells like some pretty stinky stuff man!" Added Joe.

By the time Ted got back up to the top of the ladder, Zack had some fatties rolled up. "Hey man, we gotta crank that stove up a bit, it's frigging freezing out there!" Ted shouted, as he took off his wet jacket and sat next to the heater.

"You got a fat rolled?" Ted asked Zack, who nodded as if to say yes. "Well spark that sucker up and let's get to the story then!" Said Joe. Zack handed the first spliff to Ted. He sparked it up, had a few puffs, and then passed it on.

CHAPTER 7

The Packs

"Okay where was I?" Ted took a second to think. "Oh yeah. Leroy was in his bed by now, but he could not get to sleep. He kept hearing something that seemed to be coming from inside the walls." Ted began. "Ha ha, we all know what that sound is!" Blurted out Ron. "Uh, are you going to let me continue or what?" Sneered Ted. "Oops, sorry Ted." Ron replied. So Ted continued.

"Leroy listened for a couple of minutes, and then closed his eyes to try and fall asleep. But the noise sounded like it was getting closer. So he turned on his night light beside his bed, just in time to notice some dirt fall on top of his dresser. That's strange, he thought to himself. But before he could react, the dresser came down with a thunderous crash to the floor. Leroy jumped out of bed and was about to start screaming, but it was too late."

"Hi Leroy!" "Said a voice." "How, how do you know me?" "Asked Leroy, in a shaky voice." "Let's just say, *everyone* knows about you." "Said the boy, as he popped his head out from the dark hole in the wall." "My name is Dude, and your the kid who got shot by his father. I know this, because I'm the one who had to save your butts. Well, my sister kind of made me, so I kind of had no choice." "Replied the boy. There was a short silence, and then Leroy spoke again."

"Is your sister here as well?" "Asked a curious Leroy." "Uh, well yeah, she *was* right behind me. Hold on a second. Tanantra? Tanantra! Where did you go girl?" "Yelled out Dude." "Thanks a lot Dude! Now I got dirt on my dress!" "Said a voice, coming from the hole in the wall."

"A few seconds later, out popped the head of the most beautiful little girl Leroy had ever seen. She was startled when she caught sight of Leroy, and let out a short high pitch screech." "You idiot Dude! You never told me Leroy was in here!" "Yelled out Tanantra." "You never asked." "Said Dude, as he laughed it off. He knew that his sister was shy, and that if she *did* know Leroy was in there, she never would have come this far."

"Uh, well, hi, and how are you?" "Leroy asked, as he tried to find his voice." "Um, hello Leroy." "Replied Tanantra, with a shy little voice." "Uh, well it was nice meeting you. I will see *you,* back in the Packs!" "Replied Tanantra, giving her brother an evil look as she disappeared in the darkness of the hole, which Leroy figured out was the beginning of a tunnel."

"Well Leroy, I better head back with her before she decides to tell on me or something. Hey, I got an idea, why don't you come back to the Packs with us?" "Asked Dude." "What's the Packs?" "Asked Leroy." "It's where we live silly. You know, our village, where we hang out. Oh come on, what else were you going to do tonight?" "Pleaded Dude." "Well it's just that I don't want my pops to worry about me." "Replied Leroy."

"Look, you got a lock for your door?" "Asked Dude." "Yes." "Replied Leroy." "Then let's lock it up and your dad won't even have a clue. Besides, we'll be back before you know it." "Added Dude." "Okay, well then we better get going before he wakes up." "Said a nervous sounding Leroy."

"So as Dude climbed back through the entrance of the tunnel, Leroy followed. It was a dark and eery crawl through the damp hole in the wall. Leroy was a bit nervous at first, and had a hard time trying to catch his breathe at times, but he managed to keep his cool. It wasn't until Leroy started to see light up ahead, did he really feel good about the trip."

"Wow! This is where you guys live? This is sick!" "To Leroy, this was some sort of dreamland. It was totally and utterly amazing. A whole underground city right in front of his very own eyes." "Oh man, I can't wait to show my dad this! He's gonna flip! Hey, Tanantra?" "Yes?" "Tanantra answered." "Is there another way to get here? I mean, without having to crawl through my bedroom wall?" "Asked Leroy."

"Yes and no. You see, there are only a certain few who are allowed to use the other entrance. We just refer to it as the big wooden door. That is why we asked Motimer to dig a tunnel for us." "Replied Tanantra."

"Now as far as Leroy knew, he was from a small town, and wasn't at all used to the city life, never mind an underground city. The biggest crowd he ever seen, was when a tiger escaped from a train car, and pretty much the whole town gathered around. Loaded with tranquilizer guns, ready to recapture it. But this was all new to him, and quite exciting at the same time."

"I say we go back to the house and you can meet the rest of the family. Then if you want, we can all go swimming together. What do you say Leroy?" "Asked an anxious Dude." "That sounds good to me." "Answered Leroy." "If you want, we could go for a walk and I could show where the big wooden door is Leroy?" "Suggested Tanantra." "I would like that Tanantra, but, well, Dude wanted to go swimming and, I'd kinda like to check out the sights a bit before you lead me out. If you don't mind that is?" "Oh well of course Leroy, that would be fine." "Replied Tanantra."

"It was settled then. The trio walked through the underground city called the Packs. The walk along the way towards Dude and Tanantra's place, was unlike anything Leroy had ever imagined. There were creatures of all shapes and sizes wandering the city. There were no streets like you would see up above. Rather, It was like a path in the middle of town. There were people flying by on magic carpets and everything. To Leroy's surprise, it really was quite a strange and magical place to be, and he was really starting to enjoy himself."

"Hey Leroy, you wanna go and get some ice cream?" "Asked an excited Dude." "You guys have ice cream? I'm down. It's been a while since I had any ice cream." "Replied Leroy." "Follow me then." "Added Dude. It didn't take them long to reach the ice cream shop. It was right around the corner from where they stood."

"When they arrived at the ice cream parlor, Leroy was absolutely surprised. The windows were blue, the walls were blue, and so was the floor. Even the ice cream cones were blue. In fact, everything in the whole ice cream parlor was blue. It was quite a pleasant sight for Leroy, he had never seen anything like it in his life."

"So what kind of ice cream do you want Leroy?" "Asked Dude. But Leroy could not decide at first." "I'll have blue Dude." "Demanded Tanantra." "Yeah, it's my favorite as well, so that's what I'm having." "Said Dude." "Then that is what I will have as well." "Replied Leroy. So Dude ordered for everyone."

"They didn't take long to finish off the sweet blue ice cream. Dude finished first, followed by Leroy, and then Tanantra. Before they knew it, they were out the door and down the path heading towards Dude and Tanantra's home. Leroy watched in amazement as he noticed the many different species of creature walking about. That is, until he bumped into a creature, without even noticing, until it was too late."

"Are you crazy Leroy? That is *one* creature you have to be *very* careful around. He is a dragon, and if he would have swung at you with his blade like tail, he would have cut you in two." "Snapped Tanantra." "Oh, I'm sorry, I, I didn't know." "Replied Leroy, shaking a little." "That's okay, you just stick close to me and you'll be alright." "Said Dude."

"Instead of cars, everyone seemed to take flight with the use of these magic carpets, of all shapes and sizes. But there were so many, that Leroy swore he saw a long haired man carrying a hockey stick. But he wasn't sure, so Leroy just kept *that* to himself."

"Leroy was so interested in what was going on around him, that he never even noticed where he was. Tanantra opened up a door and walked inside." "Mom we're home!" "Tanantra shouted! Then she walked up a set of stairs, followed by Dude and last but not least, Leroy."

"The home was beautifully decorated with pictures covering every portion of each wall. There were pictures of creatures he had never seen before in his life. He never even knew they existed until now. There, at the top of the stairs, was a lady wearing an apron." "You never told me you were bringing company over." "Said the lady." "Oh sorry mom. This is Leroy." "Replied Tanantra. The ladies mouth dropped and she was practically speechless. Then a tear rolled down her cheek." "Why are you crying mom?" "Asked a sympathetic Tanantra. The lady wiped the tear from her eye." "I'm not crying. I, I was cutting up onions, that's all." "Said the lady really fast, trying to hide her tears of joy. Then she grabbed Leroy and gave him a huge hug, trying to hold back her tears."

"Are you, here alone Leroy? By the way, my name is Anne." "Asked the lady, as she introduced herself." "Well, yes and no. You see I'm here with my father, but he is actually sleeping right now." "Then, he *is* alive?" "Anne asked in surprise." "Yes ma'am, but I didn't tell him where I went though. I didn't want him to worry." "Leroy explained." "Hey Leroy, you may as well come with me and we'll try to find you some shorts to wear in the pool." "Said Dude." "Okay." "Leroy replied, as he followed Dude to his room."

"Tanantra, can I have a word with you for a moment?" "Sure mom, what's up?" "How in the world did you find Leroy?" "Um, well, we didn't go through the wooden door if that's what you think? Actually, we sort of asked Motimer to dig us a tunnel, and, well, as it happened, the tunnel ended at a wall in Leroy's bedroom of all places." "Tanantra explained."

"I was wondering why your dress was so dirty. But this conversation isn't over yet! I'm going to fix dinner, but when I am done, we are going to finish this conversation." "Yes mom. Can I go now?" "But her mother did not answer. Instead, she walked back into the kitchen."

"Here! You can put these shorts on Leroy." "Suggested Dude, as he handed him a colorful pair of shorts and walked out of the room. Leroy didn't think twice, he put on the shorts as fast as he could, and before he knew it, Dude had returned." "Are you ready?" "Asked Dude." "Yes I am. So how far is to the swimming pool from here?" "Asked Leroy. But before Dude could answer, Tanantra entered the room." "You guys ready?" "Yup. Hop on and let's get going." "Replied Dude." "Hop on what?" "Asked a curious Leroy." "The magic carpet your standing on of course." "Added Dude, with a bit of a laugh, joined by Tanantra."

"You mean to tell me, you have a *real* magic carpet as well?" "Yes Leroy, anyone who's *anyone* down here has one. Now hop on and let's get out of here." "Said Tanantra." "Is it safe?" "Asked Leroy, a bit skeptic about it." "Just hold onto the sides, cause we're going for a ride!" "Yelled out Dude." Ted stopped for a second to clear his throat, then he continued.

"Without any further ado, Tanantra, Dude and Leroy began floating with the magic carpet. Leroy, still standing of coarse, almost lost his balance. Then he noticed Tanantra and Dude sitting down. So Leroy decided he had better do the same before he fell down."

"Dude had his window wide open, and before Leroy got the chance to ask how they were getting out of the bedroom, his question had already been answered. The trio soared high above the underground city of the Packs, and what a marvelous sight it was. The city varied in magnificent, as well as radiant colors. The faster the carpet carried the three across the city, the more fearless Leroy became."

"Uh, Tanantra? Did you even *set* the traps to the tunnel Motimer made?" "Asked Dude, out of the blue." "Uh, well, I may have forgotten to do that." "Said Tanantra, in an apologetic voice." "Yeah so I can tell!" "Snapped Dude, as he noticed a rather large crowd gathering around the tunnel. So Dude hovered high above the crowd. As he sat there, he noticed that everyone seemed to be standing quite a distance away from the hole itself." "Well it's a good thing I always got a backup plan." "Dude said, as he got closer to the crowd."

"He reached into his pocket and pulled out a little remote control device. Dude always seemed to have a backup plan. Then he reached into his other pocket and pulled out what looked like a string of small fireworks, which he lit. He threw them on the other side of the crowd, between the start of the tunnel and where the crowd had gathered. The loud crackling sound of the fireworks going off, frightened the crowd back far enough where Dude's plan went into effect. Then he pushed the button, and got out of there in a hurry."

"There! That's how things get done! Now let's go swimming." "Dude said. So the trio hovered high above the Packs once again." "Leroy, this may come as quite a shock to you. I don't know if Dude told you or not, but, well, you are a bit of a celebrity here in the Packs." "Tanantra started to explain." "Me? Why me? Is it because I'm new here?" "Asked Leroy." "Look, that is all I can say for the moment. It really isn't my place to tell you. So if you get some strange looks, then you'll at least know I gave you fair warning." "Finished Tanantra."

"Within minutes, the trio landed the magic carpet right next to a blue underground swimming pool. Even though it wasn't much of a warning, Leroy didn't know what to think at this point. He was a little nervous after what Tanantra had just told him. But before he had the chance to speak, a small crowd gathered around him." "Okay folks, nothing to see here! So if you will all make way here, my friend and I would like to take a swim." "Announced Dude."

"As they cut through the crowd, a familiar voice was heard in the midst." "Well hello Leroy!" "Said a voice, with the greeting of a hand shake. So Leroy shook the boys hand." "My name is Dylan." "But as soon as the hand shake was complete, he focused his attention directly towards Tanantra." "Well hello there beautiful! Where have you been all my life?" "Dylan asked, as he wrapped his hand around Tanantra's hand and gave it a kiss."

"You are *so* gross! Why do you always have to do that?" "Exclaimed Tanantra, as she pulled her hand away." "Because I get lost in your beauty my love." "Answered Dylan." "Yeah, well give it up! It will *never* happen!" "Added Tanantra, as she stormed off to the change room."

"Man, why do you always gotta do that to my sister?" "Asked a furious Dude." "Because Dude, your sister is like, so hot man." "Replied Dylan." "Leroy, this is my brother from another mother. He goes to school with me." "Announced Dude." "Cool, I never got the chance to go to school. But I have heard a lot about it!" "Leroy spoke out." "You never been to school man? Your missing out on all the honeys! Dude, we have *got* to hook this kid up with some schooling man! He doesn't know what he is missing." "Added Dylan."

"In due time my friend, but for now, he has got to get used to swimming first!" "No sooner did he finish his sentence, Dude tackled both Dylan and Leroy, and they all fell into the swimming pool at the same time. Leroy came up first, gasping for air and hanging on to the edge of the pool." "Wow! This pool is a lot warmer than I thought it would be." "Leroy said, half out of breath." "What? You can't tell me you have never been in a swimming pool before either?" "Asked Dude. Leroy caught his breathe and then he spoke."

"Well we used to go swimming down by the pond near our cabin." "Said Leroy." "What's a pond?" "Asked a curious Dylan." "It's a body of water, formed by a creek, that runs off the mountain where my father and I used to live. It was *really* cool." "What? You mean like, cold? I don't think I could handle cold water. Nope, this water is fine enough for me." "Answered Dylan. But before Leroy got the chance to say another word, Dylan disappeared back under water."

"Hey Dude, I got a question for you. Do you and your sister really hate each other? I mean, it seems like you guys don't get along at all." "Asked Leroy." "No man. Where did you get a crazy idea like that?" "Asked Dude." "Well it just seems like you guys fight a lot." "Replied Leroy." "I'll put it this way, when you have a sister, or brother for that matter, you live with them, and go to school with them, and they *always* seem to be around you, like twenty four hours a day. You would kind of get sick of them after a while too." "Answered Dude."

"Oh. Well I don't have any brothers or sisters, so I really *don't* know what you mean." "*That* conversation didn't last long at all. Before they knew it, the pool filled up with creatures of all shapes and sizes. All trying to get a closer look at Leroy. But he payed no mind and began swimming around the pool with Dude and Dylan."

"The next hour or two was spent diving into the pool, to see who could make the biggest splash. That is, until boredom set in, and Dude asked Tanantra and Leroy if they wanted to fly through town once more, before dinner was ready. So they said their goodbyes to all their friends. Then they got changed, and met at the magic carpet one more time."

"Leroy got to see most of the city, and wanted to see more, but by this time, dinner was ready. Dude and Tanantra knew *not* to be late, or they would go without. So the next stop, was back through Dude's window, and back into his bedroom."

"The trio arrived just in the nick of time, for their mother was calling them to the table." "I see you still have your little friend with you. Well, come grab yourself a seat, and Tanantra can help me set the table." "Anne said, in a rushy sort of voice. The boys sat themselves down at the kitchen table, while Tanantra and her mother brought plate after plate of food to the table."

"Leroy's eyes lit up at the feast he was about to endure. There was cut up chicken, mashed potatoes, cakes and cookies, along with puddings and vegetables. Once the table was full of food, everyone got seated and ate until their hearts were content."

"After dinner, Leroy offered to do the dishes. But because he was a guest, Anne told him under no uncertain terms was he going to do dishes. So Dude and Tanantra were elected, with no argument whatsoever. When everything was cleaned, Leroy pulled Dude aside, and suggested to him that it was time for him to go, before his dad woke up."

"So Dude yelled out to his mom that he was going to take Leroy to the big wooden door. Reassuring her that he would not be long, since it *was* a school night. Leroy thanked everyone for such a great time. He also thanked Anne for the dinner, and was on his way out the window with Dude on the magic carpet."

"It did not take Dude and Leroy long to get to the big wooden door. But before Dude dropped him off, he circled around to make sure there was no one else around to see the pair by the door. Keep in mind, that it was forbidden for Dude to be anywhere *near* the door."

"But as far as Leroy was concerned, it was the only way for him to go home, and this was the only entrance he was *allowed* to use." "Well Leroy, I hope you had a good time, and perhaps you can come back soon so we can hang out some more." "Said Dude." "I had an *awesome* time Dude. This was the best day I've ever had, thanks to you and your family. I'll try and get back here as soon as I can." "Added Leroy."

"But by this time, Dude was up and away with the magic carpet, and did not even know if Dude heard everything he had said." "Meet me here in two days Leroy!" "Yelled out Dude, and then he was gone. So Leroy grabbed the handle of the big wooden door and opened it up. The door practically scared the crap out of him. The big old hinges creaked very loudly with an echoing sound. It was a heavy door, so Leroy had to pull hard to open it, and push even harder to close it behind himself."

"On the other end of the door he found himself once again in a dingy dark tunnel. But as he seemed to get his night vision, Leroy knew that he wasn't alone." "Hello Leroy." "Said a deep voice." "Hi Motimer. Your not going to tell my father I was here, are you?" "No Leroy, I won't say anything. I would get in trouble to. I *was* the one who dug the tunnel that would lead Dude and his sister to your bedroom." "Yes, they told me, and I actually want to thank you Motimer." "Leroy gave his big hairy friend a hug."

"Leroy and Motimer set out down the dark and dingy corridor, engaging in lengthy conversations to help pass the time. Leroy was starting to know a little about this underground city, but the big pieces of the puzzle were still missing. Like why Anne seemed to be so interested Leroy's father? He *did* however manage to ask Motimer a few things, that was one question he *would* not answer though."

"When Leroy reached the door to his home, he said goodbye to Motimer, and he disappeared back down the hall. The door was locked as Leroy tried to turn the knob. But he remembered the key him and his father *had* stashed, in the hallway behind a painting. So he grabbed one key for his bedroom, and opened the front door with the other key. Then he took the spare key and replaced it where it should always be kept, in case of emergencies such as this."

"Leroy took small steps and slipped silently through the hallway to his bedroom. He opened the door with his bedroom key, as quietly as he could, so as not wake his father. He stood still for a moment, as he thought he could hear his father wake up, but he was mistaken. So he carried on to his bedroom."

"Once Leroy unlocked his door, and was back inside his bedroom, he felt a sigh of relief as he closed the door behind him. Leroy cleaned up the dirt, and put everything back the way it was. He picked up the dresser and set it back up against the wall. Then he hung the picture back up to hide the hole he had once crawled through with Dude and Tanantra. After the room was back to normal, Leroy collapsed on his bed. He was so tired, but he could not stop thinking about the adventure he had just lived, and that is how he drifted off to sleep."

CHAPTER 8

Back to reality

"Well if this isn't the most perfect time to pause the story, I don't know what is!" Exclaimed Ted. Paul, who got the munchies, decided to burn a few burgers on an electric frying pan. There was no arguing with that. The other boys seemed to have a developed a case of the munchies as well. The burgers obviously set off a couple of tape worms in the boys stomachs. Because story time was out, and the munchies were in. Paul broke out the chips. Ted got *right* into a bag of salted peanuts. Ron got out a two liter of pop. Zack on the other hand, just hit everyone else up for what they were eating.

Once the boys finished eating, there *was* no mention about Ted continuing with his story. No, that's where the story went dead for a little while. One by one the boys began nodding off. Paul was the last man standing, and the only reason he was still up, is because he wanted to eat himself to sleep. Hey, that's just the way he rolled.

The morning couldn't come soon enough. Ted thought to himself, as he rolled over onto his stomach, tossing and turning in his half sleep. As it ended up, he was the last one to roll out of bed. Ron was the first to get the fire started, and as well, he organized everything they needed for their trip in the woods today. He also managed to have time to make scrambled eggs and french toast for everyone.

But by this time, Zack and Ron were having a rather loud argument over what they called, the art of fatty passing. It was enough to wake Paul up, and *that,* was a mistake. Because now there was going to be three grumpy kids up. "If you two don't shut up, I'm gonna throw you guys in the fire!" Yelled a furious Paul, who hated to be woken up. "Yeah, and a good morning to you to *Paul!*" Yelled both Zack and Ron at the same time.

There wasn't any use trying to sleep now. Besides the fact, the smell of food was beginning to linger upwards, and *nothing* got passed Ted's nostrils. Paul chose to sleep above everyone else, literately. He took that hammock with him every time he went camping with his family. It had sentimental value to him. Paul's grandfather gave it to him just before he passed away a few years ago.

"You get any sleep last night Ted? I slept like a baby man, what about you?" Asked Paul. "I couldn't even sleep a wink the whole night. I kept tossing and turning man. Mind you, I am pretty sore." "Sore from what man? Were ya pulling it all night? Ha ha." Paul said with a laugh. Ted took a look to see if anyone else was listening.

"No man, look, if I tell you something, you gotta promise me you won't tell anybody, okay?" "Yeah man, you know you can *always* trust me." Added Paul, in a very convincing manner of speaking. "Okay man, but remember, *you* promised not to tell *anyone* else." That is when Ted lifted up his shirt and showed Paul his back.

Paul put his hand over his own mouth. He was in shock at what he saw. "Okay man, who did that to you? Let's go deal with this *right* now!" Paul yelled. "Hey man, not so loud! You want everyone else to hear? I told you I don't want anyone else to know!" Scolded Ted. Paul was a little stuck for words at first, and tried to figure out something to say next.

"I'm sorry. I just never expected *that* man. Who did that to you?" Asked Paul, one more time. "Same person it's always bin. Except this time he went a little overboard." Replied Ted. "Your *dad* did that? Holy crap man, we got to do something about this, it's starting to get *way* out of control!" But the conversation was cut short.

"So you guys gonna sleep all day? Or are ya gonna come down and eat the breakfast I made?" Asked Ron, appearing out of nowhere. "You can at least let us roll out of bed! Before you start grilling us with questions first thing in the morning!" Snapped Paul. After which he thanked Ron, and said they that would be down in another minute or two. That was fine with Ron, he just wanted everyone to at least taste his breakfast. So he threw Paul a rolled up wake and bake fatty, and went back about his task at hand, preparing for the journey.

"Look man, you gotta tell someone about these beatings! Before your dad flies off the handle so bad one day that eventually he kills you." Paul replied. "Look man! Ain't no one gonna say a word to *nobody* okay! You got it Paul!" Yelled Ted, in a harsh but serious voice.

But before Paul could spit out even *one* word, he noticed a long sad face, followed by two lone tears, streaming down each side of Ted's cheeks. Which made Paul change *everything* he was about to say. So Paul tried to comfort Ted instead. With a lump in his throat, Paul swallowed his pride and said this. "Hey man, how long have we known each other bro? You know darn well I won't say a word dude." Paul said. "Yeah?" Replied Ted. "Yeah man." Said Paul, as a matter of fact like.

With that in mind, the conversation ended, in an embarrassing sort of way. Zack walked in on the pair, just as they were giving each other a manly hug. Totally platonic of coarse, but, Zack just *had* to pull out the fag card in mid hug. "Shut the hell up man, before I knock you into next week!" Yelled Paul, who wasn't *about* to take Zack's crap at this point.

Pulling out that card on Zack's part, didn't last long. But the boys *did* eventually head down to the fire pit to grab some grub. After a couple of puffs of the prefab Ron brought up to them earlier of course.

"It's about time you guys decided to come down and join us. Huh, we were about to leave without you." Ron blurted out sarcastically. "Oh really? Well it sounds like you got the whole day planned for us eh Ron?" Asked Paul. "As a matter of fact I do. I took the liberty of filling two liter pop bottles with a food and water mixture, in the midst of preparing breakfast for you all." Ron took a bite of his french toast and continued.

"*Then,* I figured while we were out that way, we could catch a couple of fish. After all that, we can head back here for the afternoon to work on the second level of the tree house. If there's any time left? Then we will just sit back and relax. Hows that for a full days planning?" Added Ron. "Sounds like somebody has been smoking a little too much this morning to me." Answered Paul sarcastically, as he fixed a plate for himself.

"Hey, before we head out, I think we should put up that army netting I brought!" Yelled out Ron, from inside the tree house. "Well, if we're gonna get everything done that we planned, then we better get that netting up right now." Added Zack. "Zack! Why don't you start up the elevator, throw the netting on, and ride up with it?" Blurted out Ron. "What the heck are you talking about? I don't see any netting. Did you forget to bring it?" Asked Zack. "Uh, that bag that's been sitting out in the rain all night, has all the netting inside it." Added Ron.

Setting up the netting didn't take as long as Ron figured. Before he knew it, they were done, and back on the ground with the rest of the boys. "Okay then, I threw a few beers in each of your bags, along with plant food and a few munchies for the day. Alright boys, whenever your ready." Finished Ron. Paul and Ted had just finished eating, but did not waste any time putting on their pack sacks and heading out with the rest of the boys.

The first patch did not take any time at all to find. But what a sight for sore eyes, that's for sure! "Man, are you guys seeing what I'm seeing?" Ted whispered loudly to the rest of the boys. The few plants they put int the ground, were already making progress. They were starting to grow healthy and strong.

Narrator,

There are a few things in this book which I mention from time to time, that *are* true. I will leave it to you to decipher what *is* true and what *isn't* true. I will however point out only a handful of things that *really* has happened during the coarse of my life, as well as others around me. But until then, let's get back to the book shall we?

"These plants are going to be *insane* man! I never seen marijuana plants grow this fast before." Said Ron. "Well check it out man, everything that grows in this area seems to be getting a lot of sun. Look at how green the grass is here. More so then the rest of the vegetation around here." Said Paul. "He *does* have a good point Ron. Let's feed them and move on to the next patch." Said Zack.

The boys stood their staring at the healthy fat leaved, bushy plants, while Ron watered them and put the bottles back in his sack. "Okay boys, let's get the heck out of here man, this place is littered with bugs!" Said Ron. The other boys didn't argue, they were just as curious to see the next few patches as Ron was.

"Oh man, why did we have to plant our plants so far apart?" Joe complained, as they trudged through the thicket of the forest. "Well for one, you never put all your eggs in one basket. Number two, well, I *really* didn't think it would turn out to be such a jungle out here. I especially never thought there would be so much poison ivy and blackberry bushes." Added Ron.

Joe was the first to discover the second bunch of plants. He also remembered *exactly* which ones were his. He took about five or six sharpened branches, and stuck them in the dirt, surrounding each and every one of his plants, so as to steer the deer away. "Well I'll tell you what guys, we sure as heck picked a great place to grow man! These plants are already twice as big as they should be. I think this is going to be a good year man!" Yelled Joe.

Everyone got out their water bottles and took care of their own plants. It was for the best, that way if nothing turned out, no one could blame any certain person but themselves. "Hold up everybody, I got something to say." Said Ron.

"Look, if we're gonna do this, we gotta do it all the way man. There can't be no half ass way about it in the least. Which means, if you guys got anything planned for the summer, cancel it. Because this is going to take most of our summer to get done." Added Ron.

"Our whole summer?" Paul began, but was interrupted. "Oh, and a part of September I might add." Said Ron. "Holy crap man! You don't expect a lot out of us do ya?" Blurted out Joe. "Hey man, I thought we planned to spend most of the summer out here to begin with!" "Ted spoke out. "Ya man, I just kinda wanted to be a bit of an ass about it okay." Joe replied, with a bit of a chuckle.

"No man, don't you guys realize what I'm trying to do here? If we pull this off, we could be the king pins back at school, and put Freddy the free loader out of the game! We could each have our own cars, and *actually* have money for gas. You guys get why this means so much to me?" This was Ron's biggest speech of the day. But after that speech, the hype within the group seemed to calm down a bit. In fact, the boys began thinking a little deeper on their next walk.

They thought about what it would be like to be king pins for a year. There was no running on *this* walk to the next batch. Instead, the boys were in deep discussion of what it was going to be like, if it was *them* running the school for once. It was going to be awesome. "So what do you say boys? Are we going to do this all summer long or what? I mean, we *are* going to run this school man!" Yelled Ron. "I'm in!" Yelled Zack. "I'm in." Said Ted. "I'm in." Said Paul. "I'm in." Said Joe. "So it's settled. We are going to rule the school. Yeah!" Yelled Ron.

Of coarse Ron had to start the celebration off right, by pulling a beer from his pack sack. That seemed to start and trend. Once the other boys heard the sound of a beer opening, four more beers were pulled and cracked.

"This summer is going to be wicked without our parents boys!" Yelled out Ron, after taking a big gulp of his beer. The other boys stopped in their tracks and looked at each other. "What do you mean by that?" Asked Paul. "I have a plan." Replied Ron, all casual like. "Yeah, and what sort of plan do *you* have that is different from any other summer?" Paul asked, curious to see what Ron had to say *this* time.

"Simple! Welcome to camp Mary Jane!" Yelled Ron, sounding confident with his idea. "Camp Mary Jane? Man, I think it's time to check Ron into the funny farm. He needs some help!" Paul added with a laugh. "Yeah man, get some help Ron." Said Zack. Who was already feeling a good buzz after guzzling two beers in row.

"I got it all planned out guys. Hear me out, I got it all worked out. Remember the permission slips we got our parents to sign from school? Well, I made up some special ones for camp

Mary Jane. It's a religious camp with our camp leader being named, Mary Jane. What we do is, we hand our parents the permission slip, along with a payment to camp Mary Jane of course. We get our parents to sign it. Then we get them to call the phone I bought from Freddy. They have to call at different times though, so we can each disguise our voices for each parent that calls." Finished Ron.

"You know, this little idea of Ron's *just* might work. I think he could *really* be on to something." Paul added. "To tell you the truth guys, this could really work." Said Zack. "You know what man? I think we should give it a try. What have we got to lose?" Yelled out Joe. So it was settled, for the rest of the school year, they would proceed to make this plan a go. Something they would remember for the rest of their lives.

"I gotta admit boys, Ron *does* seem to be a few fries short of a happy meal. But once in a while, he *does* seem to come up with some pretty good ones." Laughed Paul. "You got that right!" Added Joe, as he and the rest of the boys, including Ron, joined in the laughter.

"Yeah, well you guys laugh it up while you still can! You ever bin to a psychiatrist before? Well I *have!* I was always bumping into stuff as a kid, and mom thought I needed some help. So they brought me into the docs office, and he sat there trying to make me put triangle blocks into triangle holes, and square blocks into square holes and such." Ron paused for a second, while everyone waited for him to continue. Just like they *all* knew he would.

"Yeah! Well I shocked the heck out of him! I began forcing square blocks into circle shapes. Eventually throwing a fit, trying to beat the blocks into the odd shapes. I think the doc kind of thought I was out to lunch, so they put me in the hallway, and mom stepped into the office with him." Ron lights a smoke and takes a puff. "So from what I was told, years later mind you. Over the next few weeks that followed, they were putting pills in my breakfast. I really didn't notice a thing, but *mom* sure did. She found me up all hours of the night rebuilding televisions." Ron takes another drag off of his smoke.

"So the next visit back to the doctor, I heard them talking about it. The doctor told mom that they should just let me go, and see how things work out. Because at that point, there was nothing they could really do about it. I was just happy to know that I never had to go back again." Ron took his last drag of his smoke. "That's *my* story and I'm sticking to it!" Said Ron, with an odd grin on his face. "That's exactly why your one of the boys Ron!" Yelled out Joe, and everybody had a bit of a laugh. "You'll *always* be my bro man!" Yelled out Paul. So they finished off a couple of beers, and hit the trail.

Narrator,

Camp Mary Jane eh? Now what kind of parent would fall for *that* scam? But you *just* never know, these kids could be on to something. It's a good thing they picked a weekend of the teachers professional day, they had one more night to go. One more thing though, that topic with the pills, was based on true events. But that's another story, let's get back to five kids shall we?

With only one thing on their minds, the boys scouted out the next patch. "Hey Ted, wait up!" Shouted Joe. "Why do you gotta walk so fast?" Joe asked, as he caught up to Ted. "Cause I wanna get something done today! Better than being a slow ass like you man!" Shouted back a sarcastic Ted.

When Joe caught up to Ted, he only had one question on his mind. "So you really think this plan of Ron's is gonna work man?" "You know what man, I think everything is gonna work out just fine. At least, that's what I think *anyways,* but who knows? I guess we are just going to have to play it by ear." Said Ted. "Yeah, I guess your right." Replied Joe.

The boys arrived at the last patch, and it *just* so happened to be the healthiest of all the patches put together. "Well I got to give you this one Ted, you sure picked one heck of a spot here. Man, would you look at the size of these babies? Looks like we hit the mother load!" Yelled out Paul. "Yeah man, we hit the jack pot here Ted!" Added Zack. The plants had fat leaves and a thick stock. The healthy white roots could be seen growing big and strong in between the blackberry bushes.

Once the boys fed and watered each and every plant, they put everything away in their back packs and prepared to head out. "Okay boys, this time we aren't allowed to call out our spots. Instead, we have a race, and whoever gets to that spot first, gets to fish in *that* spot for the rest of the day. You ready? Go!" Paul said really fast, and the race was on. But there were never any worries, no matter who got where first. They *all* pretty much got the exact same spot they felt most comfortable fishing from. So fishing was on!

"Paul, what are you fishing with?" Asked Joe. "What are *you* fishing with?" Answered a sarcastic Paul. "Well I'm using an eagle claw hook with a worm, and a few strands of red wool. So may the best man win!" Yelled Ron. "I'm fishing with a crocodile spinner and a hint of pink wool. So watch the master at work!" Paul shouted back.

The boys knew that it would be a short lived day for fishing, since there really wasn't too much daylight left to begin with. But that wasn't going to stop them from at least *trying* to have some fun while they could. That's when it happened, and I don't think the boys would forget this for the rest of their lives, no matter what happened from now until then.

"Fish on!" Yelled Paul. "Fish on!" Yelled Joe. "Fish on!" Yelled Zack. "Fish on!" Yelled Ted. "Fish on!" Yelled Ron. It was an historic event in these boys lives indeed. "Yeah right, you probably got yourself in a snag!" Yelled Ron to Paul. That is, until he seen the fish come right out of the water with a mighty splash. "Woo man! Hows *that* for a snag there Ron?" Yelled Paul, trying to play his fish out. But Ron wasn't really paying too much attention, since he had a fish on, as well as the rest of the boys for that matter.

"Okay, I'm calling it! Who ever pulls in the biggest fish, has to clean everyone's fish! You guys all in?" Even with all the yelling going on from everyone reeling in their fish, they could *still* hear Ron and agree. So it was on, biggest fish in gets to clean all the fish.

Paul was the first one to bring in his fish, and a pretty good size one too I might add. But no sooner did Paul bring his in, he began filming it for bragging rights. Then he began filming the other boys bringing in their fish. Only because he never thought that any one of their fish would match up to the size of his.

After everyone's fish was pulled up and lying on the riverbank side by side, it was settled. Paul had bragging rights to the biggest fish. But he also had to do the thing that was his pet peeve, and that was to clean *all* the fish, along with his own. It wasn't that he disliked cleaning fish. It was more like he had to do a perfect job no matter what he did, and it *had* to be done *his way,* or no way. But this was Paul, and they loved him like a brother.

While Paul cleaned the fish, everyone else decided they would keep fishing. They seemed to be catching them by the dozen. So Paul had to put his two cents worth in too mind you. "I hope you guys plan on catching and releasing! Because if you think your gonna add another fish on the pile for me to clean, you better think again, cause it ain't gonna happen!" But the other boys simply ignored Paul in his now grumpy state.

One after another the boys kept hooking on to big fish. Ron actually pulled one ashore and brought it to Paul, just for bragging rights about how big it was. That just got Paul even more frustrated. But he seemed to keep his cool, at least until he was done cleaning all five fish anyways.

Paul hollered out to everyone that it was getting a bit too dark to fish, and that he wanted to head back to camp. But everyone else seemed to be preoccupied catching and releasing fish, to *really* pay too much attention to what Paul was saying. Then it started getting darker, so that's when Ron called it. After bringing in another trophy trout ashore of course.

"You guys ready to get some food in our bellies?" Yelled out Ron, to the rest of the boys. "Yeah man, one more fish eh?" Yelled back Joe. "Well, you guys can keep fishing if you want, but I think Paul and I are going to head back. So we'll see you guys back at the tree eh!" It didn't take Joe, Ted and Zack long to reel in and pack up though. Especially since they knew Ron had the only flashlight.

The trip back to the tree house was quite a nasty one in the dark. But it would have been a lot worse, if it wasn't for the only flashlight in the crew. Carrying those fish didn't make things any easier. The boys got tangled in so many blackberry bushes and poison oak, that it was almost unbearable. When they finally caught sight of the smoldered out campfire in front of the tree house, you could hear the sighs of relief coming from each boy.

"Anyone got any prefabs rolled?" Blurted out Paul, as he gathered more sticks for kindling to start the fire. "I got a half spliff here we can smoke!" Yelled out Ron, as he pulled half a fatty from the inside of his jacket pocket. "Well spark it up man! What are you waiting for?" Yelled out Zack. So Ron lit up the joint, had a couple of puffs, and passed it along to Paul, who in turn passed it on, and so on.

Once the fatty was finished, the roach was set aside. The campfire, now burning hot with red amber's, was ready to put the metal tray over the two large rocks. Then the fish were spread open to lay flat on the rack above the coals until it was time to flip them over. Tonight would be a beer and fish night. Perhaps even another story from Ted, if they had dessert ready in time that is.

After dinner, everyone but Ron relaxed in their chairs by the fire. Ron went up to the tree house for something or other, and that's when it started. "Alright! Why does it seem like all *my* crap goes missing? Which one of you guys stole my tool belt *this* time?" Yelled out Ron from above. "What the hell are you ranting about Ron?" Paul yelled back, with a little bit of chuckle.

"Yeah it was probably *you* who took it Paul!" Yelled Ron. "Took what? What the hell are you blaming me for *now* man?" Yelled Paul. "Somebody stole my pouch man, and I made sure I put it away where none of you guys would find it! Now which one of you took it? Was it you Paul?" "No man, I never touched your stupid pouch!" Paul raised his voice as he screamed back at Ron.

"What about *you* Ted?" "No man, *I* never touched it either!" Answered Ted. "What about you Joe?" "No man, I never touched your pouch." Answered Joe. "Okay Zack! Mister joker, then *you* did it!" Accused Ron. "Look man, I never took it, and who would want to take your pouch anyhow?" Answered Zack sternly. "Well now, I *guess* we must have a ghost here then! I know *exactly* where I left it, and now it's no where to be found!" Yelled Ron, sounding quite irritated at this point.

While Ron walked back to the campfire, the rest of the boys were discussing the mysterious missing pouch amongst themselves. Ted spoke out first, as Ron joined the boys. "Look Ron, you know that story I've been telling? Well you know the stories *are* true. So maybe the same people who took the bodies are the same ones who took your pouch. You ever think about *that?*" "You know what man? I think those stories you tell, are starting to take control of your head, and it's making you believe something that really isn't true!" Ron muttered back.

"Look, I don't wanna interrupt your little squabble here. But uh, Ron, every time you seem to have something go missing, none of us ever seem to be around. Hear me out. Your pouch went missing? We were all out fishing together. When your hammer went missing? We were all out planting. Don't you get it? I don't think we are alone out here man." Finished Zack.

No one had a chance to finish another sentence. Ron freaked out and thought everyone was against him, so he took it out on Zack, and made a football tackle right directly in front of the fire. But it didn't end there, Paul and Ted got up from their chairs and went right over to Ron, and body slammed him right on top of some tarps that were laying around. Making it somewhat of an easier landing for Ron. While he was on the ground, the pair made him scream uncle. But that was just the beginning. Ron got back up and bulldozed Paul right over. Then Joe got up and plowed right into Ted. It was nothing but a good old dog pile in the end.

The novelty wore off after a good five minutes of rough housing. The boys all sat on the ground, half out of breath, just staring each other down, to see if anyone had the energy to continue. That, was a negative. It took a few minutes before anyone spoke, and then a fit of laughter broke out between the boys.

"Looks like the fish is done boys, and I *am* starving." Blurted out Paul, as he got up to get himself a plate full of fish. The other boys didn't waste any time following Paul. Then they all started digging into the succulent fish as well. Silence fell once again, as the boys devoured what was left from their catch of the day.

After dinner, Paul asked if anyone had any prefabs rolled, but there was no answer from anyone. "Well pass over the herb and I'll roll us some dessert." Paul Said, looking right at Ron, since the tray of weed was sitting right beside him.

"Hey you know what we're missing here?" Asked Ron. "What?" Answered Paul. "Beer!" Said Ron. Then he made his way to the cooler and passed everyone a beer each. "Yeah, you know what else we are missing? For Ted to finish that story he's been telling us." Added Paul. "Yeah well the sooner you get that thing rolled, the sooner I can get down to it. I should have just brought the book to show you the stories *are* true."

"Book? What book are you talking about Ted?" Asked a curious Zack. "Oh, I guess that's *one* thing I forgot to mention to you guys. The reason I never did, is because I didn't want you guys to make fun of me, knowing I'm a little bit of a book worm and all." "What book are you talking about Ted?" Interrupted Paul. "Well if you guys would pass on that fatty, and stop interrupting me, maybe I can get on with telling you the story eh?" Suggested Ted.

CHAPTER 9

Rugkey in the underground
The Packs vs the Nacucks

"I found this book a couple of months back, and I put it in my pack sack to take home and read. I knew that if one of you guys would have found it, you'd just throw it in the fire or something, so I just left well enough alone." Ted began. "Yeah, like *I* would have burnt a book like that eh?" Paul laughed. "Hey man, let him finish Paul!" Yelled out Ron defensively.

"Now if I may continue? The book must have been left behind for its secrets to get out. Or it was just forgotten. Could be a good explanation of why everybody's stuff keeps going missing. The point I'm trying to make is, that this book was meant for us to read, which is why I have been telling you what was written in it." Added Ted. "Go on." Said an excited Zack.

"It was two days after the last time Dude, Tanantra and Leroy were all together. They were supposed to meet at the big wooden door, even though Leroy had no clue of what time. So he spent most of the day by the entrance. Leroy stood there knocking and waiting, but there was no answer. He was about to give up and go back to his room, when he heard a knock from the other side. It was around three thirty."

"Leroy was all excited when he heard the knock. So he knocked back to let them know he was there. The door handle began to turn, so Leroy began pulling on the door as hard as he could. Meanwhile, on the other side of the door, Tanantra and Dude were pushing on the door at the same time." "Hey Leroy. You ready to go and watch a rugkey game?" "Asked Dude, who was apparently out of breathe." "What is rugkey?" "Asked Leroy, as he helped Dude and Tanantra push the door closed." "What is *rugkey*?" "Dude repeated back sarcastically, as Tanantra and he broke out in laughter." "Only the greatest game in the world man! Where have *you* been?" "Replied Tanantra."

"We would have been here earlier, but we had school." "Said Dude." "Now let's get going before the game starts eh?" "So the trio walked down the path towards the biggest building in the underground city. It was a roundish oval shaped building, as colorful as a rainbow, which Leroy had seen with his father on many occasions."

"Here is a ticket for you Leroy, and one for you Dude. Now let's get inside so we can get good seats." "Said Tanantra. Leroy was astounded and bewildered at what he saw once he entered the building. Aside from the many carvings, trophies and paintings that took over every inch of every wall in the whole place. Leroy had never seen so many *people,* never mind creatures all in one place. It *really* was a sight for sore eyes."

"Dude was the first one in, and didn't waste any time heading towards the best seats in the house. Right at center ice on the bottom row. That way no one got in the way of them watching the game. Tanantra on the other hand, with Leroy by her side, went to go and purchase some cotton candy, pop and popcorn."

"Well what about Dude? We'll never find him with all these creatures hanging about." "Said Leroy. But Tanantra was now talking to the creature running the concession stand." "I'll have a large popcorn a large cotton candy and three pop please and thank you." "As the concession worker got everything in order, Tanantra payed for the cost. Then she told Leroy to grab the drinks and follow her." "If Dude *is* where I think he *is,* then he got us the best seats in the house." "Explained Tanantra, as she led the way down the steps to the center ice."

"There you are Dude. Tanantra got us some munchies and some drinks. So here you go." "Leroy said, as he handed Dude one of the pops, and sat down in the reserved seat between Dude and Tanantra." "Alright! The game is about to start!" "Yelled out Dude." "Now I know what this game is. It's hockey!" "Yelled out Leroy. Everyone that was sitting around and behind Leroy looked puzzled, after hearing what he had just blurted out." "What's hockey?" "Asked Tanantra." "This is hockey, isn't it?" "Answered Leroy." "My dad used to sit around and watch this all the time!" "Said Leroy, all excited." "Well I don't know what game your father was watching, but this is the game of rugkey." "Replied Dude."

"Leroy was confused, as he looked beyond the plexiglass towards the ice. He seen two goalie nets, one on either end. Two defense lines, a center line, two penalty box's, and two separate team benches. But he didn't say anything more. He did *not* want to embarrass himself any further. So he stayed silent and waited for the game to start. Then over the loud speaker a voice spoke out."

"We have a great game for you tonight folks! I'm Jim." "And I'm Folga!" "And we're your rugkey announcers for this evening." "They both say together."

"Oh and what a day it is Folga!" "Yes it is Jim, and we have a couple of great teams playing for you today folks!" "Yes Folga we do! In one corner of the rink we have the raining champions of course, the Nacucks! Who have been undefeated so far in every game they have played." "Your absolutely right Jim, and in the opposite corner, we have the Packs."

"let me remind you at this time, that there will be refreshments, as well as hot dogs and peanuts available throughout the game. You can purchase them as the vendors walk through the seating area." "Announced Jim." "Or you can have yourself a cold one, by heading down to the concession stands provided." "Added Folga."

"Well here comes the first team out on the ice, the Nacucks!" "Announced Jim. The whole coliseum cheered them on as they flew to the ice and began taking shots on their goalie." "Well folks, make way for the Packs! That crazy bunch you all know and love." "Added Folga. Then both teams took a few minutes to practice before the game starts. Shortly thereafter, all team members line up on either side of the center line, while the underground anthem played."

"Both teams line up at center ice." "Wayner Pretzel is center man for the Nacucks" "Said Jim." "As well as Forty Howl, center man for the Packs." "Said Folga." "Referee steps up to the center line. Sticks are down on the ice." "Referee drops the key, and the game is under way!" "Forty Howl takes the key away at first draw! He passes across to Tom Chelius who has control of the key now and he brings it forward." "Tom Chelius gets checked by Stevey Sizerman from the Nacucks, but Chelius manages to get a piece of it to make the pass back to Wayner." "Wayner has control now and oh! He gets knocked to the ice by Forty Howl, and the play continues Folga."

"A scramble back in the corner for the key in the Nacucks zone." "Never Bindin gets the key and heads in behind the net. A pass to Dan Steal, and he gets the key up the left wing to Stevey Sizerman." "Sizerman goes in all alone now, he fakes a shot, goalie goes for it, he *takes* the shot, scores!" "The Nacucks get the first score on the board for the night, and the crowd goes wild!" "Announced Folga."

"Let's have a look at that one more time Folga!" "Yes Jim, here we have the start of the key *right* from the pocket to the hole." "A pass from Never Bindin up to Dan Steal, who gets the key up the left wing to Stevey Sizerman." "Sizerman flies up the wing alone, heads towards the net, fakes a shot, then he takes a shot and scores. Bringing this game to a one nothing lead in favor of the Nacucks Jim." "Well Folga, it looks like we are in for *one* heck of a game if it's already starting out like this!" "I hear you there Jim, but now, a quick word from our sponsors."

"Well Leroy? What do you think about rugkey so far eh?" "Asked Dude excitedly." "Wow man, this is nothing like the hockey game dad used to watch. I mean, it's the same thing, except for the fact that there are no flying carpets in *hockey!* They just use their skates and sticks. But this is way cooler man. I couldn't imagine missing even one of these games, there's a lot of action!" "Added Leroy, just getting to know the game."

"Oh, and by the way Leroy, rugs, they fly around on rugs, not carpets. It's a big difference as you will get to know. Hence the word, rugkey." "Said Tanantra, correcting Leroy." "Yeah man, this game is dope!" "Yelled out Dude." "The announcers are just like the ones on my dads hockey games too. Except these guys are a little more funnier." "Leroy added." "Okay quiet you guys, the announcers are on again." "Snapped Tanantra, with her eyes front. Leroy and Dude looked at each other, and then rolled their eyes forward as well."

"Okay rugkey fans, we're back, and it's already been an exciting start to this one to nothing lead the Nacucks have early in the first period over the Packs." "Yes Folga, and an exciting game it is, with Wayner Pretzel already tossed to the ice like Saturday night at the fights!" "Oh, by the way Jim, I heard tell that your mother was sick. I hope she gets better soon." "Yes Folga, and uh, thank you for that. She is doing much better now thanks."

"Referee drops the key. Wayner gets a piece of the key now, but doesn't get enough, and Forty Howl retrieves it as he heads in all alone, but with much difficulty." "Guy Lapuck goes in for a check, but Forty shoots the key between his legs and flies his rug up and over his head, so as to avoid a hard collision!" "Announced Jim."

"Forty Howl hits the ice on the other side of Lapuck and regains control. He flies in towards the net, takes a shot, scores!" "Richard Growdeer doesn't seem to like *that* goal." "Yes it looks like he broke his goalie stick on the cross bar of the net!" "Well Folga, looks like the table's have turned here early in the game tonight."

"Yes Jim, it most certainly *has,* but we haven't seen the last goal of the night *I'm sure!*" "Folga, did you happened to notice the speed and agility of that of our own team member Forty Howl? Born and raised in the Packs I might add." "Yes I did as a matter of fact Jim. Perhaps we can arrange an interview during the intermission."

"The referee was about to drop the key for the third time in under five minute of this rugkey game, but instead, the whistle blew and Wayner Pretzel has been waved back. So Stevey Sizerman takes *this* face off." "Okay, referee is holding the key back at center ice, he fakes a drop, nobodies stick moves." "Well Jim, you can sure feel the confidence in the stadium tonight. You can see *that* when the ref faked a drop. But neither teams center ice men seemed to make a move."

"The referee drops the key, and we're back in play, coming to you *live* from the Packs stadium." "Forty Howl starts things off. He gets a piece of the key and passes back to his team then let's out a scream for the crowd, with one hand in the air." "Well that got the crowd shaking. Let's see if we can get the players shaking eh?" "Marcel Dupponne has the key now, as he brings it behind his own net." "But from out of the blue Guy Lapuck steals the key, and flies back around to the front of the net, he shoots, he scores! Bringing the game score 2-1 in the first period." "Said Jim."

"For the next ten minutes of the game, there was nothing but hard hits, heavy slap shots, and high flying action. Along with some brutal slams up against the boards. In fact, the Packs defense man hit the key so hard, that it broke the glass on the opposite side of the arena. Now wasn't that one heck of a powerful shot?"

"Well Jim, there goes that buzzer and the end of the first period!" "Alright folks, I hope you enjoyed the first period of our game tonight. Stay tuned for an upcoming interview with some of the players." "Just a reminder to all you folks in the arena tonight, that there is ice cold beer in the concession stands, as well as hot roasted peanuts, and now, a few words from our sponsors."

Narrator,

This game is sure like the game of hockey we all know so well. Without the flying rugs of course. But could you just imagine a game like that? Take the puck for instance, instead of being all black, it's a clear see through puck with a golden skeleton key inside it. Now *that* could do some serious damage. Not to mention, I wonder if it's a *real* gold key inside it? Well I'll tell you, if they ever come up with a game like that, they got me sold. Game on!

"Well Leroy, what do you think about the game so far?" "Asked Tanantra." "To tell you the truth, I think it's better then the game of hockey my dad watched above ground. I think he would have a blast chilling at one of these games. He would go absolutely nuts!" "Added Leroy." "Hey, let's go get some munchies before the second period starts." "Said Dude." "I'm in. You coming Leroy?" "Asked Tanantra." "You bet!" "Said Leroy, as he looked over the arena with a smile. He was admiring the rather large gathering of creatures in one spot, *just* to watch a simple game that gave so much pleasure to so many."

"This place is wild guys! Sure wish I could bring my dad to one of these games. He would absolutely flip!" "Said Leroy." "You sure talk about your father a lot Leroy." "Said Tanantra." "I admit that yeah, and why wouldn't I? He's all that I got, and we get along just fine." "Oh well, not that there's anything wrong with that. I admire that. My mom is pretty cool as well. She is very kind and, well, she sure puts up with a lot. Especially from Dude and his hood friends. Me? I'm her little angel." "Added Tanantra."

"Yeah right." "Muttered Dude, not impressed with the conversation at all." "Like a devil in disguise." "Said Tanantra." "Yeah right ya loser." "Snapped Dude." "Bite me!" "Added Tanantra." "Woo, woo, woo, don't you guys *ever* get along?" "Asked Leroy." "Yeah sometimes, when we haven't seen each other for a few days or something." "Tanantra said, with a half laugh." "Well you guys think you can get along, at least for the day?" "Both sets of eyes were staring down Leroy." "Yeah, yeah, now let's get something to eat eh?" "Said Dude."

"Okay boys, how about some fries and a cheese smokey each?" "Asked Tanantra." "Sounds good to me." "Answered Dude." "Yeah, I'll eat just about anything." "Answered Leroy." "Hey, aren't you the kid everyone's talking about?" "Asked the short little creature from behind the concession stand counter. She was so tiny, she could barley reach the counter, never mind look over it." "I, I guess so. My name is Leroy." "But before the conversation had any chance to continue, Tanantra interrupted." "So how much will that be?" "Then the little creature hopped up on some sort of a stool, and rang everything up on her till. But when she added up the total, a bell rang throughout the concession stand."

"Well my dear, it looks like you three are in luck! You have just won the one hundredth person to order. Which means that your meal is free." "Did you hear that boys? We just got a free meal!" "Announced an excited Tanantra." "But that's not all kids. You also won free seasons tickets for all three of you. As well as a free meal each time you present your free ticket pass and attend a game." "Concluded the concession stand worker."

"With that being said, the place began to swarm with people, creatures, cameras and questions. Pictures were being taken, and the trio were all asked to reveal their names. But then something happened that nobody expected. Leroy disappeared out of nowhere." "Dude? Did you happen to see where Leroy went?" "Asked Tanantra." "Uh, I think he might have went to the bathroom." "Answered Dude." "I think there is something wrong with him, so will you do me a favor and go check on him?" "Asked Tanantra. Dude hesitated for a moment, and was about to argue with Tanantra. But then he remembered that he had agreed to get along with his sister, at least for the day." "Oh alright. I'll be back in a minute." "Replied Dude."

"Dude ducked around the camera men, and headed straight towards the first bathroom he could locate." "Leroy? Are you in here?" "But nobody answered. He proceeded to open up each and every stall, calling out his name and still no answer. There was just one stall that remained left to look in, but it was locked. Dude even looked underneath the stall door, but he never noticed any feet. But then, why was the door locked? Dude thought to himself."

"Look Leroy, I know your in there." "Go away!" "Snapped Leroy." "Well what's the matter?" "Asked Dude." "You wouldn't understand." "Try me. But before we carry on this conversation uh, your gonna have to come out of that stall. Before someone comes in here and thinks we are a *little* weird. If you know what I mean?" "Replied Dude. Just then the bathroom stall door opened and Leroy stepped out."

"Look Dude, if my father sees me in the newspaper, he is gonna flip. Not only that, but it's the fact that he doesn't even have a clue of where I am. I sort of lied to him, and I have never lied to him a day in my life. That is, until I met you and your sister." "Whined Leroy." "So what, that's *our* fault?" "Snapped Dude." "No, that's not what I mean. What I mean is, that I never had a reason to lie before, and I really like hanging with you guys and all." "Leroy paused for a second, and then continued."

"It's just that my father has been wanting me to do things with him, now that we have a little more time together, and, well, I've been sorta putting them off. I've been sorta goofing off a bit and hanging out with you guys and well, I don't wanna hurt my dad you see. He kinda thinks I'm taking a trip down to the spell room." "Finished Leroy"

"You've been to the spell room?" "Asked a curious Dude." "Of course I have." "Replied Leroy." "Wow man, that is *so* cool. I have wanted to go there all my life. But as you already know, we aren't allowed past the big wooden door though." "Added Dude." "Oh yeah, in all the confusion it kind of slipped my mind." "Replied Leroy."

"The boys were then interrupted by an unexpected entrance to the guys facilities." "Uh, you do realize this is the *guys* bathroom Tanantra!" "Blurted out Dude, when he noticed his sister enter the rest room." "Of course I do silly, but you two were taking too long, and I just wanted to find out what was the matter with Leroy." "Replied Tanantra."

"Well, like I told you." "Leroy started to speak, but was interrupted by Dude." "I'm dealing with it, and besides, it's all worked out. So go ahead back to the seats and we'll catch up." "Alright. But you guys better hurry up, because the game is about to start." "Said Tanantra, on her way out of the bathroom door."

"Thanks Dude. I really didn't want to have to explain myself again." "No problem. But she is right, we better get a move on if we're going to catch the key drop." "Okay. Eh thanks Dude, you know for." "But Leroy was stopped once again in mid speech." "Ah, don't mention it, I'll see you out there eh." "Said Dude"

"As soon as Leroy figured the crowd had left, and he could sneak back to his seat before any snapshots could be taken of him, he headed out the door as well. He took a quick peak first, then continued on his way to the seats with his head down. But not before getting a crowd of reporters snapping pictures like crazy. They asked him all sorts of questions, but Leroy just kept his head down and set his pace from a running walk to a fast jog."

"Leroy made it to the aisle where his seat was located. When the reporter's tried to enter, they were all asked for seat tickets and eventually all sent away." "Oh there you are Leroy, we thought you might have got yourself lost or something." "Replied Tanantra, with a sigh of relief in her voice." "Uh, yeah, sorry about that. I kind of got tackled by a crowd of reporters on my way out of the bathroom, and they *literately* followed me back to my seat." "Said Leroy."

"Well if I haven't already told you, your pretty much the most popular kid down here at this stage of the game, so don't be surprised if they put your face up there on the big screen. Oh, oh quiet, the game is about to start." "Finished a long winded Tanantra."

"But the game wasn't about to start, as of yet anyways. In fact, the big screen, high above the arena, lit up and the announcers appeared onscreen, live from inside the locker room."

"Here we are standing in the locker room with our home team and team member, center ice man, Forty Howl. I'm Jim."

"And I'm Folga." "And we're your announcers for this evening." "Said Jim and Folga at the same time."

"So Forty." "Yes Jim." "You seem to be having a great year so far, your the leading goal scorer of your team this season. You should be so proud. Do you have anything to say to your fans here in the arena?" "Well you know I am Jim, and it's bin an awesome season so far. The packs are a great team and a great group of players out here. They are playing like a team and passing like a team. I'm proud to be a part of the Packs. Go Packs go!" "Yelled Forty Howl."

"Hey there Forty, Folga here." "Hey Folga. How are the wife and kids?" "They are quite fine Forty, quite fine thanks. The crowd *sure* seems to love you here at the Packs stadium. Is there anything you'd like to say?" "Well Folga, it's like this, this *is* my home town, and my home based team, and I wanna thank all of our fans for taking time out of their lives to watch us kick some ass." "Replied Forty Howl."

"Oh, we can't say ass on the air, oops, now I said it." "Said Folga." "Sorry. My son is probably watching as well. Now don't you give your mom a hard time son. I'll see you after the game. No seriously Folga, just like I tell my son and all his friends, say your prayers and eat your vitamins. If he keeps to those daily rituals, then perhaps one day he will be as lucky as I am to play for the Packs in the URL. Keep your dreams big and your friends even closer." "Finished Forty."

"Well folks, there you have it, big words from a big home town rugkey hero. Everyone give a warm welcome to Forty Howl!" "Are we off the air now guys? Cause I gotta drain the main vain." "Um, Well folks, there you have it, live from the locker room in the Packs arena, where we have just interviewed one of the Packs most famous rugkey heroes." "Announced Jim."

"Thank you Jim." "And thank *you* Folga. Stay tuned now for the second period of our feature game, where the score is 1 for the Packs and 2 for the Nacucks." "Well, how did I do guys?" "Asked Forty" "You did great Forty." "Said Folga." "Uh, you can uh, go have your leak now." "Replied Jim. So Forty made his way carefully to the urinal stall." "I think he did good Jim." "Yes Folga, I have to agree with you there."

"Okay fans we're back, high up in the stands of the Packs stadium. I'm Jim." "And I'm Folga. "And we're your hosts of tonight's rugkey game between the Nacucks and the Packs." "They both say together." "Well Jim, that was a great intermission interview with Forty Howl." "Yes Folga, you can say that again. That was a fine interview, if I might say so myself. He sure is a popular guy. Let's get a replay of his last goal Jim."

"Alright Folga, here we have Forty heading up the ice weaving in and out of oncoming traffic. Now pause it right there. This ones for the folks at home. Listen to the crowd as Forty passes the key between the legs of Guy Lapuck, and takes to flight instead of causing a head on collision. Okay, let it play. Now right there, *before* Forty *even* shoots the key, the crowd is roaring with confidence." "Well I'll tell you Jim, you *h*ave a point there when you said he is a popular guy, and I think that's a bit of an understatement, according to the crowd. Ha ha." "Finished Folga, with a short laugh."

"Now it's gonna be a toss up between Wayner and Folga here at center ice. Oops, I mean Wayner and Sizerman, sorry about that Folga." "Yes Jim, but you could also sense a bit of bitter hatred between the ref and Wayner." "You could see that too eh? Must be a lovers quarrel." "Both announcers laugh." "Well fans, the key is about to drop, as we bring you the second period of our rugkey night in the underground." "Said Jim."

"Let me remind you folks at home, that this second period is brought to you in part by Viagra. As my grandfather always used to say, your never too old. Viagra, helps you stand up when times seem to be down." "Announced Jim." "Oh, and don't forget Trojan. The one soldier that will fight, when your not paying attention." "Finished Folga."

"The ref gets ready to drop the key." "The key is dropped, Pretzel gets control and passes across to Sizerman." "Sizerman ups the key along the boards, while he flies up and around Toni T. He catches the key like soap on a rope on the other side of Toni." "Sizerman's all alone now and waits for the goalie to make the wrong move." "He is running out of time, looks for the opening, he shoots, he scores!" "Yelled Folga."

"The Nacucks, *still* undefeated, make the score 3 to 1 in less than a minute of play in the second period." "Let's see that in instant replay Jim." "Okay Folga. Here we have Wayner Pretzel passing the key across to Stevey Sizerman. He brings the key across center ice, then gives the key a snap along the boards. As the key goes along the boards, Sizerman goes around Toni T." "Then he proceeds to drive that bird all the way to the nest. He waits for the right opportunity, and boom, slaps that key past goal tender Sandy Rogue before he even *knew* what hit the back of the net Folga."

"Yes Jim, and if I may say so myself, that was one *heck* of a shot! Oh, what's this? Do you think they are gonna do what I think they are gonna do Jim?" "Yes Folga, I *do* believe they are going to do what you think I think you think they are gonna do." "Well I'm sure we *all* wondered when they were gonna make *this* move Jim." "Well we can all stop wondering now Folga. For those of you just tuning in, and who don't know the Step brothers we come to call the brotherhood. They are the Nacucks secret weapon as you will soon find out." "Announced Jim."

"Yes Jim, and the name is very fitting. But don't let the name fool you. These boys are in fact *real* blood brothers, with the last name as Step." "Well here they come Folga, and the fans are going wild here in the underground."

"Well folks, here we have Sean Step as our center ice man. Over to the right of him, we have Darryl Step as the Left winger." "Thank you Jim, and over to the left front line, we have Travis Step as our right winger, and if we look way back to the net, we have last but not least, Tyler Step as the Nacucks Goal tender."

"Listen to that crowd meter roar at the announcement of the Step brothers on ice Folga!" "Yes sir Jim, there is nothing like a little brotherly love in the game." "Yes Folga, and the fact of the matter is, that this isn't even home ice to them. But these brothers seem to have a lot of love given to them by the fans, and that is enough to get anybody routing for you." "Yes Jim, and the fact that these brothers sure seem to get a lot of lady luck wherever they play." "You got that right Folga." "Both announcers chuckle."

"I'll tell you Folga, the Nacucks forward line sure didn't look none too happy after the brotherhood came out onto the ice." "Neither did Richard Growdeer for that matter." "You can say that again, but that's how the game is played, so let's get back to center ice." "Finished Folga."

"And we're off, it's Sean Step for the Nacucks and it's Forty Howl for the Packs." "The key is dropped, and Sean gets this one with a pass to Travis. Travis spins around and fakes a pass back to Sean." "Forty falls for the fake and Travis makes a long pass across ice to Darryl. Darryl now man handling that key like it owes him money, and he does a, what's this?" "A roundabout spin and a key between the five hole of one Marcel Dupponne, and then yet another roundabout." "Announced Folga."

"He handles the key like it's on a string. Takes a shot, five hole! Scores!" "Well I gotta tell you Jim, what a sensational goal that was!" "You got that right Folga, and Travis will be getting an assist on that goal as well. What a great pass through all that traffic. He must be happy about that!" "That will take *this* score up a notch. It is now 4-1 for the Nacucks over the Packs early in the second Jim."

"Would you listen to that crowd cheer for those brothers? That's louder then the home team scorers get, and look! Is that what I think it is Jim?" "If I think your looking at what I think your looking at, then yes Folga your right. Can you believe this? The women in the stands are *actually* ripping their under garments off, and throwing them on the ice for Darryl."

"I have *never* seen anything like it before in my life Jim! The only thing I gotta say about that, is it can *only* happen in rugkey!" "You got that right Folga. Close your eyes kids." "Jim clears his throat." "Well let's slide on in to an infomercial while they clear off the ice of ladies panties shall we?" "Both men had a bit of a laugh." "I'll have to agree with you there Folga." "Folga and Jim had no idea they were still on the air."

"Would you look at those hot young ladies out there Jim!" "Yes Folga, I hear you there. It kind of makes me wish I was one of them bench seats those ladies are sitting on right about now." "Both men chuckle." "Uh, guys? Um, your still on the air." "Whispered one of the camera men in the booth." "Both men look at each other." "Uh, and now a word from our sponsor." "Folga managed to say." "Uh, excuse me for a moment, I'm gonna misuse, I mean abuse, I mean, I gotta go and use the boys room." "Said Jim." "With that being said, Jim left the announcers booth."

"We're back for some more rugkey action coming to you live from the underground in the Packs arena. I'm Folga, and uh, Jim is just taking a bit of a bathroom break right now." "Just then Jim returns from the bathroom." "And I'm Jim. Well Folga, that was a bit of an unusual, not to mention illegal move in the eyes of the fans, as far as the players are concerned."

"Yes I hear you there Jim, and what a way to take the focus off the game."

"Players line up, and the referee gets ready to drop the key." "The key is dropped, and it's a stick fight right off the bat." "Forty Howl for the Packs and Sean Step for the Nacucks." "Sean wins this face off, and does a long back pass all the way down to his brother, and Nacucks goal tender, Tyler Step." "Tyler doesn't waste any time with the key and flicks it high up in the air. It looks like, yes, it's heading straight for the Packs right winger Toni T Jim."

"But wait, what's this? Darryl comes right out of the woodwork, putting some chill height on that rug and scoops the key out of the air like a frog snapping its tongue at a fly." "Man, that was fast. Do you think *that* was fast? I think that was fast Folga!"

"Darryl now in full control, brings the key down the ice so fast, the cameramen are having a *heck* of a time trying to break film." "It's a one on one between the goalie for the Packs and Darryl. It looks like he is going for a shot, no, he passes the key back behind him through his own five hole, and, no wait, a quick dribble between his skates, as well as a heel pass back to his stick. He takes a shot, scores!" "Says a long winded Jim."

"Yes sir Jim, and the crowd goes wild once again!" "Yelled Folga." "The score is now a whopping 5 for the Nacucks and still 1 for the Packs." "I have *never* seen a shot like that before in my life Folga!" "There's a lot of things happening in this game tonight, that you *or* I have never seen before Jim." "Well you gotta ask yourself, do these four brothers eat, sleep *and* dream rugkey?" "Every one of them have more talent then I think *even* the Packs give them credit for." "Said Folga."

"Okay Jim, now I think the fans would be a little more than choked up, if we didn't give a them a *replay* of *that* goal." "I think your right Folga, and I would have to agree with the fans on this one." "Let's take this one right from the face off. Here we have a *good* fight for the key, a long back pass to goal tender Tyler Step, received from center ice man Sean Step, Jim."

"Now watch how high Tyler cranks that key up in the air, like he planned to aim it towards Toni T." "Let's take this one in slow motion for a second or two." "Holy limb lifter I don't know *how* the cameraman was able to catch *this one*? It's even fast in slow motion!" "You got *that* one right Jim. Look at how fast Darryl picks the key out of thin air like that!"

"Yes Folga, it's like he magnetized his stick to the key, doesn't it?" "Alright now, speed it up a bit. Okay, pause it right here Jim. Now let's get a closer camera view and watch this *unbelievable* shot in slow motion shall we?" "It looks like Darryl is about to make the shot. But instead, Darryl hooks that key back towards his left skate and begins to dribble it like he was playing soccer Folga."

"Okay pause it right there. Now if you'll notice, he did this move like he was wearing a blindfold. Okay, now let it play. He was looking straight towards the goal tender. Yet Darryl dribbles the key from skate to skate, keeping his front skate forward. Then, a quick pass to his stick to make a skate to stick one timer. Now *that's* an amazing shot, that will probably stick in my head for the rest of *my* days Folga." "You got *that* right Jim, and I'm sure your not alone there. He must have practiced that unbelievably perfect shot in his sleep."

"Listen to *that* Folga. Now if I didn't know any better, I'd say you would probably be able to hear *this* crowd from the comforts of *every* home in the Packs!" "What was *that* Jim? It's a little hard to hear you over the roar of the crowd!" "I said it's so loud I bet the whole underground can here the crowd!" "What?" "Oh never mind Folga."

"Well here comes your favorite part of the game again Jim. Oh, did you see that? Instead of a pie in the face, Darryl got a bra in the face." "Well he's like a man on a mountain. Sorry, I mean a man on a mission." "We'll return with a most eventful game of rugkey, I don't think anyone has *ever,* seen anything like before, when we return."

"We're back I'm Jim." "And I'm Folga." "And we're your rugkey announcers coming to you live from the underground in the Packs stadium." "They both say together." "What an exciting game this has been so far Folga." "Yes Jim, it sure is, and we haven't even reached the five minute mark in the beginning of this second period. A quick reminder to the folks out in the stands, that there is a sale on cotton candy, as well as our very own tasty chilli cheese dogs."

"Referee gets ready to drop the key, both center men pose for the face off stance, and the key is dropped! This game is underway one more time, and the score is five to one in favor of the Nacucks!" "Ooh! Looks like Lander Macdonald is a little more frustrated then we thought! Did you see him knock Travis right off his rug?" "But it looks like Travis is taking the knock down like a champ. The whistle is blown and I think there is gonna be a penalty." "You got that right Jim, and what kind of a ref *wouldn't* call an attack like that?"

"Let's have a look up at the main screen in the center of the rink, and get a glimpse of our one hundredth customer in line at the concession stand. Oh, I am told we are going live to Tan Rather for a brief interview." "Tan Rather here, with the *winners* of the seasons tickets and free lunches. Here we have Leroy, which I'm sure you have all heard about through word of mouth. You have anything to say to the fans in the stadium and to the many folks at home Leroy?" "Asked Tan."

"But Leroy did *not* say a word. Instead, Tanantra stole the spotlight." "*Well my* name is *Tanantra,* and *I* am the one who *actually* purchased the ticket." "Added Tanantra, with her voice constantly getting higher as she spoke." "Well hello there Tanantra, and how did you *feel,* the moment you won seasons tickets for a year*?"* "Well you know Tan." "Tanantra began, but was rudely interrupted by none other than, her little brother, Dude."

"Man, You guys rock Tan! Thanks for coming out, and, hey mom! I t*old y*ou I was going to be on the big screen one day!" "Oh, well that's all the time we have right now, back to Jim and Folga in the booth. I'm Tan Rather coming to you live from the Packs!" "But the camera didn't leave the seats the trio occupied, until a few seconds later, when Tanantra was caught on the air giving her little brother a charlie horse."

"Meanwhile, back at home." "Why that *little* deviant! Wait until *that* girl comes home tonight and see what I got in store for *her*!" "Anne muttered to herself at home in front of the tube."

"Sorry about that folks. We tried to get the cameras back rolling onto what has taken place on the ice. It seems that center ice man, and team captain Wayner Pretzel, has decided to take off his Nacucks jersey! What an historic night *this* is *gonna be.* Wayner Pretzel has switched teams midway through second period, and what a shock this is to everyone in the building. Including me Jim!"

"Well Folga, I think this brings quite a shock to *anyone* who knows *anything* about rugkey." "I really don't know the whole background story here for the sudden change, but I'm sure it will be a good one Jim." "Hold on a second here Folga. I, I'm getting word that we *do* in fact have footage of Wayner Pretzel *actually* ripping off his Nacucks jersey. With the backup of the Packs jersey on underneath?" "Well before you say it, again I'm gonna say it this time. I have *never* seen another game like this before in my life!" "Couldn't have said it better myself." "We are going to cut for a quick commercial break." "Announced Folga."

"Meanwhile, back in the stands." "Thanks for getting the camera off me Tanantra. I really appreciate it." "No problem Leroy, anything for you. But *you!* Now that is going to be all *anybody* talks about at school tomorrow! Not to mention the whole underground! Oh your gonna get it when we get home!" "Tanantra finished, as she glared at Dude. But then her phone beeped, and she was silent for pretty much the rest of the game. Dude dared not say anything. But he knew that his mom *probably* seen everything on the tube, and sensed there was going to be some trouble back at the homestead."

"We're back again folks, for probably one of the most exciting games of this century." "Yes Jim, and it looks like Lander will get a two minute roughing penalty." "Yes Folga, and it appears that Forty Howl has been benched while Wayner Pretzel takes his place." "Well nothing comes as a surprise to me tonight Jim."

"Ref gets ready to drop the key." "It's a stand off now between Sean Step and Wayner Pretzel, neither man backing down." "The key is dropped! Sean gets the key and makes a pass over to Darryl." "Darryl quickly passes the key to Sean, ooh! What a hit by Tom Chelius!" "Wow, what a knockout! But the play continues!" "Sean is getting back up now, and it looks like he is shaking it off taking like a man. Wait a go Sean!" "Announced Jim."

"Chelius now in control of the key. He passes it up to Wayner, who flies up with Toni T out into the open." "Wayner sees him, goes for the pass, ooh, one timer, and a glove save by the hand of Tyler Step." "But before the play is stopped, Tyler quickly shuffles the key up to Never Bindin. Never Bindin gains control and slams a pass up the center to Sean." "Sean now going hard to the net. He passes over to the wing towards Travis." "Off the boards, Travis with a huge slap shot, scores!" "That makes 6 for the Nacucks and still 1 for the Packs."

"Well I'll tell you Folga, this game would give you reason to believe that fans of the Packs, would rather walk out then stick around. But am I just seeing things? Or did this stadium just get more packed then I have *ever* seen before in my life?" "You know your absolutely right about the amount of people and creatures that keep showing up. As far as statistics go, we have *never* had this many in one place in the history of the underground the Packs Jim."

"Looks like we missed the replay of *that* goal Folga." "Well Jim, the game is underway once again, and it looks like we are missing a lot of things around here." "Wayner gains control of the key right off the hop, and he races down past the Step brothers, out skating everyone in his path." "He is fast and all alone! Takes the shot, head butt! From goalie Tyler Step and the play is stopped."

"Well, you can see why they stopped the clock with only a few seconds left on the timer Jim." "Did you *see* that *stop* Folga? Tyler Step head butted that key so hard, he broke the golden key *right* in half!" "The announcers then replay the save three times for the fans, and each time it got played, the crowd screamed even louder."

"Back at center ice, the new key is dropped and fight is on. The time runs down, and this period is over! Time to start our second intermission of the night! Now, a few words from our sponsors Jim."

Narrator,

Well this game seems to be a little more than meets the eye. Now it may be hard for you to imagine, flying rugs on each player. So picture this. There is a hole cut near the front of the rug, in which it wraps around the waist of each player. Not much of the rug hangs out in the front, or the sides of each players waist. For the most part, the flying rug sticks out the back of each player. But let's see how the rest of this game turns out.

"Welcome back to the underground arena. I'm Jim!" "And I'm Folga!" "And we're tonight's hosts for the remainder of this game!" "They both announce together." "Can you believe the attraction this game has brought to the Packs tonight Folga?" "Yes Jim, and I think we had better get ourselves some crowd control, if I may say so myself." "Said a sarcastic Folga."

"Starting out for team Nacucks, we have center ice man Sean Step, along with his two younger brothers, Darryl Step on the right wing and Travis Step on the left wing. On the defensive line, we have Never Bindin on the right defense, and we have Dan Steal as the left defense man. For the Nacucks goal tender, we have Tyler Step."

"Thank you Folga. Now starting line up for the Packs, we have Wayner Pretzel as the center ice man. Joining along side of him to the right we have Toni T, and to his left, we have Tom Chelius. For the Packs defensive line, we have Marcel Dupponne as the left defense man, along with Lander Macdonald as his right defense man. Goal tender for this team tonight, is none other than our very own Sandy Rogue. Folga, back to you."

"Game on! The key is dropped and a quick stick fight ends with Sean getting this one." "He looks around to make a pass, but can't find anyone." "He decides to go for it, balls out. Sean goes straight up the middle, skating easily around Wayner like he was being schooled." "Marcel comes in for a check, but hits the ice hard. Sean goes for a double flip in mid air above Marcel, and flicks the key up still moving forward." "Sean, now back on the ice and still in full control, takes a blistering slap shot, scores! Right through the netting making a home embedded in the backboard behind the net!" "The score is now 7 to 1 in favor of the Nacucks over the Packs."

"You could feel the arena rumble with *that* shot Jim. Man, that is *some* powerful slap shot this kids got!" "Welcome to the future of the Nacucks Folga." "So what does that say for the future of our own the Packs Jim?" "Well quite frankly Folga, the Packs don't look like they *even* showed up for *this* game. What, are they drunk? Was there some sort of party last night that I wasn't aware of?" "Well we all know you wouldn't miss *that,* eh Folga?" "I think we better just get back to covering the game. I don't have time to argue with the likes of you!" "Snapped Folga."

"Both teams are back at center ice, and the referee drops the key. Travis gets a piece of it and passes the key across to Darryl." "Darryl one times the key from center, right through the traffic, scores! This game is an astounding 8 to 1, with the Nacucks punishing the Packs in a 7 goal lead Jim!" "Well there you have it Folga. *Somebody* put these Packs out of their misery, before this turns into a basketball score!" "I think we have already passed *that* by now Jim."

"Back at center, Sean wins the face off." "That's nothing unusual." "He passes the key to Travis, who seems to be having a bit of trouble gaining control. In comes Chelius, who steals the key from under Travis's nose, and begins flying towards Tyler Step, along with Wayner Pretzel." "Now that was a good steal Jim."

"The pair now neck and neck, coming in with Toni T following in behind. Chelius passes over to Wayner. Wayner takes a shot, oh, blocked by Tyler Step!" "Wayner gets his own rebound, he shoots, and the key goes wild! Right off the forehead of Tyler Step, but he shakes it off and the play goes on." "Announced Folga."

"Wayner, back in control at the back of the net. Never Bindin and Dan Steal closing in from either side. Wayner goes up and over, he shoots, he scores!" "Well I never seen that goal coming Jim." "You can say that again! Let's take another look at this in instant replay. Here we have Wayner feeling like a champ. He decides to do a rocket lunge flip right over the net with the key. Then without any realization where the key was, or Wayner Pretzel for that matter, Tyler Step gets a goal scored on him." "The score is now 2 for the Packs and 8 for the Nacucks Jim."

"I'll tell you though Folga, Tyler is really doing a tremendous job at goal tending tonight for the Nacucks." "Yes Jim, one heck of a job if I may say so myself. A most truly amazing goal by Wayner I might add as well." "I wouldn't be surprised if this goal ended up as the best goal of the year!" "Said an enthusiastic Jim."

"Well after seeing that shot, you can really sense the energy that went into *this* goal. Wayner obviously felt he *had* to get this done." "You can say that again Jim. Anything to relieve, at least some of the tension, that seems to be heating this over crowded rugkey arena tonight."

"Both teams are back at center ice getting ready for the key to drop." "The key is dropped, and the fight is on." "Sean gets control of this one and passes behind him to Never Bindin." "Never Bindin brings it up and gets checked by Wayner Pretzel." "Bindin still in control, passes the key ahead to Travis Step." "Announced Jim."

"Travis now bringing it up, he sees Dupponne heading towards him and passes the key to Darryl." "Darryl going in all alone now, and it doesn't look like anyone can catch *this* kid." "He must be the fastest kid in the league Folga." "I have to agree with you there Jim."

"Darryl, now at the Nacucks defensive line, fakes a shot, goalie goes down, quick snapshot, scores!" "He made *that* goal look easy Folga." "He sure did Jim, and the score is now a phenomenal 9 for the Nacucks and still just 2 for the Packs." "That's three for Darryl too I might add." "Well it looks like they are gonna be cleaning the ice a little longer than we think this time, after the fans finish celebrating *this* hat trick." "Just a reminder to all you folks drinking any alcoholic beverages, not to drink and fly. Let's keep the underground safe tonight eh." "Thanks for that Folga, and now we will take a short break while the ice is cleared."

"Well that took a little longer then expected Jim." "Yes, and it kind of makes you wonder if the ladies in the audience have anything left to throw on the ice." "Well as long as the gentlemen don't start throwing jock straps on the ice, I think we'll be fine." "Both men chuckle."

"Two minutes left on the clock, and the key is about to be dropped." "There is the drop, and here comes the fight." "Wayner snags the key this time." "Well you can't win em all Jim." "He passes across ice to Toni T." "Toni T back to Wayner, and he moves the key forward." "Chelius joins him in the Nacucks defensive line, and Sandy Rogue leaves the net to pole the goalie and bring Forty Howl back on the ice Folga."

"Wayner passes the key to Chelius, oh, checked and robbed by Never Bindin." "Bindin doesn't waste any time, and passes the key up to right winger Darryl step." "Darryl brings the key forward. He shoots, he scores! An empty netter and the crowd goes wild!" "Bringing this game to a phenomenal score of 10-2 for the Nacucks over the Packs Jim."

"You know Folga, you would think these ladies were packing spares, for the amount of undergarments on ice *this* time." "Yes Jim, it's no wonder the game still plays on with all these delays." "It's all in good fun Folga, all in good fun." "Yeah maybe for you Jim, but I came here to announce rugkey, not a lingerie show!" "We will return you to *live* rugkey, after these words."

"We are back rugkey fans. The ice is clear, and it looks like this could be the last face off your going to see tonight, in this most unbelievable game." "The Packs have their goalie back in, and the key is dropped." "Wayner gets control and passes it to Chelius." "Chelius moves the key up along the boards, but he gets checked by Travis." "Travis now with the key, and he passes it to Sean who takes a shot. Oh, he hits the crossbar and the key lands behind the net Jim."

"Marcel Dupponne gets to the key first, and slap shots a pass to Wayner Pretzel at center ice." "He gains control, takes a shot, *saved* by Tyler Step!" "The clock runs out, and *this* game is over folks! With a final score of 10 for the Nacucks, and 2 for the Packs! I'm Jim." "And I'm Folga." "And it was our pleasure to be your announcers for this most exciting game." "They both announce together." "Have a great night folks, and a safe fly home." "Finished Jim. After which, the crowd slowly begins to exit the building."

"Well what did you think about the game tonight Leroy?" "Wow, I have never seen anything like it in my life! I gotta get my dad out to one of these games, he would love it!" "Well I think you should bring him out to the next game, and perhaps I can convince our mom to come out to a game as well." "Replied Tanantra." "Yeah, well your gonna have to give me a little time on that. Dad doesn't even know I'm here. So I wanna break it to him slowly." "Added Leroy."

"Hey, maybe the next time you come out, we could get a few of my friends together and play a game of path rugkey." "Suggested Dude." "That would be chill. But do you guys think you can fly me back to the big wooden door? I better get home for supper, before my dad starts to worry." "Yes. We better get going as well, so I can get home and face the music with mom." "Said Tanantra." "So that was who called you earlier. I knew it!" "Blurted out Dude." "Oh shut up! I'm not done with *you* yet Dude!" "Snapped Tanantra."

"So Leroy, Tanantra and Dude exited the building, and hopped on Dude's rug, making it to the big wooden door in no time at all." "Well I wanna thank you two for a most exciting night. It was the best." "Don't worry Leroy, there will be even more nights like it in the near future." "Added Dude. It took all three of the trios strength to open the big old door, and to close it as well."

"You guys have a great night. I know I sure will. Oh, by the way, are you guys both in tomorrow? You know, to come and explore the other side of the door?" "Asked Leroy." "Well, we really shouldn't. If we got caught even helping you open the door, there would be some serious punishment!" "Said a concerned Tanantra." "Oh stop your worrying! What time do you wanna meet here Leroy?" "Asked Dude." "Well, what time do you two get out of school?" "Asked Leroy." "Three o'clock." "Said Tanantra." "So let's meet here at three thirty." "Replied Dude." "Sounds good to me." "Replied Leroy. Then they said their goodbyes, and all three of them closed the big wooden door together."

Narrator,

Well that was one sick game, if you ask me. I dedicate this game of rugkey, to the four brothers I grew up with. The brothers first names *are* real, and they have *always* loved the game of hockey. They lost their mom early in life, and had to grow up rather fast. They also lost their youngest brother Darryl, due to a fiery car crash at the age of 19. Miss you bro. I'm sure you, your mom, and my mom, are all in a better place. So may you all rest in peace. These four brothers are the reason I invented rugkey, so I just want to say, I never forgot about you and I never will.

"Well that sure sounded like one wicked hockey game, I mean, rugkey game you had going there Ted." Said Paul. "Thanks Paul." Said Ted. "Well we better be hearing a lot more rugkey stories this summer. That was awesome!" Added Joe.

"Yeah man, hearing about those Step brothers, makes me think we should a get a hockey team going. I mean, we got the whole line covered, except of course for the goalie, but I really don't think that would be hard to find." Said Zack.

"Yeah, well while you guys are stuck in la la land, I'm sobering up here, and sure could use a fatty." Said Ron. "Alright then, let's fatty up." Said Paul, as he pulled out a bag and started rolling one up for the boys. "Well boys, let's not be too hasty here, it's time to break out the rye and celebrate like men!" Announced Zack. "Now we're talking man." Said Ron. So Zack started to dig through his over night bag, and before long, he pulled out five small shot glasses and handed them out. Then the rye was poured, and the drinking was on.

"Cheers boys! Here's to the brotherhood and the rugkey league. Oh, and here is to kicking those Packs asses." Yelled out Zack. The other boys all clanked their glasses together, and cheered out loud hooting and hollering. "As well boys, cheers to all my brothers, right here in front of me. May we all live a happy and most decorated life." Added Joe. The boys clanked the shot glasses together again, with even louder cheers this time. Ron however, had been guzzling beer all night, and fell over backwards. But he did however manage to save his drink at least.

"Well that was a good story Ted. When are you gonna break out some more buds?" Asked Paul. "Uh, I think I just wanna party a bit, and stretch my eyes out to the stars tonight, since the sky is clear and the rain has stopped. But don't worry, there's a lot more story telling then just that." Ted said, with a half grin. Joe hadn't really got into the chatty mood, up until this point. Now, it was hard to get the guy to shut up.

"Man you guys are the best. We're just like the brotherhood eh? You know, if I was ever going to die, I would hope it be *right* here with you boys, and that's the truth." Added a half drunk Joe. "Oh snap boys, Joe is getting drunk!" Paul yelled out with a laugh. "Look at him man!" Yelled out Ron. "Screw you guys. But you know what? You guys are alright in my books." Said Joe, in a drunken slur.

In that moment, Zack staggered over towards Ron and put his arm over his shoulder. "Don't worry buds, your a part of the bro ship dude, and we love you like a brother man." Replied Zack. "You guys are alright. Hey man, where's that fatty? You know what guys? Your the best. Till death do us part, and to tell you the truth, I would give my life for any one of you boys. I mean it man. You guys ever have any problems, you come and see uncle R eh?" Said Ron.

"Uncle R? This kids out of control boys! Party on dudes!" Yelled out Ted, and the rest of the boys had a bit of a chuckle as well. "He's out of it dude!" Yelled out Zack. "Hey shut up man! You guys think I drank a little too much? Well maybe your right, I don't get a chance to say this too often, but you guys are the best, and that's the truth." Added Ron, after a couple of puffs from the fatty. Then Ron fell on the ground with a good thump *this* time.

"You alright man? You want me to help you to bed?" Asked Paul. "No man, I'll be alright." Replied Ron. But when Paul tried to help Ron up, he fell over as well. "Okay Paul, I think you better help me to bed eh?" "You wanna sleep up in the tree or in the tent?" Asked Paul. "I'm sorry Paul. I don't wanna ruin your drunk, so just throw me in the tent eh." So Paul and Zack both helped Ron to the tent, and then they threw a couple of blankets over him.

"You guys are the best." Slurred Ron. Paul and Zack looked at each other with big grins on their faces. "You gonna be alright Ron?" Asked Zack. "Well, I gotta bit of the room spins bro. But I think I'm gonna be alright buds." Replied Ron.

There wasn't another peep out of Ron for the rest of the night, except for the occasional snore that is. "You see how drunk Ron got tonight man?" Zack spoke out. "Yeah man, but he never gets *that* drunk, unless he's got some issues." Added Ted. "Yeah, I hear you man. Maybe his old man has been getting drunk and throwing him around again or something eh?" Said Paul. "Well, whatever it is boys, I think we gotta help him out. After all, he is family, and Ron's always there for us whenever *we* need him." Said Ted.

"Your right man, he really hasn't been himself lately." Added Zack. "I'm kind of worried about the kid myself, and I really didn't want to say anything. But now that you mention it, I think we better keep a close eye on the kid for the next while." Suggested Joe. "Cheers to that." Said Ted, raising his glass. "Cheers." Said Joe. "Cheers." Said Zack. "Cheers." Said Paul. "Then it's agreed that we all keep an eye on Ron." Added Ted. The other boys agreed, and the night slowly continued.

"You know, I'm starting to get a bit drunk myself dudes." Said Ted, with a bit of a slur. "Yeah man, I think it was the fatty dude." Said Zack. "Hey Ted, what's your problem man? You spilled beer on the grass. Never do that man, that's alcohol abuse! Besides, the grass will grow up half cut. Ha ha." Yelled out Paul jokingly. "Sorry man, must have been the fatty." Slurred Ted. He was obviously catching a buzz, because he never caught onto the joke. "Yeah, well I think we're all a little drunk here. So pass the fat, and let's see who's the first one to drop to the mat." Said Ted, and the game was on.

Narrator,

Well you can pretty much see where this night is going. Ted's slurring his words, Ron has already hit the pillow, and the other three are puffing fatties like they are going out of style. So let's see what the morning brings shall we?

The next morning turned out to be *one* beautiful and sunny day. Paul was still asleep, but was rudely awaken by Ron, who was hovering over him with beer in hand, and a fatty in his mouth. "Get your ass out of my face Ron! I ain't getting up for nothing. Just because *you* went to bed so early last night, doesn't mean I'm getting up early for you! I'm going back to bed." Snapped Paul. "Really?" Replied Ron sarcastically. Then he lit up the fatty and started blowing it in Paul's face. "Okay, I'm up." Said a half groggy Paul. This seemed to stir the rest of the boys as well.

"What time is it Ron?" Asked Ted, with his eyes half closed. "Time for you to get your asses up. It's 9:30. I got bacon and potatoes burning on the fire, along with the making of eggs and toast, when you all get out of bed." "Nice." Said Joe, as he turned over to pluck the fatty from Paul's fingers. "Oh, and I brought you guys up some instant coffee I found in my bag. So wake up, it's time to finish what we started." Finished Ron.

It was practically a dog pile to see who got the first cup of coffee. Paul got there first. He poured himself a cup, stirred in some sugar, and lit up a smoke when he was done. By the time everyone had a cup in hand, the tree house was filled with cigarette smoke. But it was enough to know, that Ron got everyone out of bed like he planned. "Okay boys, I'm going down to start the eggs and toast." With that being said, Ron climbed back down the ladder to the fire and finished cooking breakfast.

Once the rest of the boys finished up their coffee and morning smoke, breakfast was served. So all they had to do, was pick up a plate and dig in. "You sure made a sick breakfast Ron." "Thanks Ted." "Yeah man, *really* good." Said Zack, with a mouthful.

Ron had already scarfed down his breakfast and rolled a fatty, by the time the rest of the boys were done. They ate like they hadn't been fed in days. Once every plate was practically licked clean, Ron flashed up the fatty, and the day began with a little hard work. Paul and Ron worked on the walls for the second floor of the tree house, while Joe and Zack cut floor joists for the third floor.

Your probably wondering what is holding up this mini fortress. Well I'll tell you. The boys found four straight cedar trees close by, and cut them to length. Then they laminated together four sets of three two by tens, to form the outside of the bottom floor. Bracing every corner of the bottom floor, with the cedar trees, that they buried three feet into the ground. Then using two by fours, they nailed each corner post together, and braced the posts to the tree itself.

As the day progressed, so did the heat. The shirts were off, and the sweat poured off their bodies by the bucket. But that didn't stop them from doing what they had to do. Halfway through the day, the beers came out. A couple hours of working and drinking in the sun though, the work eventually came to a halt.

"I'm flipping hot man! I think we should go for a swim and cool off boys." Blurted out Ron. "I think *that* has to be the best idea I've heard all day." Replied Ted. After that suggestion, tools dropped and the work stopped instantly. "I'm in." Said Paul. The rest of the boys agreed without an argument, and the race was on for the ladder.

"Hey, before we go, I'm telling you all *right* now where I'm hiding my stuff! So you guys better not screw with it *this* time!" Snapped Paul. "We heard ya." Muttered Zack, as he slid down the rope to beat the rest of the boys down.

The hike to the swimming hole was nothing but a buzz. Beer and fatties all the way. It was quite the hike through the thick brush though. Then you had to cross the mouth of the Fraser, and walk to the base of an old landslide. Which happened about a hundred years or so ago. It was a bit of a climb to actually get up and over the once fallen rock. But since then, a regrowth of trees, grass and other vegetation had replenished the mountainside. So the boys were able to climb the slide area, with the help of small trees and roots they used to pull themselves up of course.

On the other side of the remains from the fallen rock and dirt, was a hidden valley. It was the reward the boys discovered a few years back when they were out hiking. It was *absolutely* gorgeous, once you got past the regrowth of trees. The act of God, created a more than one thousand foot streaming waterfall, that seeped from the mountainside. Eventually, forming a beautiful swimming pond. It was a truly magnificent sight to the naked eye, and not a lot of people really knew about it. It was a fluke these boys found it, but what a find it was.

Paul was the first one in, followed by Zack, then Ted, and last but not least, Ron. Joe on the other hand, stayed close to the edge of the pool, just long enough to dunk his head in. Then he headed to a grassy area and found a spot to bask in the sun. He didn't want anyone to know he didn't know how to swim.

"Come on in Joe, the water is awesome!" Screamed Ted. "No, I think I'm gonna take a break and rest a little bit in the sun." Replied Joe. The rest of the boys didn't pay no never mind to Joe, until it was time to leave. Instead, they swam underneath the waterfall until their hearts were content.

"You turd! What did you do that for?" Snapped Joe. "It's time to go." Replied Paul, after splashing Joe with water. Then he walked away with the other boys. It took a couple of minutes for Joe to wake up and catch up with the others, and when he did, the boys wished they all had earplugs.

"You guys could have woken me up without the water you know!" "Yeah, but it wouldn't have been as much fun." Paul snickered. "Yeah, real funny guys, laugh it up. I'll remember you said that when I'm cooking dinner tonight." Replied Joe. "Hey man, I draw the line when it comes down to screwing with another guys food!" Snapped Ted. "That goes double for me. I'll make dinner." Suggested Paul. But instead, the unanimous vote was in turn given to Zack, which suited him just fine.

"You see how I get out of doing things?" Joe whispered to Ron, as they hiked their way through the brush. Ted and Paul were ahead of the pack, and made a bit of a detour to make the trip back a bit more bearable. "Wow dog, you see how big these suckers got?" Said Ted. "Well you can tell they are getting enough water that's for sure." Said Paul.

"How could they not man? They are planted right in the middle of a huge marsh. When the rain comes and the river overflows, where do you think the water sits?" Asked Ron. "He does have a point there Paul." Said Joe. "Yeah, well I've seen enough, it's time to get a move on. I'm hungry." Paul muttered, as he trudged on through back to camp. The others followed, but for the rest of the walk, there wasn't very much talking amongst the boys. The only thing that could be heard, was the rustling through the long blades of grass, and the snapping of twigs along the way.

Tonight was going to be a simple dinner. Steak, cheese macaroni, with a side of mushrooms, garlic and onions fried in butter. Paul, being the first one back, headed straight to the place where he stashed his tools. By the time the rest of the boys got back, he was already up in the tree house freaking out aloud.

The boys weren't prepared for what was about to happen next. Paul came flying down the ladder so fast, it would have made your head spin. But by the time he reached the bottom where the boys were, he was gasping for air and tried to talk at the same time. The way he spit it out so fast, couldn't have been any funnier if he would have planned it. Zack and Ron immediately hit the dirt in a fit of laughter. Ted tried to talk to Paul, but he could not help himself and burst out laughing as well. Joe was almost in tears with laughter, and this just pissed Paul off even more.

"Which one of you guys stole my tools again?" But Paul got no answer from anyone, and that just made him even more angrier. So he tackled Joe to the ground. That sent Ted to his assistance and he jumped on top of Paul. Zack and Ron laughed so hard that their stomachs started to hurt, but that didn't stop them from joining in on the rumble. It was a dog fight at first. Then it started to get serious. Paul pulled out a knife used to cut the food.

Everyone's eyes were fixated on Paul at this point. He was holding the knife in the air to let the others know he was serious. "Hey man, put the knife down! Nobody here touched your tools you tool! First of all, you were the last one to leave when we left to go hiking. Second of all, you were the first one here when we got back. So what makes you think *we* had anything to do with your tools going missing?" Ron yelled back.

But Paul's eyes changed, and he looked like he was going crazy. He was about to turn around and walk away, but that wasn't good enough. Instead, he looked at Ron, and threw the knife towards his head. Luckily though, it landed just inches away from his ear.

Ron was half stunned at first. He looked at the knife, and then at Paul. Without any hesitation whatsoever, he got up and tackled Paul to the ground. To everyone's surprise, Ron was on top of Paul throwing wild punches. Ted and Zack were there in time to peel Ron off of Paul. Joe was still in mid laugh, but when he seen what was going on, he decided to try and help out, the only way he knew how.

"Hey guys! Quiet, quiet!" Yelled Joe. "You here that?" The boys went dead silent. "There's something out there!" Paul freaked out and hid behind a nearby tree. Once everyone's attention was now on Joe, he knew there was no better time like the present. He burst out laughing harder then he did before. "You should have seen your faces!" He managed to spit out during his fit of laughing out loud.

Then Paul came out from behind the tree. "You scared the crap out of me!" Yelled Paul. "Yeah! What do you think you did to me when you threw the knife at me?" Snapped Ron. "Yeah, well what about you man? You jumped me from behind!" Snapped Paul. But once the boys realized they were acting no better then that of their own parents, they blew it all off with a laugh.

It took Zack twenty minutes before serving dinner, and it was well worth the wait. The only thing you could hear for the next few minutes, was the odd sound of a little chewing, and the crackling of the fire. After dinner, the night stars began to show themselves, and beers were being cracked open one by one. Two recently rolled fatties were being passed around as well. The only thing that was missing, was for Ted to continue his story.

CHAPTER 10

This side of the big wooden door

"Okay guys, don't crowd me. Let me have a couple of more pulls off this fatty, and I'll continue where I left off." Said Ted. Ron got both fatties passed to him at once, so he had a couple of puffs from each joint, and then passed them along. After the fatty session was over, Ted got right back to his story.

"Leroy got home that night and was just about to open up his bedroom door, thinking he was in the clear, when his father called him." "Leroy? Is that you? Why don't you come out into the living room and say hi to everyone?" "Asked Andy." "Yes dad." "Blurted out Leroy, in a lazy sort of voice." "Hello Leroy." "Said a cheerful voice. It was Nina and Santose sitting in the front room on the sofa." "Well how does it go today Leroy?" "Asked Santose." "Very well thanks." "Then Leroy waited about thirty seconds before he spoke again."

"Can I go to my room now dad?" "Asked Leroy." "Why sure you can son." "Replied Andy. With that being said, Leroy didn't waste any time heading to his room. But not before noticing the newspaper sitting on the floor by the door. Now you gotta remember, this is the Packs, so newspapers came out right away after any nightly function, such as rugkey. So Leroy grabbed a hold of the paper, hoping nobody noticed him grabbing it. He wanted to make sure he took off his shoes with a loud thug, so as not to arouse any suspicion."

"There he was, along with his new friends, right smack dab on the front page of the Underground Chronicle. How could he hide *this* from his dad? He reads the paper faithfully, each and every time it comes out. This worried Leroy, because things didn't pan out like he had planned it, at all. Its not like he wasn't going to tell his dad, he just didn't want to tell his dad *right* now. According to the paper though, Leroy didn't have any choice whatsoever."

"The next few minutes that went by, was full of nothing but pacing around his room, and debating whether to tell his dad, or wait until the next day. But the more he thought about it, the more it made sense to tell his dad, before he found out and mistrusted him from here on in."

"This was something that Leroy did *not* want. After all, his dad and him *never* kept secrets from each other. He was just afraid his father would yell at him or something. On the other hand, Nina and Santose were here, so perhaps this would be the best time. Leroy flipped a coin inside his head, so to speak, and decided it would be best for him to fess up."

"Leroy opened up his bedroom door and proceeded to walk nervously down the hall. Slowly making his way to the sitting room, where his father, Nina and Santose were talking." "Uh, dad?" "Leroy began." "Yes son." "There he is! We were just talking about you little fella." "Said Santose." "*Santose!* Can't you tell Leroy has something to say." "Scolded Nina." "Oh, yes of course. Sorry Leroy, continue." "Said Santose." "Well dad, it's kinda of complicated, and I didn't want to hurt you, but here, read this, and I'll explain the whole story." "Then Leroy handed his father the newspaper."

"Well son, according to this, you seem to have won something." "Oh, what did you win Leroy?" "Asked Nina in excitement." "Okay dad, it's like this, now it's not like I didn't tell you, I just didn't tell you *yet*." "Well go on son, what is

it?" "Asked Andy, now curious as to what Leroy had to say."
"Okay dad, here it goes. It all started when Dude and Tanantra
came through my bedroom wall, through a tunnel that was
made a few days ago and I went back through the tunnel with
them, back to the Packs that is, and then they blew up the
tunnel, and they took me to a rugkey game, and I had to leave
through the big old wooden door because they aren't allowed
to go passed the door." "Leroy spit out really fast, in one long
sentence." "Woo, slow down son and hold your horses. Take
a deep breath now. So you met Dude, Tanantra and who?"
"Asked Andy."

"Well I also met Dude and Tanantra's little sister Lynda.
They also introduced me to Anne." "Anne?" "Andy interrupted."
"Uh, I met her in the Packs dad." "But Leroy stopped talking
for a moment, to notice the expression on his fathers face. He
had never seen his dad make a face like that before, and it
sent chills down his spine. The next thing Andy knew, Leroy
turned around and went straight for his bedroom."

"Will you two excuse me for a moment while I go and have
a little talk with Leroy?" "Of course." "Replied Nina." "You go do
what you have to do, and we'll be here if you need anything."
Said Santose. Andy left the room and walked towards Leroy's
bedroom. He knocked on the door and called out Leroy's
name. So Leroy told his father to come in."

"Are you mad at me father?" "Asked Leroy, in a nervous sort
of voice." "What would ever give you that idea son? Of course
I'm not mad." "Andy replied, in a soothing voice." "Its just, that
I never seen that look on your face before." "Replied Leroy."
"Well you know that Anne is your mothers name son, and,
well, it sort of took me by surprise, hearing that name coming
from *you* son." "I know and I apologize dad." "Leroy began."
"You don't have to apologize son. Your mother was a good
egg, and you should never apologize for speaking of her. So
who is this Anne that you speak about?" "Andy interrupted."

"Well father, she is Dude, Tanantra and Lynda's mother." "Hmm." "Andy managed to slip in." "Well Dude and Tanantra are supposed to be meeting me at around three thirty tomorrow, and they want me to take them on a tour. Is it okay if I go dad?" "I don't see why not." "Replied Andy."

"Then you don't mind if we swing by for a bit, so you can meet them?" "Asked Leroy." "That sounds alright with me. In fact, I'll even set out a few snacks for you kids if you'd like." "Replied Andy. But Leroy changed the subject, seeing how his father was fine with everything he had just told him."

"Dad, you gotta see this game they call rugkey." "Uh, don't you mean hockey son?" "No dad, it's called rugkey. They have skates and ice like hockey, but they fly around on these magic rugs and play. Its really a more intense game of hockey, but a lot faster." "Finished Leroy."

"You mean to tell me, the whole time I have been reading the paper, I thought I was looking at the hockey scores and I really wasn't? Hmm, I always wondered why those players seem to be on some sort of carpet. I just thought it was some sort of trick photography." "Said Andy."

"Hey dad? Would you like to come to a game with Santose and Nina sometime?" "Well, I'd be all for it. But you will have to go ask Nina and Santose for yourself." "Can I dad? Right now?" "Asked an excited Leroy." "Go ahead." "Replied Andy."

"So Leroy bolted off to the living room." "I was just wondering, if perhaps you two would be interested in coming to a rugkey game sometime?" "Uh, rugkey? What is that?" "Asked Santose." "Uh, well it's like hockey. Here, it's on the front page of the newspaper, you can have a look for yourself." "Replied Leroy." "Well I don't know about Santose, but I would love to come to one of these, rug games." "Said Nina." "Oh, and it's rugkey. Its just like hockey, but more faster." "Leroy corrected Nina." "I'd love to go with you one day Leroy." "Replied Santose."

"Okay, well thanks guys, your gonna love it. I'm off to bed now, so goodnight." "Goodnight Leroy." "Replied Nina, giving him a big hug." "Goodnight there young man!" "Said Santose, in a deep voice, holding out his hand and giving Leroy a firm hand shake. Then Leroy left the room."

"Andy was still in Leroy's bedroom waiting for him, when Leroy entered his room." "Oh, I almost forgot dad." "Without another word said, Leroy took down a picture from the wall, and pulled the dresser out far enough, so he could show his dad the tunnel that led into his room."

"Well, I'm gonna have to fix that up tomorrow. We can just leave it like that for tonight son." "Replied Andy. So Leroy hung the picture back up, and moved the dresser up against the wall again." "Well goodnight Leroy. Have a good sleep." "Goodnight dad." "Said Leroy. But just as Andy was about to close the door behind him, Leroy asked one last question."

"Dad?" "Yes Leroy." "Do you think one day I will be allowed to go to school?" "Asked Leroy." "You know son, I think that would be wonderful idea, if we were back up there." "Andy said, as he pointed above ground." "Oh, but Tanantra and Dude go to school in the Packs." "Leroy blurted out. Then Andy spoke with a bit of a chuckle." "Well then, I guess we're going to have to put you in school as soon as we can. But we'll talk about that another day. Have a good sleep." "Replied Andy, as he closed the door behind him. Andy paused for a moment In the hallway, reflecting on the conversation he just finished having with Leroy. Then he made his way back to his company."

"It looks like your boy got himself a bit of the spotlight, according to the paper here Andy." "Replied Santose." "Yes it appears that way, doesn't it?" "Yes, it says here that him and his friends won some sort of seasons tickets, to this rugkey game. It looks to me like it's just like hockey, except they are on some sort of rug. But if you look at the puck, or *key* as they call it here, it's clear, and seems to have some sort of golden key inside of it." "Said Santose." "I noticed that. It must make for one wicked slap shot eh?" "Andy said with a laugh."

"So did Leroy ask you two to the next game?" "Asked Andy." "Yes, and according to what it says here in the paper, the next game is tomorrow night at six o'clock. Well, we're in. How about you Andy?" "Yes, I think it would be fun." "Replied Andy." "It seems like somethings got you puzzled Andy. May I ask you what is the matter?" "Asked Nina. But Andy took a moment before he answered."

"Oh it is nothing, it's just that, Leroy mentioned a name I have never heard him speak of before, and, it was his mothers name. But it's nothing. Shall I make you two a coffee?" "No we're fine. I think we are going to get going to bed though, so we can rest up for the game. But its been a lovely time." "Said Nina." "Okay, well we'll see you two in the morning." "Replied Andy."

"The next morning, Leroy was up rather early. He was too excited to sleep any longer. So he decided to see if his father wanted to go exploring for the day, to kill some time before the game. He was all right with that, so they spent the day going down the different hallways. There were too many though, and the hallways were too long to see all in one day. But it *was* tiresome, and by the time two o'clock hit, Andy was getting kind of hungry, so Leroy and him split up. Andy went back home to fix the kids something to eat, and Leroy walked towards the big wooden door."

CHAPTER 11

The Four Seasons

Narrator,

I think there is something peculiar about Anne here, that Andy is not letting on at this time. But I'm sure we'll find out soon enough. To tell you the truth, I'm kind of interested in the next game. Those announcers are pretty funny. But let's see what is up with this four seasons.

"When Leroy finally arrived at the big wooden door, he gave the secret knock. He waited for a couple of minutes, and then the same knock was heard from the other side. That was his cue to pull on the door as hard as he could. At first, it wouldn't even budge. But with the help of Dude and Tanantra pushing from the other side, the door began to slowly creak open."

"Hey there guys, your right on time." "Said Leroy." "Well hurry up and help us close this door. I'm not sure, but I think we were being followed." "Said an out of breathe Tanantra." "Yeah, I think it's all in your head, ever since mom yelled at you last night." "Said Dude." "Oh what do you know! So how are you today Leroy? Are you getting stoked to come and see the game?" "Asked Tanantra, trying to change the subject."

"Oh, I'm doing fine thank you. I told my father about going to the game, and hanging with you two though, and he wants to meet you. Is that alright with you? Oh, and about the game, I invited my father and two friends of ours to come and watch it with us. So, do you think that will be okay?" "Asked Leroy."

"Sure Leroy! We are going to be in a booth anyways, and I'm sure we can bring whoever we would like." "Replied Tanantra." "Cool, this game is gonna be sweet." "Said Leroy." "Yeah, but there is one thing Tanantra never told you. The only way Tanantra is *allowed* to come to the game, is if our mom comes as well." "Dude said with a laugh." "Oh shut up Dude!" "Sneered Tanantra." "Well it's true!" "Yelled Dude."

"So Leroy quickly changed the subject, by grabbing hold of the magic carpet in his hands, and neatly unfolding it on the ground in front of the big wooden door." "Well hop on guys, and I'll show you around." "Said Leroy." "Which way Leroy?" "Asked Dude." "There *is* only one *way to* go." "Said a sarcastic Tanantra." "Yeah, just keep going straight, until you meet a bunch of different hallways going in every different direction." "Added Leroy. So away they went."

"Okay, now the first hallway to the right, and about half way down, you will see a light. That will take us to the four seasons room." "Finished Leroy." "The four seasons room?" "Dude and Tanantra both say at the same time." "You'll see." "Replied Leroy, with the wind rushing through his hair."

"So they set off down the long corridor, and passed the room where all hallways met, then Leroy spoke." "Okay guys, this is where we get off." "Once Dude landed the magic carpet in the hallway, Leroy got off and walked towards the nearest door. Dude rolled up the magic carpet and carried it over his shoulder, while Leroy held the door open for him. Then they all walked inside to view a most unique and enchanting display of eye candy."

"Wow, man. What is this place?" "Asked Dude." "Well, over here we have what people above ground call sunshine." "Leroy replied, walking around the place like he owned it." "This is where you can grow vegetables, climb trees and pick flowers." "As Leroy talked, he bent over to pick a red rose. Then he handed it to Tanantra. She had never seen a rose before, and was not sure of what to say. So Leroy took the rose and held it's beautiful fragrance up to her nose. Tanantra took it with delight after Leroy placed it in her hand with a smile. Leroy kept moving as he motioned Dude and Tanantra to follow him." "Now where you just were, is what we call summer. Where I am about to take you *now,* is called winter." "Said Leroy."

"Now keep in mind, that this was a magic room and the four seasons appeared in one great big stadium size room, but ends just like that of a movie film. So in other words, you walk along in the summer until the clip ends, and our next step is into the winter clip. You get it?" Explained Ted.

"No sooner did they get into the winter side of things, Tanantra, who had never seen snow before, quickly rolled up some in her hands and made a snow ball. Her next move was to throw it at Dude, But Dude kept his wits about him around her, and ducked just in time for the snow ball to land right directly in Leroy's face." "Oh, I'm sorry!" "Said a half panicked Tanantra, but it was too late." "The snowball fight had begun, and the next one was from Dude hitting Tanantra in the shoulder. Leroy didn't waste any time, he rolled a couple of snowballs up and ended up nailing both of them, one after another."

"The novelty wore off after a short while. So they started making snowmen. But when Dude pointed out the big fluffy pillows in the fall clip, Leroy told him that they were clouds that produced rain. So they went straight to fall. They stood in the rain for what seemed like hours. In reality though, a couple of minutes was sufficient enough for the trio."

"Can we go some place a little bit more warmer now?" "Pleaded Tanantra." "No problem." "Replied Leroy, as he began to lead them off to the spring." "Now this is about the best time of year, because everything begins to grow. The flowers bloom, and leaves start forming on the tree branches. This is when all the flowers come out and new life is born."

"During his tour, Leroy showed them the many different types of trees and flowers. But that didn't last long at all. It was starting to get a bit chilli, so Leroy suggested they go back to summer and dry off. Tanantra and Dude folded out the magic carpet without a complaint in the world. Then they all got on and flew straight to summer."

"Dude was about to land, when Leroy pointed out a row of trees up ahead, and asked them if they wanted to go for a swim." "Well, won't the water be cold?" "Asked Tanantra." "Heck no, the water will be perfect. We can change into our swim wear and hang our clothes out on the tree branches to dry." "Said Leroy." "Its a good thing we packed our bags for *this* trip." "Said Tanantra."

"Dude put the magic carpet down on the sand, but could *not* keep his eyes off the water that stretched out as far as the eye could see. Tanantra had taken her shoes and socks off on the way over to dry out, and when she stepped on the hot sand, she screeched out loud and quickly got back on the magic carpet." "What is the matter?" "Asked Dude immediately, thinking his sister was in danger."

"Its just *sand*. Look, I'll show you." "Said Leroy, as he took his shoes and socks off. Then he started running through the sand in his bare feet." "You see, it's all good." "Tanantra slowly put one foot in front of the other, and could not get used to the texture of the sand squishing in between her toes. Dude on the other hand, took off his shoes and socks. Then dropped his pants and shirt, leaving him in his swim shorts. After which, he ran straight for the giant bath tub, as he referred to it."

"While Dude's clothes dried in the hot sun, Tanantra and Leroy got themselves dressed to swim. Then they hung their clothes on a small tree that stood by itself, directly in the eye of the sun. There was nothing left to do but to go for the gusto, and the race was on. Tanantra and Leroy entered the water at the same time. Tanantra was surprised that the water was so warm."

"The trio splashed around in the water and cooled off for about a half an hour or so. Dude, who got bored easily, decided to go lay on the carpet to dry off. It didn't take Tanantra and Leroy long to follow the same example. Once Leroy figured everyone was dry enough to continue the tour, he got up and encouraged everyone to do the same thing. It didn't take much to coax Tanantra and Dude, they were pretty much game for anything at this point."

"After everyone got dressed, they all met back on the magic carpet, and flew until Leroy got Dude to stop. Leroy explained a little more about fall to them as they slowly flew by it. Then out through the door of the four seasons, down the hall, and back to the large room where all the hallways met. Right in the middle of the room is where Dude was asked to land. It was mysteriously dark in the room, so Leroy told them he would be right back to shed some light on the situation."

"Leroy ran to the wall next to the hallway which led home. Then he gave the rope that hung from the ceiling a pull. He returned in a flash, back to the middle of the room where Tanantra and Dude were waiting." "I thought you were going to turn on a light. What is the matter, you don't know where the switch is?" "Asked Dude." "I found the switch, it just takes a minute." "Replied Leroy, with a huge grin on his face."

"Then from out of nowhere, the thunderous sound of the ceiling opening up, frightening both Dude and Tanantra. But as the light began to shine through, brightening up the room more and more as the ceiling opened wider, no one spoke a word. All eyes were peering up at the amazing creatures that seemed to fly, rather than swim. They seemed to cut through the water like a hot knife through butter. Tanantra and Dude held their hands to their ears at first, but as they looked up at the glorious sight, they were absolutely dazzled."

"Leroy was now standing beside Tanantra, explaining to her, the many different species of fish and wild life that lived in and amongst the river. Tanantra listened intensely, as if she was intrigued by every word Leroy was saying. Dude on the other hand, wasn't listening to a thing. He just stood there gazing upwards at the river full of living creatures, with his mouth wide open."

"Woo guys! Check it out!" "Dude yelled, out of the blue as he pointed upwards." "Tanantra and Leroy looked to where Dude was pointing, *just* in time to see a school of fish swimming by." "Wow, everyone in my class would *love* this!" "Exclaimed Tanantra." "Mom would love this too eh?" "Said Dude." "You know what? Mom would love that Dude." "Added Tananatra. Leroy smiled to himself, his plan worked. The brother and sister he had just met, were getting along for the first time since they got together."

"They stood there for a while, like they were stuck in time and in silence, as they watched the underwater world unfold before their very own eyes. Then Leroy glanced at his watch." "Okay guys, hold on to your ears, because this is going to get loud. The ceiling above began to close off the underwater world once again. The thunderous sound was so loud that Leroy hopped back on the rug with Tanantra and Dude, and they got the heck out of there."

"Are we going to the spell room now Leroy?" "Asked Dude." "Um, I thought we would stop by my place and have a few snacks. Besides, I told my dad I was going to bring you by the house. If that's alright with you two of course?" "Replied Leroy." "Sure, I could go for something to eat." "Said

Dude." "Yes, I would love to meet your father Leroy." "Replied Tanantra. So Leroy led them down the hallway to his home."

"Leroy could smell baked goods as they neared the front door." "Wow, whatever is cooking sure smells good." "Said Dude." "Oh, Nina probably did some baking today." "Replied Leroy." "Who is that Leroy?" "Asked Tanantra." "I'll introduce you all to each other when we get inside." "Said Leroy."

"Dude was the last one in, so he closed the door after the trio got inside. Then his sister and him followed Leroy to the sitting room." "Dude and Tanantra, I would like you to meet my dad, Santose and Nina." "Announced Leroy. Everyone introduced themselves, and then Nina spoke." "Go on everybody, help yourselves, Your gonna need your energy for the big game tonight." "Dude wasted no time at all, he went straight to the feast that lay before him on the coffee table."

"So your the two who made the hole in my sons room eh?" "Said Andy, in a stern voice. Tanantra and Dude both looked at each other, and were speechless for words." "Ah, I'm just messing with ya." "Said Andy. Tanantra and Dude both looked up at him with a sigh of relief." "Oh my, have you two grown up to be a healthy pair. I can't wait to see your mom one of these days." "Added Andy. Then he walked away into the kitchen, while the trio gazed at each other with strange looks on their faces."

Narrator,

Now if you ask me, I'd say there is something mighty peculiar going on that Andy isn't letting on. In any case, let's see what happens next shall we?

"Nina had several plates of goodies spread out all over the table. Then she handed each individual a plate so they could serve themselves. Dude was the first to dig in and make a pig of himself. Tanantra wasn't really that hungry, so she only tried a few things. Leroy had a few bites of food and that was it. He just wanted to get going. Leroy didn't want to waste any time, so he went to his bedroom and got some fishing rods together. Then he returned to the sitting room, after setting the rods down in the hallway beside the front door." "Okay dad, we're going to head out to the fishing hole for a while." "Said Leroy." "Well, do you mind if we joined you?" "Asked Andy." "Well sure but, uh, Dude's got a magic carpet, and we were going to fly there because it's gonna save us a lot of time and all." "Replied Leroy."

"How about this, you kids go on ahead of us, and we'll just catch up with you." "Suggested Andy." "Sounds good to me dad. So, can I go now?" "Asked Leroy." "Of course son." "Replied Andy." "Well it was nice to meet you two." "Said Nina, as the kids opened the door to leave." "It was very nice to meet you all as well." "Replied Tanantra, in a polite voice." "Yeah, and thanks for lunch." "Dude blurted out, with his mouth still half full of pie."

"The trio closed the door behind them, and hopped on the rug." "Well that was a little awkward, if I may say so myself." "Said Tanantra." "That was a bit strange wasn't it?" "Replied Leroy." "I know right. I felt bad just leaving all of that food sitting there. But I did pocket a few items." "Dude added, as he chuckled to himself. Tanantra and Leroy just looked at each other and rolled their eyes. Dude had no clue that there was something strange going on, and Tanantra thought it best to keep him in the dark, at least for the moment."

"The trio was off down the hallway again. When they reached the fishing hole Leroy and his father frequented, Leroy got off the magic carpet and started getting the rods ready to fish. When they were all ready to go, Leroy led the way and made the first cast. After which, he laid his rod down on a tree branch, he had previously stuck in the ground. Then he helped Tanantra and Dude cast their lines in."

"He taught them how to hold the rod, and how to set the hook. He also made sure to remind them that they should *always* keep an eye on the floater. Then he showed them how to cast, so he could keep fishing himself. It took a few tries, but they seemed to get the hang of it."

"A few minutes into the casting and reeling in, Leroy was startled by the high pitch scream that came from Tanantra. He almost dropped his rod in the water." "What is the matter?" "Asked Leroy." "Um, I don't know. This rod seems to be doing tricks!" "Screamed Tanantra. Leroy laughed a bit and reeled his line in the last few feet. Then he set his rod down to go and give Tanantra a hand."

"What do I do Leroy?" "Asked Tanantra." "Its okay, this is what we came here for." "Replied Leroy, in a voice that seemed to calm Tanantra down a considerable amount. Then he stepped in behind her and showed her exactly what to do." "First of all, after you set the hook, and your *sure* the fish is on, you have to pull hard, until your rod comes all the way back. At the same time, you have to be able to reel in as fast as you can. Then you have to let the rod back down and repeat the same motion. Now if the fish seems like he wants to fight you, then you have to release this button right here." "Leroy explained." "Then you let it run for a bit, but not too much where the fish thinks it's in control. Once you think he's played out, you repeat reeling in as you pull your rod up. Then you hold your rod down and reel in again, slowly pulling your rod up again, until your fish is ashore." "Finished Leroy."

"Before long, Tanantra was doing it all by herself. Leroy wanted to go back and fish with his rod, but he knew that once that fish came ashore, she was going to need a hand getting it beached. Besides, he wanted to pull the hook out of the fish himself." "I could get used to this!" "Shrieked Tanantra. But it didn't take her long to wish she hadn't said that. Once the fish jumped close by her, she immediately gave the rod to Leroy, and told him to bring the fish in. Which he did in no time at all."

"It looks like you caught yourself a beauty here Tanantra." "Leroy complimented." "I did?" "Replied Tanantra." "You bet! You caught yourself at least a ten pound trout. That's a bigger fish than I caught my very first time out." "Added Leroy. Tanantra was all proud of herself now, and asked Leroy what to do with the fish. So he told her she could do whatever she wanted to do with it. She could either keep it for eating, or throw it back. Her face went from a smile to a frown when he mentioned the words eat it, and spoke very fast. "I am *not* eating the likes of *that* small creature. Throw it back!" "Tanantra said, in a firm voice."

"Dude was a quick learner, and was obviously paying attention to what Leroy was saying when he was teaching them how to fish. He was busy reeling in a fish by himself already." "Woo that's a big fish Dude!" "Blurted out Leroy, after throwing the fish Tanantra had caught back." "I know right!" "Was the only thing that came out of Dude's mouth. He was too busy fighting the fish to pay attention what was going on beside him."

"As far as Tanantra's fishing for the rest of the day went, it didn't. Instead, she watched the boys go at it. She caught the first fish, and that was all she was concerned about. Leroy thought Dude would need a bit of a hand bringing the fish in, but he was surprised to see the fish ashore, shortly after a quick cast."

"Will it bite me if I touch it Leroy?" "Asked Dude, sounding half excited and half nervous at the same time." "Of course not. But you have to get that hook out of its mouth, without hooking yourself." "Replied Leroy. So without any further ado, Dude had the hook out of its mouth and a rock in his hand."

"Ah, what are you doing with that rock in your hand Dude?" "Asked Tanantra." "Uh, I'm about to kill the creature, if you don't mind." "Can he really do that Leroy?" "Asked Tanantra." "Of course he can, but *only* if he plan on eating it. Do you plan on eating it Dude?" "Asked Leroy." "Uh, well, how does it taste?" "Asked a curious Dude." "Well I'll tell you, it's one of the best tasting fish I've ever eaten." "Said Leroy. Dude didn't need to hear anymore. He took the rock that was in his hand, and with one hard hit, he knocked the fish over the head. After which, Leroy took out his pocket knife and began cleaning the fish."

"Good job Leroy, I'm very proud of you." "Said a familiar voice in the distance. Leroy lifted his head up slightly, to see Santose, Nina and his father coming to join them." "That is a mighty fine looking fish you caught there Dude." "Said Andy." "You must have been watching us for a bit or something eh pa?" "Asked Leroy." "For a spell my son, for a spell." "Admired Andy, as he watched Leroy clean the fish just like he taught him how to."

"Well we can thank Dude for dinner tonight. I don't think it would be wise if he brought it back to the Packs with him. He would probably get in trouble for being here." "Suggested Leroy." "Good call Leroy." "Said Dude." "Speaking of dinner Dude, I think we better get back home, before mom freaks out about us being late or something." "Said Tanantra." "Yeah, I guess your right eh. Hey Leroy, we can check out the spell room the next time okay." "Said Dude." "Yeah and besides, we have to go home and get ready for the game tonight." "Added Tanantra."

"Hey dad, I'm going to go with them, because they are going to need help opening up the big wooden door. So, I'll meet you back at home." "Said Leroy." "Okay son, we'll get the fish started in the meantime." "Suggested Andy." "Oh, one more thing you two, uh, is your mother going to be there at the game tonight?" "Asked Andy, as he clears his throat." "Uh,

I like to make it a habit of meeting my boys friends parents." "Andy said quickly." "Oh she'll be there alright. Or Tanantra can't even go." "Blurted out Dude. Tanantra gave Dude a little slap on the shoulder, and they were off."

"The trio arrived at the big old wooden door in good time. They all pulled as hard as they could to open the door, until it was open wide enough for Dude and Tanantra to squeeze through."

"Hey, aren't you guys forgetting about the carpet?" "Asked Leroy." "No, you can use it to get home if you want. I left mine on the other side of the door." "Said Tanantra." "Okay, thanks. I guess I'll see you two at the game." "Said Leroy. Then they said goodbye to one another, and shut the door together once more."

CHAPTER 12

The Winners Box

"Leroy took a crack at flying the rug for the very first time by himself. It was a little tricky at first, but he got the hang of it in no time, and flew the heck out of it. In fact, he got back fast enough to offer his dad and his friends a ride. So they all got on the magic carpet. After a few minutes though, Nina wanted to get off. But by this time they had already reached the door to home."

"While Andy prepared the fish for dinner, Nina and Santose figured it would be a good time to get ready. They were excited to have been invited to go and watch the rugkey game. It was time to see what the Packs was all about. That seemed to be the only thing on Santose's mind."

"The fish was prepared, and Leroy had the chore of getting the vegetables ready. Andy figured in the meantime, he would go and get himself ready. After Leroy put the vegetables and the fish on the table to serve, he called everyone to the table."

"Santose and Nina sat at the table and waited for Andy. When he didn't come, Leroy got up to see what was taking him so long. As Leroy walked into his fathers bedroom, he stood there in shock for a second or two. His father was all dressed up and clean cut for a change."

"Oh hey there Leroy. Pass me some of that old spice on the dresser will you son?" "Here you go pa." "Replied Leroy, after handing his father an ancient bottle of old spice." "Santose and Nina are at the table waiting for us." "Well that's just fine son. I'll be along in a minute. After I figure out how to put this tie on. Its bin a long time since I wore one of these." "Finished Andy." "Okay dad, I'll tell them you will be right out. Dinner is ready by the way." "Okay son, I'll be right out." "Then Leroy left the room."

"Meanwhile, back in the Packs." "Are you kids almost ready to go? I thought you said that the game started a little bit early tonight!" "Anne yelled from her bedroom. Tanantra was about to speak, but stopped short as she walked into the bedroom, to find her mom standing in front of the mirror."

"Wow mom, you look absolutely gorgeous! What's the occasion?" "Asked Tanantra, quite surprised." "Oh, this old thing? What on earth are you talking about? I just so happened to have worn this *old* thing *plenty* of times." "Yeah, maybe before we were born." "Said a smart ass Dude, as he walked by and noticed what his mother was wearing." "Well, there is something strange going on here, and I can't *wait* to find out what it is!" "Sneered Tanantra, as she stammered off to finish getting herself ready."

"Okay mom, I'm ready!" "Yelled out Dude, from down the hallway." "I'm ready too mom." "Yelled out Tanantra, from her bedroom." "I am ready as well." "Announced little Lynda, as she walked into her mothers bedroom." "Then off we go." "Replied Anne. Then she went to the closet by the front door, and pulled out the family carpet. With the help from her son, she lay it out flat on the front door step. The minute it was down, the family hopped on and off they flew."

"Mom, do you mind if you drop us off at the front steps of the arena, so that we can go and meet our guests?" "Asked Dude." "Why certainly. But you make sure to hurry back."

"Replied Anne." "Yes mom. Okay, right here will be fine. Don't forget mom, we are in the winners box. Its the box right beside the announcers box." "Yes, now go on you two. I'm sure Lynda and I will have no problems finding our seats." "Replied Anne, as her and Lynda flew towards the entrance to the arena."

"About this time, Leroy, Andy, Santose and Nina had finished eating. So they were on the carpet and heading towards the big wooden door. The only problem with that was, they seemed to be getting there a bit faster than Nina would have liked to. Once they arrived in front of the big wooden door though, she seemed to feel fine."

"Leroy immediately got off the rug and did the secret knock. Before long, the same knock was heard coming from the other side." "Okay dad, now we have to pull on the door as hard as we can." "Said Leroy. This time though, with all the extra help, the door opened with much ease."

"So you guys all ready for the big game?" "Asked Dude, sounding excited." "You bet, and how about you?" "Asked an excited Leroy." "Well lead the way kids." "Andy said, after he helped close the big wooden door."

"Everyone seemed to be pretty stoked about the game. But the two I'm gonna bet my money on to be the most excited, would *have* to be Anne and Andy. For some reason, I think they got a bit of a secret to share." Ted added, trying to sound mysterious.

"It took a few minutes to climb the stairs leading to the arena. At the entrance door, they were greeted by a strange looking creature." "Tickets please." "Said the creature. But no sooner did he say that, he recognized Leroy, Tanantra, and Dude right away." "Oh, your the ones who won seasons tickets. Well right this way please. No need for introductions, I know who you are, and don't worry about your family, it is all free of charge." "Said the furry little creature."

"As soon as they got in the entrance way, they were crowded by reporters of all shapes and sizes. There was even the Canadian Underground News Network there trying to get a piece of the action. They started in on Leroy and his father right off the bat. Asking them all sorts of questions, but the owner of the stadium caught wind of this, and put a stop to that right away."

"Excuse me, excuse me." "The owner of the stadium said, as he made his way through the crowd." "Hello there, I'm Bent Forlane, the owner of the arena. Come with me and you won't be bothered by these pesky reporters." "Said Bent. So Bent led them towards the restrooms. Leroy thought it was sort of weird, that the man seemed to be talking to his watch. But then, the wall beside the rest room opened up. It was a hidden door, that just looked like an ordinary concrete wall that slid to the side. Beyond the wall was the start of a long corridor."

"Wow! Is there other secret doors like this?" "Asked a curious Leroy." "Oh, there are many my boy. You just gotta know where to look. I'm the owner, and *I* don't even know every secret entrance in this place. But I'm sure I've been through every entrance. As you get older though, the memory seems to fade a bit." "Finished Bent."

"Well sir, I wanna thank you for getting us away from those reporters." "Said Andy." "My pleasure. So you must be Leroy's father." "Replied Bent." "Yes sir I am." "Replied Andy." "Your boy has got himself quite famous down here. He takes after his father." "Said Bent, with a grin." "So I've noticed." "Replied Andy." "Well, let's get you guys to the winners box." "Replied Bent." "Oh, we can get there from here?" "Asked Tanantra." "Why yes of course. We can access anywhere we want through this tunnel. Famous creatures use this entrance all the time. In fact, the rugkey players often use this tunnel to escape the crowds, and if we're lucky, we might run into the brotherhood in our travels." "Finished Bent." "Really?" "Screeched Tanantra." "Woo, that would be *so* dope!" "Shouted Dude." "Do you think we can meet them?" "Asked Leroy" "I'm sure we might be able to arrange that." "Replied Bent."

"They took a couple of turns, and ended up walking down a long corridor. At the end of the long corridor, were several doors." "Here we are folks, the winners box. Go on inside and get yourself comfortable, and I'll make sure the snack and drink platter arrives before the game starts." "Said Bent. Then he walked down the long corridor, and disappeared through another entrance."

"Hi mom." "Said Dude, as they entered the winners box." "Hello Dude." "Replied Anne. Santose and Nina introduced themselves next. Santose of course remarking Anne on her dress." "Why thank you young man." "She replied. There was a brief moment of silence, that is, until Andy spoke out." "Hello Anne. You look even more beautiful then I remember." "You look just as handsome as the day you left Andy." "Replied Anne. Then they literately ran to each others arms. Which of course led to a long kiss." "Wait a minute! You guys know each other?" "Snapped Tanantra." "Hey! That's my mom your kissing you know!" "Shouted Dude."

Narrator,

There you have it, I think there is going to be some explaining to do here. It seems like Anne and Andy both had a secret they have been keeping. So let's see what happens next.

"I thought we *never* kept any secrets from each other dad!" "Blurted out Leroy." "Yeah, mom? What's up with *that?*" "Snapped Tanantra." "Now hold on everybody! All your questions will be answered one at a time. But first, let me explain the whole story to you once and for all. Shall I tell them? Or would you like the honors my dear?" "Asked Andy, looking directly at Anne." "Well since you got the floor, I think it would be best if you tell them." "Replied Anne."

"Andy took a deep breath, and then just let the words fall out." "Alright, here we go. I'd like to start off by introducing you to my future wife, Anne." "The whole room fell in silence, and nobody said a word. They just sat there listening intensely, with their mouths gaping open, as the more than shocking news was being told."

"It all started about ten years ago, when you were all very young. But let me first tell you, that your mother and I really had no choice in the matter. It was a matter of life and death, really. You see, Leroy was very sick at the time, and we tried everything possible, known to the Packs, to try and find a cure for him. But there was no magic spell that was going to help him. I know, we tried everything. But it was no use, and we were running out of time. He was dying." "Announced Andy."

"I almost died?" "Asked Leroy." "Oh son you were deathly ill." "Replied Anne." "Now as you all know, there is only one way to the Packs, and only one way out. But I just so happened to hear a rumor about the gate keeper planning an escape. I knew this was the answer to our prayers, so I wrapped up little Leroy in a blanket, and followed the gate keeper past the big old wooden door." "Andy continued, as he loosened his tie."

"Now back then, the door opened a lot more easier then it does these days. Anyways, I followed him to the entrance door. Before it closed behind him, I caught the tail end. I managed to keep it open until I could get Leroy above ground. Once the door is closed, it will not open again for another ten long years. Unless of course, you had the key, which the gate keeper had. I tried to catch up with him, but it was no use, he was gone. I spent years looking for him, as well as a way to get back here, but without the key, I could not return. So I had to wait it out." "Said Andy."

"Did you ever *find* the gate keeper?" "Asked a more than curious Dude." "No, I didn't son. But thank goodness Motimer had a spare key, which nobody knew about. Anne? Would you like to tell Tanantra? Or shall I?" "Asked Andy." "I think I can take it from here." "Replied Anne." "Now Tanantra, this is going to come as quite a shock to you, but it's about time you knew the truth. The gate keeper was your father."

"So, are you my mother?" "Asked Tanantra, in a soft voice." "I'm afraid not my dear. You see, your mother was my best friend in the whole wide world, and I would have done anything for her. But you see, she was sick Tanantra, and, well, she never made it. But before she passed away, she asked me if I would take care of you. So I welcomed you in my home, like you were one of my own." "Anne paused for a second, and then continued."

"But as far as your father was concerned, he was in shambles, and there was nothing anyone could do for him. He loved your mother so much, that he practically went crazy, and I don't blame him. Your mother was a very good soul, and she was my best friend. Her name was Lynda Joy." "Continued Anne."

"Is that why you named me Lynda?" "Asked little Lynda." "Yes dear, because I wanted her name to live on. Now Tanantra, you shouldn't blame your father for leaving. He just couldn't fathom the fact of being alone. *That* would have *surely* killed him. But he left me a letter for you to read, and I told him that I would explain everything, when the time was right. At the end of the letter, he said that one day he would return."

"For all I know, he could be somewhere in the Packs as we speak. But regrettably, I have yet to hear from him. I'm sorry you had to hear it after all this time has passed. But I thought it would be better this way. Your father loved you very much, and thought it would be in your best interest, to be raised in a family. Rather then by a single father." "Anne added." "So how do you explain Tanantra's crush on Leroy then mom?" "Asked Dude."

"Oh that's easy, and that is all fine, since they are no relation whatsoever. Just as your mother and I were the best of friends, so too were Tanantra and Leroy. You two were inseparable as kids. Every time your mother and I got together, you two could *not* get enough of each other. So we put you two in the playpen together, and you were fine. You even took naps together. But as soon as we tried to separate you two, the fight was on." "Explained Anne."

"Does that mean, your not my *real* mom either?" "Asked Dude." "Oh no my dear, you and Lynda as well as Leroy are all our children. But I really felt bad for you Tanantra. When Leroy left, you were so sad. You would hardly eat, and you lost a lot of weight. I thought I was going to lose you. But you eventually came through, and well, up until Leroy came back to the Packs, you have been really quite normal. But I sensed a something different, the day you brought Leroy home. For the better of course." "Anne Replied, as she winked at Tanantra."

"Tananatra was in shock. Her life just took a very dramatic turn within the last few minutes, and she was confused. So the only thing she had left to do, was run up and give the woman she grew to call her mom, a big hug."

"I'm not upset, but while we are being honest, I'm sorry I never got a chance to meet my mom. But as far as I'm concerned, I'm glad it was you who raised me, mom." "Said Tanantra. This being said, just about brought a tear or two to Anne's eyes, but instead, they hugged it out."

"Leroy and Dude could not have been any more happier to find out that they were *actually* brothers. On the other side of the room, there was a totally *different* story going on. After all the emotion, that seemed to be filling up the room at this moment, Nina had a bit of news *herself,* which she whispered into Santose's ears."

"Are you serious?" "Shouted Santose." "Yes! Seriously!" "Exclaimed Nina, in a high pitched voice. A few seconds went by and Andy spoke out." "So when are you going to tell us? So we too can join the celebration." "Nina thinks she might be pregnant!" "Said Santose, sounding excited. It was only a split second before Santose told everyone the good news, that Bent walked through the door."

"Well I believe a celebration is in order!" "No sooner did Bent say that, a parade of concession stand workers entered the room, with all sorts of goodies and refreshments." "Compliments of the house. So get used to it folks, for this is the kind of treatment you will be looking at for the rest of this season. Of course, this season is almost over. But next season, the winners box is all yours for the year." "Announced Bent."

"There was a long table at the back of the room where the food was set. In a lone corner, opposite the food table, sat a bar on wheels. It was complete with everything you needed to make your favorite drink. As well as just about every kind of alcoholic beverage you can think of."

"By the time the food had all been placed on the table, the kids had already began helping themselves. You would have thought the kids were deprived or something, the way they attacked it like vultures. But after all, isn't that what kids are all about? Nina felt an uncontrollable urge to eat herself silly as well, and while she did that, Santose decided to keep the bar on wheels company. Andy, Anne, and Bent were right there by his side, every step of the way."

"Bent went straight for the rye, and then got into the brandy. This seemed to stir up the taste buds enough, to give him a hankering for a fat cigar. So he pressed a button on the left hand side of the bar. Then a roundish glass shelf slid up through the middle of the bar. On top of the shelf sat a box of cigars. It was the display that made the cigars seem more tantalizing. It was a sky blue waterfall of some sort. The base was a glass tube, filled with water, and a pump. Still encased in glass, the water flows up from the base, and down the sides of the rounded glass display, like a beautiful waterfall. It was a very unique piece. It had a neon light affect, which made for an absolutely breath taking view that literately lit up the whole room."

"Cigar anyone?" "Asked Bent." "Don't mind if I do." "Replied Andy, as he opened up the box and pulled out a fine cigar, holding it in his fingers and smelling its sweet fragrance." "Now *this* is something I have not had the pleasures of indulging in, for quite some time." "Said Santose. Then he lit it with a match for flavor, as he rolled it through his fingertips to catch every hint of the savory tobacco leaf."

"Well I guess the cigars will be on you when the baby comes eh?" "Bent hinted, with a little bit of a laugh. The others joined in the chuckle, and the four toasted a cheer, to bringing new life into the Packs. Then they all took a drink."

"Well I think we better take our seats, it looks like the game is about to start." "Said Bent, as he filled up his glass one more time, and took a seat beside Leroy in front of the glass. Everyone had front row glass seats in the winners box. Once everyone was seated, a lady came around with binoculars for each individual."

"Welcome everyone to our game, coming to you live from the underground in the Packs. I'm Jim." "And I'm Folga." "And we're your announcers for tonight's game!" "They both said at the same time." "Well Jim, there we have it, another night in the Packs, where your lucky enough to get in the building, never mind finding a seat." "Right you are Folga. Did you get a load of the tents that were set up at the ticket booth this morning?"

"As a matter of fact I did Jim, and if it wasn't for me being one of the announcers, you can bet your life I would have been one of those campers at the front of the line." "Added Folga."

"But before we get started, why don't we get a view of our winning trio in the winners box, shall we?" "Sounds like a great idea Jim." "Well it looks the whole family is up there Folga. Let's get a close up on the winners. I don't know if you can hear me up there kids." "Don't tell me you've never been up to the winners box Jim? They can hear just fine from the one hundred and fifty inch big screen." "Said Folga. Leroy, Dude and Tanantra, were no longer sitting in their seats. Once they noticed themselves on the big screen, they decided to flaunt it a little."

"Well kids, anything you'd like to say before the game is underway?" "The trio looked at each other and nodded." "Go Nacucks go!" "They shouted." "Well there you have it folks, live from the winners box." "I'm Jim." "And I'm Folga." "And it's time to get this game underway." "They both yelled into the microphone at the same time."

"Once the players practiced, and the underground anthem played, the game started." "Referee gets ready to drop the key. Sean Step is at center ice for the Nacucks and Wayner Pretzel is the center ice man for the Packs. The key is dropped, and game on!" "Wayner Pretzel gets the key off the drop. He passes it back to Lander Macdonald." "Macdonald brings the key back in behind the net. He looks for an open man." "He sees Marcel Dupponne, and fires the key up the left wing." "Announced Jim."

"Dupponne brings the key up fast, and runs into some trouble, but he is able to make the pass across for Wayner Pretzel, who flies across center ice with Toni T." "He takes a shot on net, no, he fakes shot. Then he sees Tom Chelius fly up and in the open. Wayner passes the key to Chelius, one timer, goal!" "Wayner Pretzel with an assist, and Tom Chelius puts the first goal on the board for the night!" "The score is now one to nothing in favor of the Packs." "Said Jim."

"Not even forty seconds on the clock so far in this game Jim, and the Packs are already in the lead!" "Well you know Folga, after the way the Packs played the last game, I'm surprised they *even* showed up." "Well put Jim, well put. Ha ha." "Folga said, with a bit of a laugh." "Now let's have a look at that in instant replay. Here we have a long pass from Lander Macdonald at the back of the Packs net, up the wing to Marcel Dupponne. Dupponne makes the pass to Wayner Pretzel, who crosses center with Toni T. Then he passes the key to Tom Chelius, who flies up in front of the net. Chelius one times it, and scores on the Nacucks goalie Tyler Step!"

"Players line up back at center ice, referee gets ready to drop the key." "Wayner Pretzel and Sean Step face each other once again." "The key is dropped, and the stick fight is on." "Sean gets a piece of the key and hits it back to Never Bindin. Now *he* moves the key forward and passes ahead along the boards to Travis Step." "Travis has the key, but he can't hold on to it and passes across ice to Sean, who moves it up and passes the key to Darryl." "Darryl puts his rug into overdrive and Toni T heads towards him." "Darryl shoots the key in between the five hole of Toni T and speeds up." "*Did* you *see* that folks?" "Darryl does a dive, tuck and roll, *right* over top of Toni T! Then he gets the key on the other side, *after* landing back on his skates Folga."

"Now Darryl winds up for a left handed shot, then he quickly switches positions and winds up with a right handed wrist shot, and, scores!" "But what is this? It looks like the refs are going upstairs on *this* goal, and the fans don't seem to like that too much Jim." "Did you see how fast he switched his stick play up there Folga?" "As I told you before, I never miss a thing. I've been watching this game since before you even heard of rugkey." "So you've told me. Let's have another look at this goal folks. I think this play is gonna make the sports wall of the underground." "Said Jim."

"Now here we have the pass from Sean to Darryl. You have to wonder what was going on inside his head when he seen Toni T coming straight for him. Yet he puts steel to ice and speeds things up even more. Now pause it there, and let's watch this one in slow motion. Okay, let it play. The key goes right between Toni's legs, and before he could even blink an eye, Darryl pulls out one of the most original tuck ducks and rolls that I have ever seen." "Alright Jim, it was a good move, but give it a rest and let's continue the replay."

"Darryl makes a perfect landing on the other side of Toni, and took control of that key in one motion, *just* like it was planned." "Then Darryl *winds up,* fakes the shot, does the fastest stick hand switch I *ever* did see, and scores, to tie the game up." "Well it doesn't look like anything has been decided yet, so let's go to a quick commercial shall we?"

"So what do you think about the game so far dad?" "Asked Leroy." "Well I'll tell you one thing son, I never thought there was a game better then hockey, until I watched this rugkey game." "Replied Andy." "I know right. Isn't it awesome? Rugkey is the best game ever man!" "Added Dude, as he listened to Leroy and Andy."

"What about you Santose? What do you think about the game?" "Well I'll tell you, in my books, this kicks the heck out of hockey! Did you see some of the moves these guys make on those magic rugs? You'd never see nothing like that in regular hockey." "Finished Santose. Nina seemed to be enjoying the game as well, but she more or less had other needs and cravings at the moment. So she just got up and went straight for the food table."

"Welcome back folks. I'm Jim." "And I'm Folga." And we're your announcers for this evening." "Jim and Folga announce together." "It seems that Darryl's goal was allowed, and the score is tied at one a piece." "Both teams line up for the face off."

"But as soon as the crowd heard the goal was allowed, the horn was blown." "Okay folks, it looks like we are going to cut to another commercial, while the officials clear off the ice. What is the matter Jim? Isn't it time for your bathroom break? After all, this is your favorite part of the game." "Said Folga, with a laugh." "Uh, we will return after these messages." "Announced Jim."

"We're back here in the Packs and its another face off at center ice." "Referee drops the key, and game on!" "Wayner stick scraps with Sean Step and wins the face off." "He circles around Sean and goes in alone." "Never Bindin comes in for a check, and Wayner passes him like he wasn't even there." "Wayner now at the Nacucks defensive line, slap shot, scores!" "The Packs are ahead by one!" "That was a fast goal Folga." "Well *now* the Packs are playing like they should Jim, and there is nothing wrong with that." "Replied Folga."

"The Nacucks make a minor adjustment and bring Travis Step to center ice." "Referee getting ready to drop the key." "Game on!" "Travis gets a piece of the key, and Never Bindin is on the receiving end of that." "Yes Folga, but he doesn't hang on to the key for long, as he passes up the boards to Sean Step." "So Sean goes it in alone. He takes a slap shot, the key goes wild off the post, and Tom Chelius is there to sweep up the mess!" "Now Chelius brings the key forward, then passes over to Marcel Dupponne. Dupponne back to Chelius and Chelius passes up the middle to Pretzel." "Pretzel, now along side Toni T, and they fly in mighty fast." "Announced Jim."

"Quick pass to Toni, he shoots the key along the boards and gets around Dan Steal." "Toni catches the key on the other side, and gets it back to Pretzel." "Pretzel pulls off a one timer, scores! Bringing the opening period to an astonishing

3-1 lead over the Nacucks by the Packs." "Let's go to a quick commercial."

"Leroy and Dude were excited about the game, and could not handle the suspense of having to wait for the key to drop again. So Dude suggested that they hit up the snack table one more time, before the period ended. Leroy had no problems with that, and the race was on."

"Welcome back folks, to our feature game of this evening. I'm Jim." "And I'm Folga." "And have we got a game for you tonight!" "Jim and Folga both say at the same time." "Now it looks like there is still a bit of a delay here Jim." "Uh, yes Folga, it looks like we are gonna have to go to commercial again." "Now this is starting to get a little ridiculous Jim. Now we got streakers on the ice! I'm telling you the games going to hell!"

"With that being said, Folga threw his arms in the air and took off his headphones. They went directly to commercial, while the underground security chased the lady around on the ice. But they had a heck of a time trying to catch her. When they finally did, they wrapped her in a blanket, and courted her away through the nearest available exit."

"Why don't we take this opportunity to interview the kid who everybody seems to be talking about? Let's go over to the winners box shall we?" Said Jim. So the camera crew followed Jim and Folga into the next room to the winners box."

"Even though everyone heard what Jim and Folga were about to do, every person in the winners box seemed to be in shock as they entered the room." "Welcome to the winners box folks, let's see what Leroy has to say about the game." "Said Jim. Then he walked up to the seat where Leroy was sitting." "Hello Leroy, is there anything you wanna say to the folks at home son?" "Asked Jim." "I just wanna thank my dad, and everyone else, for coming with me to tonight's game." "Well there you have it folks, words from Leroy."

"How about you young man, anything to say to the folks at home?" "Asked Folga." "Only that this is the baddest game ever! Go brotherhood go!" "Dude shouted out." "Uh, there you have it folks, another grateful fan of the brotherhood." "Now what about you young lady? Anything you wanna say?" "Is there any chance we can meet the brotherhood?" "Screeched Tanantra, and the boys let out a cheer." "Well, I'm uh, sure we can arrange that throughout uh, some coarse of the night." "Replied Jim. He was then nudged by Folga that the game was about to start." "Now back to the announcers box." "Said Folga quickly. So the camera crew, along with Jim and Folga, all ran next door."

"We're back, and the game is under control here at the Packs stadium, coming to you live. I'm Jim." "And I'm Folga." "And we're *your* announcers for tonight's game." "They both announce at the same time." "The referee is getting ready to drop the key." "Travis Step is center man for the Nacucks and it will be Wayner Pretzel for the Packs." "There goes the key, and game on Folga!"

"Travis gets the key off the hop. He gains control and passes it way back to his brother, and goal tender, Tyler Step." "Tyler doesn't waste any time with the key and flicks it up high towards Sean, who swoops in and takes control." "Sean brings the key forward and passes it along to Darryl, who is there to catch it, after a bounce off the boards." "Now a pass back to Sean, and *he* passes back to Darryl, but he can't hold onto it and quickly passes back to Sean." "Sean brings the key to the middle, goes for the glove side, scores!" "Another great goal from the Step line Folga!"

"Well you can see why the Nacucks brought the Step brothers in so early tonight!" "Yes Folga, and *that* brings our first period game score up 3-2 still in favor of the Packs so far."

"The Packs better buckle down and create some new moves, if they wanna even consider themselves in the same league as the Step brothers, that is for sure!" "Said Folga."

"One minute left in the period, and the referee drops the key." "Travis gets a piece of *that* drop, and gets the key to Darryl." "Darryl now brings the key up and passes back to Travis." "Travis skates around Wayner and then he flies around Lander." "Travis sees Darryl in the open and makes another pass." "Darryl takes a smooth wrist shot, scores!" "Blocker side, and that makes the score a tie game, at 3 all Folga."

"Let's take another look at that in instant replay." "Here we have some random back and forth passing, between Travis Step and Darryl Step." "Then Travis flies in, and out skates the likes of Wayner Pretzel *and* Lander Macdonald, like they were standing still." "A quick pass to Darryl, and with a smooth but quick wrist shot, the key finds a home in the back of the net Jim."

"I just wanna show you folks at home, Darryl's shot one more time. He scoops that key up, and takes control like the keys on a string, and then he so effortlessly lifts that key home like he owned it. But as you look closely, he doesn't even look at the key as he shoots. He just looks towards the net. Now *that's* a play for the wall!" "Finished Jim." "Well you better find something else to *ramble* about Jim, because the ice is full of your favorite linen again." "Replied Folga."

"Woo did you see that Folga? Some girl just dropped her bra on Darryl's head, and, what's he gonna do with it now? It looks like he is gonna throw them, yes he is. He threw that bra right at Forty Howl who is sitting on the Packs bench." "Well I'm sure the Packs aren't gonna like that." "Said Folga."

"The ice is clear, and the key is about to drop." "Travis gets the key and passes off to Sean." "Is he gonna do what I think he's gonna do?" "He takes a long shot, scores from the blue line!" "Less than a minute left in *this* period folks, with a score of 4 to 3, now in favor of the Nacucks over the Packs." "Well if the crowd doesn't respect the brotherhood? Then I would be at a loss for words. Look at the standing ovation the crowd gives him on *that* goal." "Well Jim, if I didn't see it with my own eyes, I wouldn't have believed it."

"Players line back up at center ice, and the key gets dropped." "Wayner gets this one, and he passes back to Marcel Dupponne." "Marcel heads to the back of the net and gets the key up to Lander Macdonald." "Darryl comes in for the check but Lander gets the key to Wayner, and the time runs out for this period Folga."

"Man, where do you come up with this crap Ted? I mean come on, panties on ice?" Asked a sarcastic Joe. "Hey, what can I say?" Replied Ted, as he paused the story for a moments time. "What's the matter Ted?" Asked Ron. "What makes you think somethings wrong Ron?" Asked Ted. "I can hear it in your voice dude." Replied Ron. There was a short silence.

"Okay, ya bunch of dorks, you wanna know what my problem is? You guys are so dumb. Its my birthday today, and not *one* of you even remembered!" Snapped Ted. "Oh, is that all?" Scoured Paul, and then a huddle took place, leaving Ted out. It was a short huddle, and ended with Ron racing off to the top of the tree house. He returned in under a minute, with a wrapped up package in his hands. So he ran up and gave it to Ted, and everyone shouted out a happy birthday to Ted.

"You know we wouldn't forget your birthday Ted! How could you be so ignorant man?" Said Paul. "What is it guys?" "Well open it up and find out, so you can take us to the second period of the game man!" Yelled Zack. So Ted ripped into the wrapper with authority. His eyes lit up to the golden bottle of rye he had unwrapped. But he didn't think twice about sparking up the abnormally large fat one, that was taped to the top of the bottle.

"Thanks guys! Your the best." Ted took a couple of puffs and tried to pass it along, but he was rather surprised, when nobody else would except the offer. "No man, we got a fatty of our own. You go ahead and smoke that one to your head." Said Paul, as he passed out a fatty to everyone else.

"Now everybody's got a fatty, so let's get on with the game eh?" Said Paul. "Hold on a second." Said Ted. Then he took a big gulp from his bottle and passed it along. "Well you guys better not turn down a drink, or I won't continue." Added Ted. No one could argue with Ted there, and the bottle went around like water in a desert. "Okay, now that we've all had a drink, let's let Ted finish off the rest, and get on with the second period eh?" Said Paul. So Ted got back into story mode.

"The commercials were on, and it was interview time, so Jim and Folga made their way to the winners box. As soon as they opened the door, the trio's faces lit up." "Well kids, you remember the question you asked me earlier on in the game? About an interview with the brotherhood? Well, here we go!" "The door opened once again, the four brothers walked in, and the place went silent."

"I'm Jim." "And I'm Folga." "And we are live in the winners box, with none other then, the brotherhood." "Jim and Folga announced at the same time. The four brothers lined up and Jim began."

"Okay, how about we begin this interview from the oldest to the youngest. Let's start with you Sean. That was an amazing goal you scored in the last few seconds of the first period son. Where did you learn how to shoot like that?" "Well we used to play a lot of path rugkey as kids, and, well, practice makes perfect." "Replied Sean." "If you kids play the second period as good as you did in the first, then we're in for one sick game!" "Replied Jim."

"Moving along here now, to Travis. So Travis, it looks like you've been practicing in your sleep, the way you keep winning the face offs like that." "Well Folga, you know, I think we can take the Nacucks right through and win the *hell* out of this game. We *can* say, hell, can't we?" "Well there you have it folks, confidence off the ice, as well as on the ice." "Said Folga."

"So that brings us now to Tyler. So how does it feel to know that your the best goalie in the U.R.L. son?" "Tyler didn't really say too much, and when he *did* answer, he more or less looked at the floor when he spoke." "I just wanna play rugkey man. Are you guys gonna eat that?" "Said Tyler, as he looked towards the huge table full of food. Then without saying another word, he walked over and filled up a plate."

"Jim cleared his throat." "Well Darryl, you look like your playing a hell of a game out there. What is your motivation?" "Well if those girls would stop harassing me out there, we could get on with some real rugkey. Go Nacucks go! No seriously Jim, I just wanna get out there and have fun playing rugkey with my bros. This is what we live for, and this is how we do it." "Replied Darryl."

"So how did you four get into the game of rugkey, and how did you guys get so good?" "Its simple Folga, we used to play a lot of rugkey as kids. In fact, Tyler used to go to school with this kid named Bryan. He was a little strange, but we eventually grew to love him and all. Anyways, we always had team matches, until Bryan made us a challenge that he could beat us with the team he brought out." "Answered Travis, as he spoke on behalf of his brothers."

"Now Darryl was still too young to play at the time, so he was our cheering section. But we ended up kicking his teams asses. To tell you the truth, we embarrassed Bryan, and his team altogether. In fact, I seem to recall that half his players leaving him behind, midway through the second period, but he played on, so I'll give him that." "Finished Travis."

"So, does this *Bryan* guy still play rugkey?" "Asked Jim." "No, the last I heard from him, he was writing books, or something on those lines." "Replied Travis." "Well there you have it folks. We'll return you to rugkey in the Packs arena, live, after these messages." "Announced Folga."

"Well that was a great interview boys. Now there is a few kids up here in the winners box, that I'm sure are dying to meet you." "Said Jim." "You guys are the best! Can we get your autographs?" "Dude asked." "No problem." "Said an enthusiastic Darryl, who took off his Jersey and signed it. Then he handed it to Dude." "Wow! Thanks Darryl!" "Replied Dude. This seemed to start a trend between the brotherhood. So Tanantra and Leroy got a signed Jersey as well. Tyler though, was too busy filling his face, and even if his brothers *were* taking off jerseys and handing them over, it didn't mean that he was going to. He was sort of superstitious anyways. Tyler considered the jersey he wore, to be his good luck charm, and wouldn't part with it for nothing."

"The next few minutes, were spent with everybody introducing one another. More food started to arrive, and then Anne spoke out." "Tyler? Is that his name? He sure looks like a hungry fella." "Yeah, he will eat you out of house and home if you let him. Ha ha." "Replied Travis, with a chuckle." "Well you boys should come over to the house one day for a barbeque." "Suggested Anne." "That would be nice. We *are big* on eating." "Said Darryl." "I'm in." "Said Sean." "Well I guess we'll have to make arrangements after the game." "Replied Anne." "Well thank you for the invite. How about you send Leroy and Dude to the Nacucks dressing room after the game, and we'll figure out the details." "Said Travis." "Sounds good to me." "Replied Anne."

"Leroy and Dude gave each other a high five. Tananatra on the other hand, seemed to feel a little left out." "Well it was great to meet you all, but I think we better get back to the game. Go Nacucks go!" "Said Darryl, and the brothers left the room. Even though they practically had to pry Tyler away from the snack table. Jim and Folga left the winners box, shortly thereafter."

"Good evening sports fans, and welcome back to the start of the second period in tonight's game. I'm Jim." "And I'm Folga." "And we're your sports announcers for *this* game." "Jim and Folga say at the same time." "What a game its been so far Folga." "Well I'll give you that Jim. There sure has been some original plays out on the ice tonight. let's see if these boys can continue to give the fans what they came here to see." "Finished Folga."

"The players line up at center ice." "Wayner Pretzel is the center ice man for the Packs, and Sean Step is once again center man for the Nacucks." "Game on!" "Referee drops the key, and the second period is on the clock." "The sticks fight at center ice, but we got a bouncing key." "Wayner now gets a piece of the key, and passes it off to Toni T." "Toni gets checked by Darryl and the key is on its own Jim."

"Sean was there to retrieve the key, and he quickly ups it to Travis. Travis flies in and stick handles the key forward." "Marcel Dupponne comes in hard, but Travis mows him over like he wasn't even there." "Did you see Travis flip Marcel up and over, with a duck and a hard left shoulder? Wow, what a hit! But the play continues." "Announced Jim."

"Travis is still in control and he moves on." "Now he sees Sean in the open, so he gets the key to his brother and fast." "Sean gets ready to fire the key, but he catches a glimpse of two Packs jerseys coming in hard from either side. Sean ducks and oh, Lander Macdonald and Marcel Dupponne collide into each other!" "Yelled Folga."

"Holy crap Folga! I hope the Packs have some back up defense, after *that* collision!" "Sean still has the key, but passes it off to Darryl." "Darryl goes it in alone, and makes it a one on one between him and Sandy Rogue." "He does a quick round about, and keeps the key with his stick, like it's glued. He takes a shot, five hole, scores! Which makes the score now 5-3, in favor of the Nacucks." "*Yeah,* and here comes your favorite part Jim." "Announced Folga, sarcastically."

"Let's take another look at that in instant replay, while they peel Tom Chelius and Marcel Dupponne off the ice." "Well you better run that a few times, so you can work on your intermission skills Jim. Those panties aren't going to jump off the ice on their own." "Here we have a pass from Travis, over to his brother Sean. Now watch as Sean predicts his own future, and decides to go a little low." "Did you see that Folga? I think that will make the hardest hit of the year."

"Before either men land on Sean, he *actually* has the time to get away, before *even* being scathed." "Now Sean gets a pass to Darryl. Watch how perfect Darryl has *this* move down pat. He gets the goal tenders mind occupied, by working the key with his stick. Then Darryl takes a shot, and five holes the key right in the back of the net." "Yeah, well while your building up some more hot air, let's cut to commercial." "Finished Folga."

"Wow, did you see that goal?" "Yelled Dude." "I think Jim's right, that is probably the hardest hit of the year, *right* there, and this is only my second game." "Added Leroy." "Oh, he *is* a dream." "Said Tanantra. Dude just looked at her as if to say, get a life."

"We're back folks and the referee gets ready to drop the key." "Sean Step and Wayner Pretzel get ready for the stick fight." "Game on." "The key goes wild off the hop, and Wayner is there to pick up the garbage." "Travis comes in hard and fast, but he can't get the key away from Wayner, and shoulder slams Wayner into the boards." "I felt *that* hit from here Folga."

"Wayner takes it like a man, and keeps the key moving forward." "He sees Chelius in the clear and makes the pass." "Toni T now with Chelius and Wayner, making it a three on two." "Chelius passes off to Toni, Toni takes the shot, one timer, blocker save, by Tyler Step and the key bounces loose." "Wow, that kid sure has a fast reflex Jim."

"Never Bindin gets the key to the back of the net, and passes up to Darryl Step. The key goes out of reach and Wayner tries to snap it up. But he can't keep it." "The key goes high into the crowd and the play is stopped. There is going to be a face off in the Nacucks end of the ice." "Well Folga, the hard hitting *has* begun." "Now *this,* is rugkey at its best." "Well I think there is gonna be a lot more harder hits, as the game goes on." "Yes Jim, and I think there *should* be, welcome to the game of rugkey."

"Referee now with another key in his hand, and Sean Step faces off with Wayner Pretzel." "Both players line up, and the referee drops the key." "Sean Step gets a piece, and knocks the key in behind the net and Wayner flies in after it." "He goes for a wrap around, skate save by Tyler Step and the key is still in play." "Announced Folga."

"Sean moves in and robs the key now, and *he* moves on." "Quick pass to Travis, and there is no one there to hold him back." "He sees Darryl all alone, and passes up the ice to his brother." "Darryl goes it in alone, it's just him and the goalie now." "Darryl fakes the goalie out, round about, back hand, goal! Five hole, with an assist by Travis!" "The score is now 6 for the Nacucks and still 3 for the Packs." "Said Jim."

"You know Jim, I'm kind of wondering if the Packs *even* showed up for the second period. They are *sure* not playing like they did in the first period." "I can see your point there

Folga. Its like they are intimidated by the Step brothers." "You know Jim, if Darryl keeps scoring the way he is, this game could go on all night." "I think your right Folga. But let's cut to commercial while the ice gets cleared."

"We're back rugkey fans, coming to you live from the underground." "Travis is back at center ice and he faces Wayner once again." "Referee drops the key." "Travis gets the key off the hop, and gains control like he pulled it out from his back pocket." "He circles around, looking for an opening, but he goes it in alone." "He flies in around Wayner, and goes head on with Marcel Dupponne." "Travis skates around Marcel with ease, and faces Sandy Rogue one on one." "He winds up, takes a slap shot, scores!" "Announced Folga."

"Did you see that shot Folga? He fired that key so hard, it went right thru the net, and smashed the back board glass. I don't even think Sandy Rogue seen *that* shot coming. That brings the score to a whopping 7 for the Nacucks with the Packs still at 3. Let's take another look at that shot." "Finished Jim."

"Here we have Travis with the key at first drop. He skates around Wayner, and goes in full force, flying around Marcel Dupponne. We have seen some hard hits tonight, but this goal, has *got* to be one of the hardest shots I've *ever* seen! Then Travis winds up to take an unbelievable slap shot. The key rips through the netting, and smashes glass as it finds a home in the hands of one lucky rugkey fan." "Announced Folga."

"What a game we have for you tonight folks!" "Yes we do Jim, and there has been some fantastic plays made here in tonight's game. Let's take a commercial break while the glass gets repaired." "Said Folga."

"We're back folks and what an exciting game it has been." "Announced Jim." "Yeah, we would have started the third period already, if hadn't been for all these delays." "Folga added, sarcastically." "The key gets dropped, and we're back in play." "Travis gets this one, and he passes off to Darryl." "Darryl has the key, but he can't hold onto it and passes up to Sean." "Sean goes in deep, quick pass back to Travis." "Travis takes a shot, but the key hits the goal post and goes wild." "Announced Jim."

"Sean is there to pick up the rebound, he takes quick snap shot, goal! Sandy Rogue stacks his pads and gets a piece of the key, but it's not good enough, and it goes up and over him." "That will bring this score to a new height of 8-3, in favor of the Nacucks over the Packs Folga."

"You know Jim, if it were up to me, I'd just pole the goalie. He doesn't seem to be in the game at all tonight, and with the Packs back up goalie on the injured list, we are looking at a path rugkey score here." "All I can say about that is, you ain't seen nothing yet. I always wanted to say that Folga." "Folga clears his throat." "Players line up at center ice, and the game is back on track." "Travis takes this face off against Wayner Pretzel." "Referee drops the key, and the game is on." "Two and a half minutes left to play in the second period, and the crowd is still going wild Folga!"

"This time Wayner gets a piece of the key, and it goes way back to Sandy Rogue." "Sandy doesn't waste any time, and he gets the key to Marcel Dupponne." "Marcel moves the key up, and passes it along to Tom Chelius." "Chelius has the key now, that didn't last long, but *he* loses the key to Darryl, who swoops in and swipes it from under his nose." "Minute and a half left to go, and the key is all over the place." "The Nacucks form a triangle, Darryl to Travis, over to Sean, back to Darryl, one timer, oh, and it goes just wide of the net Jim!"

"Dupponne gets the rebound and he clears the key out to Wayner." "Never Bindin flies in to check Wayner, but Wayner makes the pass to Toni T." "Toni takes a shot, scores! One timer!" "The Packs get another goal on the board, to make this game score 8-4, with the Packs still trailing behind by 4 points." "You know Folga, the crowd here in the Packs tonight, seem to be cheering just as loud for the Nacucks, as they do their own team the Packs." "Yeah, well at least there are no under garments being littered all over the ice when the Packs score a goal." "Said a sarcastic Folga."

"Travis steps up to center ice, and faces Wayner Pretzel once again." "Referee drops the key, and, scores! Off the hop, and the crowd goes *absolutely wild* here at the Packs arena *tonight!*" "Let's take another look at that Jim. *That's* gotta be a first, and I have watched a lot of rugkey in my time." "The score is now 9 for the Nacucks, and the Packs with 4 on the board." "Announced Folga."

"It starts out with the drop of the key, now Travis *obviously* put some wings on this shot. It goes right under the legs of Wayner Pretzel. Then as it picks up some flight down the ice, it finds a home in the back of the net, five hole style!" "Well Jim, I think we have *just* found our most astounding goal of the year."

"Thirty seconds left to go in this second period." "Referee gets ready to drop the key." "The key is down and the fight is on." "Wayner gets a piece and the key goes to Toni T." "Toni T gets checked by Darryl, but he manages to pass along the boards back to Lander." "Ten seconds left in the period, and the key makes it back to Toni T. The clock winds down as Toni races into the Nacucks zone." "Toni heads up along the boards and goes in like a rocket towards the net, five seconds left on the clock, Toni blasts a slap shot, and Tyler picks it out of thin air with a glove save." "There goes the buzzer, and *that* brings *this* period to an end Jim!"

"Hey Ted, what's up with that Tanantra and Dude situation? I mean, brother and sister man? Come on, isn't that like incest or something?" Asked Zack. "Hey man, if it were up to me, and the chick was hot, I wouldn't kick her out of bed for eating crackers!" Added Ron. "That's what I'm talking about!" Paul said with a laugh, as him and Ron gave each other a high five. "You guys are both sick. Now do you wanna here the rest? Or should we listen to you two ramble all night? They aren't even related, so calm your hormones!" Snapped Ted. But nobody spoke, so Ted continued.

"Well folks, that was a rather long intermission, but we're back. I'm Jim." "And I'm Folga." "And we're your sports announcers for this evening, coming to you live, from the Packs!" "They both announce at the same time."

"You know Folga, if both teams put as much effort into the third period, as they did in the first and second periods, I think we are in for a hell of a finish here." "Don't count your chickens before they hatch Jim. Just because the Packs made it on the score board *this* game, it doesn't mean they are gonna break the Nacucks winning streak." "Added Folga."

"Both teams line up. Sean is back at center ice, facing off against Wayner Pretzel." "Referee drops the key, let the stick fight begin!" "Sean gains control off the hop, and he quickly moves the key around Wayner. He sees Darryl up the wing, and waits for the opportunity to make the pass." "Darryl is in the clear now and Travis passes the key." "Darryl with a one timer, scores! With only fifteen seconds gone on the clock!" "Yelled Folga."

"The game is now in double digits, at a score of 10 for the Nacucks, as the Packs lag behind by 6 points, with 4 goals in total." "Wow Folga, what an exciting start to the third period!" "Don't get ahead of yourself Jim! It isn't *that* exciting, when you come out here to watch a game, and most of your time is spent watching the clean up crew collect panties off the ice!"

"Well Folga, he must have scored *that* goal for the kids in the winners box, because that is where he was pointing. I bet you Leroy and Dude are happy about that." "Finished Jim. No sooner did they cut to commercial, both announcers heads turned around, to the sound of a knock at the door. But just as Jim was about to get up, that familiar little voice spoke out." "No need to get up boys. You just sit right back down there. I figure two hard working men like yourselves, could use a plate of food and an ice cold beer." "Said Anne."

"Oh well, thank you very much ma'am." "Said Jim." "Well uh, thank you very much. Uh, we can eat the food, but the beer would be a little out of the ordinary, and we really shouldn't, while we work." "Replied Folga." "Oh nonsense, you need something to wash down that plate of food, and besides, I put the beer in a cup, so as not to arouse any suspicion. Now you boys eat your plate of food, and finish those beers I brought you. I won't take no for an answer. I'll be back to collect your plates when your finished." "Added Anne sternly, as she walked out the door, making sure she got the last word in."

"Wow Folga, that lady *sure* is a hard person to say no to, or to get a word in edge wise." "I don't know Jim, I kind of like her." "Well I'll give her this Folga, that beer sure hit the spot." "Oh, we're back on the air Jim."

"We are back rugkey fans, and ready to rock!" "The referee doesn't waste any time, and both teams line up once again at center ice." "Referee drops the key, and the game continues." "Wayner gets the key this time and he passes off to Toni T." "Toni gets checked by Darryl, and he manages to get the key to brother Travis." "Travis moves the key up, and a pass to Sean, he takes the shot, scores!" "If you ask me Jim, I'd say an empty net would do a better job then what Sandy is doing." "Well Folga, I have to agree with you there, and it looks like Sean broke his stick on *that* shot." "Well I'll tell you Jim, I think it's time for Sandy Rogue to retire, after letting in an astonishing 11 goals, during the course of *this* game." "The score is now an amazing 11-4 for the Nacucks over the Packs." "Said Jim."

"Let's have another look at that. Here we have a pass from Darryl to Travis, Travis then passes over to Sean. Sean waits a second before shooting, then he slap shots that key in the net, and breaks his stick doing so." "I think the Packs would be better off poling the goalie, the way he's playing tonight." "Added Folga." "Um, I think that is the third time you have said that already Folga." "Well it's true Jim."

"It looks like the Packs are calling a time out here Folga." "I don't know what they think *that's* gonna solve! What, is Rogue gonna get some more practice shots on net?" "I'm in the closet as much as you are Folga. But let's see what the the Packs strategy is now shall we?"

"Well folks, it looks like the Packs have a back up plan after all. I just had a talk with the boys upstairs, and it looks like the Nacucks back up goalie, Prichard Growdeer, is coming out for the Packs." "Is this even legal?" "According to the boys upstairs it is." "I think the fans agree as well. Just listen to them as they boo Sandy Rogue, while he exits the ice Jim."

"Well here comes Growdeer, and the fans give him a warm welcome." "The players line up once again, and the referee gets ready to drop the key." "Travis is back at center ice, and he faces Wayner. The key is dropped, Travis gets a stick on the key and passes over to Sean Step." "Now Sean moves forward and passes off to Darryl." "Darryl takes a shot but it's a pad save, and the key gets away." "Travis gets the rebound, he shoots, glove save, and the play is stopped." "Looks like Growdeer is starting off on the right foot Folga."

"Players line up for a face off in the Packs zone." "Travis Step and Wayner Pretzel face each other once again. Referee drops the key, and the game continues." "Wayner gets a piece of the key this time, and Lander is there to take it away as he brings it in behind the net." "He sees Marcel Dupponne, makes the pass, and now he moves up with the key." "Announced Folga."

"Marcel to Toni T and he passes across for Wayner." "Wayner moves the key ahead and passes on to Chelius. Bindin moves forward for a check. But a quick key rebound off the boards, and Chelius reclaims the key on the other side of Never, after flying around him." "Chelius heads to the corner and makes a pass to Wayner." "Wayner takes a shot, glove save by Tyler Step! But he keeps the play going as he drops the key to the ice, and flicks it up high with his stick." "The key drops across the ice in front of the Packs net, scores! By a bouncing key no doubt!" "Yelled Jim."

"Have you *ever* seen anything like it?" "As I told you before Jim, nothing surprises me in this game." "Your right on the money there Folga. But what a first goal to be let in by the Prichard Growdeer!" "Well, I bet the Nacucks are proud of *that* goal." "Yeah well I wouldn't want to be Growdeer right now. The *failure* to stop *that* goal, will sure hit the wall of shame. Not to mention what the fans think about it!" "Well, he *is* the Nacucks back up goalie, so it wouldn't surprise me if he let it in on purpose." "Sneered Folga."

"Tyler Step seems to be happy about the goal, and who *wouldn't* be? I mean, I've seen goalie's score before, but *not* while there's another goalie in the opposite net." "I have to agree with you there Folga, I wouldn't wanna be in Growdeer's goalie gear at this point of the game, *that's* for sure." "At any rate, the game must go on, and the referee gets ready to drop the key." "The score is a miraculous 12—4, and game on!"

"Referee drops the key, and it's slapstick once again. Travis against Wayner this time. Travis gets the key, but can't hold onto it as he gets checked by Pretzel." "Here we go Folga."

"Pretzel moves the key forward with Chelius by his side." "Here comes Bindin, but Pretzel makes it through and passes off to Chelius." "Chelius flies up the wing, then he passes across ice to Toni T." "Toni T takes a shot, one timer, scores!

Glove side, and it looks like that will be the end of Tyler's goalie glove." "Announced Folga."

"Did you see *that* shot Folga? We *have* to watch *that* instant replay again." "Now have a look as the pass comes from Tom Chelius. Now Toni winds up for a one timer, he takes the shot, Tyler thinks he made the save, but the key goes right through the glove, and finds a home in the back of the net. I have never seen this much effort put into a shot before. But I'll tell you, it sure paid off." "Folga, I gotta say, in all the years I've watched rugkey, I have *never* seen a key go through *anyone's* glove before. Tyler's lucky he never lost a hand."

"The score is now 12-5, in favor of the Nacucks, but the Packs haven't given up yet." "Players line up and get ready for another drop." "Ref drops the key, Wayner gets a piece this time, and it makes it's way back to Macdonald." "Macdonald passes across and up to Chelius. Chelius gets checked, but manages to hang on to the key." "Quick pass up for Toni T, and now he brings the key forward. Toni passes over to Wayner, but he can't make it to the key in time, so Travis intervenes." "Announced Folga."

"Now Travis goes in alone, he takes a hard slap shot! Stopped, by Prichard Growdeer and the ref blows the whistle." "Wow Folga, that stop makes up for the goal he let in by Tyler Step." "I don't think anything would make up for *that* goal he let in Jim!" "Face off in the Packs end of the ice, it will be Travis against Wayner." "Ref drops the key, and it's glass smashing time." "Wayner gets this one, and a pass is made to Marcel Dupponne, who flies around the back of the net." "He goes for broke and brings the key out to Tom Chelius." "But Sean slams into Tom and the rug fights on!" "Announced Jim."

"Both players have now taken fight to flight, and the punches roll high above the ice!" "Sean takes a hit to the face, and comes back with a series of blows to the head and kidneys."

"Looks like the refs are gearing up to bring this one back down to the ice." "Six, eight, no, ten referees to bring them down, and I think each player is gonna get a five minute penalty for *this* display Folga."

"Just another day at the office for these boys." "Let's go to a commercial while the blood gets cleared from the ice Folga." "Yes Jim, and we will return, with rugkey *live*, in the underground, after these messages."

"We're back, coming to you *live* from the Packs arena, and boy did you miss out!" "Yes Jim, and what a sight to miss! First time I have ever seen a ref get taken out by a stretcher! That will cost Tom Chelius a two game suspension for elbowing the ref in the face." "Well I really don't think he meant to Folga." "Well as far as the refs are concerned it was intentional!" "Snapped Folga." "Its a four on four rugkey game here in the underground. Tom Chelius will get a two game suspension. Sean will get five minutes for roughing, and Forty Howl will take Tom Chelius's five minute penalty for him, as Tom heads to the locker room." "Said Folga."

"The key is dropped and the game continues." "Its Travis Step against Wayner Pretzel and Wayner hits this one back, as Growdeer claims the key and he quickly passes ahead to Dupponne." "Dupponne moves forward and passes off to Wayner, who flies up fast and heads for the net." "Going in alone now, Wayner takes a shot, but it bounces off Tyler's goalie pads." "Wayner is there to get his own rebound, and he gets another shot, scores!" "The score sits at 6 for the Packs and a riveting 12 for the Nacucks." "Finished Folga."

"Well I think Tyler is still playing well, and who could blame him for letting *that* goal in?" "I have to agree with you there Jim. The Packs are putting on a better show then even *I* gave them credit for." "Ten minutes left on the clock and this game has been put on high speed, late in the third Folga."

"Players are back at center ice, and the key is dropped." "Travis and Wayner battle it out, and the key gets knocked loose." "Toni T now takes it away. He moves the key forward and begins by bringing it in alone." "Here comes Bindin, and *he* is coming in hard." "Toni fakes a slap shot and Never Bindin ducks. Would you look at the flight Toni T comes up with over top of Bindin here Folga?"

"Toni T catches the key on the other side of Bindin. He moves in fast and alone. Toni takes a snap shot, no, instead he flicks the key high in the air. Toni takes some flight with his rug, taps that key with his stick, scores!" "Well I'll tell ya what Folga, I never seen a move like *that* before." "Is that move even *legal?*" "Well the ref seems to think so. Let's take another look at that." "Announced Folga."

"Now watch *this* move *here.* Toni fakes a shot, as he sees Never Bindin coming in hard and fast." "Then, *just* like Toni T *planned* it *out,* Bindin ducks. So Toni flicks the key up and over Never, taking on some flight of his own." "Toni, still going in like a bullet. Now it looks like he is about to pull off a snap shot. Instead, he flicks the key in the air, then he flies up to chase it, and feathers that key in like Tyler *wasn't* even there Jim."

"This is turning into a high scoring game tonight folks. Its a 12-7 score, with the Nacucks ahead by 5, and the Packs seem to be coming back strong!" "You can say that again Jim." "The clock is counting down but this game isn't over yet." "The crowd is on their feet and the players return to center ice once again." "Announced Folga."

"Referee drops the key, and the stick fight begins." "Travis gets *this one,* and passes back to Bindin." "Bindin has control and he brings the key back to center. He passes off to Sean, who is now out of the penalty box, along with Forty Howl." "Sean goes in deep, he can't get a clean shot off, so he gets the key to Darryl." "Darryl has the key now, and he skates it up and around Forty Howl. He heads for the net and tries to sneak one past Prichard Growdeer, but a quick glove save will stop the play." "Finished Jim."

"Face off in the Packs zone will begin with Travis and Wayner." "Ref drops the key, and Travis connects hard, knocking it all the way back across center, where Dan Steal takes control." "Steal heads to center and makes a pass to Travis." "Travis takes a hard slap shot, blocker side save, and Marcel is there to pick up the garbage. Sean comes in for a check but Marcel clears the key out of the zone." "Well that was another great stop by Growdeer Folga!"

"Dan Steal gets the key before icing is called, and he passes over to Never Bindin, who in turn passes ahead to Sean Step." "Sean is showing some fancy moves out there. Its like the key is glued to his stick, but he makes a pass to brother Travis." "Travis fakes a shot, and manages to get the key across for Darryl."

"Darryl takes a shot, scores! The Nacucks get on the board again, with this phenomenal double digit score, making it an astounding 13-7 for the Nacucks over the Packs!" "Here comes underwear on ice again!" "I think we better get a commercial or two in while they clear the ice." "Announced Folga, sounding a little annoyed."

"We're back again! Five minutes of play left in this rugkey game, and the players line up for yet another face off." "Referee drops the key, and the game is on." "Wayner against Travis but Wayner takes it away this time, and manages to get it over to Toni T. Darryl is there to intercept the key, and he gets it across ice for Travis." "Travis holds on, but decides to make a safe play, and he passes back to Bindin." "Bindin back to Tyler, he moves it on up to Steal, but he flicks the key up into the stands, and this play is put to an end." "Added Jim."

"Well Folga, it looks like the Nacucks *really* want *this* game. Their strategy of pass the key till the clock winds down, tells me the Packs are in good competition, and they don't wanna lose." "Well if you ask me, I think this is the way they should play if they wanna hold an unbeatable record." "Announced Folga."

"Referee drops the key in the Nacucks zone. Its Travis against Wayner." "Wayner gets this one and he holds onto it." "He sees a scoring chance, but passes off to Chelius. He takes a shot, wide!" "Now Bindin scrambles for the bouncing key, but Toni T is on him like a fat kid on a smartie." "Said Jim."

"Its a fight for the key in the corner, as the clock winds down." "Toni has the key now, and he gets it back to Wayner." "Wayner can't pull off a shot so he passes across to Forty Howl. Forty shoots, he scores!" "This game is in overdrive! Listen to that crowd Folga!" "Well at least we don't have to waste anymore time, never mind our eyes, waiting for panties to get cleared from the ice." "Snarled Folga."

"Let's take another look at that goal." "Here we have the stick fight in the corner, but Toni gets control and passes off to Wayner, who can't make a shot." "Wayner passes back to Forty Howl, one timer, and the goalie can't *see* the key, never mind the shooter." "A great screen shot on the part of Toni T." "Another one on the board for the Packs. Forty gets a goal and Wayner gets an assist Jim."

"This is anyone's game at this point Folga." "I don't know how you came up with that line Jim! The Nacucks are ahead by 5 goals, with a lead of 13. Meanwhile, the Packs are still in single digits, at a score of 8." "Jim clears his throat."

"Referee drops the key, two minutes left of play in the game, and the key goes wild off the hop." "Wayner is there and he gets it across to Forty, who moves the key forward." "Toni crosses center with him but Forty runs into trouble. Yet he manages to get a sloppy pass across to Toni T." "Toni takes a shot, but Tyler stops that one, and he gets the key to Never Bindin." "Said Jim."

"Bindin passes up to Dan and he makes a quick pass ahead to Darryl." "Darryl brings the key up the boards and passes over to Travis." "Travis to Sean and Sean takes a shot, but the key hits the cross bar and Darryl is there to keep the game on a roll." "Darryl looks for an opening, then passes in front for Travis." "Travis takes a shot, but a goalie pad save will take care of that shot on net, and the key bounces wild again." "Marcel is there to get a shot off and he clears the key from the zone." "Announced Folga."

"Never Bindin wastes no time in getting the key, and passes forward to Travis." "Thirty seconds left on the clock, and the Nacucks form a passing circle in the Packs zone. Travis starts things off and passes to Darryl." "Darryl now gets the key to Sean and Sean back to Travis." "Travis takes a shot, but that shot is blocker saved by Growdeer and Darryl gets the rebound. He takes a shot, oh, head shot and the key heads to the crowd." "Wow Folga, what a great save by Prichard Growdeer!"

"Referee brings out another key, with only ten seconds left on the clock." "Ref drops the key and Travis gets this one. He feeds it over to Sean, but Marcel intercepts that pass and clears the key down the ice." "That will take *this* game to its end, with a final score of 13 for the Nacucks and 8 for the Packs." "Just a reminder to the folks leaving the arena, not to drink and fly. I'm Folga." "And I'm Jim." "We'll see you *next* time, *in* the underground!" "They both say at the same time."

CHAPTER 13

The Deadly Game of Russian Roulette

"That was a wicked story man, but I'm gonna hit the hay. We got a lot of stuff to do tomorrow. I wanna get an early start in the morning so we can get back in time. I still have to get my homework done." Said Paul. "Yeah I hear you man, I think I'm gonna head to bed myself." Added Joe. It had a been a long weekend of partying and working. So since everyone else seemed to be feeling tired as well, it was off to bed they went.

The next morning, the boys did not crawl out of bed early like they planned. They got little done to the tree house, but did what they could. It was about two o'clock when the boys decided to call it quits, and pack up for the hike back home.

The trip itself was silent. One by one, they each split up in different directions. Reality was setting in, and it was time to prepare for the last week of school. They were in no hurry to get done what they had to for the week. After all, their heads were still a bit fuzzy from the weekend. They did however manage to pull through, and get done what they needed to. But in the end, they went to bed surprisingly early.

Tuesday morning was a mess, and the last thing the boys wanted to hear, was the fact that it was test day. But they kept themselves together, at least for the day anyways. The rest of the week went by as slow as the days were long. Thursday was the day they found out whether they all passed or not. The boys were all relieved to find out they all scraped by with fairly good grades.

Friday was another story all together. This was the day the boys would confront their parents, about the fake camp they came up with. Let me tell you, it came as quite a shock to each parent involved. But to let you all know, even though the parents seemed very reluctant to sign the waver, and hand out camp fees, they seemed a little excited at the same time. They thought that perhaps it would be good for the boys. I guess it made them a little proud, to think the boys were taking an interest in doing something constructive over the summer holidays, but little did they know.

The plan was to get their parents to sign the form on Friday. If everything worked out all right, they would be able to leave Saturday morning. It was just a nerve racking situation, until the phones started ringing at around eight o'clock on Friday night.

"Did you get them to sign it?" Asked Ted. "Holy crap, my parents signed it! What about your parents?" Asked Ron, sounding excited. "Yes they did! You call Zack, and I'll call Joe and Paul." Replied Ted. "Okay, I'll call you when I'm done." Said Ron. Then they both hung up the phones.

By nine o'clock that night, four out of the five boys could be reached by phone. Paul did however manage to contact Ted later on in the evening, but the conversation was rather short. Out of those four boys, each one of them got extra spending money for this, *supposed* summer camp.

Now that is not to say everything worked out for them. It seemed a little odd that when the boys were asked by each individual parent if they needed a ride, they all replied no. The only excuse they could come up with, was that they were asked to bring their bikes. But the parents didn't catch on to *that* one, until it was too late.

It was Saturday morning now, and the kids got up like it was a school day. Of course each boys parent or parents were up for a series of questions, and who wouldn't? I question my boy *every* single time he walks out *that* door. Its called being a parent.

A little breakfast, a big hug or two, and *most* of the boys were off with their pack sacks on. Nothing but the open road they traveled on could stop them now. They were in the clear, and they were going to have the best summer ever.

Narrator,

As you may have realized, these kids are only the young ages of thirteen and fourteen. I did use some *actual* real life events in this book. What you are about to read, is a true story I was told, and is what gave me the inspiration to write this book to begin with. As you read on, you will find out the tragedy of what the younger generation goes through In life. So for those of you kids struggling in life, I dedicate this chapter to you. So you know what NOT to do! So keep it real and live a long, healthy life.

The boys were to meet at the usual spot. They all knew *that,* and even though nobody but Ted had the chance to contact Paul, he knew where the meet was taking place. That is why the four out of five boys who made it there, waited so long to leave. Ted insisted that they wait as long as they did, but after Paul didn't show, he thought it would be best not to tell the others he talked to Paul.

One less person in the group, meant more stuff to carry for everyone else. But after a while, *that* just *wasn't* the case at all. Even though nobody spoke a word about it, each of the four boys that stood there waiting, knew *exactly* what was up. So after an hour went by, it was discussed, and the boys would take everything, including Paul's belongings, and head out.

The bike ride to the historical cottonwoods seemed empty, and the boys *really* didn't feel like talking about it, so they left *all* conversations to a minimum. Don't get me wrong, just like almost every young boy at that age, they still had time to wave at all the pretty ladies. Of course there is *always* a loud mouth in a group like this, so let's just say, they got the middle finger more times then they got waved at. But they all enjoyed it just the same. Anything to pass the time I guess. What? Its in a boys nature.

Nobody *really* talked too much until they got to the tree house. It was a rough hike in, and *all* the boys could think of, was catching a buzz. No sooner did the boys get a sip in, never mind a full beer, Zack would be the one to start things off. "Well I sure hope Paul makes it out here soon. I mean, we all *knew* what time to meet, didn't we?" Ted was going hold his tongue, but instead, he answered Ron.

"I talked to Paul last night, and *he* was the one who reminded *me* of what time to meet at the graveyard." Replied Ted. "Well you told me you never even spoke to him last night man!" Snapped Ron. "Because he really didn't want me to say anything. I think he was having problems at home." Replied Ted. "Hey man, let's just not think about it eh! Why don't we just catch a buzz and take a quick hike to check on the plants?" Added Joe. "Sounds good to me!" Blurted out Ron.

Then it was set, the boys rolled a couple for the road, and reached in one of the coolers to pull out a couple of road rockets each for the trip, and it was on.

By the time the four boys got back to camp, they were half cut and hungry. So even though they walked a little funny, it wasn't to say they didn't work hard to get a fire started, and get a good hot meal happening. Joe and Ron gathered wood for the fire, while Ted and Zack got out some hot dogs and hamburger patties.

When they had enough wood to start the fire, Joe went out and gathered more wood, while Ron got the campfire nice and hot, until there was nothing left but hot coals. Then Ted pulled out the metal rack they used to cook the food. He placed it on the two rocks, and put the hotdogs and hamburgers on top of it. The boys watched and waited impatiently as their food began to sizzle.

Once the smell of burgers reached the boys nostrils, more beers were being guzzled. Half a beer into the cook, Ted reached over and flipped the burgers and rolled the hotdogs over. When no one was looking, he poured beer over everything.

A couple of minutes later, Zack came along and added cheese to both the hot dogs and the hamburgers. Then he put the buns on the metal grill as well. Within minutes, the food was ready, and the feast had begun.

It didn't take long for the boys to finish all the food on the grill. But I think everyone was still a bit anxious to find out exactly *what* happened to Paul. If there was even still a possibility he might show up tonight, but *that* idea got weak, as the night progressed into the wee hours of the morning. There were no stories tonight either. Ted only told the stories if everyone was accounted for.

The next day seemed to come and go, but there was still no sign of Paul. Deep down inside though, nobody gave up hope. Beer was still on the go like it was going out of style, but the fatties slowed down.

"What was that?" Asked a startled Ted. "What? I didn't hear anything." Replied Ron. "There it goes again!" Exclaimed Ted. But this time Ted wasn't the only one who heard something moving around in the forest. "Oh crap *man,* I don't wanna die *yet!"* Whined Joe. But no one said a word, instead, they all listened intensely, wondering and waiting, until the shadow of a dark figure showed itself.

"Who, who the hell are you?" Asked Zack. Then a deep voice spoke out. "Who the hell do you *think* it is? Your *mom*?" Relief set in the hearts of the four boys sitting around the fire. "Hey man, you finally made it Paul!" Ted yelled out. The boys waited for Paul to get closer to the fire, and the answer they had all been waiting for presented itself.

"Holy crap! What the hell happened to you man?" Blurted out Joe, not even realizing what he had just said, until it was too late. But Paul never said a word. Instead, he pulled a bottle from his inside pocket. He took a healthy gulp, and then lit up a smoke. In the meantime, Joe got a good charlie horse for blurting out what everybody already knew.

Paul's face was black and blue. He had two black eyes, and his cheeks were swollen. His dad *obviously* gave him one *hell* of a beating this time. "My dads an asshole and if I ever see him again, it'll be too late!" Then he took another healthy swig from his bottle, and lit up a joint to pass around. For the next few minutes, nobody said a word. They all listened to the sound of the wakening forest.

But Paul broke the silence. He broke it *real* good, by pulling out a revolver hand gun. He pointed it at a bottle that had been hanging on a tree branch. It was still there from the last time they were target practicing with a pellet gun. Then he pulled back the hammer, and shot the bottle clean off the tree.

"Holy crap man! Where the hell did ya get that?" Asked a startled Ron. "I stole it from my fathers roll top desk. Trust me,

I walked into his room while he was passed out, and, I wanted to shoot him so bad, but, I just couldn't!" What came next, was a display that neither one of the boys *ever* thought they would see before. The sight of Paul *actually* crying in front of his bros. Ted was the first to his feet to comfort Paul and give him a hug. But he really couldn't hear a thing, his ears were still ringing from the sound of the gun shot. Paul quickly put away his tears and pulled away from Ted, he really wasn't a hands on sorta guy. But he *was* grateful he had such good friends.

Paul pulled his bottle out again and took another swig. Then he passed the bottle along to Ted, who in turn took a good swig, and passed it on for Ron. Paul wiped a tear from his cheek, and pulled out a box of shells from his pocket. He proceeded to load the revolver hand gun, after emptying the chambers of shell casings.

Once the gun was fully loaded, he handed the gun over to Ted. "Go ahead, take a shot." Ted had never shot a real hand gun before, and was a little reluctant at first, but once he felt the power in his hands, it was like his second nature. Ted pointed the gun, and with a loud bang, he shot a branch clear off the closest tree he could see. "Holy crap man! That sure packs a hell of a punch!" Ted exclaimed, after the gun snapped his whole arm back with such a force, he thought his arm had broke. The other boys lined up beside Ted. "Yeah, you guys can all try it. But after everyone gets a turn, I got a game we can *all* play." Finished Paul.

Narrator,

Yes, he has got a game to play alright. A deadly game. So you kids out there, don't EVER try this at home. Guns are very dangerous, and not to be played with like toys. ESPECIALLY, under the influence of alcohol or drugs. What is about to happen, is a true life drama, and you do NOT want this to happen to you.

Everyone got their chance to feel the embrace of cold steal in hand. But the thrill soon passed, once they heard what the game was called. The funny thing is, no sooner did everybody have the taste of a little liquid courage, it was game on.

"The game is called Russian roulette." Said Paul. "How do you play that Paul?" Asked Zack, not knowing what can of worms he had just opened up. "Its simple." Answered a staggering Paul, as he emptied every chamber in the gun except for one. Then he closed it up and spun the revolving chamber until it stopped on its own. After which, he headed for the platform of the elevator, inside the entrance to the big old cottonwood tree. The others followed him with their drinks in hand. A lantern was lit and the inside of the tree got bright.

"First of all, we form a circle around the platform. Then I put one bullet inside the chamber, and give it a spin. After that, I set the gun on the platform and give *it* a spin. The barrel end of the revolver will be our pointer. So to whoever one of us it points to, that person has to hold the gun up to their head, and pull the trigger." Finished Paul. Nobody spoke a word. Everybody was dead silent.

That is, until Paul spun the gun, and passed the bottle around to Ron, seeing as the barrel of the gun pointed directly at him. "Uh, I don't think this is a very good idea guys!" Yelled Ted, as he clenched his drink with a tight grip. But it was too late. Ron took a big gulp from the bottle of rye, held the gun to his head and, click. He pulled the trigger of that bad boy. Ron's eyes rolled back into his head, and he dropped the gun back on the platform. Then took he another big drink. His heart was pounding, so he sparked up a cigarette to calm himself down. "That was intense boys!" Yelled out Ron, breaking the silence and setting everyone's minds at ease.

Narrator,

Now do you *really* think that this display of foolishness set the other boys minds at ease? I venture to think not. It is a sick game, and Ron was one chamber away from certain death. I mean, the next boy up could *actually* die. He got lucky this time, but there are still four more boys to go. I know life can be tough, and a little overwhelming at times, but this is by far, not the answer! So kids out there, don't mix for kicks. Alcohol and weapons of any kind should never be mixed!

Paul reached into his jacket, where he had cut a hole on the inside lining, and pulled out five shot glasses. He placed a shot glass in front of each boy, including himself. He poured five shots, and he spun the chamber on the gun. Then he spun the gun on the platform. All this, without saying a single word.

This was the strangest Paul had ever acted, and the rest of the boys clued in, to the fact that he seemed a few fries short of a happy meal. But there was nothing they could say. You never knew *what* Paul was capable of when he snapped, and no one wanted to find out.

This time, the barrel pointed in the direction of Ted. Now normally he would never even *think* of doing something as crazy as this. But in his eyes, he didn't figure he had a choice. Either press his luck with the gun, or take his chances with Paul. Who at this very moment, had the craziest eyes Ted had *ever* seen. So he played the game.

Ted was scared, but he knew what he had to do. He picked up the shot glass and took her down like a man. Then his hands slowly went to the gun. Gun in hand now, he slowly raised it to his head. But he didn't hold back. He let out the loudest scream of his life, and then, click. The gun hit the platform with a loud thump. Everyone was dead silent. But Ted would live to see another day.

Ted breathed a sigh of relief. Then he grabbed the bottle from Paul's hand, and started chugging it until he just about puked. But that didn't stop Paul from spinning the chamber of the gun, and then on the platform once again. It was almost like he knew the outcome, but he never spoke a word. This time, the barrel of the gun pointed towards Zack, and he had no intentions of dying *this* day. He didn't even take a swig of rye. He just picked up the piece, held it to his head and, click. When it was all over, he set the gun back down on the platform. "Yeah! Let's get it done!" Zack screamed out. But he was alone in the cheering section at this point of the game.

Paul had no reaction whatsoever. He just did what he did. He spun the chamber, and spun that gun like it was nothing. It was time for Joe to look at death straight in the eye. You could see the fear on his face, and he turned as white as a ghost. His hand began to tremble as he picked up the gun. You could have heard a pin drop, when he picked up the shot glass, and downed it in record time. There was nothing holding Joe back now. So he just did it, click. The gun dropped to the platform. But the gun wasn't the only thing to hit the platform, Joe dropped like a ton of bricks as well.

Ted was the first to rush over to where Joe now lay on the ground by the entrance of the tree. First, he checked his pulse to see if he was still alive, after that horrific fall. To Ted's relief, Joe seemed to be fine. It took a few minutes, but Joe awoke to Ted, Zack and Ron staring down at him. "What happened man?" Joe Asked, in a bit of a daze. "Well as soon as you held the gun up to your head and pulled the trigger, you dropped like a sack of potatoes." Replied Ron. "You mean, I'm still alive?" "Yeah man, your still alive." Ted replied, with a very serious expression on his face.

Then Ted looked at Paul and gave him an evil eye. "Look man, things are getting just a bit *too* real here! Don't you think things are getting a bit *too* carried away?" But Paul spoke no words, he looked worse than Ted had *ever* seen before in his life and it was scary. *This* time, there was no need to spin the gun. Instead, Paul just spun the chamber, and then he spoke. "You guys are the best friends I ever had. I love you man and don't you *ever* forget it."

With that being said, Paul walked outside, pointed the gun to his head, and pulled the trigger. It happened so fast, no one in the group had time to react, until it was too late.

Narrator,

Well I don't know about you, but even writing about this more than horrific story, it fills my heart with anxiety. What if that was *your* boy out there? Wouldn't that make you feel terrible? Especially if you were partly to blame? Paul just had enough of getting beat up by his father. I know exactly how the kid felt. My dad used to beat the hell out of me as a kid as well, but I am still here writing this book. Kids, do NOT try this at home!

When the boys heard the sound of the gun going off, they all looked at each other in disbelief. Then they all ran outside, to find Paul laying in his own pool of blood. It was a gruesome sight, that *no* kid should *ever* have to witness. Joe, who had a weak stomach to begin with, ran to the nearest tree and began puking. All you could here were the loud grief stricken screams coming from the other boys. They had lost their best friend, and there was nothing they could do about it.

"What are we gonna do?" Cried out Ron. Ted immediately ran over to Paul, and even though he knew there was no use, he checked his pulse, to find nothing. He knelt over Paul's lifeless body, and began to weep aloud, as he rocked back and forth. Zack was hysterical, but managed to get a blanket and cover up the body. Then he literately had to drag Ted away. Joe was wandering around aimlessly, shaking like a leaf, not knowing what to do. He tried to light up a cigarette, but had *no* clue where his lighter was. Ron on the other hand, was trying hard to keep calm. So he tried to roll up a fatty. But it was no use, he was shaking so bad, that every time he tried to roll, the paper would rip. The seconds seemed to go by like minutes, but the bottle of rye was being chugged like water. It was all they could do to calm themselves down.

By now, Ted had pulled himself together, and for the sake of the other boys, he spoke out, in a shaky voice. "We're gonna have to call the police, we have no choice." "This is *not* the way the start of the summer was supposed to pan out." Cried out Ron. "I know man. What was Paul *thinking* when he brought that gun to camp?" Ted replied. "He, he was different tonight. I have *never* seen Paul like that before. His dad must have beat him *good* this time." Zack said. Then he took a healthy swig from the last few remnants of the bottle. "Well his *dad* ain't gonna be able to touch him anymore, we can *all* be thankful for that." Stated Joe.

But for a period of time, no one said a word. Ted finished where Ron had left off, and rolled the boys a fatty. They smoked it in silence, and then began to make a plan. "Well we can't just leave him there! We gotta do something!" Snapped Joe, breaking the silence. "Well first of all, we gotta come up with a story." Ted began. "Then *someone has* to go and get the police." "Well what about our parents man? They are gonna kill us!" Yelled Zack, before Ted had a chance to say another word. "Do you have to mention the word kill?" Snapped Joe. "Sorry man, it just came out." Zack apologized.

"Well first of all, we are going to have to come up with one *hell* of a story, before we *even* talk to anyone. Like why we got our parents to sign the phony christian summer camp slips. Or why Paul brought a gun to *begin* with. I mean, these

FIVE KIDS AND ONE GUN

are things we have to be able to answer to cover our backs. Those cops are going to ask questions to stumble us, and we have to be prepared for any question." Finished Ted.

"How do *you* know so much about the cops Ted?" Asked Zack. "Paul, he uh, was in trouble with the police, more than *you* guys knew, and he taught me some things." Said Ted. "Oh, I wonder why he never mentioned any of that to us?" Whined Joe. "That's because he didn't want *any* of us to know. The only reason I *knew* about it, is because I was there one day when the police dropped him off, and he made me swear I wouldn't tell anyone. It goes a lot deeper then that though." But Ted paused for a second to clear the lump in his throat.

"When Paul's parents used to fight all the time, his mom would get scared for him. So she would call the police, before his father was even *able* to lay a hand on him. But when she passed away, there was no one to save him from his father, and then this happened." Finished Ted.

Paul had often told the boys that one day he would get even with his dad. I guess this was the only way he could *actually* get even, in his own mind anyways. But what a way to go. The boys were in think mode at this point. It was all they could do to keep their minds occupied.

A few minutes had passed, by now, and it was Ted who broke the silence in the air this time. "I've gone over it at least a hundred times in my head, and I think the best thing we can do, is tell them we didn't *even* know about the gun. He just came out here and shot himself. That's all I can come up with, and, we don't even *mention* the fact that we were playing Russian roulette." Finished Ted.

"Do you really think it's gonna work?" Asked Ron, with a *really* worried look on his face. "Well, if we all come up with the same story, we should have no problems." Replied Ted. "What about the fake ass permission slips? How in the hell are we going to explain *that* one to the folks?" Asked Joe. "Well, I think we're *just* going to have to come up clean on *that* one. Unless any of you can come up with a better idea? I'm all clean out of ideas, and my head is all fuzzy right now." But nobody had an answer for *that* one. "Then it's settled, we go with my story and that all there is to it." Added Ted.

"Now all we have do, is figure out *who's* going to the police." Said Ron. There was no answer from *anyone,* until at least another minute later, and then Ted spoke. "I'll go. That way you guys can wait here and try to keep our story straight, and *don't* give the police any extra information. Just answer what they ask you, and try to keep it simple. Otherwise, they could try to pin this on any one of us, and that's *not* how I plan to go down."

"So, so when are you going down to the police station?" Asked Joe, who was still a bit shaky. "I don't know, I could wait until daylight, and then tell them I was in too much shock so I started drinking? But I don't know, I have to think this one through a bit more before I decide." Replied Ted.

The drinking soon came to a halt, and the fatties were being smoked like they were going out of style. Ted called them thinkers, but everyone knew he was just trying to avoid the reality of the situation. It was beginning to turn daylight out and still, it was undecided of what to do. "Hey, we could say we took off from camp and *found* Paul just laying here." But after a moments thought, Ted knew that wasn't going to work.

It was eight o'clock in the morning now, and Ted was beginning to nod off. That woke his ass up *real* quick, after shaking his head. He jumped to his feet and headed for his bike, but not before saying a final word to his *now* deceased friend. He knelt down and said a little prayer, got back up, and then spoke out to the rest of the boys. "Okay boys, I'm gone.

You guys remember what we talked about, and *don't* give the cops too much information!"

Ted grabbed his bike that was leaning up against the tree, and got the hell out of dodge. He had no idea as to what he was going to say to the police, but he planned it out inside his head as best he could. The bike ride seemed too fast, and by the time he reached the police station, he had a sick feeling in his stomach. But it was too late to back out now. He was there, and he knew what he had to do.

The police station was the last place he wanted to be, and there was no one standing in line, so he walked up and did what he *had* to do. "I need to speak with officer Chance." Ted said to the receptionist, in a shaky voice. "Hello Ted. Let me see if your uncle is back in the office, alright?" This was a secret that Ted never wanted any of his boys to find out. Man, it would ruin his rep if everyone knew his uncle was a police officer. So in the meantime, he took a seat on a nearby bench and waited for his uncle.

"Hey Ted, and what can I do for you this fine morning?" Asked office Chance. All Ted could do to hold back the tears was gone. But he managed to scrape up a voice, while the tears rolled down his cheek. "Uncle? Can we talk in another room please?" His uncle opened up the door to the office, and put his arm around Ted, trying to comfort him. Then he led Ted into a room used to talk with criminals. Where Ted could explain to his uncle what he was doing at the police station so early in the morning.

"Woo boy, you smell like a brewery. Let me go get you a coffee, and you can tell me all about it." By the time Ted's uncle returned, the tears had stopped. Ted immediately took a sip of the coffee his uncle set on the desk, and lit up a smoke. But his hands were shaking now more then ever, and then it *all* came out.

"Uncle, your the only one who can help us, that's why I came to see you first." "So tell me what it is so I can get you through this." Replied officer Chance. "Paul shot himself in the head last night uncle, and I'm scared out of my mind okay! There, I said it, is that what you wanted to hear?" Snapped Ted.

Ted explained the story to his uncle, and officer Chance immediately got a team of investigators together. Then he made a phone call to the coroners office. "You can ride with me Ted, so you can show us *exactly* where it all happened, and don't worry about your folks, I'll explain everything to them. I think they'll just be happy enough to know that your safe." Replied officer Chance. "So what about Paul's dad? Who's gonna tell him?" Asked Ted. "Let's get you through *this* first, and don't *you* worry, I'll go over to Paul's dads *personally,* and tell him myself." Assured officer Chance.

When Ted and the police arrived to the place where Paul's body lay, it was a rather rude awakening for the rest of the boys. Even though it had only been about an hour or so since Ted left, the other boys passed out in the meantime.

"Okay boys, it's time to get your asses up!" Yelled officer Chance. But there was no response from any one of the boys, they were passed out cold. So Ted stepped up and kicked the chair that Ron was passed out in, and it collapsed. Ron got up *immediately* when he noticed the place was crawling with police, and *that* got the rest of the boys attention *real* fast.

As the detectives pulled the blanket from Paul's corpse, Joe ran to the bushes and puked. Meanwhile, the other boys were pulled aside and questioned individually. The police were there for the rest of the day, trying to put all the pieces together. The boys were instructed to leave *everything* behind, including their bikes, so detectives could conduct a *full* investigation.

In the meantime, officer Chance gave the boys a ride to their homes, and had a talk with each of the parents. Ted was the last one to be dropped off, and he took extra time to talk to his brother and his sister in law about the goings on. Ted didn't say a word to his parents that day. He pretty much hibernated in his bedroom.

Last but not least, it was time to tell Paul's dad what had happened to his son. Officer Chance walked up to the door and knocked. The door opened a little, and that is when he seen Paul's dad, lying in his own pool of blood on the floor. He rushed in and knelt down on the carpet to check his pulse, but it was too late. There was nothing he could do. So he made another call to the coroner's office, and called the homicide investigative team shortly there after.

A house call to each one of the boys homes were in order once more. They were all taken down to the station for more questioning, and released later on that evening. The boys lives were a mess at this stage of the game, and there was nothing they could do about it. It was *just* something they were going to have to deal with.

CHAPTER 14

The Ferry Jump

In the next few weeks that followed, the boys were not allowed to have contact with one another. By order of their own parents, as well as the police. But this was no way to deal with it in the boys minds. They were stir crazy, and that is when things got *even* worse.

Ron's parents got home from work one day as they usually did, to find out the list of chores they had given Ron had *not* been done. His father called out to him, but there was no answer. So he went upstairs to Ron's room, but he wasn't there. After closing Ron's bedroom door, he could hear his wife screaming. So he rushed downstairs to see what his wife was screaming about. But she couldn't even say a word. All she was able to do, was point out the window to the backyard. Then she embraced her husband as tight as she could with both arms.

It was Ron in the backyard. He had hung himself from the cherry tree, where he and the rest of the boys sat in every summer picking cherries since they were kids. It was a tragic sight, and a nightmare that *no* parent should *ever* have to live through. These kids were more then a mess. After *this death* though, it was decided, that the rest of the boys would be subject to extensive counseling.

This would have been the second funeral Ted, Zack and Joe would attend this summer. But sadly, it would *not* be the last. Joe had refused to talk to anyone on the day of the funeral, *including* Ted *or* Zack. His parents would find him inside the family car that was parked in the garage. The engine was running, and there was a hose duck taped to the muffler that led to a partially open window on the drivers side.

The police were called, and once Zack heard about the tragedy, he went off the deep end, literately. No sooner did his mother receive the phone call about Ron, she broke the news to Zack. This was the last thing he wanted to hear, so he stormed out of the house without saying a word.

That night, Zack's parents got a call from the police, asking them to come and identify his body. It was Zack's alright. He couldn't take it anymore. So he jumped off an overpass in front of a train. He was killed instantly.

Narrator,

When I was growing up, my friend took his own life the same way Zack did. He was a good kid, and his name was Tommy. He had been picked on earlier in the night by a bunch of bullies. He had his head smashed through the glass of the local Paramount theater box window. He took his own life shortly thereafter. May he rest in peace. I did however defend his honor the next day in front of about fifty other kids. The bullies were all there, and it didn't end well for them. That is all I have to say about that.

A month passed by, and Ted was the only boy in the group left to tell the story. He was all alone now, but his parents, as well as the police, kept an eye out for Ted, and *barely* let him out of their sight. But Ted seemed different, it was like his emotions were frozen in time. But *this,* was one secret he would take to his grave.

Everyone, including the therapists tried to break free his emotions and get him to grieve. But Ted convinced them that he was alright.

It wasn't until the rainy season in mid September, did anyone get a reaction from Ted. A reaction that nearly cost him *his* life as well. Ted and his family were taking a ferry from Victoria island to Vancouver, and I guess deep thoughts drove him over the edge as well. So he jumped into the frigid waters of the Pacific ocean, without even taking a moments thought of what he was about to do. But Ted was obviously being watched over from above. A man in a small fishing boat seen Ted drowning, and raced over to save his life.

Narrator,

My friend *was* the last soul survivor of five kids and one gun. He was the one who told me his true life story. It was what gave me the inspiration to write this book. But I had to put a little bit of a spin on things of course. So let's see where this takes us.

Ted's emotions had finally got the best of him on the hospital bed when he awoke. He screamed louder then Ron did that night of the deadly game, when he held that gun to his head. Doctors and nurses rushed to his side to see what was wrong. Ted's parents had been sitting beside his bed since the day before. In need of a rest, they slipped out momentarily to get a coffee. But they came running back to the room immediately, after hearing Ted scream.

When they got back to the room and seen Ted, they knew *exactly* what was going on inside his head. He was grieving for the first time. It started a stream full of tears between him and his parents. It truly was a tearful joy.

CHAPTER 15

A Blast From the Packs

Ted's first day back at school was very lonely. He was the center of attention, from the moment he stepped on the school property though. People were pointing at him as he walked by, and some kids *even* tried to talk to him. But he blew *everyone* off like they weren't even there. He would not even talk to the teachers. This first day back for him seemed to be the longest day of his life.

So after school, he went to the place where him and his four deceased buddies would meet every day after school. This time, he would take the trip alone. I guess he needed some closure for himself more than anything. But that wasn't the only reason for his little adventure back to the historical cottonwoods. It was crop time, and he knew what he had to do.

So he set out the same way him and his bros usually did after school. Ted felt free for the first time since his boys left this world. He even made a stop at the graveyard, where they would stash things for the trip. The book Ted used to tell stories about the Packs was tucked away deep inside his jacket.

The quick stop at the graveyard didn't last long. Ted did what he felt he had to do, and then continued on his journey. Daydreaming the whole bike ride to the historical cottonwoods. It was a deep thought, consisting of his bros riding with him and waving at chicks. But it *just* wasn't the same without the rest of the boys. It was the loneliest he had ever felt. Especially when he parked his bike in front of the tree house. Flashbacks in his mind of the night everything went wrong, seemed to be swimming inside his head.

There was still yellow tape surrounding the area. This was the place where they all used to spend most of their time together, and it really hit Ted hard. But he grit his teeth, and pulled out some garbage bags he had brought, and continued his journey. It was time to pick the crop he and the other boys had planted prior to their deaths.

The first patch Ted came across, put a big smile on his face. It was probably the only smile he had made since the boys deaths. He picked the plants from this spot and moved on. After every patch had been picked clean, he made his way back to the hollowed out tree.

When Ted got back to the tree house, he thought it was only right to climb the ladder and see inside, for old times sake. As he entered the tree house, memories filled his head like they were all there together. That is when he heard a strange noise. It wasn't coming from outside the tree house, it was too close for that. It seemed to be coming from inside the hollow of the tree. So he went to investigate things for himself.

On Ted's way down the ladder, he got the crap scared right out of him. For staring up at him, was a man and a woman he had never seen before in his life. He nearly lost his balance, but managed to hang on to the ladder. However, the book fell out of his pocket.

The man looked up at Ted, and then picked up the book. "So you must be Ted." Said the man. "How do you know who I am?" Asked Ted. "I've been reading the newspaper and I knew there was still one soul survivor left. I see you have found my book." "Your book!" Snapped Ted. "Yes sir. I have been looking for this book for a number of years, and if you have been reading it, you will know that I am the gate keeper." The man replied.

Ted was lost for words at first, but then he managed to speak. "If your the gate keeper, then prove it!" Demanded Ted. Without speaking another word, the man pulled out a tiny key from his pocket, and peeled back the inside cover of the last page in the book.

Ted's eyes lit up when he noticed a tiny key hole underneath the cover, and the man put the little key inside the hole, and began to turn it. As it opened up, a big old golden skeleton key fell to the ground and the man picked it up.

"This book is full of magic Ted. I used to come out here once in a while to read what was going on in the Packs. You see, it tells the story of the goings on in the underground, and that was how I was able to know what was going on in my daughters life. That is, until you found the book. For years I watched you boys, hoping there was a chance you might leave it behind. I often sat in the bushes and listened to you tell stories from the book. I'm sorry about your friends, I really am. But Ted, it's time I get back to my home." Said the man, as he finished speaking.

"So, your the guy we thought we heard in the bushes all this time? I thought that the woods were playing tricks on us. But I knew there was something up, when things started disappearing and reappearing. So what may I ask is your name?" "My name is Bryan, and this is my wife Jessie. Tanantra is my daughter, the one you have been reading about." "So what your trying to tell me is, that the stories *are* true?" Asked Ted. "As true as you and I stand here at this very moment in *time.*" Replied Bryan.

Ted's eyes lit up, and he was practically speechless. He had no clue that the stories were *actually* true. Then Bryan spoke again. "Now, if you'd like Ted, you can come with us.

But I have to get back to my roots and see my daughter. It has been way too long." Ted was still stuck for words to say. But in the meantime, Bryan made his way underneath the platform with the golden key in his hand.

Ted watched, and followed the pair underneath the elevator platform that he and his friends had built. Using roots to climb down, they all regrouped at the bottom. Jessie had a flashlight, and while she held it up for Bryan, he started digging frantically underneath a huge tree root. When he hit something hard, he cleared the dirt away, and pulled the golden key from his pocket.

Bryan inserted the key in the hole and gave it a turn. The ground began to shake and the dirt under their feet began to stir. Ted watched in amazement, as he seen some sort of elevator rising up from the ground. Once the elevator lifted up to its full extent, Bryan took the key out. Then he covered the keyhole back up with dirt.

"This is your last chance Ted. You can either come with us, or you can leave it for your imagination. Either way, I *have* to get back to my family." Added Bryan. With that being said, he opened the elevator door. But just as Bryan and Jessie were about to take their first step inside the elevator, Ted spoke. "Okay, I wanna come, but can you wait a minute, while I get my stuff?" "No problem." Replied Bryan.

So Ted climbed up the roots back to the surface, where he had left his green garbage bags. He returned rather quickly, with a flashlight, and three large plastic bags in hand. He had no more use for the world he came from. This was his chance for a new start.

Ted was the first one to step out of the elevator, and into the dark corridor he had been reading about. It was exactly like the book had described. Bryan was the last one off the elevator, after taking the key from the keyhole. Once he gave the lock a turn, he pulled the key out, and the door began to shut on its own. It was time for the journey back to the Packs.

Meanwhile, back in the Packs, it was dinner time, and the family had sat just sat down. "So Leroy, are you excited about your first day of school on Monday?" Andy asked. "Well dad, Dude has been explaining a lot about school to me. But I am kind of nervous. Were *you* nervous about your first day of school dad?" Leroy asked his father.

"Well you know son, back in my day I never had time to be nervous about school. In those days, I had to wake up at five o'clock *every* morning to get my chores done. The cows needed milking, the eggs needed to be collected, and the horses needed to be fed. After which, I had to hitch up the team of horses to the wagon. Then I had to wake up my brother and two sisters, while mom would prepare breakfast." Andy took a sip of his coffee and continued.

"Not to mention the fact that we had a fourteen mile ride to school and back. But at the end of each day, I had to make sure there was hay in the barn, unhitch the team from the wagon, and get things ready for the next day." Leroy was about to speak, but Andy cut him off before he could say a word.

"So you see son, I never had time to be nervous, never mind being sick. No one else was old enough to do my job, and father was on the road a lot working, so I was the man of the house. Now uh, what were you saying about being nervous son?" Finished Andy.

"Okay dad, I get your point. But I *do* feel better after your little talk. Especially since I don't have to hitch the team and drive the wagon fourteen miles to school." Replied Leroy. Everybody at the dinner table had a bit of a laugh. "Are you trying to be a smart ass son?" "No sir, but you gotta admit, it *was* a pretty good story." "Yeah well don't choke on the fish bones son." Added a sarcastic Andy.

Anne and Tanantra finished their dinner and began clearing the table. "When you guys finish your dinner, Tanantra and I will bring out some dessert." Said Anne. "Nice, what are we having for dessert?" Asked Leroy. "Frog legs." Added Andy, jokingly. "Oh stop." Said Anne, giving Andy a playful slap on the shoulder. "We are having chocolate cake and ice cream, which Tanantra and I baked earlier on today." "Well that sounds good to me." Replied Andy, after giving Anne a kiss on the cheek.

Dude and Leroy finished their plates in a hurry as they waited patiently for dessert to be dished out. Little Lynda started eating her dinner even faster after she heard the words cake and ice cream. When she was finished, Anne gave her a kiss on the cheek. "I'll get your cake for you Lynda." Anne said with a smile on her face.

After dinner, the kids helped with the chores in the kitchen. Andy and Santose walked out to the patio to have a puff from their corn pipes. They watched the many different colors of magic carpets flying through the air. It was a magnificent sight to watch, and it was very relaxing.

The dishes were done by now, and the kids were about to head out the door to go and visit with friends, but they were stopped in their tracks. "Uh, where do you kids think *your* going?" Asked Anne. "Well the dishes are all done, and we thought we'd go out with our friends." Replied Tanantra.

"Well, we have a little announcement for you kids. So you can all wait in the living room for a moment." Replied Anne, in a soft spoken voice. Then she walked out to the patio and returned with Santose and Andy.

"Okay so what's the big news?" Asked Tanantra. "Well as you all know, tomorrow night we plan on having a back to school barbeque for you kids. What we didn't tell you, was that we have some surprise guests attending. Remember when we asked the Step brothers to come over for dinner? Well, they will be here tomorrow afternoon." Finished Anne.

"Are you serious? Can we invite a couple of friends over?" Asked an excited Tanantra. "You can each invite two friends over." Replied Anne. "Oh thanks mom. I'm gonna go and call a couple of friends *right* now." Said Tanantra, as she gave Anne a big hug. Dude gave his mom a hug as well. But just as Dude was about to run out the door, Andy had something to say.

"Hold on a second before you leave Dude. I have something I'd like to say, or ask rather, and I would like you all to be present." Said Andy. Then he took Anne in the middle of the room, and dropped down on one knee. Andy looked up at Anne, as he pulled out a gold box from his pants pocket, and he spoke.

"I know I have been away for a long time Anne. I wanted to marry you before we left, but things didn't work out like we planned." Andy opened up the box and pulled out a rather large diamond ring. "So Anne, will you marry me?" Andy asked, as he placed the ring on her finger. "Yes I will Andy." Replied an overjoyed Anne.

All the ladies, including Tanantra, gathered around Anne, to see the most beautiful gold ring. The diamond in the ring was absolutely stunning. So as the ladies celebrated in their own way, Andy pulled the men towards the patio for celebratory drinks.

The next morning, breakfast was served by the time the kids got out of bed. It was sort of a family tradition, which Anne and Andy used to do. Together, the pair would make for a big breakfast on Saturday morning.

On Sunday morning, Anne was allowed to sleep in while Andy and the kids made breakfast. But the kids were too excited to sleep in this Saturday. They didn't even have to be woken up in the morning. It did however take them most of the day to get the house in tip top shape, before any guests arrived.

It was around four o'clock when the Step brothers decided to show up. The kids weren't there for their arrival though. Anne had sent them all on errands to do, so they were prepared in time for the barbeque. But it was around four thirty, when an unexpected knock came from the other side of the door.

"Are you expecting anyone Andy?" Anne shouted from the kitchen. "Not that I know of. But don't worry honey, I'll get it." Andy replied, as he walked to the front door. Andy got a heck of a shock when he opened the door to an old friend. "Bryan?" "Andy you old dog you!" A hug and a hand shake were in order at this point. "Andy, this is my girlfriend Jessie, and this here is Ted." Replied Bryan. "Good to meet you *both*! My name is Andy." There was a slight pause, and then Andy spoke again.

"Well don't just stand there, come on in. Your just in time for a barbeque. Anne! You better make room for three more! An old friend has come back from the past." Anne came to the front door to see what all the fuss was about. She nearly dropped the bowl of hamburger she was mixing up for dinner. So Andy grabbed the bowl from her hands. Then Anne ran up to Bryan and gave him a big hug.

"Well your looking good these days Bryan." "Why thank you Anne, and your looking mighty fine these days yourself." "Why thank *you*." Replied Anne. "Anne, I would like you to meet my girlfriend Jessie, and this is my friend Ted." Replied

Bryan. "Well it's good to meet you both. Come on in, your just in time for dinner. We were just about to light up the barbeque." So Bryan, Jessie and Ted walked through the door, and were led into the living room where Santose was watching a movie. Everyone was introduced, and then the question Anne and Andy had been waiting for, came up.

"So how is Tanantra doing Anne?" Asked Bryan. "Oh, she turned out to be quite the young lady Bryan." Replied Anne. "Is she here?" "Well I sent her and the other kids to do some errands before dinner. But I expect them home at any time." "By other kids you mean." "Yes Bryan." Interrupted Andy. "Leroy is still with us." He said, grinning from ear to ear.

A sigh of relief came from Bryan, and more introductions were in order as the Step brothers walked in from the patio. But in that *same* moment, the front door opened up, and seven excited kids came through. Tanantra was so excited, she hadn't even noticed the other guests in the room. She seemed to be more interested in Darryl, as were her friends. So Anne led everyone to the patio where they had more room. "Tanantra, I'd like you to stay behind for a moment. There is someone I want you to meet." Said Anne. Tanantra wasn't very happy about this. She was only interested in meeting Darryl.

Once the rest of the kids and the Step brothers were out on the patio, it was time to reunite Tanantra with her father. "Hello Tanantra." Said Bryan. Tanantra looked over towards Anne. "Who is this?" "This is your father Tanantra." Tanantra's mouth dropped, and she could not find any words to say. So she did the only thing she could do at this point, she ran to her bedroom.

"I'll go and check on her. Andy, can you get our guests some drinks while I go and have a talk with Tanantra?" Replied Anne, as she left the room. "Uh, no problem dear, you go and do what you have to do." Said Andy.

Narrator,

As I write this, I think of my daughter and I wonder what it will be like when I see her for the first time, in over ten years. Her mother moved her across Canada without my knowledge. Since then, my son has moved back home, which makes me happy. I still text my daughter daily, and I truly miss her. But let us see how things turn out for Bryan and Tanantra.

Anne entered Tanantra's bedroom and sat down on her bed, so they could have a little chat. But they were interrupted by a knock on the door. Tanantra was practically in tears, but Anne gave her a big hug to try and set her mind at ease. "Is it alright if I come in?" Bryan asked, as he slowly opened the door. "Do I have a choice?" Tanantra replied, in a sarcastic voice. "Ill just step out in the hallway, so you two can get to know each other." Anne said in a soft voice.

"I know I haven't seen you in a very long time sweetheart. You were just a little girl when I left, and my apologies are in order. Now, I can understand if you have developed some sort of hatred towards me. I have gone over this speech in my head, a thousand times, and, well, here it goes." Bryan took a deep breath, and continued.

"I love you with all my heart, and it made no sense for me to bring you up with the misery I was going through. After the days that followed your mother's passing, I didn't know what to do. I just wanted you to have the best that life could offer. So, I decide to keep you here with Anne. That way you would knew what it was like to be a part of a *real* family. I wasn't in the best of shape, mentally, and I had to follow my path, without it interfering with your life." Bryan explained.

"It is the worst feeling in the world to lose someone you care for so much. So I left the Packs in search for my destiny. That is when I met Jessie, and I knew one day, I would bring her back here with me. Tanantra, I just want to start a new life, and, well, I am inviting you to come and live with us. Of course the decision is *totally* up to you. I just want to be a part of your life. But it is quite alright if you would still like to live here with Anne." Finished Bryan.

Tanantra never spoke a word after hearing what her father was saying. Instead, she began to cry. Bryan comforted Tanantra by holding her in his arms, as a tear rolled down his cheek. A moment or two passed, and that is when Tanantra was able to speak.

"Mom, I mean, Anne, never spoke a word about you, until just the other day. As far as I was concerned, I thought Anne was my real mother. But when she broke the news to me that my mom had passed away and that you were still alive, I just knew you would return." Finished a teary eyed Tanantra.

Hearing those words made Bryan feel much better. "You can come in if you want mom." Replied Tanantra, knowing Anne was listening at the door. Anne entered the room with tears of joy streaming down her face. She embraced Bryan and Tanantra with a group hug. "I am so happy you two are getting along." Replied Anne.

Anne wiped the tears from her eyes, and remembered she had stuff that was probably burning on the barbeque. So she rushed to the patio to find Andy tending to things just fine. She had almost forgotten what it was like to have a man around the house. A man who could *actually* cook.

"Its time to get this party started!" Shouted out Andy. Then he flicked a switch, and put on some good old country music. He pulled Anne into his arms, and danced around the patio until the song was complete. It was their song and Anne was very surprised Andy remembered it. After the song, the drinks were passed around and the food was put on plates.

Darryl's eyes lit up at the amount of food that was placed on the long king sized patio table. But not as much as Tyler's. His mouth watered, as his eyes veered into every dish that was placed upon the table. When everyone was seated and the barbeque was turned off, it was time to say grace. Andy, being man of the house once again, took this honor. Then the feast began.

Plates of food were being passed around, and wow, could those young rugkey players ever eat! Sean practically inhaled a plate and a half. Then he got into the homemade beer. Travis ate a full plate, and then moved onto dessert. Darryl ate three plates full before having dessert. But Tyler had four plates, and he *still* wanted more. That is, until he noticed all sorts of different desserts that were being placed on a small table beside the barbeque. Needless to say, Tyler tried a little bit of everything.

"Well it's good to see you fine young men with such hearty appetites." Replied Anne, with a chuckle. "Eat lots, there is more where that came from." Anne said to the boys. So they ate until there was hardly a scrap of food left.

Tanantra didn't eat nearly as much as anyone else. She took little bites as she kept her eyes on Darryl. Bryan caught wind of this and it put a smile on his face. It was enough to know that perhaps this was his daughter's first love. Besides, he thought Darryl was a nice young man.

The night was a total success. Darryl got Tanantra's phone number. Bryan was reunited with his daughter. Anne was with her husband again, and Ted got a girls phone number as well. Tanantra was too busy chatting it up with Darryl, to notice her girlfriend handing Ted a phone number on a piece of paper.

The rest of the evening was full of drink and laughter, but as every great moment has its endings, so did this. The wee hours of the morning had begun, and it was time to say

FIVE KIDS AND ONE GUN

goodbye to the Step brothers, but not farewell. The Step brothers were considered a part of the family now, and were welcome back anytime.

The only ones to leave though were the Step brothers. Tanantra had her two friends sleep over in her room. Dude had his two friends, along with Leroy and Ted, in his room. Nina and Santose got one of the spare bedrooms. Bryan and Jessie slept in Lynda's bedroom. Last but not Least, Andy shared a bedroom with his wife Anne in the master bedroom. Lynda slept on the floor in the same room.

CHAPTER 16

The First Week of School

The rest of the weekend went by rather quickly. That always happens when it's time to go back to school. Or in Leroy's case, the first time *ever* to be in school. Now Ted on the other hand, knew he was here to stay. So he decided to enroll himself in school as well. But he seemed to take quite an interest in rugkey. That was all Dude ever talked about and Ted loved hockey. He was even more stoked about being invited to the next rugkey game.

Monday morning was here, and breakfast was on the table before any of the kids got out of bed. Tanantra was usually the hardest to wake up. But even *she* was up before Anne came in to wake her. Ted, Leroy and Dude were busy getting dressed when Anne knocked on the door.

"Breakfast is ready boys." Said Anne. "Okay mom, we'll be right down!" Shouted Dude, as he put his new kicks on. "So Leroy, are you excited for your first day at school buds?" Asked Dude. "I really don't know what to feel. I've never been to school before. What if the other kids don't like me?" Whined Leroy. "You just stick with me and I'm sure everything will be fine." Dude assured Leroy. That made Leroy feel a bit better, but he still had the first day jitters.

There wasn't much chat at the breakfast table. Anne was going to have to go down to the school to register Leroy and Ted. So after serving the kids breakfast, she went to her bedroom and got herself ready. Dude and Tanantra thought it would be for the best to leave a little earlier than usual. They wanted to save any embarrassment of having their mom show up to the school. So they finished breakfast rather quickly and left.

Entering the schoolyard for the first time was an adventure in itself. Ted was fascinated by the different species of creatures that stood around waiting for the bell to ring. Leroy didn't know what to think. He was being stared at and pointed out by everyone, and it made him kind of nervous. So he just simply looked ahead and tried not to pay any attention.

It was a simple registration. Anne signed some papers, and the boys were handed school books. They were also given a map of the school, with directions to their classrooms, and then they were off. Anne wished the boys good luck, and she exited the building.

As Leroy and Ted exited the office, all eyes were fixated on them. It was so crowded that they could hardly move but a few feet at a time. Dude and Tanantra arrived to guide them down the hallway through the crowd. But even that didn't help much. In fact, one boy stepped out in front of them, and spoke out, as he held up a piece of paper in hand. "My name is Johnson, and I would be honored of you'd sign this for me." Said the boy.

Leroy didn't know what else to do, so he just signed the piece of paper for the boy. After which, the boy ran down the hallway screaming in excitement. "I got the first signature!" That seemed to start some sort of a trend. Everyone lined up to get a signature from Leroy, and he was more than thrilled with all the attention he was getting.

But after a while, Tanantra got a little annoyed, so she just spoke her mind. "Okay guys, you will all have lots of time to get to know Leroy. So if you will let us through, we'll be on our way." Leroy was thankful for that, because his hand was starting to cramp up. As Tanantra and Dude led the two down the hallway, the crowd literately split apart to give the foursome walking space. All eyes were still fixated on Leroy and he was loving every minute of it. But that soon changed when the school bell rang. The hallways emptied rather quickly as everyone shuffled off to their classrooms. Tanantra said goodbye to the boys, and she was off.

Ted used the map to guide him to his homeroom class. Dude knew where he was going, so he told Leroy to follow him. He already looked at Leroy's papers and found out they were in the same class together. This set Leroy's mind at ease, knowing he wasn't going to be alone.

The last morning bell rang and the announcements were about to begin. There was to be a morning assembly in the gymnasium right after the announcements. A special guest would be appearing. The mayor of the underground was here to welcome Leroy back to the Packs.

Once the morning announcements were complete, all the students slowly unfolded into the hallways and made their way down to the gym. When everyone was seated in the bleachers, camera crews began to enter the gymnasium as well as photographers.

Then a special guest made his appearance and literately shocked Leroy. It was a hero of his fathers, and one who's movies Leroy had enjoyed watching, ever since he could remember. It was none other then the famous Hollywood actor, John Wayne.

Leroy turned his head towards Dude. "Do you have any idea who that is?" "Yeah, he is the mayor." Replied Dude. "Yes well not only is he the mayor, but he is also presumed to be a dead actor. My dad and I have seen just about every movie he has *ever* made. Everyone up above ground knows who he is." Exclaimed Leroy. Then John Wayne stepped up to the podium that had been set up in front of the students, and he began to speak.

"I wanna, thank everyone for showing up on, such a short notice. First I wanna start out by saying, go Packs go." All the students started cheering and once everyone settled down, John began to speak again. "We have a special guest in our school this morning and I, would like to introduce him to you all. Leroy? Would you like to come up here son?" Asked John Wayne.

Leroy didn't know what to do, he was sorta stunned for a moment. Until Dude gave him a bit of a nudge. After which, Leroy stood up and made his way to where John Wayne stood in the center of the gym. But as he stood in front of the whole school, he was speechless. So John Wayne spoke out. "First of all, I would like to welcome you and your father back to the underground. To show our appreciation, and as the mayor of the Packs, I would like to present you and your father, with the key to the underground city." Announced John Wayne.

Then he presented a box with a golden key inside it. Leroy started to go red in the face and could not speak a word. But to his surprise, Leroy's father entered the gymnasium and walked towards the podium. He walked right up to John Wayne with a manly sort of walk, and he held out his hand. "Mr. John Wayne sir, it is truly an honor to meet you." Said Andy. John Wayne shook Andy's hand with a firm yet strong grip.

"I have seen every movie you have ever made. I have even watched all the black and white movies. Man, you have been a hero of mine ever since I was a kid, and still are as a matter of fact. My son Leroy and I enjoy your western movies most of all." Finished Andy. "Well that's a, mighty firm hand shake you got there son. You know I, got the original copies of every movie I ever made in my house. Perhaps one day, you would have the pleasure of coming over for a visit." Replied John Wayne.

"It would be *my* pleasure! You know what movie I have been waiting to see, and haven't been able to catch the whole movie from start to finish, ever since I was a little kid?" Asked Andy. "No son, but I, have a feeling your gonna tell me." John Wayne said, with a huge grin. "Big Jake." Replied Andy. "Well I guess I'll, have to give you a copy of that one son. What say, you and the boy come over Friday night around six. Perhaps we'll fry up the barbeque, and make some good old fashioned wilderness stew. You know, like Katherine Hepburn made for us in Rooster Cogburn." John Wayne replied. They both shook hands again with a bit of a laugh.

A few more announcements were presented by the principal of the school, and then students were sent back to their classrooms. Once again, Leroy was caught in the middle of a mob trying to get a word in edge wise to him. John Wayne stood there watching the display of madness that was going on around Leroy, Tanantra and Dude. So he figured he would to do something about this. John Wayne knew about fame and crowds gathering around him. Taking this into account, he began to feel bad for Leroy. So John Wayne walked into the principals office and picked up the phone. He made a call to the one answer that would solve this problem, the U.S.S. The Underground Secret Service.

An hour and a half had passed by and the bell rang for break. From the moment Leroy walked outside his classroom he was guided by men in black. They had on black shiny suits with black ties and black shirts. They were wearing black wrap around sunglasses along with black dress shoes.

"Hello Leroy. My name is Dan, and this is my twin brother Stan. We have been called out by the mayor of our fine city and instructed to be your body guards. We are here to give you round the clock protection." "Are you sure I really need that sir?" Asked Leroy. "Well according to the mayor of the Packs, you seem to be having a little trouble. So until everything settles down, we are here to stay." Replied Dan.

During the course of the break, everything seemed to take a dramatic change of course. There were still lots of students asking Leroy for his autograph, but Dan and Stan made sure no one got close to him. If they wanted something signed, they were going to have to place it in either Dan or Stan's hand. Then *they* would give it to Leroy so he could sign it. The twin brothers were huge, so there was no argument whatsoever.

The break seemed to go by real fast. Before the kids even had a chance to get anything done, the school bell rang. The crowd immediately separated themselves from Leroy and Dude. They had no choice, Dan and Stan cleared the path right away, making sure the boys weren't late for class.

Dan and Stan stood at the back of the classroom with their arms folded. Their mission was to keep a close eye on Leroy, and that is *exactly* what they were going to do. But Dude had his own troubles to deal with, as he watched Frank and Tod walk in the room. "Those are the guys who bullied me all last year and took my lunch money." Dude whispered into Leroy's ear.

"So I see you have a new buddy this year eh Dude? Well that's good to know. You here that Todd? It looks like we got ourselves even more lunch money this year. So, up it Dude!" Snapped Frank. But Dude never spoke a word. Frank was getting angry as he stood there waiting for Dude to reach into his pocket. He grabbed a hold of Dude's shirt and made a fist like he was going to punch him. But as Frank was about to swing a punch at Dude's face, his free hand was being clenched with a much larger hand. Frank turned around to see Dan and Stan towering over either side of him.

"Who are you two supposed to be? Huh, bodyguards?" Frank said, with a smart ass laugh. "As a matter of fact we are. Now if you will kindly remove your hand from Dude's shirt." Replied Dan, with a calm yet deep voice. Frank was a little more than shocked as he looked over towards Tod. Tod just shrugged his shoulders and shook his head. Now the boys were about to turn around and walk away, but Dan spoke in a deep masculine voice.

"Before you go anywhere, there is a matter for us to discuss. The matter of lunch money. Now according to my calculations, the average kid gets approximately five dollars a day for lunch money. That is twenty five dollars a week, one hundred dollars a month, and twelve hundred dollars a year. So empty out your pockets and put the money on Dude's desk, both of you!" Demanded Dan.

Frank and Tod began digging frantically in their pockets for the stolen lunch money they had already stolen from other kids. "Ah, forty dollars eh? Now you kids better get yourselves a job after school, because you owe my man here another eleven hundred and sixty dollars. Not to mention every other kid in this school you two have stolen lunch money from. Meet me at the rug racks after school, and I'll give you a much more accurate figure. Have a nice day." Replied Dan.

Frank and Tod never said another word. They quickly went to their seats and just sat silent. Dude had like the biggest grin on his face for the rest of that day. After school, Dan gave Frank a more accurate figure. It totaled up to around fourteen thousand dollars. Frank and Tod didn't know what to say. But as you can see, it really doesn't pay to be a bully.

Shortly thereafter, the teacher came in and the students settled down. "Hello class. My name is Miss Grigg, and I will be your teacher for the remainder of the school year. So I welcome you all to my class. I notice as I look around, that some of you are new. As well as I also notice that some of you are absolutely *huge*." Said Miss Grigg jokingly. But there was no humor in the eyes of Stan or Dan. They were professionals so nothing phased them. Miss Grigg did however mention the fact that if students got out of line, perhaps Dan or Stan could assist her. They both answered yes, with a nod of their heads. For the rest of the period, Miss Grigg went on about how she runs things in her classroom. If you stepped out of line, there would be consequences. But now that Stan and Dan were there, not one student said a word.

There was only two classes on the first day of school. Dude and Leroy made a plan to grab a slice of pizza and pancakes from the Pizza and Pancake House, which was across the street. Hey, what can I say? It was the *in* thing to do.

When Dude and Leroy finally found Tanantra, she was busy signing autographs in front of the library. Hmm, Dude thought to himself. Why was *she* signing autographs as well? I mean, she *is* popular, but not *that* popular. As Dude thought this out in his head, he was approached by some of the popular girls in the school. They asked him to sign the pictures they were holding of Leroy, Tananatra and Dude together. So naturally, Dude put a big smile on his face while doing so.

The girls each gave Dude a kiss on the cheek after signing their pictures. He felt like he was literately in heaven. So he had to tell somebody. "Dam bro! You just put us on the map my brother from the same mother!" "Well, I don't know how. I just came back to the Packs with pa. I never even really knew about this underground world, until I passed out and woke up down here." Replied Leroy.

"What, you mean, dad never told you about us?" Asked Dude. "No. I guess he figured the door to get back here was shut forever or something, and he didn't want me to get my hopes up. You see, I don't remember anything about *ever* having lived here. I did have these dreams though, and knew that one day they would lead me home. I just had no idea where home *was*, until now." Finished Leroy.

"Well you are home my brother. You are home." Dude answered Leroy. "Okay Tanantra, it's time to move if we wanna make it through the rush for pizza and pancakes." "Yeah, yeah. I'm ready." Said Tanantra. Then all five of them paraded off to the Pizza and Pancake House. As they walked across the street, Dude let Tanantra have a piece of his mind. "You know it's not *your* popularity that everyone is concerned about eh?" "Yeah, well this year *I'm* going to be the most popular girl in the school." Replied Tanantra. Dude tried his hardest to hold his tongue, but it didn't last long.

"let me break it down for you. Leroy was the one who brought fame to the family, so don't go thinking your all that. Besides, I figured out why everyone wants our autographs. You notice how people are starting to bring pics of us? Well the way I see it, is they think the pictures will be collectors items. Perhaps even worth money one day. So don't go thinking it's all you, baby cakes." Dude finished, in a sarcastic voice. Tanantra walked ahead without saying another word.

The pizza and pancake hot spot was absolutely full by the time they arrived. Every cash register had a big line up of students. This wasn't a problem though. Once everyone noticed the rather large shadows of Dan and Stan above them, they quickly moved aside. In fact, Dan and Stan were *so* intimidating, they cut to the front of the line in no time.

Leroy ended up getting his meal for free, and why not? According to the people of the underground, he deserved it. He *was* the kid who saved the underground from an epidemic. Of course, if it wasn't for Andy taking his son out of the Packs, things could have been a lot worse. Who knows how many others could have died from the deadly illness? They were both heroes, and that is how they were treated.

They spent the better part of the afternoon lounging, visiting with friends, and signing pictures. The place was constantly swarming with creatures. So out of respect for others waiting to be seated, Tanantra and Dude figured it was time to split the scene.

The walk home seemed faster than usual. Even though they usually flew the rug home. As it was, Tanantra had no idea when Dan and Stan were going to part ways. It wasn't until they got to the front door, did she realize how this secret service thing really worked.

"Leroy, if you need us for anything at all, you just press the button on this watch, and we'll find you immediately." Dan said, as he handed Leroy a small box. Leroy opened the box without hesitation. "Thank you very much." Replied Leroy. "We'll be right outside the front door if you need us." Said Dan.

As the trio got in the door, Tanantra had to get something off her mind. "Don't you guys find it just a *little* weird that these guys are with us twenty four seven?" "I find it quite *fine* to tell you the truth. I got a whole years worth of lunch money coming to me." Replied Dude. "Yeah, well *you* would. How do you feel about it Leroy?" Asked Tanantra.

"Well it was a little uncomfortable at first, but then again, so was the crowd that seems to gather around me everywhere I go. But yeah, I could get used to this kind of life." Replied Leroy.

Tanantra went into the kitchen to see where Anne went, but all she could find was a note.

Dinner is in the oven. We are gone for the afternoon to get some groceries and make plans for the wedding. So clean up after yourselves and we'll see you kids when we get back.

P.S. We will probably be going out for dinner so don't wait up on our account.

Dude and Tanantra took advantage of this, because there was hardly ever a time when they had the house to themselves. So they ate what they wanted, and cranked the tunes while dancing around the house. They even invited Stan and Dan in for some dinner and brownies. But that was as far as it went. Once the pair ate, it was back on duty for them. They each stood on either side of the entrance to the front door, with their arms folded.

It was around eight o'clock before the adults arrived. By now, the music was turned down, and the trio could hear laughing and giggling, as the adults walked up to the entrance of the path to the house. But that soon stopped when they approached Dan and Stan, who closed in shoulder to shoulder so as not to let anyone get by. The first thing that entered Anne's mind, was if all the children were safe or not. Then the commotion started. So Tanantra stepped out to clear the air. "Its alright Stan and Dan, they live here." So they both stepped aside to let the party in.

After the door was shut and the adults entered the living room, it was on. "Okay kids, you got some explaining to do! Who and what, are those big burly fellas doing in front of our house?" Yelled Anne. She was one to never raise her voice unless she was concerned.

"Look mom it's alright, everyone's safe. In fact, our mayor John Wayne made an appearance at our school assembly this morning, as you may already know. Anyways, I guess he felt bad for Leroy. Mom, it was getting to the point where Leroy couldn't even walk down the school hallways in peace. So the mayor decided that Leroy needed a couple of bodyguards." Finished Tanantra. "Look, you have no idea of what an amazing day we had today with Dan and Stan hanging around." Said Dude.

"Yeah dad, it was an unbelievable day! Well, not at first. But once everyone found out I had registered for school, they surrounded me. The only time I got any peace, was when the school bell rang and everyone went to their classrooms. As soon as Dan and Stan showed up though, they would not let anyone near us. So can we keep them dad?" Leroy asked, as he tried to explain his situation.

"Well, your gonna have to let me talk it over with your mother before this matter goes any further. In the meantime, do you kids have any homework that needs to be completed?" Andy asked. "Uh dad, we never get homework on the first day." Replied Dude. "Well when I was going to school, *we* got homework on the first day." Said Andy.

"Well dear, times *have* changed a lot since we went to school. But nevertheless, if it's gonna make things a little easier for the kids at school, then I'm all for it. Perhaps they can straighten things out with those bullies who picked on Dude last year." Replied Anne. "How did you know about *that* mom?" Asked Dude curiously. You don't think I keep tabs on my kids at school?" Asked Anne. "Yeah, Tanantra probably ratted me out!" Snapped Dude. "She did no such thing. It just so happens that I know people, and I'm not afraid to ask what's going on in my kids lives." Anne replied, as she gave Tanantra a wink of an eye.

The conversation ceased to exist after Andy gave his condolences as well. Then Anne prepared a fine dessert for the kids, and the topic of the wedding began. Her plan, was to have Tanantra as her maid of honor. She also asked Nina and Jessie to be her brides maids. They said yes with no questions asked. Lynda was to be the flower girl.

Andy took this time to inform them all that the wedding would take place in the winners box, during an intermission of the next game. "Oh, there is something I forgot to mention to you. I ran into those Step brothers you kids like so much. They were practicing down at the arena. So I pulled them aside and asked them if they would like to be ushers during the wedding. To my surprise, they all agreed." Andy said, with a wide eyed grin.

"Are you serious?" Screeched Tanantra. "Serious enough that they will be there in the Packs special tailor made suit and tie jerseys. The owner of the arena ordered them up on the spot." Replied Andy. "Wow dad, that is sick!" Yelled Dude. What's so sick about *that?* I thought it was very nice of Mr Bent." Replied Andy, sounding confused. "No dad, it's just an expression kids say these days. It means cool dad." Added Leroy. "Oh." Andy said, with a bit of a laugh.

So it was settled, Andy's side of the wedding party was a little full, but complete as well. His best man was Bryan. Along side him, will be Santose and Dude, with Leroy being the ring bearer. Ted was also asked to be an usher, and he was more then happy to be in the wedding party. Especially after learning he would be ushering with the Step brothers.

After dessert, the kids were unusually tired, so they pretty much went right to bed. They said their good nights and hit the hay. This seemed like a good time to hit up the old corn pipe. So, Andy poured two glasses of some good old fashioned homemade whiskey he had made prior to having left the Packs. It was aged quite well and packed one heck of a kick.

"Anne, would you and Nina like to join us on the patio for a drink?" Asked Andy. "Oh no sweetheart, you two go right ahead. Nina and I are going to make plans for the wedding. After that, I'm going to have a long hot bubble bath. But you can come on in and join me if you so desire." Anne replied, with a big smile and wink of an eye. Andy nodded with a smile. "I wouldn't miss it for the world." Replied Andy.

After a couple of drinks Andy decided to cut his visit short. He was off to go and get himself some. The night ended abruptly, but it ended well. Nina and Santose enjoyed time together on the patio watching the cities lights. They too began to feel a little frisky after a while, and decided to finish things off in the bedroom. Bryan and Jessie were out on the town. So for them, it would be a late night.

Tuesday morning was here, and the kids had to be woken up by Anne this time around. But she didn't mind, after all, it was a part of her motherly duties as far as she was concerned. All three children arrived at the breakfast table in good time. Andy was busy making everyone bacon, fried potatoes and eggs with toast this morning. What a way to start off the day. Ted was up early as well to give Andy a hand.

"So did you kids have a good sleep?" Asked Andy. "I had a great sleep dad." Said Leroy. "It took a little bit to get to sleep, but I slept alright dad." Said Dude. "Well unlike these two. I had a terrible time getting to sleep. When I finally was able to sleep, I had a nightmare that seemed to keep me awake for most of the night." Replied Tananatra. "Well that is too bad Tananatra. Perhaps the breakfast will do you good and get you off to a good start for the day." Replied Andy. "Oh I'm not tired, I just feel like I haven't even slept." Tanantra replied, with a bit of a chuckle.

Anne walked in the room just in time to hear the whole conversation. "Well I believe it has something to do with everything that has taken place in the last few days dear. It happens, and it will get better, don't you worry." Said Anne. "Oh thanks mom. You always seem to know the *right* things to say." Tananatra replied, as she gave Anne a hug and kiss.

Dan and Stan had an oversized throw rug laid out for the kids when they came out this morning. The bodyguards escorted them aboard, and they were off. Anne and Andy stood at the front window watching as they flew out of sight.

"Well I hope those kids are going to be alright." Said Anne. "I'm sure they are going to be just fine dear. But in any case, if you want to keep track of them, you could always flick on the tube. Those reporters seemed to be keeping an eye on them more than we ever could. If that will set your mind at ease." Replied Andy. "No, I think I will just keep my mind occupied by planning this wedding. Your not getting out of marrying me *that* easy this time." Anne replied.

The arrival in front of the schoolyard was as expected. Immediately the crowd gathered around to greet them. Dan and Stan rolled up the rug in a hurry. When they felt the crowd was imposing just a little too close, Dan and Stan cut a path through to the entrance doors.

At the entrance doors, reporters and news crews were there to greet the trio. They had literately camped out for the night to get even so much as a glimpse of the trio. But fearing for their safety, Dan and Stan pushed right on through towards the school doors. Once everyone was inside, they proceeded to make sure the doors were locked behind them.

"Wow, this is so cool!" Exclaimed Dude. "You can say that again." Replied Leroy. "I hope the cameras don't get my bad side." Said Tananatra. Dude and Leroy both looked at each other and shook their heads slightly, as they rolled their eyes. "What? I could handle this sort of lifestyle *any* given day. Its awesome!" Screeched Tanantra. "Oh man, I love it! You should have seen the look on those bullies faces when Dan and Stan walked over to put them in their places. Now *that* was sick!" Said Dude. "Yeah, and to top it all off, they gave *you* lunch money *this* time. Oh, don't look now, cause here they come." Said Leroy.

The two bullies Frank and Todd walked up to Dude. "Here Dude, this is all the money we took from you last year. Sorry we took it. We got every other kids money here as well." Said Frank. "Well, thanks guys. How did you guys get it so fast?"

Asked Dude. "We had it the whole time. You see, Frank and I want to get into the rugkey league really bad. So we came up with the plan of taking lunch money. But after our confrontation with your bodyguards yesterday, we decided to think things over. I mean, who is gonna wanna watch us play and cheer for us, if all they remember is us taking lunch money?" Finished Todd.

"Yeah, well our parents can't afford to send us, and, well, this is how we thought our dreams would come true." Said Frank. "Well that is a fine thing you boys did. Remember this though, you have to work hard to make your dreams come true." Said Dan. "Hey man, if that is all you guys want out of life. Then I'm sure I can hook it up for you." Said Dude. "How? We don't have any money left." Said Todd. "I'll tell you what. The next rugkey game is on Saturday, and if you guys want to come, you can be our guests in the winners box. I'm sort of in tight with the owner of the arena and he has been scouting for new talent. I'm sure he would give you boys a chance." Replied Dude.

"Are you serious? But what about money?" Asked Frank. "Well the way he told it to me, is that he was looking to give students the opportunity of a free scholarship. If they are good enough to make the team. As well as a chance to play in the U.R.L. All you have to do, is play your heart out." Finished Dude.

"Wow man, that sounds dope. Well you can be sure that Todd and I will show up. But how are we gonna get in?" Asked Frank. "You leave that up to me. All you have to do, is meet us at our house on Friday night, and we can go over the plans." "Hey man, your alright Dude." Replied Todd. "Thanks. Then we will see you there then." Replied Dude.

The boys walked away happier then you could imagine. As for the trio, they were shocked to see the boys they came to know as the school bullies, with such a change of heart.

But in any case, the day was starting off better than any of them could have planned. Now that's the stuff that dreams are made of.

The first bell rang, and students began flowing indoors. The teachers stood guard at the entrance doors to make sure that no reporter could sneak in. Once every student was accounted for, the doors were locked to keep the reporters out. Dan walked side by side with Leroy and Dude. Stan on the other hand, walked along side of Tanantra. Then the second bell rang and announcements started.

"Good morning underground high. This is your principle Mr Clarke. Now as you all have noticed, since school started, a certain trio has gained much popularity in and out of school throughout the underground. We as teachers do not think of it as a bad thing. In fact, it has brought more publicity towards the school and something we count our blessings on." Mr Clarke clears his throat.

"If it works out, perhaps it will help our funding for more activities. All that we ask, is that you as the students be very careful as to not let any of the reporters or news crews inside the building. This has become quite a concern amongst some of your parents. So we as the teachers, will make sure no unauthorized persons may exit or enter the building." Announced Mr Clarke.

"On to address other issues. Now we seem to have an ongoing littering problem here on our second day of school. Mr Barry had to stay a little late last cleaning up. So anyone caught littering on school property, will be subject to detention. I only have one final announcement for this morning. It seems that a generous donation has been given to our fine school. The owner of the underground arena has given seasons tickets to every student body of underground high. I would also like to add, that teachers will get box office seats! Go Packs go! That is all." Finished Mr Clarke.

Narrator,

Wow that is awesome! Free tickets for a game? All we got from the school was free entrance passes for the P.N.E. In Vancouver. But these kids got it made, and the teachers as well. It was nice to see the school bullies change their attitude mind you. I mean, kids go through a lot growing up. If life were really like that, it would sure make the world a better place to live. Kids can be pretty cruel to one another, and it's sad to see. But let us see what the rest of the week has in store.

The trio thought it was going to be a walk in the park. Being famous and all, that is until they hit their classes. They may have increased their popularity by ten fold, but the teachers gave them no special attention. In fact, homework was coming from every single class they attended, and this was only the second day.

Near the end of the day, Tananata, Leroy and Dude were called down to the office. They thought there was something wrong. But when they arrived with Dan and Stan of course, the principle pulled them *all* into his office. "Hello kids, and how was your day?" Asked Mr Clarke. "It was alright. Aside from all the homework we got." Said Tananantra. "Well the reason why I called you down here, is because the mayor asked me to give you kids the celebrity treatment." Said Mr Clarke.

Then he pushed a button that was hidden underneath his desk top. Behind him, a wall of trophies and awards slid to one side. There behind the wall, was a staircase leading upwards. "Now this will be the best way for you to enter and exit the building. This staircase leads to the roof. I know it is hard to focus on your school work at this point. Especially when your being bothered by all the pesky reporters and students wanting your autographs." Finished Mr Clarke.

"Wow, would you look at that? We have our own private entrance!" Exclaimed Dude. The bell rang, and two teachers brought in the oversized throw rug. So Dan and Stan brought it up to the roof top. They unrolled the throw rug, said their goodbyes and flew off like the wind.

As far as the rest of the week went, it was slower than molasses in January. But the good news was, it was now Friday night, and the big day was just one more sleep away.

There were no *actual* plans made for any sort of stag party. But a surprising phone call that afternoon, seemed to decide how the night was going to go. John Wayne got news of the wedding, so he asked Andy to bring along some friends. Of course Andy invited John Wayne to the wedding as well. He was honored to except the invitation. Andy also invited Frank and Todd to come along if they wanted, which they did.

So while the boys were off to spend the evening with John Wayne, the girls decided to have a little party of their own at home. It was a night of movies and cocktails. Of course Nina didn't drink. That's not to say her cravings didn't satisfy her though. She was content enough knowing she was going to have a baby.

CHAPTER 17

The Big Day

"Welcome come come sports fans fans fans to tonight's nights nights game game game." The echo sound for the microphone had to be adjusted. Once that was done, Jim and Folga continued. "Hello there sports fans. I'm Jim." "And I'm Folga." "And we're your rugkey announcers for this evening!" They both say at the same time.

"Oh and do we ever have an exciting game for you tonight folks!" Announced Jim. "Yes we do Jim, and also tonight during our intermission, we have a special wedding, which will also be displayed on the big screen." "Yes Folga, and from what I hear, the Step brothers will be in the wedding party as well."

"Here comes the players Jim, and what is this? I have never seen any sort of jersey like those, have you Jim?" "I can't say I have Folga. It looks to me like they wanna be well prepared for this wedding, so they decided to dress accordingly." "I've seen It all now. The Packs jersey suits? What will they come up with next?" "Let's take a quick break, with a word from our sponsors." Finished Jim.

"And we're back. I'm Jim." "And I'm Folga." "Welcome to rugkey in the underground!" They both shout into the microphone at the same time. The national anthem played and the key was about to drop for the first time tonight.

"Referee gets ready to drop the key. Game on!" "Travis Step will start off at center ice for the Nacucks and Wayner Pretzel will step up for the Packs." "Travis gets a piece of the key and passes it back to defense man Never Bindin, and he brings the key forward." "Tom Chelius goes in for the check, but Never Bindin passes the key up to Sean Step along the boards." "Sean moves up the boards and makes a quick pass to Travis Step, but he can't hang on to it, and gets a quick piece of the key as it makes its way towards Darryl." Announced Folga.

"Darryl goes in for the kill. He fakes a shot, passes the key off his right skate and it goes through the legs of Marcel Dupponne." "Darryl catches the key on the other side, he shoots, he scores!" "Well that fancy move sure paid off." "The Nacucks lead in just over a minute of play, and it looks like we are going to cut this one for a commercial." "Yes Jim, your favorite part of the game is being displayed all over the ice again." Jim clears his throat. "We'll return with live rugkey in the Packs, after officials clear the ice." Announced Jim.

"Well Jim, if this is the way the night is going to go, then I think we are in for a long one." "Yes Folga, and I hope you packed a lunch for this game, because I don't think this will be the only goal Darryl pulls off tonight."

"Okay folks, we are back, the ice is clear, and the players set up for another face off." "Referee drops the key, and they are off." "Wayner gets it this time, and he spins around with the key on a string. He gets the key across to Toni T." "Toni T now in control, and he takes to flight as the key goes between Darryl's legs. With his stick still on the ice in one hand, Toni T takes to the roof as he does a flying summer salt over the likes of Darryl Step, while he does a tuck and roll finish back to the ice!" Announced a long winded Jim.

"Toni T catches the key on the other side of Darryl and is still in full control." "What a play Folga! Did you see that?" "I don't miss a thing thing Jim." "Now he flies up the boards and passes back to Wayner Pretzel, who moves the key towards the net." "But Wayner is not there alone. Chelius is in the open as he moves in closer to the net." "Wayner goes for the pass, no, he takes a shot, oh, Tyler Step stops the key with a knee pad save!" "Tom chelius gets the rebound, he shoots, he scores! Five hole!" Announced Jim.

"The Packs are on the board, and that will tie *this* game up, with a score of 1 for the Packs and 1 for the Nacucks." "Let's take another look at that play Jim. Here we have the spin around at center ice from Wayner. With a quick pass over to Toni T, who miraculously does the unthinkable, and takes to flight over the head of Darryl Step. Now with his stick still on the ice in one hand, and the key skating under Darryl's legs, Toni does a summer salt over Darryl and regains control as he lands." Finished Folga

"Then Toni makes a pass to Wayner, who fakes a pass and takes a shot. Tyler makes a knee pad save, but Tom Chelius is there to get the rebound. He takes a slap shot, and the key finds a home in the back of the net, five hole style!" "Yes sir Folga, I gotta say, this is rugkey at its best!" "Hold on to that thought while we cut for a quick commercial." Replied Folga.

"We're back here in the underground arena, where we have a real treat for you tonight!" "Yes Folga, and a treat it *has* been so far. Two high octane goals in less than four minutes of play!" "Well the fans are sure getting their moneys worth tonight!" "Referee gets ready to drop the key. The key bounces to the ice, but not for long. The fight is on and the battle begins." "Travis breaks this one loose as the key makes its way towards Sean." Announced Jim.

"But Chelius knocks the key loose and gets it to the boards." "Both players chase the key, but what's this? Woo! Another high flying move!" "Tom Chelius knocks Sean Step to the ice. Then he does a wall climb with a back flip, and returns to ice *still* in control, as he moves the key forward." "Well I gotta tell you Jim, I haven't seen moves like *that* since Gerald Schwepp's, and man could that guy move."

"Chelius heads up the boards and streamlines towards the net, as he passes Never Bindin like he wasn't even there." "Chelius passes across ice to Wayner, who can't hold on to the key. So he in turn passes off to Toni T, who races in towards the net like a rocket." "Chelius winds up for a shot, no, a back pass for Wayner and he takes a shot. Oh, that one hit the post!" "But Wayner is not done yet, he races towards the net as the key goes wild. Then he takes to the roof as he does a flip over the traffic in front of the net." "He catches the key on the other side, he takes a shot, scores!" "That will bring the Packs to lead for the first time tonight, with a score of 2-1 over the Nacucks." Announced Jim.

"Well I don't know what has gotten into the Packs in tonight's game. It looks they just got out of a circus, with all these high flying moves they seem to be coming up with. The Nacucks are being out played and out smarted in these first six minutes. They better get their ship together, or this one is gonna be over before first period ends." "I couldn't have said it better myself Folga." "This is Jim and Folga, and we are coming to you *live* from The Packs arena. But now, a quick few words from our sponsors." They both announce together.

Narrator,

I'm going to give you a little heads up. This is where the Nacucks take it up a notch, with some old school rugkey. According to the rugkey rule book, this is what we above ground call, dirty hockey. But every player in rugkey is taught this, and *then* they learn the rules. There is just one problem with that though, the ref is going to make it an anything goes rule, so he can make sure his team wins. Hmm, there is much to be said about that, but let's get you back to the game. In any case, go Nacucks go!"

"We're back folks, and the referee gets ready to drop the key." "The score sits at 2 for the Packs and 1 for the Nacucks." "Referee drops the key, and the whistle blows as Travis gets waved off. Sean Step will take back his position against Wayner Pretzel." "Ref drops the key, and Sean gets it back behind center. But not before giving a hard hit to Wayner, as he skates by him and moves forward." "Bindin has the key and seems to know the play. He slaps the key to Sean and he takes control. Sean bullets towards the net alone with the key in hand." Announced Folga.

"Lander and Marcel form a wall, but Sean gets the key through the pair of defense men and does a twisting flip over the Packs defensive line." "Both skates back on ice now, and Sean presses forward, full steam ahead." "Sandy Rogue, confused now, seems to be losing sight of mind." "Sean takes a slap shot as he bursts forward and does a flip over Sandy Rogue. He lands skates to ice in behind the net, scores!" "Jim, I do believe this game has gone old school!"

"Well I gotta say one thing about this game Folga, it will keep you on your feet." "Well if you wanna play with the pros, then you gotta know what your dealing with. The Packs started something that they won't be able to finish. I happen to know the Nacucks coach personally, and he absolutely lives by these rules. These players are veterans when it comes to old school rugkey Jim." "Now your gonna see a different side of rugkey like you have *never* seen before. So what do you think that is gonna bring for the start of *next* years season? Brutal rugkey, and I said it right here, *live* in the Packs arena folks." Announced Jim.

"Now we just watched an instant replay of Steamboat Sean pumping up towards the net, and as you look at his face, you definitely see a different side of him." "Well that's the Sean coach Gillis brought out and prepared him for all these years. This is old school rugkey here, where just about anything flies." Finished Folga.

"The players line back up at center ice and the fans go wild." "Referee drops the key, and this play goes to, a fight?" "Sean Step drops his gloves and the key stays put." "Wayner on the other hand, takes to flight, gloves off and ready to fight." "Well that is how they do it when the game goes old school. To the roof let's knock out a tooth! At least that is what they used to say back in my day." Announced Folga.

"Both players up in the air now, and they start this one off by trying to knock each other back down to the ice." "Here we go, and the fists start flying. Sean takes a couple of shots to the face and oh, this game has turned into a blood sport!" "You can say that again Jim. It looks like those blows might have broken Sean's nose, but he is not going to take *that* one lying down." "Sean shakes it off, and comes back with a series of flying fists, and it looks like *this* fight is all over but the crying Jim."

"You can say that again Folga! You see how many refs it is taking to pull Sean off of Wayner?" "Yes I do Jim, and it's all a part of old school rugkey. The Packs made the first move, and it looks like the Nacucks are going to make sure *they* get the last." "Let's cut for a quick commercial while the referees sort this out Folga."

The crowd is going wild, but some of the onlookers from the winners box seemed to feel a bit different about the whole situation. Anne was none to impressed by the fighting. Especially since the Step brothers are in the wedding party. But hey, you can't always control rugkey. After all, it is a hard hitting blood sport.

Both players were placed in the penalty boxes. Then the referee came back to center ice to call the penalties. "Wayner Pretzel from the Packs, five minutes for fighting. Sean Step for the Nacucks, five minutes for fighting." Then the crowd went wild and the booing started. But before they could even start the game, the clean up crew had to step out and clear the garbage from the playing area, which the crowd threw out on the ice.

"Well we're back folks, and it's game on." "Both teams line up for the face off, and it will be four on four." "Travis Step will start this one off for the Nacucks, and Toni T will take center ice for the Packs." "Referee drops the key, Travis Step takes this one and passes it along to Darryl. Darryl moves forward and Lander races in for the check. But that doesn't stop Darryl, he does an ice slider underneath the legs of Lander, while he keeps the key with his stick. He gets up on the other side and makes a quick pass to brother Travis." Announced Jim.

"Travis, who has been sticking to Darryl like glue, now goes in alone. He blasts off a shot, wow, what a slap shot! Rogue makes a glove save, but *that* shot was so hard, he could not control the force of the key, as his glove and all pass the goal line, making this a two all tie!" Said Folga. But the referees never blew the whistle. I think this one is a call for the boys upstairs.

"Let's take another look at this play Folga. Here we have the face off pass from Travis to Darryl. Darryl moves the key forward, where Lander tries to intercept, but fails to do so after Darryl does a five hole slide and passes back to Travis Step." "Now folks at home, watch this cannon Travis fires. Its literately a train stop shot. Here's the pull back, and there's the shot. Okay, pause it right there for a second. Now let's play that one in slow motion. There, the force of the shot is so powerful, that it nearly lopped off Sandy Rogue's hand at the wrist. A steel plate wouldn't have stopped the likes of *that* shot." "Well I'll tell you Jim, I wouldn't want to be the one in the line of fire when Travis shoots, that's what I call a power house shot!"

"Well it looks like the boys upstairs have made the call, and the referee is about to announce it. "Shot from Travis Step, goal for the Nacucks making the game score tied at two!" Announced the ref. The crowd goes wild.

"You know Folga, it's hard to say who the fans are really cheering for here. Every goal so far as brought the crowd meter up to around the same hype." "Well Jim, we got two very good teams here, and both from the west underground. So it's hard to tell who is the favorite team here, but I'm sure we're gonna find out."

"Players line back up and once again it's back to center ice for a face off." "Ref drops the key, the stick fight begins." "Toni gets this one, and circles back as he makes a pass back for defense man Marcel Dopponne." "Marcel now across to Lander Macdonald, who in turns passes forward to Tom Chelius." "He breaks the ice and takes to flight with the key on a chain. He quickly flies in and out of traffic. He sees Toni T in the open and passes off to him." Announces Folga.

"Toni gets the key, swiftly moving forward, and a quick pass back to Tom. Tom goes for a one timer, no, a fake and a back hand back to Toni. Toni one times the key, scores!" "Its like Tyler didn't even see that one coming." "Well in his defense Folga, there was quite a bit of traffic in front of the net." "Hold that thought Jim. That will make the score a total of 3 for the Packs and 2 for the Nacucks early in this game."

"Let's have another look at that replay Folga. Now here we have Tom Chelius rocket blasting in and out of traffic, like they were standing still. Tom sees Toni and makes a pass. Toni takes the key forward and then another quick pass back to Tom Chelius. Now Tom goes for a fake one timer, then a reverse back hand as he passes back to Toni T, who takes full advantage, and one times the key in the hole. Now how is that for rugkey Folga?"

"Five more minutes left in the first period and five goals on the board! We keep this up, and it's gonna look like a football score." "You can say that again." "Replied Folga, a grumpy old free spirited fella." "The crowd goes wild, and the roof is on fire in the arena tonight!" "The key hits the ice and another stick fight begins." "Travis gets this one and passes the key back to brother Tyler. Tyler keeps the play going and passes the key to Never Bindin, who puts this one against the glass and flies around Tom Chelius. He catches the key on the other side of Tom and gets it across to Travis." Announced Jim.

"Like a bolt of lightening, Travis streaks across the ice with his blades on fire, he sees Darryl, but presses on towards the net." "Travis makes like he is going to shoot, but then he passes back to Darryl. Darryl quickly flies in with a turnaround, here comes that fancy move. Halfway through the turnaround he back hands the key between his own legs and off his skate. Then he takes a blistering slap shot, scores! The key goes in between Sandy Rogue's legs, five hole style, and this ones in the bag! That will tie the score up at 3 a piece." "In the bag?" Asked Folga. "Well, so to speak." Said Jim, as he clears his throat.

"Well you should be happy about *this* goal Jim. I'm surprised your not down there helping the officials clear the ice." "Be my guest Folga. Your the one who keeps talking about it. Uh, well, we'll return you to rugkey night in the underground, after a few words from our sponsors." "Be a little more then a few words *this* time, after cleaning up all *those* under garments." Announced Folga, not sounding impressed in the least.

"We're back, so let the game continue!" "The ice took a little longer than usual to clear." "You said it Jim. To think, all those ladies walking around out there without any undergarments on." Jim clears his throat. "Referee gets ready to drop the key, and both teams are back in full force, as Sean Step along with Wayner Pretzel are out of the box Folga."

"Sean gets this one and he presses forward around Wayner like he wasn't even there." "Darryl is with him and so is his brother Travis." "The trio pulls off some speed, then form a triangle in front of the net, and play a little cat and mouse." "Sean to Travis and Travis to Darryl. Darryl back to Travis and Travis back to Sean. Sean shoots the key with authority, scores! Right off the mask of Sandy Rogue!" "Well it looks to me like a goal there, but that will be the end of Sandy Rogue's face mask." "You said it Jim. Let's fly to a commercial while Sandy Rogue gets checked out."

Narrator,

Well it looks like the goal is good. But is that the end of Sandy Rogue for the night? He looked like he was In pretty rough shape. He was hit pretty hard in the side of the head, and his mask was shattered completely in half. A hockey puck is hard enough, but a clear see through puck with a golden key inside? That could do a lot of damage. Let's just see where this takes us in the game.

"Well folks, it looks to me like the Packs are going to be out of luck, as far as a goalie is concerned for tonight's game." "Well let's just hope that isn't the case Folga." "Well you seen it Jim. The guy could barely walk off the ice, never mind skate." "Yes I sure did Folga. The score now sits at a tie game. The Nacucks with 3 and the Packs with 3."

"Oh, this just in folks. It seems that the owner of the arena has offered free hotdogs for everyone in the arena tonight." "Well I think I'll go and get myself one." "Uh, Folga I think that was just for the fans." "Well I'm the one working around here!

I'm going to get me a dog! Hold the fort down for me will ya Jim?" Then Folga stormed out of the room.

Meanwhile, up in the winners box. "Well I can't believe I ever let those kids even *think* about watching this game!" Said Anne in disgust. "Well uh, it's a little rougher then uh, hockey! But everyone's got their favorite sport honey. I don't think you should judge the whole game of rugkey, just because of a few people who try and ruin things for the rest of us, uh who like watching this sort of sport." Replied Andy.

Andy sort of squirmed back in his chair after saying all that, but was quite frankly surprised what Anne's answer was. "You know what Andy? That's why I love you, because you always seem to have the right answer for just about everything." Then she ran over to give Andy a great big hug and a kiss. "Oh dear! We have to get ready! I have to put my wedding dress on." Screeched Anne.

"Well you go on and get yourself ready. I'm already dressed there baby cakes." Replied Andy, as he gave Anne a big friendly slap on her left butt cheek when she turned to walk away. Anne turned around, and with a high pitch screech, she gave him a wink. "We've got lots of time for that after the wedding, *baby cakes.*" Anne replied, as she left the room.

"You two make quite the happy couple after all those years away." Said Santose. "That's true love for you Santose." Andy replied, as he lit up his corn pipe and took a healthy puff. "Well I sure hope Nina and I endure the same happiness and affection you and Anne do." Said Santose. After which, there was no further conversation about the matter, it was game time.

"Well fans, we're back to a rather untimely chain of events here in the underground arena tonight." "Now it looks like the Packs are going to continue the play without a goalie." "Uh, I think I'm going to have to disagree with you on that one Jim."

"Low and behold, the man is coming back folks!" "Well now every fan in this arena tonight is on their feet in respect to Sandy Rogue. He is *actually* coming back out on the ice to finish where he left off." "Well my hats off to you Rogue. Play on, and let the game continue!" Said Folga.

The crowd goes wild and the place explodes with cheers, after Sandy Rogue returns to the net. He was a true gladiator in the eyes of the crowd, and to all who knew the sport. As for the players, they formed a sign of respect themselves, by way of forming a line on each side of Sandy Rogue, all the way to his goalie net.

"Well if this isn't old school respect, I don't what is Jim." "You can say that again Folga, you can say that again." "Players line back up at center, and the game is underway once more. Coming to you *live* from the Packs arena." Said Folga.

"Referee gets ready to drop. Game on!" "Wayner scoops this one out of the air after a bounce and gains control of the key. He skates in hard and plays the key around Sean, streaking towards the Nacucks goalie." "Toni T is with him, and a quick pass will take the traffic away from Wayner." "Toni one times it, glove save, by Tyler Step and the play is stopped." Said Jim.

"Face off in the Nacucks defensive zone and it is Travis Step against Wayner Pretzel." "Referee drops the key. Travis gets this one and brings the key in behind his own net." "He sees Darryl up the wing and passes forward." "Darryl gains control and passes on to Sean Step. Sean moves ahead and sees trouble, so he makes the pass to Travis." "Travis takes the shot, wide, and the scramble for the key in the corner begins." Announced Folga.

"The key is locked up against the boards underneath the feet of Lander Macdonald, and the fight for the key is on." "Sean Step uses his body to try and gain control of the key by ramming Lander hard against the boards, but Darryl is there to break the key free." "The key is loose and it's a stick fight between Travis and Chelius." "Travis makes some fancy moves and gets control of this one, as he heads towards center ice." Announced Jim.

"Travis circles back and then heads for the net one more time, as he now goes in alone. He skates around defense man Marcel Dupponne, then he stick handles the key trying to fake out Sandy Rogue." "He takes a snap shot, blind side, blocker save and the key is still in play." "Forty seconds left of play in the first, and Darryl is there for the rebound. He shoots, pad save and the key hits the glass and bounces back into play. Sean is there to get this one and he battles it out with Tom Chelius." Announced Folga.

"Chelius gets the key out of his zone and the race is on. Its Toni and Travis but Never is there to push the key forward again." "Sean Step gets the key and time is running out. He sees Darryl, quick pass and now Darryl goes forward." "Another pass back to Sean, he takes the shot, glove save, and there goes the buzzer, bringing this exciting first period to an end." Announced Folga.

"What an ending to the first period of this final game of the season Folga!" "Well I have to agree with you there Jim. Just a reminder to the fans in the arena tonight, that there will be a wedding taking place in the winners box during this intermission. It will be displayed on the big screen for your convenience. So if you'll remain seated in respect to Anne and Andy, we will begin. That is all." Then the lights began to dim, and four big screens unfolded down towards the ice.

"Well folks, I guess our job isn't done as of yet. Here we are in the wedding box, um, I mean uh, winners box, where we are waiting for our mayor to announce the special guests that are about to appear." Said Jim. "Speaking of guests, that sure is a gem John Wayne brought with him to the game tonight."

Added Folga. "Yes well, let's have a chat with John Wayne, and see what we can find out shall we Folga?"

"Uh, Mr Wayne?" John Wayne turns around. "Well hello there." John Wayne replies, in his deep low voice. "Hey Katrina, these are the fellas I was just talking about. This is Folga." "How do you do ma'am?" Folga says, as he kissed Katrina's smooth hand. Then he gave John Wayne a manly hand shake. "And this fellas name is Jim." "How do you do?" Asked Jim, as he gives John Wayne a firm hand shake. Following Folga's example, he kissed Katrina's hand as a sign of respect.

"Well I'm, glad I could finally meet the pair of you. The little woman and I are big fans of yours." Said John Wayne. "Well it's an honor to hear that Mr Wayne. Jim and I are even bigger fans of yours, if you wanna know the truth." Said an almost excited Folga. "Well perhaps we can, exchange autographs after the game." John Wayne said, with a little laugh. Jim and Folga both joined in on the laugh.

Then an announcement came from the podium. "Excuse me gentlemen, while I get this wedding off to a start." Then John Wayne made his way down the aisle. You could hear the whole arena cheer, as John got ready to announce his guests. Every fan in the building were off their seats for a standing ovation.

"Welcome to the underground arena!" Said John Wayne, as the crowd roared throughout the arena. When the crowd settled down, John Wayne continued to speak. "Now your, all probably wondering what sort of, special guest I brought with me today that you, haven't already run into. Well here's to a man who needs no further introduction. Would you please put your hands together, and welcome back the original gate keeper, Bryan, and his beautiful wife Jessie."

Then an entrance like no other, Bryan and his wife walked through the doors of the winners box. It wasn't until John Wayne put his hands together, followed by Katrina of course, that the audience began to shout, clap and cheer. It was like the sound of a goal in the arena. Then they stood up for another standing ovation. How is *that* for a welcome home? So Bryan and his wife walked up to the podium. Bryan said a few words, after the crowd settled down mind you.

"You are all too kind. I wanna thank my friend the mayor, for spilling the beans about me here tonight." After which, he and John Wayne had a bit of a chuckle. "But I don't wanna take any thunder away from my best friends Andy and Anne on their wedding night, so let's give up a warm welcome, to the future newly wed couple, Anne and Andy Pearson shall we?" Replied Bryan, trying to make it short and sweet.

The music started to play, and the two couples stepped to the side, so the wedding could begin. Jessie however, ran back down the aisle and out the door. John Wayne followed her as he passed Leroy, who was making his way to the front. Then the Step brothers, along with Ted, stood on each side of the entrance door. The lights were dimmed slightly in the winners box, and the minister made his way to the front.

Andy made his way to the mini stage and to the right of the podium. Then the doors opened and the ladies made their way down the aisle. First to lead the way down the aisle, was the lovely Tanantra. She looked beautiful in her rather pretty pink silky dress. In similar pink dresses, Nina followed, and behind her was Jessie. Bryan could not keep his eyes off of his beautiful wife.

Last but not least, came little Lynda, with her long hair done up in a bun. She was carrying a silky white pillow, laced and outlined with pink and white roses. On top of the pillow, glistened a stunningly beautiful diamond ring encased in a gold wedding band.

Now being the fact that Anne and Andy had no living parents to give away the bride, John Wayne was elected to perform this honor. This was the show stopper of the night. The crowd fell absolutely silent, as John Wayne walked arm in arm with Anne down the aisle.

John Wayne had been fitted with a luxurious silky black tuxedo. While Anne held up a gorgeous white wedding dress. It was long enough to pretty near stretch out down the whole aisle of the winners box. It was etched with a silky lace around the cuffs of her sleeves, as well as a veil covering her face.

Anne was nervous at first. But once she reached the end of the aisle and stood next to the man she loved, everything seemed to fall into place. She forgot about her surroundings only to focus on her man. Andy looked stunning in his black tuxedo with a white frilly dress shirt, sporting a black tie.

Then the minister began. "We are gathered here today, to witness this wonderful matrimony between Anne and Andy. Then he says a few more words before turning it over for Andy to say his vows. Andy gets down on one knee and cameras begin flashing. Anne began to blush as Andy looked into her eyes.

"Anne my dearest, it has been many a moon that I have longed for your love. I missed our long talks until the wee hours of the morning, and your soft touch against my skin as we lay down to bed with each other nightly. I promise to love honor and obey you, until death do us part. You are my one and only Anne, and it is my privilege to take the last step and devotion to our everlasting love. Will you take my hand in marriage on this grandest of occasions?"

Then Leroy stepped up to hand his father the ring. Anne stood there speechless, and almost in tears, as she nodded her head yes, allowing Andy to place the ring on her finger. "Now Anne will say her vows." Said the minister.

"If you'll excuse me for a second." Anne began, as she wiped the rolling tears from her cheeks. "Andy, I have waited for this moment all of my life, and it is more than I ever could have asked for. You are my one and only, you always have been, and I am proud to call myself Mrs Andy Pearson."

Then Lynda walked up to her mother. Anne took the ring from on top of the pillow case, and placed it on Andy's finger. After which, the minister said his final words. "I now pronounce you Andy and Anne Pearson, as husband and wife. You may now kiss the bride."

Andy knew this part all too well, and couldn't wait to pull the veil away from Anne's face and kiss her. Halfway through the kiss, Andy tilted Anne's body to one side and kissed her with all his heart, full on the lips, so the camera men could get every angle. It was a memory he wanted to endure for the rest of his life.

During the kiss, the whole auditorium went wild and happiness filled the arena. Couples began kissing and confetti was being thrown. It truly was a grand occasion. But before exiting the room, the newlyweds were called up to the front of the stage where they were to sign the wedding certificates. After that was done, the ladies were called to the front of the room for the throwing of the bouquet. Tanantra was the one who caught the bouquet.

"Well folks, it looks to me like anything can happen tonight. Let's take a short break while the ice gets cleaned, for the next exciting period of the last playoff game of this season, between the Packs and the Nacucks." Announced Folga.

Andy and Anne made their way down the aisle to the winners box door, for the first time in matrimony. Jessie takes this time to get to know Tanantra. "Well you look very beautiful today young lady." "Thank you. You look amazing in that dress yourself." Replied Tananatra. "Why thank you my dear." Replied Jessie.

"Well I see you two ladies seem to be hitting it off." Said Bryan. "Doesn't she look stunning Bryan?" Jessie asked. "Of course she does. She is a complete vision, just like her mother was." Replied Bryan. "Aw thanks dad." Then Tananatra gave her dad a big hug.

John Wayne steps forward now and walks up towards Tanantra and Bryan. "Hello there my dear. You look as beautiful as your mother once looked. If I hadn't seen it for myself, I'd say you were the spitting image of your mom. God bless her soul." Then he took Tananatra by the hand, and kissed it ever so gently. "Why thank you Mr mayor." Replied Tananatra.

"At the back of the winners box, waiters and waitresses began bringing snacks and desserts of all shapes and sizes. It was time to endure a feast while the ice was being cleaned. Tyler was the first one to fill up a plate and dig in. So for the next twenty minutes or so, the reception took place.

"Welcome back to the second period of our game tonight. I'm Jim." "And I'm Folga." "And we're your hosts of tonight's game, coming to you live in the underground arena, where the Packs face the Nacucks." Jim and Folga announced together.

The players get a feel of the freshly cleaned ice, and the referee makes his way to the center line. "Now according to the word from the locker room, Sandy Rogue seems to be playing the rest of the game with a blind eye. He should have been out for the rest of the game, but he decided to man it out." Announced Folga. "Well you have to give the man credit for the effort." Replied Jim.

"Referee drops the key, and it's game on!" "Stick fight at center ice between Wayner Pretzel and Travis Step." "Travis gets a piece of this one and Sean receives the key." "But he doesn't hang on for long, and passes the key across ice to Darryl Step, who races forward with the key like it's glued to his stick." "Lander comes forward with a check, but Darryl gets by him with ease. After a rebound off the boards and an interception on the other side of Lander, Darryl brings the key closer to the Packs net." Announced Jim.

"Darryl sees Travis open in front and goes for the pass." "Travis, with lots of time to shoot, decides to pass off to Sean and he takes a slap shot. But a stick save by Rogue keeps the key in play." "Travis is there to get the rebound, but Marcel Dupponne gets there first and snaps the key out of the zone." "Darryl turns around and races towards Nacucks half of the ice, but just misses getting a piece of the key. Toni T intercepts it instead, and slices ice towards Tyler Step." "Toni goes in alone on a one on one with Nacucks goalie. He takes a shot, scores! Blocker side, and an opening goal for this second period breaks the ice!" "Well I sure didn't see that one coming!" Said Folga.

"Yes Folga, and what a goal it was! But I'm sure that one choked up the referee. He is already back at center ice waiting for the face off." "Well it's not hard to tell what team he is cheering for Jim." "Yes Folga, and that will take this game to a score of 4 for the Packs and still 3 for the Nacucks."

"Players line back up at center ice, and the key is dropped." "Wayner gets a stick on this one, and the key heads to Toni T." "Toni can't hang on as Darryl steals the key." "Darryl breaks on through and takes to flight. Skates off the ice like his rug is gas powered, and Darryl is still in control. He bypasses Lander and heads for the corner Folga."

"Darryl flies ahead and looks for the next play. He sees Sean in the opposite corner and passes the key behind the net." "Sean doesn't hang on to the key for long, and passes up the middle to Travis." "Travis takes a powerful slap shot, glove save, no, he scores! Rogue couldn't hang on to *that* key, and it drops behind the goal line. That will make this number 4 for the Nacucks and it is another tie with the Packs at 4 as well." Announced Folga.

"Let's take another look at that in instant replay." "Here we have a pass from Darryl, who flies into the corner alone. Then a pass behind the net to brother Sean, who in return passes to Travis in front of the net. Now watch as Travis winds this one up. His feet literately leave the ice as he winds up this cannon and boom, slaps that key towards the net Folga."

"Meanwhile, Rogue thinks he made the save, but was a little confused when the horn blew." "Well Jim, you have to give him credit for the effort." "I have to agree with you there Folga. We'll return after these messages."

"We are back folks, where it looks to be an anything goes game here in the underground." "You notice how the ref isn't in such a hurry to drop *this* key?" "No comment Jim, its starting to make me sick!" "Referee drops the key and Travis pulls this one from his hat." "He circles back and then he heads for the net." "Well Folga, the Step line seems to be pacing themselves as they pass the key back and forth skating into the Packs defensive zone."

"Travis to Darryl and Darryl across to Sean. Sean back to Darryl and he gets it back to Travis." "Travis heads for the net and reaches the outskirts of the goalie's crease. He fakes out the goalie and it looks like he is going to shoot." "No, he drop passes back and Sean is there to snap the key in and it's another goal by Sean Step! With an assist by Travis Step, making it a 5-4 lead for the Nacucks over the Packs Jim."

"I never seen that coming, and what a play by the Step brothers! Talk about taking control of this game in a hurry early in the second." "Well the Packs wanted to play old school, and that's exactly what they are going to get." "You got that right

Jim, and if the Packs wanna get back in the game, they had better pack a lunch, because those Step brothers are here to win the cup. This isn't rugkey camp, and this sure as hell ain't the minor leagues, so they really gotta try and step up this game, so to speak." "I couldn't have said it better myself Folga."

"Game on, and the key has been dropped." "Well we can scratch that face off, after the referee blows the whistle and Wayner gets waved off. Toni T will take his place." "Ref gets ready once again, and here we go." "This ones good Folga, and Toni T gets the key off the hop."

"A controlled pass to Tom Chelius and he gets the key passed center ice." "Wayner is with him, and Tom makes a pass but the key has wings. So Wayner takes to flight and knocks the key back down with the use of his rug." "Still in control and back on the ice, Wayner goes for gold, stick handling like never before." "Wayner takes a shot, scores!" "I don't know how he pulled that shot off Jim, but I think we should have another look at that goal!" "Yes we should Folga. The game score is 5 for the Packs and 5 for the Nacucks."

"First of all, we have a pass from Tom Chelius, which went high. Then Wayner takes to flight, and using the bottom end of his rug, he knocks the key back to the ice. He regains control of the key and then takes the shot. Now let's play this one in slow motion so we can get a better look at this goal. The key looks like it's heading towards the face mask of Tyler Step, but it takes some sort of an air bending drop, and lands five hole in the back of the net. Wow, what a goal folks!" Announced Jim.

"Back at center ice, a change is taking place. Wayner Pretzel is trading positions with right winger Toni T and Travis Step is trading positions with, Darryl Step?" "Well this one should turn things around a bit. I don't think I have *ever* had the pleasure of seeing Darryl Step take control at center ice."

"Well Folga, if Darryl is anything like he plays on left wing, then I'm sure we are in for a real treat."

"Players line up and the key hits the ice." "Darryl gets a piece of the key to start things off." "The key bounces off his left skate and Darryl is able to gain control it off the rebound." "Darryl doesn't waste any time as he skates around Toni T, leaving him behind in his ice chips, heading straight for the net Jim."

"Marcel and Lander decide to go for a crunch play. Darryl sees this, and decides to do a suicide carpet roll with a full body extension, right over the heads of the Packs two defense men. His skates are back to ice as Darryl finishes off with a twist in mid air!" "Are you getting this Folga?"

"Lander and Marcel fall hard to the ice after a hard collision with each other, which was meant for Darryl." "But Darryl regains control after *that* landing, and takes the key in alone as he races in toward the net." "Here comes that famous skate to skate dribble Folga. Then a pass to his stick, he shoots, he scores!" "6 goals on the board for the Nacucks and 5 for the Packs." Announced Folga.

"Well this is getting just a little too ridiculous Jim! The fans pay good money to see this game, and for what? To watch the arena staff pick up more items for your collection?" Jim clears his throat as he gives Folga the stare down. "I resent that Folga! Uh, we'll return you to live rugkey in the Packs arena after this short break."

"We are back folks, coming to live from the underground." "You know, I've seen some high flight and fancy foot work Folga, but I have to say, this one really takes the cake." "Let's have another look at that play Jim. Here we have Darryl catch the hop at center ice, and with a back pass to his heel, he passes the key along his right side to keep control. He whisks around Toni and brings the key in alone, leaving brother Travis to fight the pack."

"Now this play here is what gets me, and to tell you the truth, it looks good on them. Lander Macdonald and Marcel Dupponne come in for what we call the crunch play. But Darryl out smarts them and breaks out some old school of his own. He does a full sideways extension carpet roll as he spins around constantly like a drill bit. Then he adds a twisting round off as he lands back on the ice skates down. But he is not finished yet. Darryl speeds towards the net where he pulls out his move, and with a slap shot, he puts another goal on the board Jim."

"I have to admit Folga, when it comes to old school, you have to use every play to your advantage. Darryl pulled off the right shot there as he aimed the key towards Sandy Rogue's blind side." "Its not Darryl's fault he has such a blistering shot!" Snapped Folga, getting a little on the offensive side. "Right you are Folga, and we'll be back with more high flying rugkey, after this commercial."

Meanwhile, back up in the winners box, Leroy and Dude figured it was fair play to go and hit up the goody bar while they had the chance. Then there was a loud knock coming from the entrance door to the winners box. One of the arena security guards walked in and pulled the owner aside.

But as Leroy and Dude walked by the door to see what was going on, they noticed it was Frank and Todd with the security guard. "Excuse me sir?" "If you'll just hold on for a minute Leroy, I'll be right with you." Replied Bent. "Uh, but sir, that's what I wanted to talk to you about. You see, those boys in the hall are my guests tonight, and better later than never, if I may say so myself." "Oh, well if that's the case son, then my apologies are in order. Okay Dennis, you can just lead the boys on in and get back at it. Thank you." Said Bent.

The security guard let go of the boys, and they were introduced to the owner, after the doors shut behind them. "Thanks Leroy. We owe you one. We couldn't get away in time and they wouldn't let us through the gate, so we had to sneak in." Said Frank.

"Yeah man, we know every inch of this arena like the back of our hands. But when we got to the secret entrance in between the two bathrooms, we got chased by security." Added Todd. "Yeah, that's how we ended up with such a grand entrance." Said Frank. The boys laughed it off and Leroy invited the boys to indulge with them for dessert.

"So have you guys had a chance to catch any of the game?" Asked Dude. "Of course. We caught everything on my portable radio." Replied Todd. "Yeah, well that's too bad about Sandy Rogue. I was really hoping the Packs would take the cup this year. I mean, don't get me wrong, he is an awesome goalie. But with his blind eye? I just wish there was some way they could put me in. I've been the best goalie in our whole junior league. I only let in four goals this season." Replied Frank. "Really? You know, I think it's time we had a little talk to the owner." With that being said, Dude asked Leroy to walk with him. They returned within a few minutes, with huge smiles on their faces.

"So, you think you can still hold that record through tonight's game?" Asked Dude. "Well of course, since I'm not even playing." Frank replied. "So what if we were to tell you that the Packs could sure use you for the third period?" Asked Leroy. "Yeah, well like that's ever going to happen." Said Frank. "Don't be so sure of yourself." Said Leroy.

Then there was another knock on the door, and the owner walked over to answer it. After shutting the door behind him, Bent walked over towards Frank with a rugkey bag in hand. "Well son, if you ever wanted to do something for your city, the time has come. Do you think you can be in uniform by the end of the period?" "Uh, I, I don't know what to say." Frank replied, as he stumbled on his own words.

"No pressure son, but I do have to inform Sandy Rogue, so he can get to the doctors before he loses sight out of that eye for life." Said Bent. "Well, well yes sir. I'm in!" Said an excited Frank. "Well what are you standing there for? Let's get you off to the players locker room, because you have got a third period to play, and an eye to save." Replied Bent.

The other boys cheered him on as he left the winners box and hurried off to the locker room. "Wow, can you believe that? My bro has just gone pro." "Thanks guys. You think you could hook me up for next year?" Asked an excited Todd. "Well it isn't going to hurt to ask. But we better grab a seat, the game is about to start again." Replied Dude.

"We're back folks, *live* in the underground. I'm Jim." "And I'm Folga." "And we're your rugkey announcers for this evening." They both say together. "Players line up at center ice, and to start things off for this third period, Darryl Step will face Toni T." "Toni gets this one and tramples through Darryl like a ghost through a wall." "Wayner is with him on the wing as they reach Nacucks defensive line. Toni passes to Wayner and he goes in deep." "Quick pass to Tom Chelius, he takes a shot, scores! That will bring this game to another tie, with a score of 6 for the Packs and 6 for the Nacucks Folga."

"Well this is no surprise. It looks like the referee is trying to hurry this face off after *that* goal." "You know, someone should take that ref out back and teach him a lesson." Snapped Folga. "Well it just goes to show you what happens when your father is high up in the underground rugkey League." Said Jim. "You got that right." Replied Folga.

"Ref drops the key, and we're back in play." "The stick fight begins and the key goes wild, but Sean is there to open *this* door." "Sean puts fire to ice and heads for the net." "Marcel heads towards Sean and Sean steamboats ahead. If these two don't stop playing chicken, it's gonna add more blood to the ice Jim."

"Four feet from each other, three, two, oh, what a move by Sean Step! He takes an ice slide right under the legs of Marcel Dupponne. With one smooth motion, Sean gets back up on his skates, *still* in full control of the key." "Sean heads to the net alone. He takes a slap shot, scores!" "What a magnificent goal Folga, and that brings the score up to 7 for the Nacucks and the Packs with 6."

"Five minutes of play left in this second period, and both teams are playing their hearts out." "You can say that again Jim." "This game has *got* to go down in the history books as the most high flying goal scoring game, I've ever witnessed anyways." "Thanks for that Jim, I couldn't have said it better myself. Now we have something we can both agree on."

"Players line back up at center, and the key is dropped." "This time Toni T gets the chance to show us some moves, and oh, what a move that was. He gets a piece of the key after the first bounce. Then Toni flicks it upwards, and with a head butt, he knocks the key forward." "After which, he follows through, catching the key after another bounce to gain full control." "But Toni is not alone, Wayner Pretzel is with him and Tom Chelius is not far behind Jim."

"Toni goes for broke and spins around Nacucks defense men like a tornado." "Now with a quick pass back to Wayner, who rushes in with the key behind the net. He sees Tom in the open and makes the pass." "Tom goes in deep and alone he takes the shot, no, another pass to Toni T. He winds up for a one timer, he shoots, he scores!" "The Packs add another goal to the board! It is now a 7-7 tie." "I tell you Folga, this is going to be a close game in the end."

"Let's take another look at that goal shall we?" "Uh, I don't think we're going to have time Folga, the ref is back at center ice again." "Well then the head of the U.R.L. should be up here announcing the game! Instead of having his son, the ref, running things around here." "I can go with that Folga."

"Here we have the face off where the key makes a single bounce. Toni T flicks the key to give it wings. Then he proceeds to head butt the key to knock it forward. Toni gets around Darryl, then flies passed Nacucks defense line. A quick pass to Wayner, who brings the key behind the net. Wayner passes the key to Chelius, who in turn gives it to Toni T. Toni one times it, and the key finds a home in the back of the net." Finished Folga.

Meanwhile, the game continues without the announcers, so Jim steps up. "Travis Step has the key now at the Packs defensive line, he takes a slap shot, oh, off the knee pad of Sandy Rogue, but Sean is there for the rebound. He shoots, he scores!" "Listen to that crowd Jim! You know, it's hard to tell who the fans are actually going for here in the underground!" "Yes Folga, and that brings the score to a whopping 8 for the Nacucks and 7 for the Packs."

"Players line back up at center ice." "Uh, Folga, aren't we going to show the instant replay?" "Not on my watch! As far as I am concerned, the ref is going to be waiting all night for *this* replay! So if he can hear me, then he better drop the key. I mean, who does he think he is?" The ref looks up at the announcers box. So Folga makes another comment. "Why don't you call your daddy if you don't like the way I run things up here?" The ref just shakes his head and gets ready to drop the key.

The fans cheer Folga on, and in the same breath, they boo the ref. But there was *really* nothing he could do about it, so he dropped the key. "Game on here at the Packs arena, and Darryl gets this one." "He moves around Toni T and passes off to Travis. Travis passes back to Darryl and he heads straight for the net, but Lander Macdonald heads straight for him at full speed. Its going to be a hard collision!" "What a move by Darryl Step!" "He does the splits, and Lander Macdonald takes a tumble over Darryl. With a tuck duck and roll, Macdonald hits the ice hard!" "Now this is rugkey Jim!"

"Darryl slides back to his feet with such agility, and yet he is still in full control. He takes the shot, five hole, and in the key goes!" "Well Folga, we haven't seen this display in a while." "Yeah well, you wouldn't want to miss your favorite part of the *whole* game Jim." Jim clears his throat. "We will return you to rugkey in the underground, after a few words from our sponsors." Announced Jim.

"We're back folks, *live* at the Packs arena, and the ice is clear." The ref stands at center ice looking up at Jim and Folga, waiting for them to go to instant replay. But Folga stands his ground and folds his arms. The crowd starts booing the ref, and it just isn't good enough because the ref isn't budging.

"Wait a minute, what's this? Folks at home, this is something you just *have* to see. The fans are climbing over the plexiglass and making their way towards the ref! Well if I hadn't seen it for myself I wouldn't have believed it. The fans are literately taking the ref out of the game *themselves*." "I have never seen anything like it Folga! The fans seem to be carrying him back to the bleachers."

The crowd goes wild as the ref is being held against his will. He was hauled off and forced to sit in the stands. "Well I wouldn't want to be the ref right *now* Jim. Those fans don't seem to be the type you want to be messing with." "Well this game has gone *way* out of control! So let's take a quick commercial break while we figure this one out Folga."

During the commercial, officials came out of the box and tried to make their way down to get the ref back in the game.

But the fans were making up their own rules. They would not let *anyone* near the ref.

"Well we're back here in the underground, and what a turn of events. The fans have taken the ref hostage, and are making him sit in the stands to watch the game." "Not to mention the fact that they won't let *anyone* near him." "Well here comes a new ref and the fans show enthusiasm for this one Jim."

"Game on, and the crowd is wild folks at home! We are *live,* as the new referee drops the key, and the period goes on!" "The stick fight begins, and Darryl gets the key to brother Sean." "Sean takes a huge slap shot, scores! What a goal from Sean Step!" "Darryl is going to get an assist out of this one Folga." "Yes Jim, and this game is about to reach double digits, with a score of 9 for the Nacucks, and still 7 for the Packs."

"We *have* to get an instant replay out of this one Folga." "I agree with you there Jim. That goal was absolutely *sick.*" "It starts off with a drop of the key. Darryl gets this one, and makes a pass across to Sean Step, who takes a huge slap shot from center ice. The key goes just above Sandy Rogue's goalie stick, and finds a home in the back of the net." "Short and sweet Folga. *That's* what I like to see." "You can say that again Jim."

"What a score for the last game of the season folks!" "With just two minutes to go in the second period, this one goes back to a face off." "Referee gets ready to drop the key, and the fans are on their feet." "The key is dropped, as this one heads for Travis after Darryl gets a piece of the key." "Travis makes his way through, but gets checked by Wayner, who can't pry the key away from Travis's stick." "Up against the boards now, Travis rolls the key along the plexiglass and breaks loose from Wayner." Announced Jim.

"Lander is there to catch the key and tries to clear it, but Travis grabs the left over garbage and keeps it in the Packs zone." "He plays the key towards the corner and passes in behind the net, where Sean is there to retrieve it." "Sean gets checked, but manages to shoot the key towards the side of the net. The key hits the goal post and Sean is there to pick up the pieces. He passes off to Darryl right in front of the net. He shoots, he scores!" "He made that look like it was easy Folga."

An instant replay was in order at this point. While that was going on, the fans blocked the referees view of the replay, to teach him a lesson. "Don't you have a bathroom break to attend to Jim? We all know how much you like *this* display." "I'm not even going to bother commenting on that one Folga. Um, let's take a commercial break while the ice is being cleared." Announced Jim.

"We are back folks, and the score has reached double digits here in the underground. The Nacucks with 10 and the Packs lagging behind with 7." "A minute and a half left to play in this second period, and the referee drops the key." "Toni T gets this one and he passes back to Marcel Dupponne." "Marcel has the key now, and he passes across to Lander as he makes his way towards center ice." Announced Jim.

"Lander reaches center ice and makes a quick pass to Toni, who crosses the center line with Wayner and Tom by his side." "A pass to Tom and then another pass to Wayner." "Tom heads for the corner and Toni heads to the front of the net, while Wayner streaks along the boards to bring the key forward Jim."

"Wayner passes the key across ice in front of the net to Tom." "Tom passes up to Wayner from behind the net and now Wayner has control. He looks for an opening, but back to Tom it goes." "Tom now being guarded by Never Bindin, so he gets the key in front to Toni T. Toni shoots, he scores!" Announced Folga.

The instant replay is shown once again and the fans block the refs view from the stands. "The score is now 10 – 8 and the ref drops the key." "The clock winds down, and you can hear the crowds anticipation as they count the seconds down out loud." "Darryl has this one and he takes the shot, save by Sandy Rogue, and this period is over!" "We'll return, after these words from our sponsors." Announced Jim.

The commercials start, and then the camera crew takes quick interviews with individual players from each team. After the interviews, Jim and Folga, along with the camera crew, decide to head up to the winners box. They were just in time to catch the first dance of the newly wed couple, Mr and Mrs Andy Pearson.

"Welcome back rugkey fans, to the third and perhaps the last period of tonight's game. I'm Jim." "And I'm Folga!" "And we're your hosts tonight, for rugkey night in the underground!" Jim and Folga both say at the same time.

"Now we are just getting word, that there has a been a change of goalies for the Packs. Uh, from what I am getting back, yes, it has been confirmed." Folga is getting feed back in his ear piece at this time from the boys upstairs. "It seems that Sandy Rogue has been taken to the underground Hospital, in need of immediate medical attention."

"Yes Folga, and here comes the new kid on the block, Franky Bonner." "Well let's hope this kid does as good a job as Sandy Rogue did, even though he was fighting a handicap." "Well Folga, Rogue manned up and did the best that he could. So if this kid wants to prove himself in the U.R.L, well then there is no time like the present." "The kid does seem to be stopping everything that comes his way. Look at all those keys being shot at him. To tell you the truth, I don't think I have even seen one key make a home in the net so far." "Well, maybe the Packs still have a fighting chance Folga."

CHAPTER 18

The Last Period

"Players line up, and the ref gets ready to drop the key." "The key is dropped, welcome to the third period, and we're off!" "Sean Step back at center against Wayner Pretzel and Wayner will snag this one Jim." "Wayner gets the key between his legs and Lander Macdonald picks up the garbage. He passes off to Marcel Dupponne, and he hangs back." "Travis Step goes for the check and Marcel gets the key to Wayner. Wayner now takes to flight, pulling off flying splits over top of Sean Step's head as the key flies between Sean's legs! Did you see that Folga?"

"Wayner lands back on the ice like a cat, still in control of the key as he races towards Nacucks net." "Tom Chelius is there to back up Wayner and Wayner makes the pass. Chelius shoots, pad save! Wayner gets the rebound, he takes a shot, scores! This one is *on* the board!" "The score is now 9 for the Packs, and double digits for the Nacucks, with a score of 10."

"Let's have another look at that goal. Here we have the pass from Marcel to Wayner, who packs on some heat, and pulls off the most athletic set of splits, I've ever seen, right over the head of Sean Step. Then he bolts on into the Nacucks zone like the key is on a chain, and just before getting to the net, he makes the pass to Tom Chelius. Pause it there for a second Jim."

"There, now Tom had lots of time to shoot. Okay play it again. Now he takes the shot, knowing that if he misses, Wayner is right there to pick up the rebound. Tyler stops that one, but the key goes wild, fast, and Wayner slaps the key to make the kill." "Well said Folga, I couldn't have announced it better myself."

"Back at center ice, the ref drops the key, and rugkey sticks fly once again." "Sean hooks the key this time, and turns back towards his own net, but fakes out Wayner and bolts right through, with Darryl and Travis along side him." "Quick pass to Travis and then back to Sean. Wayner comes in from behind and tries to check Sean, but he was able to pass the key to brother Darryl." Announced Jim.

"Darryl skates around Lander and heads for the net. From his stick to his heel, and back behind him on his opposite side to his right, Darryl takes a quick snap shot, as Franky Bonner closes in on the corner and hugs the post." "The key rockets towards the open side of the net, Bonner snaps his arm into action at full reach, with a glove save, and the play is stopped!" Announced Folga.

"What a glove save that was Folga! Did you see how far, and how fast his reflex's were with *that* glove save? Unbelievable!" "Don't count your chickens before they hatch Jim. Just because the kid stopped his first shot on net, that doesn't mean he *has* what it takes to become the Packs number one goalie. I'm sure the Step brothers will give the kid a run for his money." "On the upside Folga, if it wasn't for this new rookie goalie, and from what I am getting word about right now, Sandy Rogue could have lost sight in his left eye. But as it turns out, he received medical attention just in time, and it sounds like he is doing quite fine." "Well we can be thankful for that Jim."

"Its a face off in the Packs zone. Wayner Pretzel will take this one, and so will Travis Step." "Referee drops the key, and

Travis is able to get it across for Sean, who gets the key to Darryl in a hurry." "Darryl back to Travis and from Travis over to Sean. Sean takes the shot, blocker save, by Franky Bonner! Darryl gets the rebound, he shoots, goalie pad save!" "Sean takes another crack at it. He takes a slap shot, blocker side glove save, and Franky Bonner holds the key to stop the play. This kid has a fast arm on him that's for sure Folga."

"This time, on the opposite side of the Packs goalie, Travis Step will be facing off against Wayner pretzel." "Players line up, and the ref drops the key. The key gets knocked to the boards, and bodies get slammed against the plexiglass in a desperate fight for the key." "Both teams surround the battle against the boards, waiting for signs of a loose key." "Darryl breaks the key free, but not for long, another battle of the boards breaks out between Wayner and Sean, who stick to each other like glue." "But this one ends with the key being sent all the way back to the Nacucks zone. Tyler gets to the key before icing is called." "Wayner races in before Tyler can get rid of it, but he doesn't get there in time and now Bindin has the key." Announced Jim.

"Bindin looks ahead and passes up to Travis, who heads up the boards. Sean is with him now as they both pass center ice. Travis passes to Sean, he takes a shot, stick save, by rookie Franky Bonner!" "Marcel is there to get the key out of the Packs zone." "Well he got that key clear across the ice Folga."

"Never has the key now, and *he* starts out. Wayner races forward for the check, but Never passes the key to Sean and from Sean to Darryl." "Darryl moves forward, but gets checked by Toni T, and now he makes the turnaround. Toni races towards the net with Wayner by his side." "Toni passes off, Wayner with a one timer, scores! The Packs get another goal on the board!" "Its a double digit tie here in the underground arena. The score is now 10 for the Packs and 10 for the Nacucks." Announced Folga.

"Players line back up for the face off at center ice. Ref drops the key, and game on!" "Wayner gets the key between his legs, but not fast enough. Sean belts on through to take control of the key as he heads for the net to try and make a break away. Lander Macdonald and Marcel Dupponne try to close in, but Sean blows by them like they weren't even there." "Sean gets in close as he throws around some sneaky moves. He winds up, takes the shot, another glove save by Bonner, and this rather short play is at a stand still." Announced Folga.

"Well you gotta give the kid credit. So far in this third period, there has been about 15 shots on Franky, and the Nacucks can't seem get one passed him." "Both teams ready themselves for another face off in the Packs zone. Its Wayner against Travis, and the ref drops the key." "Travis gets a stick on this one, and manages to get the key over to Sean, who stick handles the key towards the back of the net Folga."

"The brothers form a triangle and the passing begins. Sean to Darryl and then over to Travis. Travis gets it back to Sean and then Sean gives it back to Travis." "Travis looks like he is going to pass across to Darryl, no, he winds up and takes a powerful slap shot, another great save by Franky Bonner!" "Darryl gets the rebound, he takes a shot, *oh*, Bonner extends his body and does the splits, catching a skate on the key and it goes wild!" Announced Jim.

"Marcel is there to back this save up and he tries to clear it out, but Sean scoops it away and *he* takes a shot on Franky." "Another great save and the key heads towards the corner." "Lander has the key now and he starts out towards center along the boards. He gets checked by Darryl, but the key moves on." "Toni T gets in there and breaks the flood gates across center ice with Wayner by his side." "A pass to Wayner as they head into Nacucks defensive zone. Its a two on two and Wayner gets it back to Toni. Toni takes a shot, scores!" "The Packs are ahead by a goal again! This double digit score is now 11 to 10, and the Nacucks are down by one." Announced Jim.

"Let's have another look at that shall we? It starts off in the Packs zone, where Lander Macdonald brings the key towards center and he gets checked by Darryl Step. The key gets through, but Lander is tied up along boards. Toni is there to bring this one home as he and Wayner make the break across center. Its a two on two and the passing begins." "From Toni to Wayner and then from Wayner back to Toni. Toni takes a shot from Nacucks defensive line, it looks like a save, but the key manages to sneak its way underneath the legs of Tyler Step. Making this one a five hole goal Jim."

"It looks like this one is anyone's game folks. Wow Folga, can you believe this score in our last game of the season?" "Well Jim, it will make for an interesting start for next season, that's for sure." "Back at center, the players get ready for the face off, and the key is dropped. Wayner desperately tries to get it back behind him, but Sean gets this one and he heads towards his own net." "He passes over to Bindin and he makes a stand at the back of the net. Tom goes in from the left and Toni goes in from the right, but Never sees how this ones gonna be and clears the key up to Darryl along the boards." Announced Folga.

"Darryl can't hang on to it and makes the pass to Sean. Sean moves on and the brothers race across center back to the Packs zone." "Sean heads straight for Bonner and then passes over to Travis. Travis now in control, heading towards the side of the net. He winds up for a shot, but makes a quick pass to Sean in front. Sean slaps one towards the net, but Franky makes the stop and the key is on the loose, while the time runs down." Announced Jim.

"Macdonald clears the key down the ice and Dan Steal has the key now. He passes over to Bindin and then Bindin back to Steal." "Darryl is in the open now so Steal gets the key to him." "Darryl crosses center with Travis and Sean as they form the triangle. This play that hasn't let them down yet." "Darryl to Sean and Sean to Travis. Travis then rolls the key along the boards behind the back of the net, and Darryl is there to receive it." Announced Jim.

"Darryl looks at Sean and notices that the Packs are trying to break the triangle, so another pass back to Travis and Travis skates for the net. He takes a snap shot, but it hits mid goalie stick and drops in front of the net. Bonner tries to cover up but it's too late. Sean gets a piece of the key and knocks it towards the top shelf, blocker side." "Bonner pulls off an extension of his right leg pad, where his skate *actually* touches the top hand corner of the goal post, and makes a miraculous save!" Announced Folga.

"But he is not in the clear yet. The key is loose and Darryl comes in to make this pick. He takes a hard slap shot from the front side of the net. The key heads glove side, but the play is stopped, after ninja hand Bonner makes this save." "Well I'll tell you Folga, it looks like the Packs have got themselves a keeper. Think what this could mean for next season!" "Well first we gotta get through this game before we can think too far ahead Jim."

"Ref gets ready to drop the key, and Wayner faces Travis Step once again." "Game on, and the stick fight begins. The key is loose, but ends up getting jammed in the corner, and the brawl against the boards takes wind." "While Travis and Marcel try to unlock the key from the corner, Lander flies in and tries to break it up with a body slam against the boards." "But Sean steps in the way as he bends over, and using his shoulder like a shovel, he scoops Lander upwards with such brute force, he ends up over the plexiglass to join the fans!" "Well Folga, lucky for him his rug takes to flight and nobody gets hurt."

"The key is loose and Sean gets it in the front of the net. Quick pass to Darryl, Darryl takes a shot, but another great save from Bonner, blocker side, and the key goes wild." "Sean gets the rebound, he shoots, pad save! Travis is there to get *this* rebound and snaps one to the net, but after yet another glove save, this one stops the play Jim."

"This kid is dynamite Folga! I'd sure like to know where he came from." "Well I'm sure we'll have plenty of time to find that out Jim. The face off starts and the key is on the hop. Marcel gets this one and clears it down the ice." "Never Bindin has the key now and passes along to Dan Steal." "Steal moves forward and Toni T is there for the check. But he can't break the key free and it's back to Bindin." "Bindin now to Travis and the brothers pass center ice in sync." Announced Folga.

"Marcel breaks out his stick, getting a tip on the key, but Travis pulls back to regain control." "Now a pass to Sean, he shoots, just wide of the net, and Lander has the key in the corner. He sees Toni and makes the pass forward." "Then Toni, Wayner and Tom go for broke and it's a three on two." "Toni sees Wayner heading for the net but passes off to Tom. Tom heads for the corner and then flies towards the net. He sees Wayner in the open and makes the pass. Wayner shoots, five hole shot! But Tyler Step gets his blocker down in time and makes the save." Announced Jim.

"The key is still on the loose but Toni is there to get a shot off. He one times it, but he is gonna have to get off a better shot then that to catch Tyler off guard." "The Step brothers fly in to help out brother Tyler, and it's a battle to clear the key out of the zone." "Steal gets the key in behind the net and the brothers form the triangle. Sean stays back while Darryl and Travis take to front." "Steal fakes a pass to Darryl and belts it in front for Sean. He then meets his brothers at center ice and they cross the line in synchronicity once more." "Here we go Folga."

"Darryl and Travis break out like lightening bolts, while Sean holds back and the triangle goes back into effect." "Sean to Darryl and Darryl across to Travis. Travis rips off a one timer, easy stick save for Franky Bonner." "Darryl gets the rebound and passes to brother Sean. Sean takes a shot while Travis and Darryl move in towards the net, and Franky stops the key with his chest." Announced Jim.

"The key drops in front of the net and Travis gets off a poke, but Bonner isn't letting nothing in tonight. Glove save! No time to clear the key this time folks, and the referee blows the whistle to stop the play." "You gotta admire the stamina this new rookie goalie for the Packs is showing Folga." "Yeah, well the game isn't over yet! We still got ten minutes of play left, and this double digit score is too close for my liking Jim."

"Wayner and Travis take another one together, and there it is!" "Just like Chinese in rugkey, every time they get in the corner they wanna start up a store." "Where are you getting your lines from Jim? I think you better just stick to announcing the game. Thousands of comedians out of work and your still trying." "Well it looks like these boys are setting up shop, the way they are roughing each other up against the boards." "But it doesn't last long, as Travis gets this one out and along the boards." "Tom picks this one off the tree and clears the key Folga."

"Well that didn't get very far Jim. Sean gets to the key before it crosses center ice and keeps it in the Packs zone. Wayner is there to try and steal the key, but Sean gets it over to Travis." "Travis looks towards the net, but there is too much traffic in front to shoot, so he gets it across for Darryl." "Darryl can't hang on and he makes a pass back to Sean. Sean one times the key, Lander takes a swan dive and gets a shoulder on this one. But the key looks like it broke *this* lock, and yet the play is still good." "Lander is down on the ice Folga, so I don't see why the ref hasn't blown the whistle!"

"Darryl winds up, takes the shot, Bonner catches this one in the glove and makes it look easy, as the play is stopped, *just* for you Jim." "Darryl shot that key over the lifeless body of

Lander Macdonald and he isn't getting up." "Well let us hope he can continue, since the Packs already have one player injured Jim."

The first aid attendant enters the ice with a stretcher, followed by the coach. "Well you had to have seen that coming. Lander may play a bit dirty for my liking, but I gotta admit, he's got the dedication to keep the Packs in the game." "You got that right Folga, and he is willing to risk injury for the sake of the team."

"Well it looks like we have movement by Lander Macdonald. I'm getting word that the first aid attendant wants to put Lander on the stretcher, but I'm afraid that one is not gonna work for him." "Well in spite of that just being said, it looks like Lander is making a stand, literally." "Well you can tell that by the way he is pushing everyone away as he gets up." The crowd rumbles the building with feet to floor, as a sign of respect for Lander. "You can tell the fans are glad to see Lander sticking to his guns Folga."

"Another face off in the Packs zone will begin with Travis and Wayner." "Ref drops the key, and Travis smacks it towards Darryl. Darryl gains control and Lander drops his stick during the fight for the key." "Darryl skates back towards center ice as Lander picks up his stick." "Yes Folga, and it looks like Lander seems to be favoring the shoulder where the key hit him. There he goes, he just dropped to the ice!" "Yes Jim, but the game plays on."

"Darryl is back at center ice and he gives the key to Sean. Sean can't shoot, so he gets the key to brother Travis who takes a shot. But that goes wide and the key heads behind the net and off the back boards, for Lander to clear it." "The key crosses center, where Dan Steal doesn't waste any time in getting the key back to Sean Step." "Sean with a quick pass over to brother Darryl. He takes a slap shot, another great save by Bonner!" "Bonner tries to cover up the key but Travis picks his pocket and heads for the back of the net." "Marcel is with him though, but Travis moves along with the key like rugkey tape on a stick." Announced Jim.

"He goes for a wrap around, but it's stopped by Bonner's right skate tight up against the goal post." "Sean skates in to get the rebound. He winds up, takes a slap shot, oh, it hits the crossbar and Franky gloves the key as it hits the ice, and the play is stopped." "If this kid keeps playing like he is Folga, the Packs have a good chance of winning the cup tonight." "Yeah well don't get your hopes up. There is still lots of time and anything can happen Jim." "You do make a good point *there* Folga."

"Ref gets ready to drop the key, but Travis gets waved off and Darryl will take *this* face off with Wayner." "Ref drops the key, and Darryl tips it over to Sean." "Sean breaks away towards the back of the net." "Woo, I can't say I've seen a play like *that* before! Sean does a walk up the backboards and does a backwards flip in the air." "I know right! After flicking the key over the net." "Sean is back on ice in front of the net along with the key. He takes a shot, scores! Five hole Folga!"

"Yeah well you can't blame Bonner for *that* goal Jim. Who knew Sean was going to pull off a move like *that*?" "You can say that again Folga! Its another tie here in the Packs arena. That will bring the game score to a whopping 11 for the Nacucks and the Packs with 11 goals as well." "The next goal could very well take this game Jim. But as I said before, let's not count our chickens before they hatch."

"Let's have another look at that goal Folga." "Here we have the face off, where Darryl gets the tip of his stick on the key. Sean takes control and he streamlines it to the back of the net." "Then he does a wall walk up the backboards, as he flicks the key towards the front of the net. Sean does a flip over the goalie *and* the net, as he lands in front of Bonner with the key by his side." "Then he takes a quick shot before

Franky Bonner even had a chance." "Yes Folga, and that will tie this game up with a high score."

"Players line up at center ice. Referee drops the key and Sean will start things off." "He slaps the key to Darryl, and the brothers cross center together as they head into the Packs zone." "Darryl gets checked by Lander but manages to get the key to brother Sean." "Sean heads towards the net with the key and he makes a pass to Travis." "Travis has the key now but Marcel Duppone comes in, and the key is held up against the boards." "Marcel looks like he seems to be tiring out a bit Folga."

"Marcel gets the key out from along the boards and clears it down the ice." "Bindin has a hard time controlling the bounce, and he ends up chasing it. Never gets to the key before icing is called and heads back towards center ice." "Tom comes in to keep him on his toes, and Never scrambles to get the key across to Dan Steal." "Steal in control now, and he skates backwards after seeing Toni chipping ice towards him." "Well I don't blame him for that Folga, Toni is a big boy."

"Steal plants one over to Sean and the brothers cross center ice." "What's this now? This is something new. Travis pulls out in front and Darryl pulls in behind him with Sean at the back." "I haven't seen this locomotion play since the Step brothers started using it back in rugkey camp. I have to tell you Jim, I never thought I would see the Step brothers use this last resort strategy."

"A straight line formed by the brothers from center ice to the Packs net. Travis clears the path and Sean moves the key ahead to Darryl. Darryl quickly passes up to Travis once there is no one left in his path." "Travis shoots, blocker save!" "Darryl comes in for the rebound and *he* shoots for the hole, but Bonner blocks that shot and the key goes wild." "Last but not least, Sean moves in with a powerful slap shot. He shoots, he scores!" "Yes Folga, and what a great ending for *that* line dance!"

"The Nacucks are ahead again, with a score of 12 and the Packs with 11. Well Jim, that is the second goal Franky Bonner has already let in tonight." "Yeah well you can't blame him for the way *this* game is being played Folga. The Step brothers are a tough line to beat." "You can say that again Jim." "Let's take another look at that goal Folga."

"Here we have the Step brothers crossing center ice. Then they form a line as Travis leads the pack and clears the ice." "Travis takes a shot but Bonner makes the save. Darryl retrieves the rebound and he takes a shot, but Bonner saves this one as well and the key goes wild." "Then Sean comes in with a blistering slap shot, and scores the goal to break the tie." "Well you have to give the kid credit for at least two out of the three shots on net Folga." "I have to agree with you there Jim."

"Sean will take center ice to switch things up, and he will face Wayner Pretzel once again." "Sean takes control off the drop as he turns around to look for an open man. Quick pass to Never, and *he* hangs on to the key." "Chelius races in to check Bindin, but he gets the key across to Dan Steal." "Steal has the key now as he flies up to center and makes a pass to Darryl along the boards." Announced Folga.

"Darryl in control now as he flies towards the Packs defensive line. Lander is there to check him, but Darryl passes the key to Travis." "Travis has the key and Wayner blocks off any chance of taking a shot. Travis passes the key for Sean, but it's a race with Chelius." "Sean gets a piece of the key as it heads to Darryl. Darryl one times it, and the key goes off of Lander's stick, but still heads towards the net." "Oh, what a save by Franky Bonner, and the play is at a stand still." Announced Jim.

"If the Packs are going to have any chance to further themselves in this game, they are sure going to have to pick things up. I mean, who knows how long Franky Bonner is going to be able to keep this up?" "Well Folga, quite frankly, in my opinion, the Packs *really* don't seem to be doing a lot of anything here but relying on Bonner." "There is still less than five minutes left on the clock, so let's see what happens Jim."

"Travis will take this face off in the Packs zone, along with Wayner." "Referee drops the key, and Travis clears it back across center, where Steal brings it forward and passes up to Sean." "Sean heads straight for the net and gets off a shot. But it goes wide and Lander is there to pick up the garbage." "Lander starts out for the Packs. He gets the key up for Toni T, as Wayner joins him and they cross center ice in sync." Announced Jim.

"Dan Steal stays back as Darryl tries to twist up the play." "Toni sees this one coming and passes over to Wayner who flies in like the wind. Wayner goes around Sean and makes it to the clear. Wayner skates towards the net as he tries to fake out Tyler Step." "He pulls off a wrist shot, goalie pad save! Chelius is there to receive the rebound and he fires a shot. But the play is stopped, while Tyler Step covers the key after making that huge save." Announced Folga.

"Great stop by Tyler Step!" "You can say that again Jim. He hasn't had a lot of action in this third period and after witnessing that save, you can tell he hasn't lost his touch either." "Face off in the Nacucks zone with Sean against Wayner, and the key is dropped." "Sean gets a piece of this one, and he snaps the key off the boards where Wayner is there to pick it up." "The pressure is on in the Nacucks zone late in the third Folga."

"Wayner doesn't hold on for long before passing off to Tom Chelius." "Tom hangs on and Never Bindin heads in to try and make a hard hit against the boards. But Chelius moves out of the way and gets the key back to Wayner." "Wayner breaks away towards the net after sneaking past Sean. He winds up and takes a shot, but Tyler saves this one with his blocker and the key gets deflected to the corner Jim."

"Never gets to the key first but Tom rams him up against the boards and the key gets locked between the two pairs of skates." "Sean goes in to try and stir the pot, but the door is locked." "Never manages to unlock this door and the key rides free towards the back of the net, where a stick fight begins with Dan Steal and Toni T." "Toni wins this one and gets it in front for Wayner. He takes a shot, ooh, just wide of the net, and the play continues as the clock winds down." Announced Folga.

"Dan Steal catches the key off the rebound. He tries to clear the key down the ice, but Toni is there to keep the key in the Nacucks zone." "He plays the key forward and the Packs go in full force. Toni to Wayner and Wayner across to Tom." "Tom goes in behind the net and then he makes a pass in front for Wayner Pretzel." "Wayner takes a shot, but that one hits the post and the key makes its way over the glass and into the stands. The play is stopped while the ref grabs another key." Announce Folga.

"The face off begins with Sean and Tom now as Wayner gets waved off." "Sean gets a piece, but Tom gains control. He heads for the net, goes for the shot, no, a fancy back pass for Toni to pick up. Toni shoots, but Tyler makes a pad save! Then it hits the goal post and flies back out in front." "Sean is there and he manages to clear the key all the way down the ice." Announced Jim.

"A bouncing key in front of the net catches Franky Bonner off guard, but he makes the save." "The play continues as Bonner clears the key and Marcel takes control." "Dupponne now to Macdonald and he passes ahead to Wayner." "Wayner in full control now, as he busts a move towards the net. He passes everyone in sight and heads for a breakaway. Its just Wayner and Tyler now, but here come Steal like a lightening bolt in behind Wayner who tries to take a shot." Announced Jim.

"Oh! Wayner goes down hard in front of the net after Steal gets a stick between his legs, and the key goes in five hole style!" "The buzzer goes off but I really don't think this is going to be a goal Folga." "I have to agree with you there Jim. Wayner was in the crease when the key went in, and I think Steal should get a tripping penalty after *that* play!" "Let's take a quick commercial break while this call goes to the boys upstairs Folga."

"We're back folks, and it looks like the ref has our results." "No goal. Tripping has been called, and a penalty shot will be taken by Wayner Pretzel for the Packs." "Well the fans are a little disappointed with that almost goal. But they sure seem to be cheering on Wayner Pretzel as he waits for the whistle Jim."

"The whistle is blown and Wayner is off. He races towards Tyler Step like a streak of lightening. He pulls off some fancy foot work as he nears the net." "Wayner takes the shot, glove save by Tyler Step!" "Veteran Tyler Step shows the fans he can perform under pressure, and the game is still 12 for the Nacucks and 11 for the Packs Folga."

"The players are back at center ice, and the ref gets ready to drop the key." "The key is dropped, and this game is underway, with four minutes left of regulation time for the last game of this season." "It is still anybody's game here in the underground, and Sean gets this one after a quick stick fight. He passes to brother Darryl, and they start off together heading into the Packs zone." "Game on Folga."

"Darryl goes in along the boards but circles back trying to avoid the check by Lander. Sean is being guarded by Wayner, and Travis skates away on Marcel out into the open. Darryl gets the key to Travis and he moves in." "But Travis can't seem to find any room to shoot, so he gets a pass back to Sean. Sean gets a shot off, goalie stick save, and Franky Bonner manages to give the key some legs. Toni T is there to back up this play." Announced Folga.

"Its a breakaway and Toni goes it in alone! He passes both Nacucks defense men and makes it a one on one between him and the goalie." "Tyler readies himself, Toni skates in fast, winds up, no, Toni changes his mind at the last second and tries a turnaround back hand. Stop by Tyler Step and he clears the key!" "Never has the key now as the clock winds down. Now across to Dan Steal as he gives the key up for Sean who passes center with his brothers." Announced Jim.

"Now they form the Step brother line from center to the Packs net, as Travis clears the path." "Darryl breaks wind behind him with Sean in the rear. Sean makes the pass but he doesn't pass to Darryl this time. Instead the key goes right through his legs and straight to Travis." "Travis takes a shot, but a stick save was made. Darryl comes in for the rebound and tries out his luck, but he also gets denied. Now Sean takes a huge slap shot, glove save, and the play is stopped!" Announced Folga.

"You know Jim, I have watched that same play a hundred times. To tell you the truth, this is only the first time in the brothers history of making this play, that they haven't scored." "Yes Folga, but it's only the second time they have tried it against rookie Franky Bonner. We got some good talent in the Packs net, which could lead to the start of a great career."

"Two and a half minutes left in the game folks, and the ref drops the key as Travis and Wayner fight for control." "Wayner gets the key to the corner and races forward, after slapping the key in behind the net." "Marcel has it now and pushes it forward to Tom Chelius. Tom gets the key and he moves ahead with Wayner on his side. They pass center ice and go for gold." "Tom passes off to Wayner and he goes in deep. Toni slides in and it's three on two Folga.

"Quick pass to Toni, he takes a shot, wide of the net, and Tom steps in to make a play. He passes the key to Wayner. Wayner takes a shot, stick save!" "Steal picks up the garbage and he clears the key out of the Nacucks zone." "Lander has the key in the Packs zone and he gets the key back to Wayner. Time winds down with less than a minute of play and a desperate Wayner takes a shot, but a blocker save stops that almost goal, and Tom recovers the key in the corner." Announced Jim.

"Tom sees Toni in the open and makes the pass. Toni one times it, but he can't get one passed Tyler Step." "The key goes wild and Steal is there to clear the key." "Now if Marcel gets the key back across center in time, the Packs still might have a chance in this last thirty seconds of the game Folga."

"He does it and Tom takes a long shot with Wayner up front to try and get the rebound. Wayner has the key, quick shot, and another great save by Tyler Step!" "The crowd goes wild as this game nears its end with the Nacucks ahead by just one goal." Announced Folga.

"But the play hasn't stopped yet, and Toni T presses on to get off another shot, but this one hits the post." "Never gets the key now and tries to clear it. But the key doesn't make it far before Wayner steals it right from under him and heads for the net, with the key on a chain. This could be the last shot of the evening folks! Wayner gets off a shot, glove save, and the buzzer goes! This game is over folks! The Nacucks take the cup! Nacucks take the cup!" Jim and Folga announce at the same time.

"Nacucks haven't lost the cup yet, and this game just goes to prove that they are still the best." "Well it looks like the fans are escorting the ref in the stands out of the building, and here comes the red rug."

The players line up and show signs of respect, by both teams skating towards each other and knuckle punching it up. Then the Packs take the walk of shame, and exit the ice. After which, the officials enter the ice with a cart full of champagne, followed by the underground cup.

The end.

This book is inspired only in part by a true story as well as some real life incidences. Be sure and read my next book called rugkey in the underground. This time we will explore the secrets behind the doors on the other side of the big wooden door. Doors that will take you to places beyond your imagination, and remember kids, always wear a helmet.

I am thirty eight years old. I am a single father of two beautiful children. I am a survivor of horrific events in my life that should have left me for dead. In response to these more than horrific events,

I would like my name to live on through books I have written. My dream is to literately climb into the minds of millions across the globe.

As well, I hope to inspire young minds in a way that might change the outcome in troubled young teenage lives.